www.theforgot

Thank you so much
I really ap
Enjoy the book.

CW00517125

The Forgotten Mission

The Return

....

By
Jonathan Taylor
Copyright © 2010

....

Cover designed by
In House Aliens
Copyright © 2010

....

Copyright © 2010
All rights reserved.

J Taylor
The Forgotten Mission, The Return©
© copyright 2010. All rights reserved.

www.theforgottenmission.com
themission@theforgottenmission.com
Published by: In House Aliens©
(J Taylor)

Thank You

There is a few people I'd like to thank who have helped me along this turbulent path.

• I'd like to thank my wonderful wife and two fantastic children, for putting up with me for the last couple of stressful years. They are my rocks, my inspiration, my positivity, giving me strength and support throughout my treatment for cancer. I couldn't have done this without them, this also extends to my close family members. My Auntie, for her strength throughout everything, my wife's family who have supported me throughout everything, massive hugs and kisses to you all.

• A special thank you goes out to my wife for painstakingly proofreading the final copy. Thank you X.

• If you've read the author profile you'll know that since 2012 I've been battling with a rare form of lymphatic cancer (NLPHL). I'd like to thank all the staff at North Tees Hospital, for their amazing work, all the consultants, all the nurses and everyone who helps to diagnose and treat this worldwide disease. And lets face it if all these countries stopped raging war on each other and started pooling their resources into finding a cure against these fatal diseases, we could all live in a better and more peaceful world. Life is fragile.

• A special thank you to the front-line nurses in the chemotherapy day unit for all their hours of dedication to the patients, if it wasn't for all of you this experience may well have been very different.

• A massive thank you to all my friends who've been there for me throughout my life, especially the ones who've helped me and taken the time to see me through everything.

• Thank you to all who help spread the word about theforgottenmission.com let's see if it can go viral, don't forget to like, tweet, pin and everything else you can do;-)

• One more thank you and that's to apple, if it wasn't for you this book would never have happened, inspiration through technology, the iPad turned this book from an idea into reality.

About the Author
Jonathan Taylor

Well, where do I begin?

One of the things that grabs you when life gets tough, is just how strong the human mind can be! I was sailing through the stresses and strains of modern life, when right out of the blue, my seemingly great life was blown apart by the news of the Big C word! Yes, I had that unimaginable diagnosis, the one you never hope to hear (hence my epic hairstyle).

It's at that point, you wonder what's next and what to do! Well, in my case, I dug deep, the deepest I've ever dug in my short life, and believe me I've been through some things I wouldn't want anybody to have to go through.

Have you ever thought something has happened for a reason?

This was my thought exactly. Here's how this book and hopefully many more to come, came about.

I had the idea whilst on a family holiday to Florida, USA, back in 2010, it stayed an idea for a few months after returning. Until my wife, or should I say my rock, my best friend and mother to my two fantastic and talented children, encouraged me with the words; "You have to write these down, they are fantastic!" as I made up yet another story for our children. Well, I kind of took her advice this time and started putting pen to paper, or should I say fingers to tablet.

After a few thousand words, the idea sat there waiting for me to carry on, never finding the time to do so. This is where that thing happened for a reason. My former job was very demanding and physical, and with the kind of Cancer I had and where it was, this stopped me from continuing in this line of work. Then unfortunately I had a reaction to the chemotherapy, leaving me with severe nerve damage all over.

All that aside I've never once lost my positivity. I took the bull by the horns and danced to the rhythm of the drip-stand. Making the most of what life had to throw at me! After all this isn't a trial run! So here goes.

Thank you for taking the time to read my profile, I hope you enjoy the books.

J Taylor.

Foreword

There are lots of what ifs out there, but what if everything you ever thought to be true, or had been told was right - wasn't? What if all those conspiracy theories you'd frowned at, turned out to be true? The lies, the cover ups, the events marked throughout history, we've all believed them at one time or another.

That's just what Scott Salvador thought when his whole life took a path he wasn't expecting, a turn of events that shattered his naivety. Everything he'd ever believed in, or thought to be true, had suddenly been pulled out from under his feet, his unblemished innocence, stolen by what was about to happen.

Scott couldn't believe the things that had been going on under our noses throughout history, that was until he became part of it all. His suspicious nature had got him into a predicament he just couldn't escape from. Whether he likes it or not, he's now in so deep he can't get out!

The history of evolution as we know it, is about to change, the truth has been out there for millions of years and we are just about to find out where…

YEAR : 2067

. . . .

Date : July 3rd

. . . .

Day : Sunday

. . . .

Time : 16:16

• • • • • • • • •

The year was 2067. In a dusty, dark and gloomy room, where nobody had been for quite some time, there stood an old control panel. It had been made at the beginning of the technology race for space supremacy, with big flashing lights and reels of memory tape that spun round whenever there was information to record. The lights and reels had seen better days. This state of the art computer was still switched on, but never monitored. Hardwired into the old mainframe computer system, along with a few other machines by its side, the system had never been connected to the new interface which had been established in the early Two Thousands. They'd lain dormant in the museum they called the Kennedy Space Centre, concealed and hidden away for decades. A distant reminder of the early missions into space. This control panel had a very special job on a mission that was never made public, just mothballed and forgotten, after years of no contact.

UNTIL NOW...

Beep...Beep...Beep...Beep...Beep...Beep...

The reels of memory tape spun into action once more, throwing over seventy years of dust particles that had settled on the top of the vintage machine, into the air, before falling lazily back down in the stillness of the storage room. Finally coming to rest on top of some already dusty large coloured lights, which suddenly burst into life on the old control panel. They started to blink in unison with the piercing sound of...

Beep...Beep...Beep...Beep...Beep...Beep...

....

Chapter 1

July 16th 1969, the launch date for the planed Apollo 11 Mission, to land and walk on the moon.

Or so we thought…
…………

Thirteen months earlier.
1st June 1968

Scott Salvador, the newest employee at NASA, a Harvard graduate, sporty, very fit and extremely technically minded, had his whole life in front of him. He was 21, but never really knew where he had been born. All he could remember from his early childhood was that it was very hot wherever he grew up. He managed to land a great job, with masses of potential in the space exploration race for the future. The perks were fantastic, smart cars, hot chicks and an apartment with everything you could ask for. He started his job at the beginning of July 1968. Scott had been given his first brief, to write a new program, for the planned Apollo missions, in his new office with his own desk, computer and large window overlooking the massive NASA complex, which was to play the biggest part of the space race to date. With the planned lunar landing and moonwalk mission's launch date in 12 months, he had his work cut out to get it finished in time. It had taken him the best part of a day to get his new office in order, that meant sorting out his certificates, files and his photos. He finally got his office just right; certificates on the wall, a picture of his top of the range Corvette Stingray taking pride of place on his desk; he was in his element, it doesn't get much better than this. He thought.

The program he had started to write was for the new mission to the moon, Apollo 11. As Friday ticked on, Scott found himself struggling with one part of the program. He gazed out of the window, deep in thought, subliminally watching one large truck after another drive away with a full load covered by a tarpaulin. His daydreaming thoughts were quickly shattered by a knock at his door. It was the chief of the department, Bill Sanderson. He had just been moved out of Scott's new office, as his promotion had given him a new office on the top floor, with all the big wigs. But with his new promotion came the new stress of looking after the newbies, like Scott. That's the nickname the older employees gave any new brain in this department, especially when they came in and jumped a few steps of the ladder like Scott did, it seemed to piss them off. Bill wanted to know how Scott was getting on with the new program.

"Fine!" he said, trying to shadow the fact that he had spent what he thought was five minutes looking out of the window, when in fact it was more like one hour five minutes.

The program he was trying to write was for the lunar module, so it could send a signal from the

Moon back to Earth, when it was roaming on the surface. This was so it could be tracked from Earth. Well, that's what Scott and his boss thought they were doing.

Bill asked Scott if he fancied joining him for lunch, to meet a few people and see how he was settling in at his new job. Scott thought it would be a good idea to clear his clouded mind and start afresh after meeting some of his new colleagues. He hadn't been down to the canteen at lunchtime yet, he had been too busy all week, grabbing a snack when he got the chance. As Scott walked down the hallway, he looked at the walls full of pictures from the past rocket launches and images of all the astronauts, past and present. They had been on some fantastic journeys over the last decade, pushing the boundaries of mankind to the extreme limits. The hallway seemed to last forever with picture after picture passing them by. Bill was giving him a brief explanation of each photo. That was until he saw somebody down the hallway;
"Come on," he said in his low chilling voice which would have sent shivers though any newbie, "there's somebody you need to meet".
There, in the distance was an angel in Scott's eyes. She could well have been an angel, she seemed to glow and glide as she walked, she was beautiful. Blond hair, tight, slim, fit looking body, she must work out thought Scott. Her skirt was just above the knees and she wore a matching suit jacket. Her walk was as beautiful as her looks, sultry and sexy. She was heading for the elevator. Scott and Bill were about twenty yards away, they quickened the

pace slightly so they could get the same elevator, the faint, calm music flooding the hallway which played for its guests. Scott was hoping she was going for lunch so he could continue grabbing the odd quick glance in her direction. The canteen was one floor below ground level.

"Hold the door!" Bill said as he nearly broke into a jog, skidding to a halt on the polished marble floor as his feet hit the elevator threshold. The lady calmly placed her hand on the door to stop it closing and asked Bill which floor they wanted.

"Minus one please," said Bill, as he straightened his tie.

"You going for lunch now Bill?" the angel said in a voice that could have melted a thousand hearts and made many a man turn his head in wonder as to who was talking. Then there was her scent! She was wearing the most aromatic and hypnotic perfume Scott had ever inhaled, it pushed all the right buttons! Scott's senses were shot, for the first time in his life he was speechless, in awe of this perfect lady who stood beside him in the elevator. He had his head slightly bowed as to not draw attention to his glances and he delayed blinking to save the images in that special part of the mind. Scott wasn't normally shy, but for some reason this woman had stolen his confidence with her looks.

"How rude of me," said Bill, "Scott, this is Kimberly, Kimberly this is Scott".

Their eyes met, her head tipped slightly forward as though she were a little shy and her smile, well her smile finished the picture for Scott, that was it! He was on a new mission. They had both felt that instant attraction the moment their eyes had met. Scott had to get to know her and he wouldn't give up until he did.

"Yes, we are going for lunch," Bill replied, "will you be joining us?"

"No, not today unfortunately," she gave a cheeky glance towards Scott, "I have to go to a meeting."

"Ok, well maybe another time?"

"Definitely!" came the reply as the elevator stopped at Bill's floor.

....

On the elevator control panel Scott had noticed that Kimberly had inserted a key and pushed a button next to it, which was now illuminated, it had no number on it, just the words;

Security Controlled Zone
Development Area One
No Unauthorised Access

Scott's curiosity got the better of him so he asked Bill about the button. He received a quick glance from Bill, the look stopped Scott dead, it would have stopped anyone for that matter.

"We don't talk about that area. It's off limits to our section. Only people with Development Area clearance can gain access. Then only a select few of them know what really goes on there. Kimberly must have clearance for that section," Bill told Scott, and then he changed the subject before he could ask any more questions. Being a very inquisitive person Scott thought he would bide his time before asking anything else about that area, but he wanted to know what went on down there for sure.

At lunch Bill and Scott sat at a big, round canteen table with food they had picked from the buffet. The food looked great, very healthy, just up Scott's Street as he was a fitness fanatic. He would be off to the gym after work to do his daily routine of running and weights, which kept him trim and fit. He prided himself on his fitness, he had always been very good at sports of any kind.

Bill started to introduce Scott to the other people on the table, starting with John who worked on the launch systems for the rockets. Then there was Colin, he was the odd looking one of the table, very shy with thick rimmed spectacles, which had lenses thicker than the bottom of a jam jar. He would talk whilst looking down at his plate and push the bridge of his spectacles up every so often, as if he had a nervous affliction. Fiona was next, she was in her late forties, very intelligent, as described by Bill and was a doctor of physics. They all chatted about their jobs at NASA and seemed to get on very well; apart from Colin who spent most of lunch muttering to himself, probably trying to work out an equation for the next space flight or something. Scott asked all the relevant questions about what they all did and how they all came to work at

NASA. Each had a very different story, but they were all the best in their field of expertise. He was most intrigued by Fiona - she seemed to be very down to Earth, married with a few kids. She seemed to gel with Scott the moment she saw him, like she'd known him before somehow.

After they had all finished their lunch they headed back to their offices for the afternoon. Scott tried to ask Bill about the lower area again, but it fell on deaf ears. As the elevator stopped on Scott's floor he stepped out and turned to say bye to Bill, but just before they parted company to get on with their work, Bill did say something to Scott before he said goodbye,

"Most of the people you have just met work in the section you were bugging me about!" With that last comment, Bill pushed the top floor button and the elevator doors shut in-front of Scott as he heard a muffled goodbye.

Scott headed back down the marbled hallway to his office. He opened his door then leaned back on it to close it, thinking about all the unseen people that must work here. What do they do? He slowly walked back to his chair and sat down to work on his program. His first day of real work had been an eye-opener for him.

Scott got back into his work and things were going very good now, he was back on track after his break. Although one thing was at the forefront of his mind. Kimberly! He couldn't stop thinking about her and longed for their next encounter, hoping it wasn't very far away. His thoughts of Kimberly had replaced his curiosity of the top secret area.

The overflowing trucks continued coming out from one of the buildings, without Scott even noticing. NASA was preparing something special and it included Scott in a way that would change his life for ever.

Chapter 2

Scott had a very disrupted family background, he never knew his real parents. He found out he was adopted at the age of sixteen when his adoptive parents were both killed in a tragic car accident. This didn't send him off the rails like it would have done to some people. He had a very strong personality and learned to deal with his emotions at a very early age. He had never tried to find out who his real parents were and nobody had ever tried to get in contact with him, so he had left it that way.

As Scott left NASA, he was heading towards his Corvette Stingray with a big smile on his face. When he was distracted by another big truck pulling out of the building in the distance. This time he looked at it, hearing the noise and feeling the rumble as the truck got closer, passing on the other side of a wire fence next to the parking lot where his car was parked. He watched the driver go past with his worn out NASA baseball cap and sunglasses on. The truck's window was open. Scott watched as the driver leaned out and spat a mouthful of what looked like black tobacco, he must have been chewing on this while his truck was being loaded.
But loaded with what and from where?
The driver looked straight at Scott as he passed, he

flicked the underneath peak of the baseball cap and tipped his head forward as not to be seen clearly. Scott tried to acknowledge the driver by slowly raising his hand and gave it a slight cautious wave, more like a salute than a wave. The driver turned back and rumbled off out of sight. Not really paying that much attention to the situation, Scott carried on heading towards his car, only to see Kimberly across the car park heading for her car. He quickly jumped into the Stingray to drive past her before she reached hers. As the key turned in the 435 Big Block Tri-Power Engine, he felt the Stallions explode under the hood in a frenzy of anticipation as to how fast they could carry their master.

He reversed his beauty out of his parking space and roared towards Kimberly. As he drew in closer she turned to see what the noise was. She looked shyly excited when she realised it was Scott. Her hair was gently blown in the butterfly effect caused by the rush of wind from the Stingray as it stopped right in front of her. Scott savoured the moment and admired the stunning picture of beauty that stood before his Stingray. One hand on her hip, her right leg slightly bent showing the top of her knee, she slowly tipped her sunglasses forward, checking out Scott in his car.

"Hi, its Kimberly right?" said Scott, "We met earlier in the elevator with Bill!"

"That's right!" Kimberly exclaimed, (as if I would have forgotten, she thought). "Nice car!" she said taking a step back to admire it (and Scott for that matter).

"A Corvette Stingray, Tri-Power, very nice," said Kimberly.

Scott was now just blown away with her.

"You know your cars Kimberly," he said.

"My father worked at the Corvette factory when it opened in St. Louis in 1954. That's where I come from, so I've grown up with these cars, they are fantastic," she said. "So where you heading Scott?"

"I'm off to the gym, try and blow away some of these cobwebs!" Scott exclaimed. "How about you? Do you have any plans?" he enquired hoping she wasn't going to say she was meeting her boyfriend.

"I sure do, I'm going out with a few of my girlfriends tonight for some drinks, we're going to Mickey's downtown. If you're around you could always call in for a drink!" Kimberly said shyly.

"You never know, I might just do that," replied Scott.

"Well, I'll have to get going if I want to make myself look beautiful!" she said as she opened the door of her car. A beat up old yellow VW Beetle. As she started the car it coughed like a sick kid and a plume of black smoke erupted from the tail pipe behind the car. Kimberly waved as she pulled out in front of Scott and sped off down the parking lot. Scott said goodbye and gave a shocked little wave as she drove off, I hadn't pictured her in a car like that, he thought. Scott put his foot down and started to follow her out of the parking lot, with a smile at the thought of maybe seeing her again that night.

Scott slammed his foot on the brakes, as a black Sedan pulled out of a parking space right in-front of him. He thrust his hand onto the air horn, that should have grabbed everyone's attention, but the two people in the car didn't even look round, they just slowly drove forwards towards the security check point. Scott waited behind the black Sedan as Kimberly had just been cleared to leave, the barrier went up and she drove off. The black Sedan pulled forward to the check-point, they seemed to take for ever, the guard was talking through the window to the driver, then he looked up and looked straight towards Scott. What was that for? The barrier finally lifted and the Sedan drove off in the same direction as Kimberly.

Scott tentatively pulled forward towards the check-point, wondering what had been said. "Identification please!" said the guard.

Scott handed his ID over to the guard who looked at the card, looked at Scott, then looked back at the card.

"Wait here please!" he said as he turned to his hut, still holding Scott's ID card.

"What's going on here?" Scott questioned.

The guard didn't say a word, he had picked up a phone receiver and was talking to someone. The guard didn't actually look like he was talking about Scott, he was laughing and fiddling with Scott's card in his hand, he hadn't even looked at it since he made the call. A queue of cars had formed behind Scott now, waiting to get home.

"Excuse me," Scott questioned, "is there a problem?"

The guard finished on the phone, stood up and walked back over to Scott.

"Which department do you work in?" he asked.
"Ermmmm, programming, why? It's all on the card." Scott replied.
"There you go sir, have a nice day." With that he raised the barrier and ushered the next car forward as Scott pulled away looking very confused. Kimberly's Beetle and the black Sedan were long gone by now, he'd been ages.

At the gym, Scott wasn't having a very good workout, he was pumping weights and thinking about Kimberly and her invite to join her and her friends for a drink.

"Should I go?… Or should I play it cool?… But then I don't want to miss my chance with this angel that has been sent to me. All these thoughts!"

Go.

No, play it cool.

Go.

No, don't go!

The thoughts were battling in his mind like he had some kind of Jekyll and Hyde syndrome making him switch from one to the other. He thought if anyone could read his mind at that moment they would have him sectioned at the nearest mental facility.

He finished his workout feeling like he needed to try again, without any distractions, but that wasn't going to happen until he could make a decision about whether to meet Kimberly. In the changing room he got out his towel and was ready for the shower that awaited him. His perfectly toned body had taken some stick in the gym, he was ready to feel the cool water raining over every sweat soaked pore, like the blade of a freshly forged samurai sword being cooled ready for the battle. The force of the shower rinsed away the sweat and left Scott feeling refreshed as if it had melted away his old skin leaving him with a new revived skin to replace his own. If only it could have the same effect on his mind, he thought. He got dressed and packed away his things in his kit bag, and headed out of the gym.

He fired up the stingray once again. The feeling of turning the steel in the barrel and unleashing the stallions under the hood always excited Scott, knowing they were there to take him wherever he wanted to go, at anytime. He pulled out of the parking lot with the same roar that had stopped Kimberly in her tracks earlier that day. Thinking of this made the mind tricks start again. Trying to usher them out of his head he pushed his foot down on the gas pedal, the rear wheels span and the Stingray started to drift to the side. In complete control Scott powered into the drift and sped off down the road leaving a faint cloud and the scent of burning rubber in the air.

He drove for a while, trying to make up his mind about whether to go and meet Kimberly or not. It was 8:30pm, he still had time to go home and get ready if that was his decision. What the hell, I've got nothing to lose, he thought. He turned his car around and headed back to his apartment in Cocoa Beach.

He hadn't had his apartment long. He moved into the apartment when he started the job at NASA, this was another perk of his new position. This was one of his favourite places in the whole world, mainly because he loved to surf and Cocoa Beach was fantastic for that. His apartment looked out over the sea and from his little balcony he had a view that was so spectacular it was a dream to wake up and see the sun rise on the horizon. It was like being reborn every morning. Scott had been left everything when his adoptive parents died so he wasn't short of money, he liked the good life, but he also liked his work and now was the time he was making mega bucks at NASA.

Pulling his car into the parking space that came with his apartment, he rushed up the stairwell to get ready. In his rush as he ran around the corner of the stairwell and bumped straight into his neighbour Karl, knocking him flying backwards, smashing the bottle of beer he was carrying.

"I'm so sorry Karl! Here let me help you up bud!" said Scott apologetically. "I should have been watching where I was going."

"Where are you going in such a rush? Is the building on fire?" Karl said frantically.

"No, I have to get ready I'm going back out to meet someone." Scott mumbled in some form of garbled response.

"Hang on! By the way you're running around like a headless chicken and trying to beat the world record for the most words spoken in ten seconds, it wouldn't be a girl by any chance, would it?" asked Karl.

"How did you guess?" Scott said, wiping down the front of his T-shirt that had been splattered with the eruption of beer from Karl's Bud that now laid smashed into a thousand pieces on the floor at their feet.

"I have more beer in my fridge, come on in and I'll grab you one, it's the least I can do!" said Scott, "No, it's ok, you're in a rush buddy." replied Karl. "Honestly Karl, please let me get you another beer and I'll get a brush to clean this mess up as well, I won't take no for an answer!"

"Ok." said Karl.

Secretly Scott was trying to find an excuse to change his mind about going for the drink with Kimberly. His nerves were starting to kick in now after he had told himself he was going.

   While Scott was sweeping up the broken bottle, that had managed to get just about everywhere, Karl was admiring Scott's apartment. It was much bigger than his. It had a fantastic kitchen dining area, huge living room and bedroom with a balcony that Karl would have given his right arm for. Karl's apartment faced another building to the right. The only plus was that there was a very nice girl who lived there she had the same view, but towards Karl, but that's another story. It only took a few minutes for Scott to clean up the mess he had created. Once done he came back inside and grabbed himself and Karl a beer out of his fridge.

"Wow! This place is awesome my friend, it must have set you back a fair few bucks?" Karl said excitedly.

"It's not bad is it? It was the view that did it for me! Perks of the job my friend." said Scott.

"Yeah, mine too!" laughed Karl. Scott looked puzzled, knowing that the view Karl had, was of the building next door.

"The view I get every morning is hotter than the sun!" Karl laughed again, "Haven't you seen the girl next door Scott?"

Scott put two and two together and laughed out loud with Karl.

Scott had only met Karl a few times in passing in the corridor since moving in, he seemed a nice guy, very funny, someone you could have a good drink and night out with! Scott thought for a moment; "What are you up to tonight Karl?" Scott asked.

"Nothing, I was on my way to the beach to drink my Bud when you steamrollered me like a freight train with a late load, why?" Karl replied frowning.

"How do you fancy coming with me downtown to Mickey's bar?"

"Oh, I don't know, we've only just met." Karl said.

"Seriously, come with me, you'll be doing me a huge favour," Scott said before Karl had chance to think about it. "There are girls there!" he added.

"Well, that's that then, what are we waiting for?" Karl replied.

"Give me a minute to get changed." said Scott.

"Yeah, good plan. I have beer deodorant at the moment, I'll meet you in the hall in two minutes," laughed Karl necking his replacement bottle of Bud before rushing out of the door.

Scott quickly freshened himself up and went out into the hallway to wait for Karl. He had beaten Scott to it, with another few beers in hand he passed one over to Scott and they headed off down the stairs and out to Scott's car. Karl had heard the stingray start up on a few occasions, he would swear it made the glasses vibrate in his cupboard, like a distant earthquake waiting to unleash its power. They drove off into the dusky evening, hesitant of what lay ahead in the downtown drinking den. It was only about a thirty minute drive to Mickey's Place in downtown Palm Bay, this was the place to hang out. Scott headed straight down the A1A past Satellite Bay across the 518 and into Palm Bay, he turned onto Pineapple Avenue and there it was, in flickering blue neon lights as if there was a short circuit somewhere in the wiring; "Mickey's Place" as large as life. They were there! Scott felt like he'd been kicked in the stomach by an angry mule that had missed it's supper, his adrenaline had started to flow.

"What am I doing here? You bloody idiot!" Jekyll said to Mr Hyde!

"What did you say?" asked Karl frowning at Scott with a puzzled look on his face.

When Scott realised he'd said his thoughts out loud, he quickly tried to make amends while digging his hole deeper! Karl realised what he had done and they laughed about it like a couple of school boys who'd got into trouble for giving the new boy a wedgie. That helped the situation, he felt more relaxed now after releasing the adrenaline and laughing it off.

They got out of the car after some careful manoeuvring around all the other vehicles in the parking lot. Scott parked beside a Ford Mustang, his next favourite car on the road. Being careful as he opened his door so he didn't get a ding, he quickly glanced into the Mustang to check out the interior. With a cocky tongue-in-cheek gesture, "It's not a patch on mine!" he said as they walked towards the bar, laughing as they went.

There were four steps leading up to the doorway. Scott thought he would be sure to trip on one of them. Even though he was as cool as Steve McQueen he was very clumsy. Thankfully he didn't trip and he made it to the front door. The handle of the door was metal and was stickier than the wax on his long board, from years of surfer's hands haunting the bar for that thirst quenching beer, after a long afternoon hunting down that killer wave. As he opened the door for Karl to go in first, he thought he might have trouble peeling his fingers off the metal work.

"Whatever that is, I want some for my board, I'd never fall off with that on!" Scott exclaimed.

As they walked a few steps into the bar, it was clear how busy this place was. There was a sea of heads and the garbled white noise of a hundred people talking at the same time, each one trying to speak just that little bit louder than the person next to them and then there was the pumping music coming from the jukebox.

They stood on a raised part of the room and there were more steps leading down into the bar area. Scott scanned the room like a lion on the prairie looking for his dinner. It was clear to Scott that this bar was the place to be! They walked down the stairs into the devil's nest, where alcohol fuelled bodies raised the temperature of the already humid and smoke filled air. The bar was six deep, all waiting to be served by the sexy bar maids who worked for Mickey, with all the customers shouting their orders at the same time it was hard to see who was getting served and who wasn't.

As Scott scanned the room for Kimberly he saw a few familiar faces from around the surfing beaches who all give the friendly nod of the head when noticing one of their own.

There she was!

She seemed to have a hidden spotlight picking only her out, making her glow from head to toe, standing out from every other beauty in the room. Their eyes met. It was like she knew where to look just at that split second when Scott caught a glimpse of her. She smiled that shy, sexy smile. Scott slowly swam through the sea of people in the room, weaving his way through the shoal of beer fish gasping for liquid instead of air. Finally he made it through, he reached Kimberly. Fearful of their meeting, his adrenaline kicked in big style! He thought he wouldn't be able to speak when he stopped, but Karl put paid to that. He was just behind Scott and broke the silence straight away with a quick cool comment about how NASA can fly to the moon but you still can't get served in Mickey's Bar. Kimberly laughed and Scott just shook his head and thanked Karl for that input. Kimberly's friends were all good looking girls so Karl was in his element. Instead of waiting for the formalities he started kissing the cheeks of all her lovely friends, but leaving Scott the pleasure of kissing the one cheek that he'd come to see.

"Hi!" shouted Kimberly over the loud music from the jukebox. "This is Jenny, Doris, Valerie and Gwen."

Scott shouted back, "This is Karl, he lives in the same apartment block as I do on Cocoa Beach". Karl had them all laughing in seconds which was a great ice breaker. Before they knew it they had moved towards the bar in the wake of people brushing past and moving out of the way. The lucky ones that had been served. They were next. Scott asked the girls what they all wanted to drink. An easy round, they all came back with Bud. Scott tried to get served for what seemed like ages. With Kimberly standing beside him he was starting to feel a bit useless, until Karl muscled in again! He shouted, at the next bar maid who walked past, for a round of Buds, the bar girl smiled and said; "Coming up!" Karl just winked at Scott and that said it all.

When the bar maid put the last Bud on the bar Scott shouted up, "Chase that with a round of Tequila shots!"
There was an excited, "Oh Yeah!" from the girls and the bar maid.
Lined up along the bar were the Tequila shots. They all got ready.
Scott said the countdown! "Three - two - one - down!"
They all raised their glasses and downed the tequila in one. The glasses were brought down with a cool sense of achievement and slammed upside down on the bar.
"This is the life!" shouted Karl.

They had managed to get a table right beside the jukebox, so it was a bit loud, but lots of fun. After countless beers and god only knows how many more tequilas, Kimberly walked over to the jukebox and put a dime in the slot. As she did it she looked round at Scott, gently biting her bottom lip and holding onto the jukebox. With one knee bent, she raised her foot to balance on her toe. Scott hadn't seen anybody in his entire life look so beautiful and so sexy as that picture of Kimberly at that moment! There was a slight pause before the music started. Then with a sensual walk back towards Scott, Kimberly slowly reached out to take Scott's hand. She gently pulled him up out of his seat and led him to the area used as a dance floor beside the pool table. She slowly started to dance around in front of him, in a sexy way that left Scott speechless. She caressed Scott's shoulders and wrapped her arms around his neck to pull him closer. Their bodies finally touched as they started to dance. The temptation of moving his hands onto Kimberly's body was too great for Scott, as he started to caress her curvaceous back and hips. His imagination ran wild. The thought of doing this to Kimberly's naked body was at the forefront of his mind. They slowly danced to the mystical voice of Van Morrison, getting more sensual by the minute. Staring deep into each other's eyes they slowly felt themselves falling into that inevitable place. Kimberly tucked her head into the snug gap between Scott's head and shoulder, it fit like a glove. Kimberly slowly nuzzled herself closer until her lips were just grazing Scott's neck. Scott gently tilted his head towards Kimberly as they moved in unison to the music. Scott couldn't believe that it was only just this morning when he had met Kimberly in the elevator, he was now dancing with her like this in a bar.

What a day to remember!

As Scott looked back to where Karl was sitting, he began to smile. There was Karl sitting in the middle of four beautiful girls, his arm around the back of two of them as he lounged like a prince with his harem. Every now and then he would say something and they would all laugh, it made Scott smile even more. Karl was having so much fun, knocking back the Buds and Tequila he was so glad Scott had bumped into him that night! Literally!

It was getting late and the last few bar flies were kicking around Mickey's. The waitresses were chatting at the bar as they tidied up, getting the place ready for the next day.

"I suppose it's time to go," Scott slurred.

Scott tried to stand up from his seat, he felt like he was at sea, swaying this way and that! "I don't think I can drive!" he chuckled, and fell back into his seat, nearly missing it.

"We better grab a cab!" said Kimberly.

"At 2 am, it's going to be a pain!" exclaimed Karl. "I'll get somebody to ring for one, we are all going back the same way."

There were only four of them left now, Valerie, Doris and Jenny had reluctantly gone at about 12 o'clock, when Valerie's boyfriend had come to pick her up and given the other two a ride home. Karl told Scott that he would bring him back for his car later that day if he didn't mind riding on the back of a motor bike! Scott's face was a picture at this suggestion! They all got into the cab when it arrived. It was there pretty quickly considering the time of night. The girls' places were on the way home so they swung by there first.

Scott was in the back with Kimberly and Gwen, while Karl was in the front chatting away to the cab driver in a funny drunken manner, slurring his words and getting all the directions wrong back to their neck of the woods. When they reached Gwen's apartment Karl turned around and tried to lean over from the front to give her a kiss goodnight but slipped and fell on the cab driver. He started to laugh but the cab driver was getting a bit sick of this and said, "Hey man, you'll be walking soon if there's any more fooling around!"
They all started to laugh! The cab driver sounded stoned out of his mind!
"Wow man, ok I'm sorry!" Karl returned in his best stoned voice making them all laugh even louder. He got out of the car and brushed himself down as if it would help him sober up. He concentrated on trying to walk around, to be a gentleman and open the door. They all thought it was such a funny sight, he put so much effort into each step that it looked like he was taking his very first steps again. He opened the door and held out his hand for Gwen to take, so he could escort her home, she giggled and played along with the drunken comedian. When they reached the door, Gwen opened it and gave Karl a big kiss on the cheek then quickly closed it laughing as she did so. He hovered there for a moment swaying in the cool night breeze, before leaning on the door bell. He jumped off it and put his hand over his mouth and

held a laugh in like a naughty little boy who had just done something mischievous. Just then, Gwen opened the door before he could make his getaway back to the cab. As he turned to see Gwen there, he released a laugh unique only to Karl and the hyenas. Gwen burst out laughing too, "Go home you drunken bum!" giving him another big kiss on the cheek.

Karl asked if he could give Gwen his number before he stumbled back to the cab. Scott and Kimberly were laughing at Karl.

"You're crazy!" Gwen giggled.

It was Kimberly next, she lived about three km away from Scott and Karl in a lovely beach front apartment.

"This is the place to live!" said Karl.

As Scott got out of the car to walk Kimberly to her apartment, he could hear the distant whispers of the surf calling him, luring him into nature's hypnotic power. As the waves crashed in the distance, he could see the faint spray bursting off the crest of the waves, riding the moonlit highway towards the horizon. The shimmering light reflected off the ocean like a heat wave on the long road to nowhere. He couldn't quite see the breakers but he longed to ride them. They were beckoning him to try his best, but they knew they could churn him up and spit him out whenever they felt like it. He walked with Kimberly to her door, she gazed into his eyes longing for the chance to have him hold her tight one last time, before she left him.

"I have enjoyed every moment with you tonight Kimberly, I'm so glad I came!" Scott said softly as he reached around the back of her neck, gently smoothing her long blonde hair with his hand, slowly pulling her towards him for that long awaited goodnight kiss. As Kimberly moved forwards, their lips gently pressed together, relieving that insatiable passionate feeling they both had longed for the whole evening. In the moment of their passion, time was nonexistent and extremely irrelevant. Scott said his goodbyes. They had both hoped to have this night over again, very soon.

"I hope I see you at work soon Scott!" Kimberly exclaimed passionately while pressing a piece of paper into the palm of his hand, "Call me if you can't wait that long!"

"I might just do that!" replied Scott.

"Wait!" he shouted just as Kimberly was shutting the door, "Have you got a pen? I'll give you my number."

Kimberly handed him her lipstick and said, "Use the back of my hand!"

Scott attempted to write his number down in his drunken state.

"There, I hope that's right!" he said as he handed her lipstick back.

They had one last kiss before Kimberly pulled away and slowly closed the door, whilst peering through the ever decreasing opening, until it clicked shut. Kimberly leaned back pressing her back gently against the door. She smiled, then a tear welled up in corner of her eye and rolled down her cheek. She wiped away the tear with the back of her hand. Pull yourself together girl, she told herself, you have a job to do.

With his head still spinning from the cocktail of alcohol flowing through his veins, Scott slowly turned to walk back to the cab, where Karl was waiting for him. He was scared he would never see her again. Scott made it back to the cab to find Karl chatting away to the cab driver, he turned to give Scott a cheeky wink before carrying on talking to the driver. He had the cab driver laughing; god knows what he had been saying! He didn't want to know!

Scott was very quiet all the way back to their apartment, Karl knew why! He was love struck. "Hey man, come on, snap out of it, we're home!" Karl laughed.

Back to where the night took a turn for the best, if Scott hadn't bumped into Karl, things may have been very different tonight. Scott and Karl paid the cab driver and tried to walk to their apartment.

The two of them were a picture, hanging onto each other so they didn't fall. They made it up the stairs to the place where the evening had begun. Recalling the moment they started to laugh all over again.

"What a night Scott!" Karl slurred.

"Yeah, it certainly was my friend!" Scott replied.

"I'll see you in the morning bud, so we can go and get your car!" said Karl.

"Ok." Scott replied.

Fumbling with his key, Scott tried to insert it into the lock. He had a few attempts before he finally got it in! He stumbled into his apartment after saying goodnight to Karl and closing his door. He fell flat on his face in his bed. Still fully clothed Scott fell into a deep, alcohol induced sleep.

Chapter 3

Thump! Thump! Thump!

Scott woke up thinking it was his head pounding from drinking the night before. His eyes tried to focus on the clock beside his bed, his eyes were glazed and blurred like a steamed up mirror. He rubbed them and tried to focus.

Thump! Thump! Thump!

It was 7:07am, his alarm had been going off for 37 minutes. On a Saturday he normally got up at 6:30am to go and catch the surf on Coco Beach, not today though.

Thump! Thump! Thump!

This time he realised it was the door of his apartment almost being knocked off its hinges. He rolled over and crawled off the bed, still in the same clothes as he was wearing the night before.

Catching a glimpse of himself in the mirror as he walked to the door, he stopped, confused as to why he was still in the same clothes. As he walked towards the door he had a furry feeling in his mouth, like he had been licking the carpet all night, "This is not good!" he said.

Scott nearly missed the door handle as he reached for it. When he managed to grasp and open it, there stood Karl, bright and chirpy almost as if he hadn't been out at all. "Morning love machine!" Karl said, the words seemed to boom around Scott's head like he was in a cave.

"Uuurrrr!" Scott groaned back to Karl.

He turned his back and ushered Karl in with a weak flick of the wrist. Karl followed him into his apartment.

"Hey, you look like shit man, here get your mouth round that, that'll sort you out!" Karl exclaimed as he handed Scott an ice cold Bud.

"Thanks a lot! I can't drink that!" replied Scott.

"It'll sort out your fuzzy head. Are we off to get your car buddy?" asked Karl.

"Yeah, just let me freshen up a little before we go, I might be a while!" said Scott.

"Ok, I'll make us a coffee, and put the Bud in the chiller."

Scott staggered into the bathroom to take a shower. It's a good job its Saturday and I'm not at work! Scott thought.

  After a refreshing shower and sorting himself out in the bathroom, Scott got dressed in his jeans and a white t-shirt, ready for a relaxing trip on the back of Karl's motor bike.

"Coffee is ready!" Karl shouted from the other room.

"Ok!" came the quiet, sombre reply.

  Scott and Karl sat on the balcony overlooking Coco Beach drinking their nice fresh coffee.

 "This is the life!" Karl said.

 "You're right there, except for the bad head! Look at that swell, it's a ripper today!" Scott said with a touch of; I want to be out there riding those waves.

"Why did we say this early?" asked Scott, as he rubbed the side of his head.

"We should stop off at The Diner on the way for

some breakfast," said Karl.

"Hell yeah, that'll perk me up! Let's go!" replied Scott.

They both drank up their coffee like two dehydrated camels finding an oasis in the middle of the desert. The two of them walked through Scott's apartment and out of the door before they could swallow the last remaining drops of coffee from their cups. Taking their places on Karl's motorbike they fired up the Triumph and sped off down the road. Holding on in fear of losing his life, Scott managed to get his balance sorted out before they reached the first corner.

"I wasn't expecting that!" fretted Scott.

"Feel the wind in your hair!" shouted Karl.

"WHAT?" hollered Scott.

"I said feel the wind in your hair!" screamed Karl.

Scott held on for dear life. It's not my time to go yet, he thought to himself. The Diner was only about three km away from their apartment, so they reached it in no time at all. They came to a sudden stop outside The Diner as Karl slammed on the back brake and skidded round to a halt right next to a lovely Harley Davison, throwing a dust cloud over the piece of true precision and craftsmanship. It was a lovely glossy black and chrome Harley, parked just right for all to admire. Now, it was tarnished with a light covering of sand and dust from the car park, kicked up from one of it's rivals. Scott thought that if these machines could communicate they would have had a fight there and then. They walked into The Diner still feeling worse for wear but the ride had cleared their heads a little.

Finding a booth they walked past a really muscular guy, wearing a leather jacket with the arms ripped off, to fit his extremely large biceps in. Scott instantly knew he was the owner of the Harley that Karl had just showered with dust, good job he was facing away from his bike, Scott thought. After sitting down as far away as possible from Harley man, Scott and Karl were greeted with a sour faced old woman who threw two menus on the table and said in a surly voice;

"Specials are: eggs, eggs Benedict, poached eggs, scrambled eggs, fried eggs, boiled eggs and waffles…"

"Wait for it…" said Karl.

"With eggs!" she finished.

They both burst into laughter, the waitress turned on her heels and walked off, Scott had to shout after her for two coffees, and Karl added:

"With eggs!"

That made them laugh even more!

"You know what will happen now don't you? We'll get two coffees with a poached egg on the top man!"

A few minutes later the waitress returned with a clear coffee pot, the kind that's left simmering on a hot plate for hours at a time ready for the next caffeine junkie to walk through the door, gagging for their next fix. Scott and Karl ordered their breakfast, they had eggs with bacon, sausage, tomatoes, waffles and toast on the side.

"This is just what the doctor ordered!" exclaimed Scott. They devoured their food like it was their last meal, like two starved wolves, and then filled up on the free refills of coffee. Scott got up to go to the rest room, when out of the window, behind Karl's head, he saw Harley man standing beside his bike outside, kicking the dirt in a fit of rage and looking around to see who could have covered his precious bike in a film of sand and dust. Luckily, Karl hadn't parked right next to him so it wasn't that obvious. Scott started to laugh and Karl asked what was up."It's Harley man and he's looking mighty pissed!"Just as Karl looked round, Harley man looked into the window, where they were sitting. They did the wrong thing and ducked down giggling at each other. They heard the deep rumble of the Harley start up and as they dared to peek back out of the window, they saw Harley man open the throttle up and spin the back wheel round just in front of Karl's bike! His too was now covered in sand and dust! As the Harley man reappeared from the dust cloud he had just created he sped off out of the car park laughing. Scott and Karl both looked at each other and started to laugh.

"Man, that could have been nasty!" said Karl. Scott finally went to the rest room and when he returned they jumped back on the bike to get Scott's car. When Karl pulled into the car park at Mickey's, there it was, Scott's pride and joy. His Corvette! The time was now 10am, after a lazy start to the day, Scott was planning on hitting the beach when he got back to his apartment. The swell looked great as they were riding down the highway. Scott started to day dream as he was driving his car back, about seeing Kimberly again. Wow! He couldn't believe his luck. Scott arrived back at his apartment, pulled on his wetsuit and headed for the beach. The swell was great! He paddled out and sat up on his long board and waited for a wave to carry him back in. He didn't have to wait long. There, out of the corner of his eye, he saw it! An awesome swell forming about 100 yards behind him. He started to paddle, as the wave caught up with him, it took him on the adrenaline ride of his life. He beat the water as fast as he could. Trying to catch the white tipped wonder of the world, just as it started to break. What a wave! He thought. Catching one fantastic wave after another, Scott stayed out there for hours, every wave as good as the first.

Scott needed to get back and pluck up the courage to phone Kimberly. He carried his long board back to the apartment and took a shower to freshen up. Cracking open a Bud he sat on his balcony with the phone on the table beside him, the cable stretched tight from the kitchen to the table on his balcony. There had been no phone calls. He had another Bud and plucked up the courage to phone Kimberly. Taking the piece of paper, where Kimberly had written her number, from the front of the refrigerator door, he began to punch the numbers into his state of the art phone. No spinning dial just a very cool twisted cord with a handset that sat on the base covering the numbers 1-0. His mouth suddenly went dry when the phone started to ring at the other end... four rings... six rings... he was about to give up when a sweet voice at the other end said, "Hello?"
Lost for words, there was a brief pause.
"Hello, is that Kimberly?" he asked cautiously.

"What took you so long to call?" she said in a sexy voice that had Scott melting again at the other end of the phone.

"I... I..."

She didn't let him finish.

"I'm only joking!" she exclaimed. "How's your day been?"

"Well, where do I begin...?"

Scott started to tell her the events of the past twelve hours. She was laughing and giggling at the other end of the phone as he went through all the things that had happened on the way to get his car. It was a busy weekend for Kimberly, she was going to visit her mom that night and all day Sunday, so they couldn't meet up.

"I'll have to see you at work on Monday," she said with regret.

"I can't wait!" said Scott.

They said their goodbyes and hung up, arranging to meet for lunch in the cafeteria on Monday.

All being well...

Chapter 4

The rest of the weekend seemed to drag for Scott. Checking his watch every ten minutes, which to him had seemed like an eternity. Scott had arranged to go out early with Karl on Sunday evening for a few beers, to help the time pass quicker, but it didn't help.

As Scott was sat in the bar he started to think about some of the events that had been happening lately, for some reason he started to think about the black car, the one that had pulled out in front of him at work. Then something clicked as he thought about it a bit more, he seemed to remember seeing it everywhere he had been. He wondered if he was going mad. Scott hadn't taken much notice at first but he remembered passing a black car when he left his apartment to go surfing yesterday. There were two men in it with black suits, white collars and dark sunglasses. He remembered thinking they looked odd because it was a very hot day to be dressed in dark suits. It wasn't quite beachwear, he'd thought to himself as he walked towards the surf. Not taking that much notice of the car they were in, he just remembered it was black. He wondered if it was the one that had pulled out in front of him at the parking lot at work.

The car had been parked near to his apartment, facing the sea. When he returned from surfing the Sedan had gone. All that was left in its place was a pile of cigarette butts at either side of the car, with one still smouldering away on the top of the pile!

That night when Scott was having a beer with Karl in the bar near their apartment, he was sure he'd seen the same car parked down the street with the two black suited men sitting in it. He drifted off into a daydream for a split second, trying to work out if it was the same car or not. Was it his mind playing tricks on him? Or was it just because he was so distracted with wanting to see Kimberly again? He mentioned it to Karl.

"What? Are you mad Scott! Why would there be a car following you?" exclaimed Karl laughing as he said it.

"I know. I must be mad. What the hell am I thinking?" Scott joked back to lighten the mood.

When they had finished their drinks they headed back to their apartments, passing where he thought he had seen the black car, he noticed the two piles of cigarette butts on the floor again. It was definitely the same car. He pointed out the cigarette butts to Karl, but he just curled the side of his mouth up and gave him a concerned smile.

It was getting late on Sunday evening. The sun had set leaving a clear star lit blanket with the moon so low, it looked like it was balancing on the horizon, casting it's silver presence across the ocean, like a path to a new world. Scott stopped and just looked at this moon-lit vision before him as Karl had carried on walking.

"What you doing now Scott? You've been on another planet tonight bud. Come on I wanna get back," shouted Karl.

"Yeah, yeah I'm coming!" replied Scott, saving the image he'd just seen.

Daydreaming about Kimberly, he suddenly realised that Monday at work was going to be hard, wondering if he was going to see her at lunchtime. Scott and Karl reached their apartment and said their goodbyes. Scott turned the key in his door and went into his apartment still daydreaming.

"That's funny!" he exclaimed.

A faint smell of cigarettes hit his nostrils and then he felt a breeze on his face. The door to the balcony was open!

"I'm sure I shut that before I went out today," he told himself.

Shutting the door he checked the apartment. Nothing was missing and nothing was misplaced.

"I must have forgotten! I'm going crazy!" he muttered under his breath.

The next morning he got up as usual. Same routine as most days, heading for the gym and then to work, still with just one thing on his mind, Kimberly! He had never felt like this before about anybody, and it was driving him mad.

That morning the hours seemed to drag, it took forever to get to lunchtime. Finally, Scott headed off down the corridor past all the great pictures of mankind's ultimate achievements once more. Reaching the elevator he pressed the call button and stood, waiting for it to arrive. The arrow above his head pointed up, telling him it was on its way. It seemed to take for-ever, as if it had been summoned from the bowels of the earth.

When the doors finally opened there were three

faces he hadn't seen before. As Scott stepped into the elevator, any talking had stopped dead. He noticed the man in the middle looked very edgy, his brow dappled with beads of sweat. He had a man standing either side of him, one of them looked like he had his hand on his back. All three were dressed in black suits, white shirts and thin black ties. Scott said, "Hello!" and nodded his head to acknowledge his fellow workmates, then he turned to face the doors. There was no reply from anybody, just a slight stumble from the man in the middle, as if he'd been pushed from behind. As he went to push the button on the control panel he noticed there was a key in the Authorised Personnel Only point.

"Which floor?" said Scott as he waited for a reply, with his finger hovering next to the panel of numbers.

Nothing but deadly silence was the reply.

Scott pushed the zero for the ground floor and the elevator doors shut tight. You could have heard a pin drop on its descent. When the elevator reached the ground floor, everyone got out. The men rushed past Scott and hurried off in a different direction, there were a few glances his way as Scott had said, "Take it easy fellas, what's the rush?"

The man who looked very scared in the elevator had slipped something into Scott's pocket without him noticing, as they all brushed past. Scott walked on slowly wondering what had just happened, he felt a little bit awkward, as if he had walked into a conversation about something he shouldn't have heard, or something out of his clearance level. As

Scott got near to the canteen he felt his jacket's breast pocket and realised he had forgotten his wallet. He'd left it in his desk draw.

"Damn!" he sighed.

With his mind all over the place at the moment he was forgetting everything. He turned around and headed back to the elevator, the doors had just started to close as he approached them. There was nobody in so he ran towards it, his slippery shoes skidding to a stop on the polished floor. He just managed to get his arm in before it closed, this opened the door again. As he pushed the button he noticed the key had gone!

Once he reached the floor of his office he hurried along the corridor back to his room. His phone was ringing as he entered, not knowing how long it had been ringing he rushed to lift the receiver.

"Hello?" he said whilst trying to catch his breath.

"Hi there, it's Kimberly!" the sweet voice said on the other end of the line.

"Hi, how are you doing? I've just popped back into the office, I forgot my wallet," Scott said excitedly.

"How was your weekend away?"

"It was ok, but my mom's not very well. She is very sick at the moment. I'm staying here a few more days to keep her company." Kimberly's voice sounded very emotional.

"Oh no, I hope she gets better soon Kimberly! Is there anything I can do?" Scott replied. "No, unfortunately there's nothing anybody can do, she is beyond help now." Kimberly said, sounding like she was trying to hold back the tears.

Scott felt sorry for her and wanted to give her a hug

to comfort her. There was a moment of silence on the other end of the phone. Scott couldn't find any words to help the situation. He could hear a faint whimper on the other end of the line.

"It's ok Kimberly, I wish you were here, so I could comfort you."

"You're so kind Scott, I'm sorry for getting upset, I just can't help it. I'm going to have to go, she's calling for me," she said.

"Ok Kimberly, you take care and I'll see you soon." Scott replied. "Oh, by the…" He didn't have time to finish before the phone went dead at the other end, he was going to tell her what he had just seen in the elevator. But on second thoughts, she's got enough on her mind at the moment. Scott sat back in his office chair and gazed out of the window into the distance. As he got lost in the moment the time flew past, and he forgot all about lunchtime, and all about the incident with the man in the elevator. He was just thinking how upset Kimberly sounded when he spoke to her.

Scott got stuck back into his work and before he knew it was 7pm. He'd missed lunch and going to the gym! There was a faint murmur coming from the hallway outside his door, he could see through the obscure glass that it was the cleaner with the floor polisher, making his way down the hall, cleaning the tiles so they shone like new ready for the next morning.

When Scott finally got ready to leave the office it was getting dark. He was on his way out towards his car when he checked his pockets for his car keys. His fingers tickled the foreign object in his pocket,

unknowingly nudging it around whilst he fumbled for his own keys, "What's this?" Pulling it out of his pocket he studied what was in the palm of his hand. "A key! But for where? It's not mine."
He put it back in his tweed jacket pocket and finally pulled out his car keys. His car was on it's own in the middle of the parking lot. It was so late, most of the people who worked there had gone home. As he neared his car he did notice another car in the distance. The black Sedan again! Scott could see the faint orange glow from the end of a cigarette behind the windshield that had been tinted by the night sky. Then the rumble of a truck behind the fence surrounding the parking lot startled Scott. Just like the one he saw last time, headlights blaring nearly blinding Scott through the wire mesh fence as he got into his car. He looked back towards where he had seen the black Sedan, it was gone! Scott drove home, thinking about the events of the day. The men in the elevator, the phone call, the car and the truck.
Was it just him, or was there something happening here?
   When Scott reached his apartment he put his smart tweed jacket on the hook by the door. Fumbling around in the jacket pocket he pulled out the key. Where did that come from and what was it for? As Scott walked through his apartment he left the light off, he had a plan that if someone was following him, this way they wouldn't know he was home. He walked to the window, pulling a slight gap in the side of the blinds so he could spy up and down the road outside to if he could see the black

car again. As he looked up and down the street he saw it! About half a block up. He knew it was the same car because the windows were halfway down, so the two men inside could flick the ash out from their cigarettes. There was a faint smokiness in the air oozing from the open car windows. What was happening?

Why was that car following him?

The day had been tough. Scott was tired out. He got showered and hit the sack ready for the gym in the morning. He tossed and turned in bed for a while, thinking he'd seen one of the men in the elevator before, the one in the middle who looked very edgy. But where? Then it came to him. He had parked his car a few spaces down from where Scott had normally parked. He'd said hello to him that morning!

Scott was up early the next morning, he spied through the corner of the blinds again, the car had gone! He tried to put it behind him so he could get on with his day. Scott put the new found key on a fob he'd had for years. The fob was given to him in a box full of items when his adoptive parents were killed in a car crash, he'd kept his keys on it ever since.

Scott would never lose his car keys.

That morning started just like any other morning. He hit the gym and drove to work to carry on writing the program he had been assigned to. Scott had the feeling he was being watched again, he just hadn't seen the car yet. When he parked at work he passed another truck on his way in and thought to himself, they must have moved a lot of soil or whatever was in the trucks from somewhere, they are going all day and all night.

Things weren't making much sense at the moment to Scott. He pulled into his parking spot at about the same time as yesterday and noticed the space where the man from the elevator had parked was empty. As he was walking into the building, going through the security checks he asked the guard, "What's in all the trucks? Is it soil? Where's it all coming from and what are they building?"

The guard just looked at him and said, "What trucks? What soil?"

"Come on, you must have seen the trucks? They are going out of here all the time!" Scott replied.

"We don't ask questions around here. Things happen to people who ask questions." The guard said with a, have a nice day smile.

....

"We need to find the missing object soon agent, or we'll all be out of a job! Has the key been placed"

"Yes sir!" replied the edgy agent.

The echoes of this sentence could be heard throughout Area 49. The agent turned on his heels and headed out of the automatic frosted glass doors into the marble hallway that seemed to go on forever. You would never have guessed that they were a 100 meters below the swamps that surrounded the Kennedy space centre.

The lunar missions were just a cover for the real mission that had been in the planning since 1947... the Roswell Incident.

Chapter 5

The Roswell Incident.

In July 1947, an unidentified flying object was reported to have crashed on a ranch in Roswell, New Mexico. The 509th Bomb Group recovered the flying object before anyone had the chance to see it. It is believed that the craft had hit a radar tracking balloon, which somehow got caught around the craft and made it crash. This was a great cover up, to throw the public off the scent of a crashed UFO. The debris from the radar balloon was spread all over the ranch, so it was easy to mislead people.

The craft wasn't very big, about eleven yards in diameter and about five yards at its thickest part. It looked to be the same shape as a doughnut curving in on the top. It didn't look very aerodynamic. It was smooth like chromed silk. The speed of the impact had buried part of the craft, so it wasn't obvious whether it was completely round. The body of the craft didn't look like it had any seams or windows. To the naked eye, it was like mirrored glass, liquid metal reflecting anything that was near to it, making it virtually invisible. From the side you couldn't see onto the top very well, most of it was covered with soil and pieces of cacti from the dry ranch ground. The impact had scorched the ground for about fifty yards behind. Where the craft had come to a rest it had built up a mound of earth covering the top. A few small brush fires were still smouldering, tinging the air with the scent of charred wood.

On first arrival at the crash site, the 509th Bomb Group set up a security perimeter, so nobody could enter. They did an inspection of the area and they noticed that there wasn't any damage to the craft's external surface. That led them to think there must have been some kind of shield that surrounded it, or it was made from an extremely unusual material. A low frequency humming noise could be heard from around the area of the craft. There was only one visible opening, but there wasn't any sign of a door in the wreckage from the radar balloon or in the area around it. A light glowed from the opening, a multi coloured light with a beautiful array of different colours reflected around the inside of the craft, shielding the view from outside.

A wooden ladder was placed against the side of the craft up to the opening. Tentatively, a member from the 509th Bomb Group climbed the steps and peered inside. Looking through the craft's opening it was like one big circular room, filled with light. The high powered beam from a military vehicle's spotlight shone into the craft, everyone very wary as to what might lay ahead. As the soldier peered into the opening, he was met with the image of a being just inside the doorway. He froze, looking straight at the being from another planet's face. The soldier's reflection glared back at him from the being's large black eyes. The rainbow of coloured lights flowed over the being's body, like the mirage of an oil spill in a dirty puddle. Its outline became distorted with all the shadows. The frozen soldier on the ladder didn't move a muscle, he was transfixed by the sight of this being. Was it alive? he wondered.

Finally, he moved up the ladder and stepped inside the craft. The being didn't move! There were what looked like pods coming from the floor. Each one housed a form of being, stagnant in appearance, frozen in time. These must have been encapsulating the beings when it crashed. Four in total. One of them was damaged and a clear jelly-like substance had oozed out onto the floor of the craft. The being inside the smashed pod must have managed to open the access door before dying from injuries caused by the crash, or our atmosphere. On first examination, the being's appearance was the typical impression of an alien, big black eyes that started near to the bridge or a hump which looked like the nose. The face was completely smooth, with no openings for a mouth, ears or nostrils. This area around where our nose and mouth is, was protruding and what looked like two thin veins were going round the neck and down the back to a raised section on either side of the being's back. There were also two thin lines going down the side of the being to the hip area where there were some dark patches, like fingerprints, three on each side, these looked like they were glowing very faintly.

The being was a light grey in colour, it's height was approximately 6′ to 7′ and very well built all over. The exact height was hard to tell, due to the position the being was in. The skin was very smooth. You could make out every muscle shape. They all looked very similar, strong and powerful.

Every muscle was visible, the forearms looked really powerful and the chest was very well defined, very similar to the physique of a body builder. There was no visible clothing on this being, or on the ones in the pods. The amazing array of colours was coming from a ball of spinning light at the centre of the craft, it stood out like a mystical multicoloured sun.

A recovery team joined the soldier in the craft, they too were faced with this being from another planet as they entered. Transfixed at the lights and the amazing sights before their eyes, it took them a few minutes to pull themselves together. Once they had collected their thoughts, they tried to remove the being, they turned it over and also noticed two veins from the face and neck going down its back into what looked like two large shoulder blades on each side of the back. It was very odd and made the being look like it had a kind of hunched back. There was an indented impression to the bottom of the pod that the being had come out of, which looked the same size and shape, as if this thing on the being slotted into it. The back of the head looked bulbous and slightly elongated. There were weird shattered glass fragments all over the floor mixed in with the jellylike substance, which may have been the liquid from inside. The soldier kneeled down and discreetly picked up a piece of the glass, it melted into the jellylike liquid and rolled off his hand back onto the floor of the craft.

"Wow, this is… Have you touched anything soldier?" questioned one of them.

"No Sir! Not a thing Sir!" The soldier said, as he

thought best not to mention about the glass on the floor.

"Good keep it that way soldier, stand guard at the opening and if that thing moves, you've got our backs. Right?"

The soldier moved cautiously back to the opening, and watched as the men looked around the craft.

The pods were tube like, rounded at each end and half clear, the back section was the same colour as the rest of the craft, they looked like they moulded into the floor, projecting up into the area around the spinning ball of light. Four of them in total. It gave the illusion that they didn't touch the floor of the craft, they seemed to hover there like magical clear cocoons waiting to produce an unknowing being. On first glance around, there were four odd looking shapes. Chair like, all connected by a bright blue circle of light, each one facing a pod. That was it, there wasn't anything else in the room from what they could see, apart from the sprawled out dead being. There wasn't enough time in this location to do a full investigation, so the inside of the craft would have to wait till they moved it to a secure place. It wouldn't be long before people got wind of the incident and tried to come out and see what had happened. Photographs were taken of the whole area before anything was moved, just incase something was missed.

A number of samples were taken from the wreckage before anything was contaminated with human contact. They took jars full of the liquid off the floor and samples of the glass fragments that lay scattered throughout the craft. As they carefully picked up the glass, using some large metal tweezers, they could feel a strange force pulling on them. They placed the glass specimens into small jars, the items rattling as they hit the base.

The team had been told to take the whole craft, as it was, back to a place called Area 51 after they had finished taking their samples. This operation had to be kept completely secret from anyone. All personnel that had attended the crash site had been briefed with a code red conduct file, and told not to mention a word about what they had seen to anyone or they would be facing military action or a court marshal.

Chapter 6

This is the mission that NASA had been working on for the last 20 years.

The task of getting the craft back to Area 51 was mammoth! It had to be done as quickly as possible. A team started digging under and around the craft. Some of the men had to get on top and clear off the soil and debris that was covering it. A few of the men had reported that they hadn't been feeling too well whilst they were digging, some had nose bleeds and headaches. They were told to get on with it. When anybody wearing metal got too close to the craft they could feel a slight pulling sensation.

After they had been digging for a while, the men clearing away the debris from the top discovered the craft looked more like a doughnut than first thought. A shaft of piercing light blinded one of the men as he reached in and cleared the last few bits of debris away. They could see straight through to where the ball of light was spinning! Finally the men working on the bottom half had broken through the piled up earth, they were able to pass some thick high strength straps underneath, so it could be pulled out and lifted onto the truck.

The craft had to be made to look like it was something else, before it could be moved. It was covered with more of the shiny silver aluminium balloon material that the Air Force and NASA used for high altitude weather observation balloons. It was then placed on the back of a very large army truck by a military crane, ready to be transported to Area 51. As the craft was being lowered onto the back, the suspension of the military truck started to lift slightly, it groaned and creaked, as if it was being pulled towards the craft somehow. It was then covered with a dark green tarpaulin so nobody could see what was underneath.

The Roswell crash site was about 1400 kilometres away from Area 51 and would take a few days to drive. Some of it would be done under the cover of darkness, to limit the amount of people that would see the convoy of army trucks. Once they had left the crash site it would just look like any other convoy of trucks and shouldn't bring that much attention.

Every inch of the crash site had been checked and rechecked, to make sure nothing had been left, except some of the debris from the radar tracking balloon that had caused the crash in the first place. This was left to show the reporters a decoy crash, to throw them off the scent of a crashed UFO. It all had to be completed before anybody from the newspapers or television was allowed in, to report on what had happened, so the window of opportunity was very short. The location was mapped and the direction of the landing channel was logged, just to see if it was heading anywhere in particular. The crater and the landing channel were filled in and all that was left was a load of tyre tracks from the military vehicles.

Back at Area 51 the task of finding out who they

were and what they were doing here began.

....

Area 51 is situated in the middle of the Nevada desert just near Death Valley. Of course Area 51 does not exist, so everyone who works there, doesn't! That's the way it's got to be.

Most of Area 51 is in vast underground chambers deep below the flat salt lakes. Looking from above it just looks like a few hangers and an airstrip! But under the flat salt plains there is a vast network of tunnels and chambers full of secrets. All personnel have been sworn to secrecy, so they can't talk about anything that goes on there. Some of George's friends have worked there in the past and for some reason or another they've just disappeared without a trace. So now George just gets on with his job and does what he is told. He is a top scientist and has worked his way into Area 51 so he can help with unexplained events like this.

There are 51 areas around the USA which do not exist, they range from Alaska to New Mexico, even Hawaii. These areas are there for one reason and one reason only. To explain the unknown, house diplomatic personnel in times of emergency and develop technology for the future. They keep and research interesting finds from around the world and gather intelligence and information on the unexplainable.

Area 51 is the largest of these areas, the second largest is Area 49 in Florida, Merritt Island to be precise. They hope to extend Area 49 and use it as a testing base for future space travel. These plans come direct from the S.I.S. (Secret Intelligence Service) an organisation set up by US President Grover Cleveland in 1894. With a select few people he started this sector to follow up on a large number of UFO sightings that had been reported around his time in office, to investigate any unexplained events and any unexplained findings. Some of the other secret areas include the Hoover Dam, Mount Rushmore, Niagara Falls and the White House to name but a few. They all have deep underground areas that house unexplained things and gather intelligence on events around the world. They are in places you just wouldn't think of.

Very few of the US presidents even knew of the areas existing in the past, unless they needed to know, they were kept in the dark when it came to the S.I.S. Government money supported the building of these places and was done under the cover of other projects, like the Hoover Dam and Mount Rushmore, so they were able to build the areas with great ease.

The S.I.S is known to very few people as the Secret Intelligence Sector, it's aim is to keep the world from unexplained events and try and find explanations. The people who work for the S.I.S don't always know it, they think they work for the government in very restricted areas. Which in a way is true!

....

The three pods containing the other beings, remained intact at the crash site. They had been kept as they were in the craft. On the side of each of the pods was a series of lights and graphs, they were thought to be monitoring the vital signs of the beings inside the pod. The power supply to the pods was somehow still active, it was unknown what was still powering the craft. The open pod's lights were flashing, it just showed a bright red circle and an unrecognisable symbol blinking away. In the centre of the craft was the glowing ball, trapped inside what looked like a glass sphere, a clear material contained the light inside. It was a kind of cloudy white, blue, red, green and pink, a rainbow of different colours, all mingled in together. It was spinning at a very high rate, too fast for the naked eye to see. This must have been the power source for the craft, they must have found a way to harness the ultimate form of energy to power the craft. There were no other moving parts of any description. Above and below the glowing ball was a tube, which was the same colour as the craft, very shiny and smooth. It splayed out, moulding into the ceiling and the floor. Through it you could see lights or particles of light that were coming from the ball and moving up and down the tubes, coating all the areas of the craft. The lights seemed to separate into their different colours and flow off in different directions throughout, some to the front, the side, the back and the ceiling. They looked like veins under the surface, taking life to various parts of the craft. It was an amazing sight. Somehow the ball of light was contained inside this material, open to the top and bottom of the craft, where the light was visible.

At Area 51, the being that died in the crash was taken to the specialist surgical team, which had been put in place as soon as the discoveries were made. The six strong team was being led by a man called George Wilkinson, a well known scientific brain.

The lab at Area 51 was deep below the surface, about a hundred yards down. The only way to reach it was in the massive elevators that were in one of the hangars. These were big enough to take aircraft down. Beside the mammoth elevator there was a smaller one, for cleared personnel only.

The being had been transported to Area 51 in a different truck, more like a medical ambulance, strapped down to a surgical trolley. The vehicles had been taken down to the hangar together in the large elevator. The truck with the craft was in front of the ambulance carrying the being. The truck slowly moved off the elevator, taking care to not spill its load. It drove into the hangar, past all the other objects and parked up under the winch. The ambulance moved next, but this didn't go too far into the hangar, it stopped just off the ramp, so they could remove the being and the ambulance could go back up. Once they had managed to get the truck down into the chamber below ground, they had the unnerving task of getting the craft off the truck. In the underground hangar they had winches fixed to tracks on the hangar ceiling with pulleys and chains, so they could be used to lift and move things around. The craft was secured using these chains.

In turn they were linked onto the straps that had been left in place around the craft and lifted into the air. It was placed on a rolling base so it could be moved around easily. There were lots of other prototype aircraft down here, things that looked out of this world, craft that would never be able to fly and others that people had spotted flying around, thinking they'd seen a UFO.

As the being was wheeled out of the ambulance they pushed it past the craft, something strange happened! The trolley seemed to be pulling towards the craft, some kind of invisible magnetic force. The four soldiers pulling and pushing the trolley, guided the being, which had been draped in a white sheet, past the craft. This unusual force grabbed one soldier's attention, "Did you feel that?" he said to the others helping.

"Yeah, maybe just a problem with one of the wheels!" exclaimed the soldier.

Unknown to the team, the spinning ball of light inside the craft had started to gain speed, the low frequency hum becoming less audible to the human ear as it span faster.

The laboratory was down a long cave-like corridor, with lots of lights along the ceiling and a rough man-made floor. Door after door passed the soldiers by as they headed for the lab. The being was laid out on a stainless steel table, lots of implements surrounded the surgical team, on separate tables and trolleys. They started the autopsy of the extraterrestrial, hoping to gain some knowledge as to who or what it was. The scalpel was the first instrument to be used. They tried to

cut open the skin, but to no avail. It just took the sharp edge off the blade as if it had been used on a stone instead. The next implement was like a sharp disc coated in diamonds that was attached to a mechanical device that span it at very high speed. It was normally used to cut through metal or bone. This didn't work either, it just wound the skin up and stopped the disc. Then the skin spread back out, slowly going back to normal. They rolled the being over onto another trolley, which they had positioned beside the one it was on. It took four of the lab workers and the soldier standing guard to do this. They then looked at the section on it's back, it was hard to the touch with a scalpel, seeming to send a tiny arc of electricity from its razor sharp point, yet when one of the technicians touched it with his pencil it felt soft, the skin seemed to burst with light. It didn't look like the thing on the back was part of the being but looked like a separate back pack, underneath the skin. Nothing they were doing could break the skin encasing this being.
"Maybe we should try taking it back to the craft?" a voice from one of the team said.
"In the craft where the beings were cocooned, this exact same shape must have connected them to the pod somehow and maybe even to the craft," he added.

The team decided to take the being back towards the craft for inspection. It was rolled back onto the other trolley and wheeled back to the chamber. They were going to try and fit the being back into its pod.

When they got back to the hangar they slowly

wheeled the trolley towards the craft until it started to feel like it was being pulled again. They then stopped and held the trolley steady waiting for things to be put in place. Inside the craft some lights on the side of the pod started to glow and some unusual lights started to squirm around the indented part in the back of the pod. It looked like the inside of a walnut shell. These lights hadn't been seen when they pulled the being from the craft at the crash site. The lights were flowing faster around the craft now, since the ball had started to gain speed. Some unusual lights started to glow on the fingertips of the being. Just like humans they had four fingers and what looked to be a thumb, bigger in size and just like the rest of the body they were covered with this skin. No finger nails were visible, just light patches on the fingertips which were now known to glow.

"Pull it away!" shouted one of the team. "It must be magnetic or something, it's getting harder to hold the trolley, something is wrong. This didn't happen at the crash site. Maybe the craft is gaining power! Something might have caused it to lose some power in the crash," he added.

"That was close!" stressed George, the head of the scientific team as they moved the being away from the craft.

They didn't know what to do, so they decided to take the being back to the lab again for further investigations. As they were pushing the trolley back to the room, the pulling eased off and the lights on the finger tips went dim.

Back in the laboratory they were trying all sorts to

get this being to reveal its true identity, but with no joy. They were all starting to get really frustrated, they had been working on it for hours now.

"Nothing is working! We are just not equipped for this, it's no use. We are drawing blanks with everything we try!" ranted Tom. "What can this material be?" He motioned to the rest of the surgical team.

   George was looking at the fingers again where they had seen the lights. He brought over a microscope and set it up so he could take a closer look at the finger tips, fiddling with the eyepiece, as he focused in on this skin like material covering the middle finger. George slowly moved his eye away and rubbed it, then took another look.

"Take a look at this Tom," said George.

Tom walked over to the microscope and looked through the lens, taking his time and fiddling with the focus ring again, he also moved slowly away.

"What the hell is that stuff? I've never seen anything like it in my life!" he said.

"I don't know Tom, I'm with you on that."

The rest of the team took it in turns to look at the findings, all excited about what they might see. Through the microscope the material took on a whole new form. It was built up with what looked like tiny little hexagon shapes, not visible to the naked eye. Minute hexagons interlinked to form this super tough skin, impenetrable to everything they used to cut it. George stood, tapping his pencil, thinking.

"Have you got an idea?" asked Tom.

"I wonder…" he said out loud. "Soldier, take a shot

at the being."

"What?" replied the soldier.

"Are you mad?" someone shouted.

"I think that if a shot were to hit this material it would not penetrate it!" George said. "Soldier, take the shot."

"Sir, no Sir, I will not shoot that thing Sir."

"Give me your side-arm soldier!" ordered George.

"I cannot do that Sir."

"You can have mine!" came a deep rattling voice from behind them.

It was the new Head of Investigation at Area 51!

"If you're wrong about this, then we'll have some explaining to do."

Luckily, George had been trained with firearms so he was able to take the shot. He was used to shooting desert rats though and not beings from another planet. He pointed the gun at the thigh of the being and slowly squeezed the trigger. The bang from the gun echoed around the room, down the corridor and into the hangar. Everyone's ears were ringing in the room now. The bullet had hit the thigh dead on, as it did it ricochet off and went straight across the room smashing a jar filled with an animal specimen from years ago, turning it to mush as it hit the stainless steel lab top. The gooey decaying remnants splattered some of the men standing close to where it fell, it seemed like the only thing holding the specimen together was the liquid in the jar. The rancid smell filled the nostrils of all the men in the room, overpowering the odour which had started to set in from the decaying being laid out before them. The room fell silent, as

everyone was trying to get their hearing back.
"You were right George, good work, we have some progress. Or maybe not! We now know that these beings can't be shot. How are we going to get past this amour-like skin?" questioned the chief still rubbing his ears.

They all stood in silence. George was holding his chin, in a deep pondering trance. Then he suddenly spoke up, "Maybe these lights on the fingers have something to do with it?"
"How?" came a reply from another team member.
"Well, maybe this isn't the skin after all! Maybe it's just a protective layer! Like our clothing!" he replied.
"What, like a space suit?" laughed the team member. The laughter filled the room and George wished he hadn't said anything.
"I'll have none of that here! If you hadn't noticed we have an alien of some description in front of us, so a space suit doesn't seem out of the question or out of the ordinary now does it?"
The room fell silent once more, his voice more deadly than the crack of the gun.
"Tell me more about your theory," he enquired as he looked around the room fixing his eyes on the team member who joked about it.
"W-w-well S-S-Sir," he stuttered in complete fear of being shot down.
"Take it easy, I don't bite!" the Chief butted in.
"When we took the being into the hangar, where the craft is, the fingertips started to glow Sir. I was just thinking that the pod could somehow be transferring energy into the being because that's

where it should still be. If the being has to get out of it's protective layer that might have something to do with it! Just a thought Sir!" he sighed a huge sigh of relief getting that off his chest.

"You have a very good point man, we should try that immediately don't you think?" he proposed in a raised voice to prove a point to the rest of the team standing there looking at the floor wishing they had thought of it now.

"Well... what are you waiting for?"

They all started rushing round trying to look busy.

"What's your plan then?" whispered the big Chief into George's ear, "You do have a plan don't you?"

Chapter 7

The Chief was new to Area 51, transferred here as soon as the word got out about the craft. He hadn't really had a chance to properly meet the new team yet, having had only one quick briefing with them before it was due to arrive. There was no way he'd be able to remember who they all were, he was hopeless with names and usually just said, you there or you man. This investigation had brought him here from Area 36, and anybody who knew Area 36 would have known this young highly ranked military person wouldn't have seen much action, went straight to the top by shouting at people, but he came highly skilled and highly recommended to work with all these secret events. He'd investigated many UFO sightings and worked on numerous unexplainable artefacts, which had been found around the world. Area 36 is deep inside the mountains, under Mount Rushmore in South Dakota. The vast cave and chamber network had been found whilst they were surveying the national park, well before the building of the famous four presidents' sculptures into the granite face. A great cover-up for the real project that was going on in the background.

"W-w-well Sir, if we take the…" he was stopped dead.

"DON'T TELL ME MAN! TELL THEM! What's your name man?" the Chief bellowed furiously, his anger showing as a red mist descended over his face.

"G-George sir, I'm the head of the laboratory testing facility here, we met..." stuttered George as he didn't get the chance to finish.

"Well, G-George, it's your call. You're in charge!" he said.

George had worked in Area 51 for seven years. He lived just outside Las Vegas in a small place called Indian Springs, relocated to there to work on a government program for this facility. Indian Springs was a town used to house people by the United States Air Force who worked in the Air base and at Area 51, the advantage being it was only a 105 kilometres away, so it was easy to commute.

George had been married to Linda for five years and they had just found out that she was pregnant with their first child. Things couldn't be better for him at the moment, he was on cloud nine. Linda didn't really have a clue what George did at Area 51, she thought he just worked at a military base as an aircraft mechanic for the Air Force. George had been sworn to secrecy years before he met Linda, so it was easier to keep the act going, this was the same with all the Area 51 personnel, plus they'd all been given other normal job titles.

George told them about his plan to take the being back to the craft again on the surgical trolley but not to get too close, as the being might be pulled back into the pod. Just close enough for the lights on the being's fingers to glow again. Then they would get a better idea of what to do next. The being was placed back onto the mobile trolley and secured down with straps around the head, wrists, chest, waist and each leg, then wheeled back towards the craft. Once they had noticed the lights starting to glow they stopped and put the brakes on. The attraction seemed to get stronger, as if it was recharging the being somehow. They thought the trolley would be fine where it was, but when they let go, it started sliding towards the craft, making a screeching noise from the wheels that sent shivers through their bones, like a grimacing teacher, pulling her finger nails slowly down a black-board, trying to get the class' attention.

"Quick, grab it!" shouted one of the team. "It's moving!"

They all grabbed it again and it stopped.

"That was close!" he panted.

"We need something to weigh it down, something heavy!" shouted a team member.

"How about that?" someone pointed towards a big truck that was in the hangar.

"Ideal!" exclaimed the Chief. "Someone reverse that frigging truck over here now!"

One of the soldiers from the 509th Bomb Group, who was on guard in there, heavily armed to provide back up just incase things got nasty with the beings, jumped into the truck and reversed it up to the trolley. They hooked it to the trolley with a massive chain, which was attached to the back of the vehicle.

"That's not going anywhere now!" the soldier insisted.

"Maybe it's just the metal trolley that is being pulled and not the being!" shouted one of the team.

"Whatever it is we need to stop it!" came the reply from the Chief.

They noticed the fingers were glowing brightly now, but only three of them.

"Why are there only three of them glowing?" George muttered as he rubbed his confused head, "What's going on?"

"What's that under the straps on the side? It's glowing!" Tom said as he was pointing to under the waist strap.

"Can you reach the buckle and take that strap off the waist Tom?" shouted George.

The strap was undone and the three patches on the side of the body, that looked like fingerprints, were glowing the same colour as the fingertips of the being. The lines that went up the body to the hunched section on the back were starting to glow as-well, just under the skin-like material. Particles of light, like the ones in the craft.

"What do we do now George?" asked Tom.

"How the heck should I know?" he declared as he shrugged his shoulders.

The trolley that the being was laid on started to shake. The rifle the solider was holding, was ripped from his hands, flying across the room and into the craft. Discharging as it hit something inside, making a muffled bang, as if the gun had a silencer on it! The trolley was shaking so much, it took four men, one on each corner, to hold it steady. It was at this point that George had an idea.

"Lets put the fingers that are lit up on the marks at the side of the body!" he urged.

Tom grabbed one of the being's arms and undid the

wrist strap, pulling the hand down towards where the lights were on the side of the body. He spread the fingers out to fit the glowing imprints, but nothing happened.

"Try both of them!" shouted George, whilst trying to hold one end of the trolley still.

"Here, hold this trolley down soldier!" George barked the order at the soldier standing next to him. George let go of the trolley just before the soldier got hold, which made it shake even more. He fumbled with the strap around the being's other wrist, struggling to open the buckle. The trolley was shaking so much it was hard to get hold of the strap, it was being wrenched from his hand each time the trolley was thrust this way and that. Finally managing to get the trolley under control, George grabbed the buckle once more, finally undoing the strap and pulling the other wrist over to where the lights were glowing on the side of the being to see what would happen.

The trolley stopped dead as soon as the being's other hand made contact with the area that was glowing. The fingers seemed to lock in place, and that's when something that can only be described as unbelievable happened. Standing in complete silence, they all watched intently.

The grey coloured skin that encased the being started to look like it had veins of light all over it. Then it glowed brightly like a beacon, a sheer white light, which blinded everyone watching. The skin started to disintegrate, it was like a burning piece of paper without the smoke, bright orange smouldering edges, slowly burning and disappearing into thin air. It started from the soles of the feet and slowly moved up towards the ankles. It crept over each foot at the same pace, leaving no debris in it's burning path. The edge was uneven in appearance and moved up steadily, unveiling the being below. The being's skin looked light, an off white colour, like a lifeless human who'd been dead for weeks. It slowly crept up the being like the smouldering amber edge of the Chief's burning cigar but without residue, just a faint orange glow around the edge. It had moved past the ankle, uncovering a pair of feet that looked very similar to humans, only longer and more stable looking.

The being had what looked like black toe nails that were shaped very similar to ours. The skin was tight and followed every contour of the foot, showing all the muscles, tendons and veins. It looked like the life had been sucked out if it. The edges of the suit slowly disintegrated up the being's legs, well past the ankle now and over the calf muscle to reveal a very well structured leg. The dead, lifeless grey coloured skin, pulled very tightly over every muscle in the being's leg. As it slowly moved up past the knee and headed towards the thigh, all the surgical team looked more shocked as every inch was revealed. In the thigh, there seemed to be something shiny, an object running down from the upper thigh to just above the knee, not part of the being. It looked the same colour as the craft the beings had crashed in. It was a kind of liquid chrome colour and followed the same shape as the muscles on the leg, it seemed hard to the touch, as one of the surgical team found out. He was holding

an instrument and tried to touch the leg, when it got about an inch away it sent an arc of light between the two objects, like a streak of lightning, which gave him an electric shock as it hit the object on the being's leg, making a dull tinging sound, like metal on metal. This made the man jump and drop the instrument on the floor. It lay there shaking, whilst what looked like little fingers of electricity wrapped around it's shape, trying to reach out and find something else to connect to. Then, it left the floor and flew past Tom into the craft. One of the surgical team on the other side tried to touch it with a pencil and the chrome coloured material compressed and felt flexible, like touching a muscle.
"Interesting, very interesting!" murmured Tom as he was still getting over the near miss.

The material that covered the being had disintegrated to just above the waist now, it had no visible reproductive parts, just a smooth pelvic area that was coloured and covered with the chrome looking material. The areas to the sides, where the fingers attached to the glowing lights, were the same liquid chrome colour again. The fingers were still connected to this area and they still had the suit covering them.

The suit stopped on the sides under where the fingers were, then started to move more centrally up the body of the being now. It was forming an orange line from the lower part of the abdomen to just below the area where our chin would be. The orange line then followed the outline of the jaw bone around the back side of the head and then slowly from underneath the suit started to disintegrate again. First revealing this chrome colour again, it looked like some kind of head protection that covered the top part of the head and followed the cheek bones around to the eyes. The forehead was also covered with the chrome material. When the suit got past the eyes it showed them in more detail. The large black eyes actually looked like some form of eye protection, like our sunglasses, they were fixed to the chrome coloured head plate. Gradually the disintegrating suit passed the nasal area, this part was also smooth, blending around the nose and mouth, making it protrude. This material continued over the cheek bones and around the jaw, all very smooth and the same chrome colour. Finally the disintegration of the skin had revealed the head, all encased in this unusual material, showing the distorted reflections of the team looking on, as the being was revealed. At the sides of the being's head, where our ears would be, there were two vein like tubes that came down either side of the neck and round the back, heading down to this odd section on the back. It was like a complete helmet made of an unknown material. With the skin on covering the being, it gave it the appearance of a stereotypical alien, just like everyone describes. But without its skin or suit it looked much more alien. The tubes or veins were similar in colour and seemed as flexible as the chromed body parts. They had a faint movement of coloured light in them, just like the colours moving throughout the craft. The devise and vein like tubes around the being's mouth and nose, looked like some kind of breathing apparatus, like a space helmet. The material or membrane that was over the being was so tight, like a skin, it made the being look like all these things were parts of the body. As the head was completely revealed now, some of the surgical team gasped as they watched the being unveiled right before their eyes. The head was slightly larger towards the back, a bit bulbous in appearance and much larger than our heads, but in keeping with the size of the being.

The orange line crept down the centre of the being's body, then started to move to either side, unveiling the chest area. This too was covered in the chrome colour forming the muscle shapes that the team had seen through the suit. The team member who had touched the material with the pencil tried again on the being's chest. It did the same, quite soft and flexible. Like it wasn't really there. Like it was part of the being! Tom picked up another steel instrument and wrapped a cloth around it, he then went to touch the being's chest and the same thing happened as before. An arc of light like an electric spark made the connection and a dull ting when it hit the surface, as if it was as hard as a rock. Just like the last time, it sent the instrument flying across the room, pulled from Tom's grasp, slipping out of the cloth holding it, making the chief duck out of the way.

"What the..." he stopped himself mid sentence as the instrument landed crackling and shaking on the floor of the hangar, it then sprang to life and flew through the opening into the craft.

The chrome coloured plates that formed the chest went around to the back. This coloured material was also visible on the abdomen area, in the form of the ten large looking muscles that stretched across the abdomen. The dissolving of the suit had started to go down the arms now, showing this colour again.

"It seems to me, that this coloured material, what ever it may be, is covering the areas that we have our major muscles and organs," one of the team highlighted.

"You're right! It's like a form of body armour under the outer body's protective layer!" exclaimed George.

Once all the suit had disappeared around the back, the being laid there, lifeless. The areas that weren't covered by the chrome coloured material were an off white, grey colour. The only thing that had any life in it, were the chrome coloured shapes all over the body, which all somehow linked to this odd looking shape on the back, by either tubes or vein like structures with a dim light running through them. The plates seemed to mould from one into the other. The backs of the hands, fingers and finger tips were chrome in colour too. The tips of the three middle fingers were glowing brightly and were still attached to the side of the body. An outline of light could be seen around the edges, like a solar eclipse. The arms suddenly released and fell outwards, swinging down beside the trolley. The lights dimmed. It gave the surgical team a shock, making them jump backwards. The hands were large, the grasp looked strong. Each large finger was covered in this molten armour. Everything was just slightly larger in size than the human body. The hands seemed more powerful but still practical to use, they looked like they could crush a rock, or grab onto something really tightly. Who knows what they were capable of doing, covered with this strange coloured material?

After the hands dropped from the side of the being, the shaking started again. The instrument table that had been brought in after things calmed down, started to roll across the floor towards the craft. The instruments vibrated off and fell to the floor, shaking with the dancing lightening wrapping around their structure, suddenly they all flew into the craft. A few team members grabbed the other trolley and ran with it out of the hangar and into the corridor. They could see the other men struggling with the trolley the being was lying on, even though it was chained to the truck.

"Get into the truck soldier and drive this thing forward!" shouted the chief.

The soldier jumped into the truck, but as he got the keys out of his pocket they were pulled from his fingers and started to fly towards the team. George jumped up and caught the keys.

"Good catch!" The Chief cried out.

He ran towards the soldier and handed him the keys. It only seemed to be having an effect on metallic objects, so the team could to move around ok, apart from Tom who was standing the closest to the craft. He had a metal belt buckle on which was ripped from the leather before he could get out of the way. Another team member who was wearing a pair of glasses also saw them ripped from his head and fly across the room into the craft. The soldier started the truck up and put it into gear to move forward. It felt like the truck was being held back by an invisible force, it's wheels spinning on the spot, sending a cloud of burning rubber into the hangar. It finally got a grip and moved forward, pulling the trolley that the being was on away from the craft. The shaking started to ease. He got far enough away and then stopped the truck. The team followed the truck, grabbed the trolley and wheeled the being back into the operating room. One of the team went to the opening in the craft, he walked up the timber steps and looked in. There had been no noise when the items had flown into the craft, other than the discharging of the weapon. He ran into the operating room panting and trying to catch his breath.

"Hey you guys, you gotta come and take a look at this," he said whilst pointing back towards the hangar where the craft was.

George, the Chief and Tom, walked back to the hangar. They too climbed the wooden steps of the ladder. One at a time they entered the craft and each just stood there looking. The items were floating just above the empty pod the being had come out of. They hadn't hit anything, they were just floating there. Philip who had his glasses ripped from his head, walked further into the craft towards the empty pod. He tried to reach for his glasses and as he got nearer, he noticed there was a faint arc of light wrapping around them in mid air, like tiny tentacles of static electricity. He turned to the others, "Have you seen this? It looks amazing." He said.

He plucked his glasses out of the air from above the pod, the gentle arcs of light laced his fingers like a spider spinning an electric web. He turned and faced the others looking completely stunned. He placed them back on his head, the small streaks of lightning easing off as they stroked his scalp, finally stopping as he moved away. The magnetism didn't seem very strong when the being wasn't near to the craft or when they were inside it.

"Well, I have never seen anything like that before!" exclaimed the Chief.

They all made their way back and stood horrified in the operating room, looking at the being that had been unveiled right before their eyes.

"Well, how the hell am I gonna explain this one to the President? Maybe he doesn't need to know, it won't be the first time!" The Chief grunted whilst lighting up a massive Cuban cigar.

"Ermmmm, Th-th-there's no smoking in here chief!" George stuttered.

"I write the rules down here G-G-George, let's get on with things!" he commanded through a thick cloud of smoke which orbited inches away from George's face.

George started coughing.

"Oh, what the hell!" he said whilst putting the cigar out in the coffee cup beside him.

They all looked at George and then back to the chief.

"Times against us on this one, let's undo this thing and turn it over." George said quickly, "Let's see what this thing on its back is all about!"

They undid all the straps and started to turn the being onto its front, putting the other trolley beside the one it was on, they rolled it over. The back of the being was more complex than the front. The tubes that came from the head area went to the centre of the back and down into this pack-like thing. They noticed as soon as the being was rolled over, it had symbols etched into this strange looking pack, the likes of which no one on the team had ever seen before, similar to hieroglyphs. The back section was a weird shape and could only be described as looking like a brain cut in half and the pieces placed side by side, but slightly more oval. It was ribbed all over with a faint stream of light flowing around the inside.

"What the hell is that? I've never seen anything like that before in my entire life! And I've seen some pretty horrific stuff since arriving here!" George exclaimed.

"Get somebody here now who knows about symbols like this. I don't care which government area they have to come from, just get them here and keep it quiet. Make sure to get them Area 51 clearance!" exclaimed the Chief as he pointed at the soldier who drove the truck in the warehouse.

"Yes Sir!" he shouted as he saluted the Chief and ran off down the corridor to find someone...but who?

Around the edge of the section on the back, was a brighter, more white light. Not the same as the colours inside the pack or the ones from inside the craft! It was a more stable light like it enhanced the edge of the section. The multicoloured array of flowing lights squirmed around at the bottom of the ribbed sections, as if the back pack was full of an unusual spectrum of colour. Unlike the plates around the body, the back section was harder to the touch and was extremely cold, it was very unusual and looked like two large ribbed shoulder blades joined in the middle.

Looking at the being from the back these veins of rainbow lights were somehow attached to the plates that covered the chest and abdomen. The tubes followed the contours of the body and blended in around the being's sides. They looked really tight to the skin, almost flattening out against the body. There were still slight slithers of the dead grey skin showing through in areas that weren't covered by the chrome looking material. When the team rolled the being back over, the grey coloured skin areas felt slightly thicker. Cold and leathery but soft and flexible to the touch, just like when the team member had prodded it with a pencil earlier. Their findings were becoming ever-more fascinating, yet more frustrating by the minute. How were they going to find out about these beings from another planet?

"Where could these beings possibly come from, and how are we going to get this armour off?" Tom asked.

"That's what we're here to find out!" stated the Chief.

"How are we going to find that out, when we can't get anywhere near the damn thing with anything that's metal, which is what most of our instruments are made of?" replied Tom.

"Good point man!" the Chief exclaimed whilst scratching his head, "we'll have to think of something, meanwhile a few of you make a plan to see if you can find out how the beings are stored in those pods! Time is getting away with us today we need to start afresh first thing tomorrow. I'll see you all in the morning," he added. With that the Chief turned and walked out of the room, leaving the team to sort out what to do with the being, so it wasn't left out all night without its protective suit on in our atmosphere.

The surgical team strapped the being down again and wheeled it on the trolley over to the containment area, this was through some double doors in the lab which had, 'Cleared Personnel Only,' written on the front of the frosted glass. George opened the door and flicked a switch on. One light after another lit the vast area. A huge store room appeared before them, an area which some had never seen before. Straight ahead were racks, full of wooden crates, filled with findings from around the world. The wall to the right had massive steel doors on a roller system, leading into the hangar where the craft was being kept. Large tracks disappeared through the door at the top, allowed things to be transported from the hangar to the storage area. The wall to the left, housed the refrigerated warehouse, where the being could be securely stored for the night. The warehouse had a large rectangular steel door which towered above them, slightly rounded at each corner. It had a handle that looked like a steering wheel and large shot bolts that could be seen around its face. This door could only be opened from the outside. It had been specifically designed to hold anything unknown and anything unusual inside. These items included any meteor samples, plants, animals, anything beyond normal, that had been found around the world. Tom had never been in there before.

George had clearance for the area. He took out a key which hung on a chain around his neck, inserted it in a keyhole next to the big steel door and turned it one click to the right. He waited. A red light appeared. Then he turned the key another click. At each quarter turn a light was illuminated at that position, going from red to amber then yellow and finally green. He then pushed a few buttons on a keypad. There was a computerised voice that acknowledged his action, "Security clearance accepted!"

George turned the massive steel wheel on the door, it was like the big handle on a bank vault. As the huge door opened, a red strobe light started flashing and spinning around above the door with the computerised voice saying, "Warning, warning, warning!"

The voice stopped and the door seal let out an almighty hiss.

"This door must be at least thirty feet wide and fifty foot tall!" said Tom, jumping as there was another loud hiss.

The pressurised freezing air that was inside, was blown out right around the door as the seal was cracked, creating the visual effect of a snow storm as the frozen air met with the warm air of the lab. Looking like the ground had a light dusting of manufactured snow over it, which melted instantly as it hit the warm surface, leaving a light skin of water on the concrete floor. There was a ramp up into the refrigerated warehouse. The door slowly opened revealing a mammoth chamber. It wasn't clear just how large this storage area was with the warm air rushing in, it had created a bank of fog that laid stagnant in the icy air.

"This may seem like a stupid question, but why is the door so big and so thick?" asked Tom.

"This is a secure area Tom, we have samples in here that could change the world as we know it! We wouldn't want them getting out now would we?" George explained to everyone.

As the trolley was wheeled up the ramp, the wheels passed through the water on the floor, creating a trail into the icy cold warehouse. The track from the wheels froze instantly on contact with the freezing cold concrete floor, leaving a slippery ridge for a few feet into the ice cold area.

Tom was first to enter the room, guiding the trolley from the front as he walked in backwards, he could see his breath from the moment he walked in. He noticed that the chrome coloured material had clouded over as it entered the chamber, the black eyes of the being misted up as the freezing cold air made contact with the unknown material. The fog inside had started to disperse and he could see all kinds of things in there. Behind some glass doors there was what looked like a frozen section, he could see plant samples frozen in blocks of ice, different animals too, they had all been researched or kept for analysis at some point. There was a brief description at the base of each specimen, saying where it had been found and how old it was, along with a serial number which corresponded with the number above the sample outside the glass door. The dates when some of the samples had been found dated back to the early 19th and 18th century, and the age of some samples dated back thousands of years. There was an animal that Tom had never seen before. It was white with long fur and had four really large sabre like tusks around it's mouth area, two on the bottom and two on the top. It stood taller than a man on it's hind legs. It was staring straight at Tom, it looked like it had been frozen instantly in a big ice cube. As he backed up, something made Tom shiver, he didn't know if it was the temperature or the beast encased in the ice, ready to pounce. He continued staring at it as he walked slowly backwards into the wide open room. With the freezing air still creating a mist far back into the area, he still couldn't see how big it was. It was about at least 50 feet wide Tom thought, and God knows how long, it just seemed to go on and on into the distance. They had walked about 30 feet into the room when George explained, "This is a refrigeration area behind this door, we don't want the being to freeze! We just want it to stay cool!" The room was brightly lit and was slightly warmer than in the main section, They draped a big thick sheet over the top of the being, which covered it from head to toe and fell right down to the floor. "There, that should keep it warm!" laughed George.

They closed the door to the small room, this door also had a pressure seal around it, as George left he pushed a button beside the door on the wall. Tom heard it seal shut for the night.

"What else is in here?" asked Tom, sounding fascinated.

"Have a look, but don't take too long, they monitor who comes in, who comes out and how long they've been in. Just incase there is any form of radioactivity given off from the things stored here and to make sure you don't remove anything! You are being watched all the time!" George pointed up at the cameras placed high on the ceiling and around the door.

The cameras had a faint red light on the front and they were following their every move, they were slightly smaller than the one used for television at the time, but still very large. Tom had a look in some of the other cases, everything had been frozen in blocks of ice.

Why? Tom thought to himself.

Inside another block was a shiny metal object, it looked like an arm, a mechanical arm with lots of shiny tubes and pulleys. It had what looked like an elbow joint and fingers. On the side of what looked like the forearm was a pad which looked damaged, scraped but he could make out some symbols on it. Tom had never seen anything like that before.

On the corners of all the blocks of ice, there were four metal rods that attached to a cross on the top and the same on the bottom, encasing the massive ice cubes. In the centre of the cross was a big steel link with a thick cable running to a screen on the outside of the glass door, the screen had a digital readout of the temperature inside the unit.

"What are these for George?" questioned Tom.

"Those are to keep the blocks frozen and to melt them rapidly incase we need to!" replied George. "What about the link on the top?" Tom bombarded him with another question.

"That's to lift them in here. After they have been frozen they weigh a ton! Look up there." George pointed to the ceiling. There was a track that led right down the centre of the room. Above the door was a big chain with a hook on the end. There was another control panel at the side of the door to operate the hook and chain. It was clipped to the wall and a thick black rubber cable stretched upwards to the ceiling through the swirling mist, it attached to the end of the chain, linking into a motor. This allowed the operator to walk with the block, to where it would be housed until needed. Tom also noticed that the things, animals and objects inside the ice had monitors attached to them, with the wires running up to the cross at the top, which must also have led across to the screen on the front of the glass.

"Why are they monitored?" Another question. "Surely they are dead?"

"We hope so!" came the reply, "If you want to see something weird Tom, take a look down there at number 214."

Tom walked about 30 feet into what was left of the mist, passing numerous weird artefacts and animals until he came across the number 214.

"Oh my God!" Tom said, as he slowly walked backwards with his arms lifeless beside his body, still looking at what was behind the glass door, frozen for eternity. As he neared the other team members, he turned. All the colour that was left in his face after being in this cold temperature, had vanished. He was snow-white in complexion, the vision that had been before him had sucked the very life from his soul. He walked straight past the other people, slightly slipping on the frozen ridges, left from the trolley wheels just a few minutes earlier, which made him stumble out into the warehouse.

"What was it?" whispered one of the others.

But Tom kept walking, through the doors back into the lab and sat down on a chair just inside the room. Tom sat there staring into thin air with a vacant, harrowing look in his eyes.

"What's up with him?" a voice came from behind a cloud of frozen breath.

"I couldn't even begin to explain! Come on, everyone out now, we've been in here too long as it is!" George held out both arms while saying this to usher the other people towards the door.

"Can't we see it?" pan other voice asked, shivering in the cold.

"Not today, some of you shouldn't even be in here!" replied George.

George pushed the buttons again on the keypad and the door began to close. The red strobe light started to flash again, with the same warning message as before. There was a thud and a loud hiss as the door shut tightly and regulated the pressure inside the room. The light mist that had been squeezed out of the room, turned to snow again, it floated down from the edges of the door, falling once more to form a light carpet of snow which melted instantly. He reversed his original key turn and the lights went back through the sequence from green to red. George removed his key and put it back around his neck.

They all walked back through the doors and into the lab, there was only George who had clearance for this area in the containment room, the others could only gain access accompanied by him. They had found many things in the past, the odd piece of unexplained technology, fossils, the odd weird space rocks and plenty of extinct plants and animals that just crop up in the polar ice caps, or unearthed somewhere in the world every now and then.
But this was the biggest find to date!
A perfect space craft from another planet, with alien beings on board. This was the greatest discovery ever in the history of the mankind.

This was a new team, formed especially for this finding, only the Chief and George had observed what Tom had just seen in the frozen chamber. They knew why he'd had the life sucked out of him. The other three members of the team were still trying to get Tom to talk.

Tom had been brought over to Area 51 with a colleague called Henry. They had worked together on numerous cases in the past. He was a fantastic research man in this field, his input was vital to the project.

The day had drawn to an end and everyone was so tired, wanting to get rested, ready to start first thing in the morning. The team waited to go through a vigorous decontamination process at the elevators. This consisted of standing in a cubicle wearing eye protection, whilst steam consisting of various chemicals was blasted at them to help reduce the risk of contamination. Once sprayed, the team were free to go into the elevators and return to the surface. This process also happened to the vehicles in the elevators when they had been carrying anything unusual.

Most of the team returned to the surface after the long day underground, they got changed into their other clothes ready to leave the none existent Area 51. Looking forward to what may lay ahead tomorrow...

Chapter 8

The next morning George woke with one of the team prodding him with a pen. He stayed at the lab so he could be there if he was needed.
"Wake up George it's morning!" called Tom.
"What? Already!" George mumbled, whilst rubbing his eyes to look at his watch.

As George prepared the lab for today's task of looking at the being, the rest of the team slowly started to arrive at the lab. There was a high presence of soldiers on guard down in all the areas on a night to make sure that nothing got tampered with, especially the being and the craft. Some guards stayed outside the lab so George could get some rest. The craft was ok over night, nothing had happened or moved. The mysterious ball of light in the middle of the craft was still spinning and the lights were still travelling all over, but nothing had changed.

The sound of the elevator could be heard in the distance, the faint rumbling and the opening of the massive doors echoed through the hangar. As the elevator descended to the chamber, it felt like there was an earthquake going on above. Once down here, there were loads of tunnels and chambers, rooms full of things like guns, food and anything you could think of incase war escalated and people had to take cover or incase of any other unexplained events. You could easily live down there for quite some time, these places, which were all over America were prepared for every eventuality.

It was 8am and George was sipping on a cup of hot coffee when the phone rang in the lab, it was the chief of operations wanting to know what the plans were for the day. Once George got off the phone he was chatting to Tom about where he had been transferred from. Tom was a very good lab technician, he had just been introduced to George the day before the craft was due, when the team had arrived from all over the USA. Tom had been flown to Area 51 from Florida (Area 49). At college he had specialised in biology with a special interest in extinct animals and had left with all the degrees you could ask for in his field of expertise, a truly remarkable young man full of knowledge. He had been headhunted to join the team just like the others who'd arrived, helping in any-way possible with his expert opinion and research capabilities. He had worked at area 49 for two years without even knowing. He'd been researching all sorts of things and he was reporting his findings back to the S.I.S. without realising it. After leaving college, his path in life had somehow just fallen into place. Or so he thought. It's amazing what doors can be opened if you have been spotted by the right people at an early age.

"The animal life forms of this planet are very alien to us humans and very little is known about most of them," explained Tom, "I was asked to come here with an open mind! I need more than an open mind in this place!"

A team had been brought in to move the craft to a

special holding area in the chamber, so it could be worked on and down here security was crucial. They had suspended the craft from the ceiling on a track which lead to another room in the corner of the massive chamber. They had left the straps, that the military had used when loading it onto the truck, around the craft. The team guided the craft through the chamber and into the room, they placed some wooden steps leading up to the open doorway. Some timber supports were put in place and a frame was built underneath, to keep it steady when people were working on it. There were two lead lined doors on the front of the room, big enough to get the craft in and out so it could be moved at a later date if needed. The walls and ceiling were also lead lined, to stop any radiation leaking out if it contained any and so it wouldn't attract any metal objects. Everything metal that was not fixed down in the room had been taken out. Somehow this attraction from the craft was not as active when the being wasn't near. The ones that were still in their pods didn't seem to have the same effect. But they weren't taking any risks, it only seemed to have the magnetising effect when the being had been brought over to the craft for some reason. There were huge cables leading into the room, all encased in a rubber protection. Their plan was to see if they could get any information from this craft or the beings in the near future, they knew it wasn't going to be a quick job. They needed to be far more technically advanced to be able to understand the technology that had been presented to them.

George, Tom and the rest of the team donned their surgical masks ready for another long day. As they headed to get the being out of the refrigerated area, Tom asked George about all the things stored in there. Especially what he had seen in 214!
"I can't tell you much about all the things that have been found, although I've been here for some time, I've not worked on a lot of the things," explained George.
"But that thing it 214, can't be real! Can it?" questioned Tom.
"As far as I'm aware it's real alright," answered George.
"Most of these things have been kept in this facility since it was opened in 1932, the place was built for these kind of items, also for soldiers and men of power incase of emergency. It was a lot smaller back then and has been added to since. When they started the work to extend the facility, they found a network of underground tunnels and chambers which they were able to use without creating new ones. That's why a lot of the walls are just jagged melted rock, a bit like old lava tunnels. There's miles and miles of under ground tunnels and a few large chambers which were still left. They go right under Mount Wandell and Papoose Mountain. The salt plains way up above are an ideal cover for the facility below." added George.

George had seen a lot of changes in his seven years at Area 51, there was always something new going on. Testing of this and testing of that, new things being brought in, some you'd never believe existed.

"Things get found all over the world, all the time and people and governments don't know what to do with them or where the things have come from, that's where we come in! We take it away and brush it under the carpet as such," sighed George. "Take that thing there!" George pointed at the metal looking arm. "That was found in the North Pole by Robert Pearly in 1909. When he and his team got lost trying to find the North Pole they stumbled on a glacier with deep caverns of towering ice walls, this was twenty meters below the surface! Which means it had been there for centuries." explained George.

"What? And the public doesn't know anything about it?" voiced Tom.

"Nope, not a murmur!" came the reply through his frosty breath.

There were hundreds of artefacts in this facility, too many to mention, but now Tom was part of the team, he would be seeing a lot more weird things.

"Now you're here, there is no going back!" George laughed, as he walked through his misty cloud of icy breath.

As everyone had arrived, George called a meeting with the assembled team.

"We need to crack on with things today! They want answers upstairs!" exclaimed George as they stood around the being again.

The being was cold to the touch, it had a faint mist coming off it, like a lake on a fresh winter's morning. Most of the tools they were using today were plastic or ceramic, they found out that this didn't react with the shiny, coloured material that

covered the being's body.
"Let's start with the face area, I want to see what's under that helmet and breathing apparatus." George ordered, "and let me know if there is any progress on the pod area in the craft, we need that information ASAP!"

They started by trying to lift the part off around the mouth. It wouldn't budge, not even a bit. All the areas that were covered with the coloured material were stuck on somehow. As if they had been fused to the skin. They didn't want to cut the being to take it off, so they had to think of something else. After a night in the cooler, the being looked more human than first thought. The only difference being that it looked taller and very muscular.

"Maybe we need to do what we did yesterday with the fingers on the side of the body?" suggested Tom. "That might work!" exclaimed George, "Right, now undo the arms from the straps, but leave the rest of the body strapped in and see what happens!"

The straps where reluctantly undone, the arms were a bit stiff, like they had frozen slightly in the chiller or rigor mortis had started to set in. Eventually, they were able to move the fingers to the imprints. As they were getting closer, they noticed that only two of the imprints were glowing this time, the two on the edge, leaving the one in the middle dark. They put the two outer fingers of the right arm on the imprints and that's when everyone jumped! The forearm started to light up, the symbols along the bottom lit up one by one around an area that was like a small screen, it was harder to the touch, curved around the forearm, a bit like black glass. It wasn't rock hard though, it could still be compressed slightly like the chrome material. There was one of these screens on each forearm. The one on the left arm flickered, then a blinding bright blue light, which started as a piercing dot in the middle, crept from side to side on the screen and slowly started to move to each end, revealing a view of the being's body on the screen. Illuminated symbols were positioned on the screen next to all the parts shown on the being's body.

"Could this be something to do with the protective armour the being is wearing?" George suggested.

"Maybe if we try touching the symbols next to the items on the screen, they will release the parts on the body?" replied Tom.

"It's worth a shot!" George exclaimed.

Tom touched the head part on the screen with a pencil, he took a step back and waited. Nothing happened.

"Well, it was the fingers that made everything else happen on the body, let's try that! Let's try touching the sides again." John, one of the scientists on the team, proposed.

"Hang on! I've had a thought. Maybe it has something to do with the lights that are at the ends of the fingers?" suggested Tom.

"Let's give that a try, bring that arm across here and see if that does anything." George said excitedly, in his muffled voice from behind his mask.

The team was ready, they grabbed the arm of the being and started to bring it over.

"Slowly does it now," George whispered.

"There!" shrieked Tom, "The finger tip, it's starting to light up."

The light had started to glow in the end of the finger, next to where a human thumb would be. They brought it closer to the forearm of the being to see what would happen. As the finger got closer to the screen, the light intensified, even the symbols on the bottom of the screen started to glow brighter too. These graphics on the screen slowly started to illuminate one by one, next to each part of the armour or device the being was shown to be wearing. They touched the glowing finger tip onto the symbol, next to where they thought referred to the helmet area. There was a loud hiss and a blast of mist from around the being's breathing apparatus. The black eyes seemed to dissolve and ascend into the head plate, disappearing but to where? The material seemed to turn from solid into a molten form, but how could this be?

The space helmet slowly followed in turn, melting like an ice-cream on a blistering hot day. Then the molten form seemed to be sucked down by the vein like structure on the side of the neck, which in turn was sucked into the part on the being's back, turning into an array of faint multicoloured lights. The team stood frozen to the spot, bewildered as to what had just happened before their eyes.

What was left in front of the scientists was remarkable? A truly unexpected life-form. The facial structure was as human as any one of us. The skin was so perfect, blemish free, wrinkle free and hair free. The features of this being looked male, not feminine. They were all in a state of shock.

They were expecting something out of the ordinary, something strange, something horrible, but to be presented with this form was more of a shock to everyone than had been expected.

The hands were dangling beside the body, everyone had let go when the hiss from around the mask had happened. The eyes on the being were closed, they had eye lids but without any lashes - very smooth. George took a step forward to the trolley that the being was laid on and with the end of his pencil he opened one eye lid. There it was! The eye! Almost human, surrounded by white but with a slightly larger and more elongated cat like pupil with bright blue surrounding. The being's appearance had shocked them all, just a slightly larger and more muscular form than human, with very little or no hair at all.

They lifted the arm across to the screen again, the lights intensified once more and this time they put the finger that was glowing onto the symbol that looked like the chest. Again, the solid material on that area started to turn from the solid state into the molten form and was then taken into the part on the being's back. This then revealed the chest area, which was very muscular, everything was very similar to a human, just larger, and the skin was a grey colour but that could be because the being was dead. There before them was a being from another planet, but from where? Nobody knew. They continued to press the other symbols on the screen one at a time, standing watching as the being was getting stripped of its amour.

With all the shiny chrome like shields retracted

into the back part, the being looked completely different than on it's initial examination. At first, the being took on the typical form we would say an alien from another planet would look like. But now, apart from having no hair and a more muscular skeleton, it was remarkable how similar to human it was.

"We need to get the being X-rayed, to see the internal skeletal structure, now that it's free from all the protection," said Tom.

The only things left on the being now were the pack on its back, the glove like things on its hands, which looked like they were attached to the things around the forearms and some kind of material covering the groin area a bit like a pair of tight briefs but made from the same shiny material as the shields. This part was the part that had the fingerprint impressions in, just on the hips. They decided to turn the being over to see how the section on its back was attached. Not taking any chances, they made sure the being's fingers were kept well away from the screens. It's feet overhung the end of the trolley. They brought over the other trolley again and tried to turn the being over onto it. As they did this, they noticed that this section was now loose. It must have been held in place by all the tubes and armoured parts that surrounded the being. George held the pack like section so it wouldn't fall to the floor, it was light and felt pliable, soft but cold to the touch it wasn't as hard as it looked. The lights that weaved in and out of the ridges on the pack were still glowing. A flowing light similar to the one in the craft, faded and then intensified.

George placed the back pack on a trolley beside the being, it was still attached by some of the veins. As he went to place it down, it seemed like it was attracted to the trolley as if it were magnetic. When he was a few inches from the trolley it was finally pulled from his grasp and it slammed down, sounding like metal hitting metal, but to the touch it didn't feel like metal. He noticed on the underside of the back pack there were some of the symbols again. They needed to see if they could find out what they meant.

Some symbols had been lighting up on the sections around the forearms, they had been getting brighter since the protective suit had disintegrated, a bit like glowing lines of the same multi-coloured light again. Looking at the fingers, they noticed the same lights on the end of the finger tips, they were embedded into the shiny chrome coloured glove. There were tiny intense bright lights, that when contacted with the screen, were obviously used to control all the parts on the being's body. These sections all blended into the shape around the arm. They were similar in structure, so it was hard to see them under the tight protective skin of the being. The team didn't know what to expect as the X-ray room was being prepared to scan this thing from another planet.

Chapter 9

"The X-ray room is ready George! We need to move the being to the X-ray machine in examination room 31!" announced Tom from under his surgical mask.
"Ok, let's get a sheet over this thing and wheel it down there." George replied. "We don't want anybody seeing anything they shouldn't."

With the being prepped ready for the X-ray room, George had asked the two guards to go and make sure the route to the room was clear and make certain that everyone was wearing their surgical masks. They set off along the corridor.

The dark, cave like structure cast jagged shadows on the walls of the corridor from the blast-proof bulkhead lights that lit their way. It was about 700 yards to examination room 31, past a few other interesting rooms on the way. They also past some of the store rooms where food, drugs and water were stored. Other rooms were full of files of past unexplained events that had happened. There were rooms and rooms down here, full of unusual items.

One of the soldiers stood guard while the other one went back to tell them that the route was clear. The team set off down the corridor with the wheels of the surgical trolley rumbling along the uneven man-made concrete floor of the cave-like tunnel. There were big steel beams that had been put in place to strengthen the structure, a bit like the old timber beams in a mine, used to stop any cave-ins. About half way down the corridor, the vibrations from the rumbling had allowed one of the beings arms to come free from beside the body. It flopped down at the side of the trolley and swung back and fourth. The soldier was at the front of the trolley with his firearm crossed at his chest. A few yards after the arm fell out, one of the doors to the other rooms opened and out stepped a woman wearing a surgical gown with a name badge on. She was carrying a file under her arm. The soldier immediately brought his gun up and aimed it at the woman.

"Halt!" shouted the soldier.

The woman dropped the file to the floor and screamed.

"At ease soldier!" ordered George, "This is Fiona, she has clearance down here." George apologised to Fiona as she bent down, mumbling something under her breath along the lines of;

"What the bloody hell am I doing working in a place like this? It's not worth it!"

George and the team carried on along the corridor, but as they did, Fiona looked at them pushing the trolley whilst she picked up her papers that had scattered on the floor from the file. She noticed the arm dangling out from below the sheet. It was the lights on the forearm that she noticed first, then she saw that they were attached to a hand. She put her hand over her month and gasped! As she did, George noticed the arm swinging beside the trolley, he quickly came to the side and was trying to lift the arm back into place when he turned around and saw her looking. He continued to look at her until he had walked into room 31 and closed the door. As the door closed a red light came on outside above the door with the words, "Do not enter X-ray in use!" One of the soldiers was left outside standing guard.

Fiona managed to pick up all the pieces of paper that had fallen out of her file, she was very shaken and annoyed at what had just happened. What was under that sheet on the trolley? She wondered. She had seen many weird things down here but nothing like that before.

Inside the X-ray room George and the team were preparing the being, they had to position it just right to get the best results.

"First the head!" Tom ordered.

The being's head was placed under the X-ray unit and all the team went behind a lead wall, with a thick glass window in it, so they could see what was happening. The machine made a loud reverberating hum, like a faulty door buzzer. After they did the head, they moved onto the body. This took a long time doing every part of the being. Each time moving the being into a different position and retreating behind the lead wall for safety. Making sure they got it right. They couldn't risk any mistakes on this operation.

After they had finished X-raying the being's body they returned to the lab to continue their research, whilst waiting for the X-ray results. By this time it was nearly lunch and all the scientists were ready for a break, so they all decided it was a good time to stop for a short while. George and Tom stayed in the lab whilst the others went to the canteen for a coffee and some lunch. George still couldn't believe what was going on, it was so surreal, like he was reading a book or being told a science fiction story.

"Do you think we will ever find out who they really are George?" Tom questioned.

"I'm not sure about that my friend, let's take it one step at a time!" George replied.

"Where do you think they came from?" Tom pondered, whilst rubbing his eyes as if he'd been up all night.

"I haven't got a clue! I wouldn't know where to start. One thing I do know is that they are not of this world!" came his reply. "This will change life as we know it Tom, nothing will be the same from this day on! I can promise you that!" George added.

"That's for sure," sighed Tom.

"What's the plan when the team gets back George?" asked Tom?

"We'll have to see what these things are on the forearms of the being, the sections with the screen and symbols on and wait for the X-ray images to come back, then we will have more of an understanding about these beings!" answered George.

   With that, the team started to return, each with a kind of bewildered look on their face. They had all been discussing the investigation at lunch and none of them could believe what was happening.

"I cannot stress how much this has to be kept quiet! You cannot mention a word of this to anyone. Your level of clearance has allowed you to be here on this project and you should feel very privileged to be part of it! If you have any questions or you feel you cannot carry on with this investigation, then please tell me now!" George said to everyone when they had returned from their lunch, he looked around the team to make sure they had all heard. Nobody said a word! George had been warned by the chief to make sure everyone on the team understood the secrecy and clearance level of this finding.

The team moved back to the being. The sleeves on the being's forearms were made out of the same kind of material as the back part. The only difference was that when a metal object touched it, it wasn't as hard as steel like the other parts. It was pliable and soft, even the parts which lit up on the end of the fingers were flexible. On the underside of the forearm where the screen was, the symbols looked just like the ones that were on the section on the back. The gloves on the being were the chrome colour again, they only covered the back parts of the hand and wrapped around the finger tips to where the lights were, the material looked very flexible allowing the hand and fingers to move freely. When they turned the hand over they could see the skin on the underside, the finger joints were very similar to humans, allowing the fingers to move in much the same way.

They brought another two trolleys in and spread the arms out at each side, so they could get a closer look at the controls and lights. The small screen area curved around the underside of the forearm, allowing the arms to keep their shape. This part was hard to touch with a pencil, yet was soft when pushed. All these parts were invisible with the protective skin on. When the skin was on, the being just looked a dull grey colour. They thought these parts on the forearms must have given the being vital information, like a form of communication device, allowing the being to breathe and protect itself whilst on alien planets. They couldn't tell this for sure, the team were all arguing about what these sections could do.

"Ok, ok, let's calm down a bit here. We'll find out what they are for soon. But first we need to see if we can remove these things from the being," announced George.

"You're right George. We also need to get the formaldehyde chamber ready to house the being, so it doesn't start to decompose after we have removed the last few parts!" added Tom.

A clear cylindrical container was brought in and placed in the examination room, a few of the other team members had the job of filling the container. But first they checked the formaldehyde liquid on an exposed part of the being's body to see if it had any reaction to it. It didn't, which was good to know. Now that the body was nearly in its natural state they took a few blood and tissue samples from it and started to run some tests on them. The blood was nearly black, but it had a dark red tinge to it, very deep maroon in colour. It was a lot thicker than the blood of a human, but this could be because it had been dead for a few days now. The teams had to work quickly. As the bloods were taken to another area in the room to be analysed, the samples were placed into their known testing procedures. A drop of blood from the being was put between two slides and placed under the microscope. Henry was one of the top scientific haematologists in the country, he had been chosen because of some of his former work in Area 49 along side Tom. They had worked together for a number of years now, mainly in the field of animals, analysing specimens of different species. They came to Area 51 together, they were a team in this field, examining new finds from around the world. As Henry placed the slides under the microscope, he was very shocked at what he saw. A very similar blood make up to human, not what he was expecting. The bloods would take a lot of testing to see if it was identical to human, so they were in for a long wait before they were going to see any kind of results.

They couldn't put the being into the formaldehyde before they had done all the tests needed and before they had taken the forearm parts and groin cover off. After the imprints on the side of the body had helped them to remove the other shielded areas, they had a better idea as to what to look out for, to remove the other parts. It all seemed to be controlled by the lights on the finger tips. It seemed to be getting its power from the section on the back or from the craft somehow. George was taking a closer look at the forearm parts.

"Can you bring the other arm over to this one please Tom?" asked George.

Tom tried to bend the right arm over towards the left but they had started to stiffen up, it creaked as he moved it over. George was looking to see if there were any other parts on the forearm that lit up like the ones on the side.

"Look at this Tom!" George said.

The arm slowly moved towards the other, the lights grew stronger again, the screen got brighter, the symbols started to pulsate with light.

"These parts have to come off somehow," George said as he studied the symbols, "are there any other lights lighting up anywhere?"

What they had failed to notice, was that on the top of the screen, on each arm, there were two symbols, the one to the left was lit, the one to the right wasn't. Why?

George accidentally pulled the finger over the screen and the screen changed. A new picture on the screen had emerged, the two arms and the groin area of the outlined body were glowing intensely.

"Look!" George shouted. "The screen has changed."

They all looked in amazement at the screen. The symbol to the right was now lit up.

"Those symbols around the screen must be for the different parts to be removed, or different things to be added!" George said excitedly.

He moved the finger to the part that showed up as the groin and touched the symbol. The same symbol appeared on the front of the material covering the groin. It glowed brightly for a few seconds and then the chrome coloured part that covered the groin melted, just like the other sections, and flowed from the back to the front. The being was left naked, with what looked like a belt around it's waist, the section that had the impressions on was still there, and the symbol on the front still faintly glowing.

"This is fascinating!" exclaimed Tom.

All that was left were the parts on the arms now. George pressed the symbol and the same thing happened. The chrome looking material melted and flowed into a section that was left on each arm, resembling two chrome coloured bracelets with a screen between the two.

The lights had disappeared on the fingers now, but the screen was still active. They saw that a symbol on each arm next to the screen had lit up and the one in the centre of the belt started to glow brighter again, but this time it was red. Bright red. They had a round glowing light encircling the symbol in the middle, moving around and around. George pressed the finger onto the belt symbol and it opened. Somehow the flexible material had taken on a solid form that now hinged from each side where the imprints were. As with the arm screens, they touched each symbol and they released in turn feeling hard and yet cold to the touch.

George placed the other three items alongside the back section pack on the trolley. A similar thing happened when he went to place them down, it seemed like they were pulled from his hands. They had finished taking all the parts off now. The being was completely naked and resembled a human form in most ways, just on a slightly larger scale. The reproductive organs were all in the same place as humans. The only distinctive feature was a lack of hair and the apparent size and strength.

"I really hope this thing is dead!" Tom said whilst remembering what he'd seen in the ice cube in 214.

Chapter 10

The results from the X-rays had been delivered back to George via Tom. He pulled one out and held it up to the bright lights of the lab for a quick glimpse as he walked towards the light box in the lab.

"The images show a few remarkable differences! But the similarities are astounding George!" Tom remarked.

George pushed the X-rays up onto the light box to see them better. First, the head and brain view. They could see the skull structure was very similar to humans, with the eye sockets, nasal passage and the mouth area being the same. The brain filled the skull, but there was something else that stood out straight away. Two dark looking objects. They were each side of the head, just behind each ear, about one inch in size, kidney shaped, with some tubes going behind the ear and into the brain. The same at each side. They took another look at the being and noticed that there weren't any visible scars behind the ear. George stared at Tom with a puzzled look on his face.

"Are these objects part of the being or do you think they have been implanted?" George asked Tom.

"They don't look like part of the natural structure of the being George," replied Tom, "what do you think?"

"I think you're right Tom, but they must have got in

there somehow!" George said.

"We will need to remove them and see how they are connected, before we put the being into the formaldehyde." Tom pointed out.

The X-ray they were looking at started from just below the neck, to the top of the head, it showed the two implants very clearly. They could also see a third implant, it was in the neck area near the larynx.

"That part will also have to be removed." Tom added as he pointed with his pencil to a section on the X-ray.

This part was a different shape, about two inches in length, it looked like a long pill sitting just behind the throat, with strands or fibres that seemed to disappear up and down the throat. It must be linked to the larynx somehow.

"That could be some kind of communication device!" Speculated Henry from near the being. He was examining the being now that everyone had stopped prodding and poking it. He looked into the ear with the otoscope, it all looked clear. He opened the jaw and shone a bright torch into it. Everything was so similar to humans, the teeth, the tongue, it was amazing. George looked at the rest of the X-rays. Those were the only three things that could be seen inside the body of the being. The other X-rays showed that the structure of the being was the same as humans. Organs were in the same place and the skeletal structure was the same too, just larger in size.

"Now, how do we get these things, that have been implanted into the being, out?" asked George.

"Are you sure there wasn't anything on the screen that pointed to any objects in these areas?" asked George.

"Not that I noticed." Tom replied.

Tom had a look at the screen on the trolley, it was still lit up when he turned it over. After he had managed to prise it from the trolley, he brought it back over to the being to see what would happen. Nothing!

"We only used the left arm screen to release the parts from the being! What about the right arm screen?" questioned Henry.

They brought the right arm screen over too. As they did, the screen started pulsating, then it stopped. There it was! A picture of the head and neck area, with some symbols on it, these symbols matched the ones below the screen, and just like before they were encircled by a moving red light. Tom used the finger from the left arm to press the symbol for the implants next to the brain.

"Hey, have you noticed we seem to be able to push these red light symbols with just the finger, it doesn't need the chrome finger tip on!" exclaimed Tom as he jumped back when something weird happened.

The head jerked suddenly to the left, then to the right like a spasm. Then everyone took a step back. Just as they did, it stopped. George walked towards the being with his arms out wide keeping everyone behind him, except for Tom who was the other side of the trolley. He walked slowly towards the being. The spasm happened again. Then they got the shock of their lives when a glowing liquid thing oozed out from each ear. With four vein like fingers stretching forward, giving the appearance they were feeling their way out. As diaphanous as the tentacles hanging form a jellyfish. Once out, the veins were sucked into it somehow and the thing reformed into its original kidney shape on the trolley in front of them. They all stared at the object, it laid motionless now but alive with a dancing rainbow of lights inside. The objects then strobed very brightly for a few seconds and turned to the solid shiny chrome colour that the craft was made from.

What had just happened?

The team was in a state of shock.

None of them had ever seen anything like that before in their lives. The unusual objects lay motionless on the trolley beside each ear.

"So that's how they got in there!" stated George.

"What are they?" Tom questioned.

"Your guess is as good as mine!" came George's reply.

The things looked like they had some kind of gooey gel-like substance covering them, but still shiny like chrome. They were smooth in shape and had fit snugly inside the being's head, just behind the eardrum.

"Can we get these into some jars ASAP please?" asked George, whilst pointing his still shaking finger at the things.

Henry came over with two specimen jars. Tom picked the things up with some plastic tweezers and placed each one in the bottom of separate jars, it sounded like he'd put a stone in the clear jar. The things didn't move as Henry screwed the lids back on and placed them on the trolley beside the other sections.

"Well, at least we know what's going to happen when we press the symbol next to the neck of the being!" announced Henry.

Again, Tom pressed the finger of the being onto the symbol. This time the head jerked backwards a few times, then stopped with the head back and the mouth open wide. This time, the spectrum of lights flowed into the mouth. The tails from each end of the object wrapped around, feeling its way inside the being's mouth, then it formed into a solid ring around the end of the being's tongue. It too flashed and then stopped, laying motionless in the being's mouth. The team just watched, standing still for a few minutes just to make sure there weren't any more surprises. Tom used the tweezers again, picking the thing out and placing it in another jar. He then lent over the body, looking into the mouth of the being with a light.

It sounded hard as it landed in the bottom of the jar, and again covered in a gel-like substance. Henry quickly screwed the lid on and placed it on the trolley next to the things out of the ears and with the other parts off the body and slowly walked backwards in shock. The whole team stood there, shifting their gaze from the being to the trolley and then to each other. Watching, astounded, not knowing what to do next. They were all in complete shock.

Another day had passed so quickly and George had to document everything that had happened in the lab and make a full report.

"How in the hell am I going to report what I have just seen?" He wondered.

The blood results were back now and they were astonished again at how human like the beings were.

"It's as if a human had come back in time and crashed his craft in the desert!" remarked Tom. George looked at Tom with that very same thought in his head.

"Well, I can say one thing. We are not going to be cutting this being up. We will be storing it in formaldehyde for a while before it is put into deep freeze with the rest of the finds from around the world. But first, we need to drain the blood and embalm the being, so it doesn't decompose too quickly. I'll leave that to you Philip and Darren!" George ordered, as he went to the sink to scrub up.

George returned to the hangar after he had cleaned up to see how far they had got with trying to find out anything about the pods the beings were in. The craft was amazing. The spinning ball of light was mesmerising with it's beauty. The craft looked huge inside, very open. Each pod had it's own moulded, reclining seat facing towards their pod and the sphere in the centre. This had baffled them all since they had found the craft, there were no windows at all inside. Just a flat, sloped area that protruded into the craft and flowed round most of the outer walls, apart from where the opening was. Like a control panel without any controls, very smooth, made out of the same chrome coloured material. The chairs seemed to be moulded into the floor of the craft, encircled by the same veins of light. An impression the same as the section on the being's back was imprinted into the back of the seat. There were four of them in total, all positioned, facing a pod around the centre of the craft. The four pods surrounded the ball of light that was moulded seamlessly into the floor and ceiling, giving the illusion the sphere was floating. This is a work of art, thought George. We will never be able to find out how this works! Not in a million years George thought to himself.

The team of technicians working on the craft still hadn't managed to find anything out, they were hitting dead-ends all the time.

"There doesn't seem to be any way of making anything work!" One of the technicians pointed out.

George explained that they might have trouble, after what they'd experienced in the lab getting any info on it wasn't going to be a quick or easy job!

It was 7 pm on Friday and George still had the two hour drive home. He'd been up since the crack of dawn and he wasn't looking forward to telling his wife his weekend's leave had been cancelled.

"It's time to go home, the craft isn't going anywhere tonight. I'll see you all in the morning!" yawned George, "I haven't been home in days!"

Chapter 11

George took the long drive home that night to arrive to the usual question from his wife;
"How has your shift gone darling?"
How can I answer that one with everything that has gone on over the last couple of days, George thought to himself. Sworn to secrecy, George couldn't say a word about what he'd been up to, so he said what he always said;
"You don't want me to bore you with my mundane job honey! What's for supper? How are you feeling today? Has he been kicking?" George bombarded Linda with loads of questions to stop her asking him about his shift.

He put his arms around her from behind to feel her bump. George couldn't be happier at the moment, all he had worked for his entire life was falling into place and with the imminent arrival of their baby on the horizon he couldn't have been happier.
"I'm ok! Stop with all the questions already!" she said.
Linda grabbed his hands and snuggled back into his loving grasp. She turned and kissed him as she put her hands around his neck.
"You need to sit down, your supper is ruined, it's nearly ten-o-clock!" she whispered into his ear.
George smiled and turned towards the table. As he walked to his seat he started to feel dizzy, as if he'd

stood up too quickly. He had a loud ringing sound in his ears and his knees buckled, his legs giving way. He quickly grabbed the back of the chair to steady himself before he hit the floor.

"George! What's happened!" Linda shouted as she rushed up behind him.

"George!"

"George!"

George was just staring at Linda with a vacant look in his eyes. He could hear her voice, but it sounded all fuzzy, like she was way in the distance trying to shout to him. His eyes went all cloudy, like the white noise on a TV, as if he was just about to pass out.

"George!" her concerned voice started to sound clearer, "Can you hear me? George! Please George, say something!" She cried.

His lips started to move! "I… I… I..m. I'm ok!" he mumbled, as his vision started to return. He was still holding onto the chair for dear life, his knees bent. Linda turned another chair round for him to sit on.

"Here George, sit down. You're working too hard. You need a break. You're there all the time. You don't get 5 minutes off!" Linda pointed out, "Are you ok?"

"Yes. I'm fine now, thanks darling! Well, that's never happened before!" he exclaimed.

His legs felt fine now, as if nothing had happened. He stayed in his seat and Linda gave him a kiss on the cheek as she walked away trying to compose herself.

"Don't do that to me, I nearly had a heart attack!"

she sighed. "You sit there, I'll fetch your supper. What do you think happened?"

"I haven't got a clue, I've not felt like that before!" he remarked. "Maybe I'm hungry, I haven't really eaten much the last couple of days!"

George finished his supper and they talked about how things would be different when their little baby arrived.

"I don't like you working out there on that military site George!" said Linda.

"Why? It's fine, there's nothing wrong with it!" he replied.

"But you hear of all sorts of things going on there! All sorts of things!"

"What have you heard? Don't go believing everything you hear, honey, there's nothing to worry about. It's just a military airfield, it won't be there that much longer now that the war is well and truly over!" George said through gritted teeth.

"I just don't like it, I get a bad feeling about that place, there are rumours that people who work there go missing!"

"We are in the middle of the desert, people should stick to the roads!" he laughed.

"It's not funny George! I don't want you to go missing! Not now! Not ever!" she said with a tear in her eye.

"Come here, I'll be fine! Oh, by the way!" he hesitated as he held her hand. "I have to work the weekend!"

"What! Not after that episode you're not!"

"I have to and that's that! Let's not let it spoil the night honey, let's go to bed now! I have an early

start in the morning again, these aircraft aren't
going to fix themselves now are they?"

. . . .

The next morning, George woke up to the sound of
his alarm clock's bell. It was 5:30am already. He
flopped his arm in the general direction of the noise
and knocked it off the bedside table. It made more
of a noise when it hit the floor, Linda stirred,
"What's all that racket?" she mumbled as she awoke
and tried to open her eyes.
"It's ok, it's just the alarm clock! I have to get ready
and go." George said as he gave her a hug.
"Is it morning already? I'll get up and do your
breakfast honey."
"No, you won't! You just stay right where you are.
You and the baby need all the rest you can get!"
George exclaimed.
Linda paid no attention to George, so when he had
gone into the bathroom for his shower, she got out
of bed and went downstairs into the kitchen to
make him a nice breakfast before he set off to work
again. When George had finished in the bathroom
he came back into the bedroom, only to see the
empty bed and the imprint of where Linda had been
lying. He could hear her cooking in the kitchen
downstairs. Then, a few minutes later when he was
getting dressed, he could smell the lovely aroma of
fresh pancakes being made. George loved
pancakes. They were his favourite for breakfast. He
would pile them up and smother them with maple
syrup, then eat them all, while they were still lovely

and warm, washed down with some fresh coffee.

As he walked down stairs, after getting dressed, the smell got stronger and stronger, his mouth started to water in anticipation of the taste of pancakes.

"I thought I told you to stay in bed honey! You need the rest." George said, startling Linda as she put the last of the pancakes onto George's plate.

"I know you did George but I like to get up and see you off to work, I never know if you're coming home on a night! So I want to see as much of you as possible honey bun!" Linda said, squeezing his cheek as she placed his pancakes in front of him, along with the maple syrup a few seconds later.

As George carefully poured the maple syrup all over the pancakes, Linda pulled out a chair and sat beside him. He made sure that there wasn't a part of the pancake's surface that didn't have syrup on, then he picked up his fork and using the side as a blade he sliced into the top pancake and pushed right through until he hit the plate. He then did the same again and scooped up a large portion of oozing syrupy pancake and shovelled it into his mouth.

"This beats anything from the canteen honey." George said, whilst putting another load in his mouth.

"Take your time, you'll get indigestion eating that quickly!" Linda remarked.

It was now 6:30am. George had finished his pancakes and was heading out of the door. He gave Linda a big hug and kiss. She started to well up as George was leaving. She always did this when he was going to work.

"Hey, please don't cry honey, I'll be home before you know it!" George smiled, squeezing her tightly before he walked out.

"When will you be home?" asked Linda.

"I'm not sure, depends on work, honey, I'll ring you later babe. You take care, and look after that bump." George shouted as he got into the truck.

Linda stood at the door drowning in the morning sunrise and waved goodbye to George. It was another lovely morning, not a cloud in the sky. She took a deep breath in, wiped the tears from each eye, then went back inside and slowly closed the door.

Chapter 12

Year 1951

Four years had gone by with George and the team working less and less on the project. The craft, biopsies and the samples, had all drawn blanks, they'd been over and over everything, time and time again, but had come to no conclusion as to where the beings had come from and what they were doing here. The beings that were in the pods when the craft had crashed at Roswell were still in there. Their life support system was still active, flashing away on the screens at the side of the pod. They had analysed the substance that had been found on the floor when they returned from the crash site four years ago, so they knew that the beings would be preserved indefinitely.

The conclusions they had come to, were that if the beings had been travelling long distances in space, they would need to be comatose for great lengths of time. They knew they were in a kind of cryogenic state, but not frozen, more like suspended in time. The gel-like substance that the beings were in, was thought to reduce the effects of travelling at, or beyond the speed of light. They still had no idea of how the craft was powered. There were no visible working parts, just the spinning ball in the centre and all the tubes of light everywhere, these somehow kept the pods maintained.

There had been talk of a new project that would involve the craft again. A top secret mission that none of the team knew much about. All they knew was that they had to try and get some more answers and quick. News of the space race was circulating, with talk high on the agenda of building rockets. The USA did not want to be beaten into space by the Russians. Especially with the advantage of having a crashed unidentified flying object. The Russians had tried on numerous occasions to get into Area 51 with spies, but to no avail. The secret was safe so far.

A breakthrough came when George and Tom were chatting one day about the parts they took from the being. The arm pieces and the back section. Were these the answers to all their questions all along? "What if we tried them on and see what happens?" Tom wondered, "It's worth a shot isn't it?" George retrieved the arm and the back section from the secure storage area. They hadn't been out for a while. The men had been busy working on the craft and other projects that were prioritised. The sections were kept in a vault in a high security room. George volunteered to try the objects on. He slipped each arm into the sleeves, which had the screens on and then asked Tom to place the section on his back.

Nothing happened!

"Remember when we first started this investigation? We had all the problems when the being was near to the craft!" Tom explained.

"That's right!" replied George.

He removed the parts and they both went to the room where the craft was stored. The doors hadn't been opened for a while. George looked on the check sheet at the front, near to where the lock was. The last date someone had been in there was six months ago.

"Has it been that long since anyone has been in here?" Tom remarked.

"Time flies down here." George answered.

It had been very well secured, with only a few people given clearance for that area. Once the lead lined door had been opened, they walked in and immediately the lights on the back section started to glow. The lights moved very slowly and were very faintly squirming around inside the ribbed area. Not like when they first found the being, back then, they were moving at an incredible speed and intensity.

The room was just as it had been left six months ago. George had been the last person in there. He could remember where everything was, nothing had been moved. Standing side by side at the base of the wooden ladder just in front of the opening to the craft, they could still see the ball of glowing light throwing its eerie shadows around inside. Just like four years ago. The floor inside the room had a light coating of dust on its surface.

"Don't you think that's a bit weird Tom?" said George brushing his shoe in the dust.

"What?" replied Tom.

"This dust on the floor! Yet look, there's not a speck on the craft." he remarked, pointing to the craft's surface.

The exterior shell of the craft didn't have an ounce of dust on it! They both raised their eyebrows at each other.

"Are you ready for this George?" Tom asked.

"Not really!" George hesitated in his reply, "Here goes!"

George placed the back section at his feet and put on the sleeves with the screens. First the right, then the left. They were far too big for him. The screen did exactly what it did four years ago. It started with a bright light in the centre, moving from side to side then showed the body-form of the being. George wasn't expecting what happened next. The bracelet section around his wrists tightened and the molten chrome material flowed down to the ends of the fingers and started to form round to fit his hands. His finger tips started to glow. The symbols had lit-up on the screen, just like all those years ago. The back section, on the floor, looked like it was trembling. He bent down to pick it up and as he did, the light flowed faster around the ribs on it, he backed off, slightly hesitant. Straightening up again he asked Tom to pick it up. Tom bent down and picked up the back section, it felt like it was vibrating. It also felt like it was being pulled slightly towards the craft.

As Tom lifted the back part towards George's back, the lights started flowing really fast around the object. He placed this section onto George's back. Two straps came from nowhere and hooked up and over his shoulders, it seemed to mould into him. George stood there in his white technician's jacket, his sleeves rolled up with the screens on and this weird thing on his back.

"What am I suppose to do now?" asked George.

"How the hell should I know!" laughed Tom.

George smiled at him with a concerned smile, he could feel the vibrations on his back as he neared the opening of the craft.

"Right, I'm going in!" George pointed to the open doorway into the craft.

"Are you sure you want to do that?" Tom replied.

"No!" George said as he took a step forward.

He stepped up onto the first rung of the wooden ladder. Taking his time, he slowly reached the top and walked into the craft. Nothing had happened inside the craft, all this time the team had been working on it, until now.

Tom walked up the wooden ladder to the opening and stepped inside the craft. The glow from the mysterious spinning ball in the middle, sent ripples of multi-coloured light around the interior surface, like shimmers of moonbeams bouncing off a lake on a clear night. Walking towards the ball of light, George cautiously looked all around the craft. Getting ever closer to where this unusual object had spun continually for years. George moved a hand towards the sphere and the lights on his finger tips started to glow. He inched one of his hands closer to the ball. An arc of light reached out from his finger tips and caressed the glowing sphere's surface.

"Look at this Tom! Can you see it?" whispered George excitedly, "It's amazing, come and have a look."

Tom slowly followed the path of George over to

where this magical event was happening.

What happened next shocked both of them. George brought both of his hands towards the sphere to see what would happen. Arcs of light that looked like electricity or lightning oozed out of each finger tip and rooted him to the sphere. Each arc of light was creeping and crawling around the sphere. Where his hands were positioned the lights flowing around the back section intensified and started squirming around all the channels, as if it was recharging the unit. Then, one of the screens on his arm changed from the body display to more symbols and images. One looked like the sphere of light. He hovered his finger over this symbol and the light grew stronger.

"Should I touch it?" asked George.

"I don't know!" came the reply.

George hesitated for a second and then touched the symbol on the display. The sphere flashed. One bright flash, that blinded both George and Tom instantly. Rubbing their eyes and regaining their sight slowly, they noticed they were standing near to some kind of image. A display, which was hovering and spinning very slowly above the flat section which was presumed to be the control panel around the side of the craft. Spheres like planets flying around, cloudy in some parts with tiny specks of intense light, as bright as stars, were all moving around another brightly glowing ball, placed at the centre, just like our sun. The colour drained from both George and Tom's faces, they slowly started to walk backwards, Tom began to turn and immediately dodged out of the way as he noticed something out of the corner of his eye was just about to hit him.

"Woah! What was that?" shouted Tom, ducking straight into the path of another object. "I'm getting out of here."

"Wait, look!"

George placed his hands on Tom's back as he held him still, the object hit him head-on in the chest, it looked like it dissolved into him. He slowly turned his head round, with George's hands still on his back, he wondered what the hell was happening. The object slowly started to re-emerge from the other side, it passed straight through and out of his back. The odd fragment finally left Tom's body, catching up to reform the image. Tom started to move, slowly at first. Still with George's hands on his back, they made their way out of the image and looked at each other, then back at the display.

"Do you know what that is Tom?" George said.

"If I'm not mistaken, I've just been hit by a planet! Is it our Solar System?" Tom looked at George for clarification.

"I believe so!" confirmed George, "it's our Solar System, the ball in the middle representing our sun and there are all the planets, in the perfect order in our galaxy!"

Tom lifted his hand up and passed it through some of the display. The planets seemed to turn into electrical particles, like fragments of light or pixels which wrapped around his hand and followed it briefly like he'd run his hand through some water and the ripples were following in its wake. Then the objects reformed in the exact same

place. It was like they were really there but see-through, a three dimensional hologram.
"Amazing!" observed George.

The detail of this Solar System was fantastic. The clarity of the image was like nothing they had ever seen before and the planets had so much detail, right down to all the continents and the seas on Earth, to all the rings on Saturn and cloud formations on Jupiter, even the solar flares from the Sun could be seen as the sphere in the centre had turned a burnt orangey-yellow colour with bursts of fire reaching out into the image. There were symbols at the side of each planet.

George pointed at the symbols, "I wonder if that is their name for each planet?"

He put his hands towards the planet he thought looked like Earth, it was positioned directly in front of them. George seemed to be able to manipulate the planet between his fingers. He cupped it up and held it in front of them both. Tom's hand had just gone straight through when he had done this. The arcs of light from George's finger tips caressed the planet he had just plucked out of the air. The planet was still spinning in-between his hands. They could make out every detail, the polar ice caps, all the oceans and it was even on a slight tilt. George opened his hands and the planet Earth just floated back into its place in the Solar System image, the symbol followed it back to it's place at the side, then it continued spinning around the Sun. It even had the Moon spinning around the Earth, all the other planets that have Moons had theirs too. He tried it with some of the other planets, Jupiter then Saturn.

Each doing the same thing, the names stayed on the display moving around as if the planet was still there.

George then looked at the screen on his arm again. He tried touching another symbol. The image of our Solar System grew into the galaxy, The Milky Way. The planets shrunk down in size and our galaxy was opened up before their eyes. The Sun had turned from the burnt orange into a swirling volatile nebula. They both just stood looking in awe at what was being revealed in the craft. Our galaxy seemed to look like it had lots of other Solar Systems in it. They were all there, spinning and moving around. There were lots of massive Suns and different Solar Systems by the look of it. "After all this time, we had the means to access this information from the parts on the being, right under our nose!" George stressed.

These weren't the only symbols on the screen that George could see. There was another one. He brought his arm over again and touched the next symbol. The display slowly seemed to evaporate down, so only one Solar System was left floating around a bright sphere. Small at first, then it grew to a scale size and formed before their eyes.

Firstly a sun formed, then the formation of another solar system started to revealed itself. It looked far more complex than ours on first glance but that was just because it was forming. There were a few more planets and moons than in ours but they all moved around this sun, just like we did. The sun seemed to be larger, much larger. There looked to be two planets, very similar to ours in this

Solar System, one larger and one that looked about the same size as Earth. The large planet looked further away from their Sun than our Earth, but it matched the scale, it was blue, like the colour of ours. There were even white parts to the top, which must have been the polar ice caps. These parts seemed to cover a larger area around the top of the planet. Land seemed to stretch from these parts towards the centre of the planet, there was a part in the middle, blue, which looked like our oceans. George cupped this planet and brought it closer for examination. It looked like it had been solid at one point and then pulled apart in the middle, the ocean went right around the planet, with sections leading up to the white areas. He let go and it floated back into position around the sun. He then placed his hands around the smaller planet and scooped that into his hands. This planet had more land than water on it and it was closer to the sun, it still had white parts to the top and bottom just like the previous one but they were very small. The men looked at the projected image for some time trying to find a hint of information that could tell them whereabouts in the Universe this could be. They didn't have a clue. George then touched the other symbol again to bring up the Galaxy. It showed the two Solar Systems in the Galaxy, they looked close on the display but hundreds of light years apart, no-doubt.

"Do you think we'd better tell the chief what we have found?" uttered Tom.

"I'm not sure yet Tom, let's just take our time here and see what we come up with!" George replied.

"They will have to know about this, it will change everything! This is the first real explanation as to where these beings have come from and we've been sitting on it for four years!" Tom pointed out. "Let's just see what else we can do here, before we start getting everyone excited about this!"

George looked at the screen on his arm again, there were two lines that formed a link between the symbols side by side. He pressed it. A connection appeared between the two Solar Systems in the display. Some more symbols had emerged across the top of it. The line was on a slight curve and then under it was another image but not a straight connection, it was still slightly curved, a wavy line with peaks and dips. It was pulsating, compressing and then straightening. It concertinaed up shortening the distance of the top image with a straight line through the middle and other symbols at the side.

"What does that mean?" George muttered, "Do you think this is where they are positioned in respect to each other in the galaxy?" he suggested.

There was what looked like a vast empty space, filled with stars and darkness between the two Solar Systems. These were the two closest Solar Systems shown on the image, there were others, but they didn't have any symbols or connections going to them from what the two men could see.

"I wonder how long it takes to reach their solar system?" questioned Tom.

"About 200 million years for us!" George joked.

"Well at least we know one thing…"

"What's that?" came George's reply.

"They came from within our galaxy!"

George touched the symbol on the screen and the display vanished into thin air. He then looked at the screen on the other arm. This screen just had symbols on it. He touched one of them to see what would happen. A square, odd looking section appeared on the area they had thought was some-kind of control panel. This area was on a slight tilt, the section was square at first then it stretched and followed the unusual flat surface around the craft. About two feet in length and one foot deep. It displayed the pods inside the craft, on the control panel, the beings inside them including the empty pod. This pod had a flashing red outline! Each one had the vital signs for the beings inside and more mysterious symbols. George had walked over to the screen, he placed his hands over the top of one of the pod displays and just like with the planets, he could move them round and look at them, then they just floated back into place. It was so detailed in the projection, unlike anything they'd seen before. He touched the symbol again and the pods disappeared. George then touched one of the other symbols on his screen and where the pods had been, appeared three different craft design. One that resembled the one they were in and two other designs.

"Take a look at this George!" Tom gasped from behind George's back.

"These must be other forms of craft they have." George stared at the other designs for a while and then said, "If this back section, these arm pieces and what we have just seen here is anything to go by, then these could be different designs of spaceship that this craft could turn into, or different designs that these beings have in their fleet. What do you think of that idea Tom?"

"Really? Do you think so?" frowned Tom.

"Look, anything is possible here! I'm baffled by the whole situation as it is!" George exclaimed. "We have made more progress in the last day, than the whole team has in the last four years Tom!" added George.

George placed his hands near to one of the other craft's images, but nothing happened. He could pull the craft out of the display and spin them around and look at them in the palms of his hands but as soon as he opened his hands they would float back to the display. The craft designs were all different shapes but relatively the same size, the same colour and each craft showed the same flowing lights radiating from a central sphere. One of the craft looked like it had a larger sphere in the middle, moulded into two wings, that bent round, nearly forming a circle. Then another was the craft they were in and the last one had a big opening at the front, a large bulbous section behind, then it went thin in the middle, only to open out again into what looked like a flat disc, with the same bulbous shape at the other end. This last design showed a faint straight light coming from the ends, projecting into the distance and disappearing, like it was travelling down the line. They all had this one thing in common, the sphere of light in the centre of each craft.

They were still no closer to understanding how

the craft worked or what kind of propulsion system it used, all they knew was it must have had to travel long distances and at great speeds, to get from their planet to ours.

"The other symbols on the screen must show us how to use the craft!" suggested George.

They spent a good few hours in the craft trying to work it out, but couldn't seem to be able to make anything else work. They left the craft and the room, making sure that it was all secure once more. George had Tom help him remove the back section. As he took the objects off his forearms, the straps that held the back section seemed to release from the top of his technician's coat. It seemed to be easier to take these sections off once the doors to the room were closed. They went through the same sequence and George took the items back and replaced them in the secure storage room.

"I'll sort these out Tom, you get yourself off and we'll have a briefing with everyone tomorrow about our findings. I'll write up my report before I go tonight." George said, as he wheeled the trolley with the items on back through the hangar, after covering them with a sheet.

Chapter 13

George was in the room putting the items back in their relatively secure places, when he noticed that the screen on the left arm section still had a symbol lit. It was a ring symbol. George scratched his head for a moment.

"I've seen something like that before!" He said to himself. Then it clicked! It looked just like the part that had flowed out of the mouth of the being years ago.

George stopped the trolley next to the secure cabinet that stored the items. It had a special drawer that contained the objects that had oozed out of the mouth and ears. He used one of the keys on his key ring to open the lock. Pulling open the steel drawer, it made a loud squeak, they hadn't been opened for a while, in fact he thought that they had been forgotten about until now! He placed his key ring, which had the keys for the room and storage areas on the tray next to him, he used this key ring to click his truck keys onto everyday so he didn't lose them. He looked over his shoulder to make sure nobody was with him. The door had closed behind him, he was alone.

George pulled the arm sleeves on once more and they tightened like earlier. The light that flowed around the back part was very faint now. He left it laying on the trolley next to him. It was like the craft instantly recharged it when it was near, then it would take years for the lights to fade out completely.

George picked up the ring section between his glowing finger and thumb and placed it on the top of the tray where the wrist sections were. It was as brightly coloured as it had been four years ago. Untarnished and unmarked from age.

Touching the symbol on the screen with his other finger, the object on the tray seemed to turn into a molten form again. It went from a solid, shiny chrome looking ring, to a molten puddle of what looked like mercury on the tray. A shiny liquid. He then touched the symbol again and it turned back into the ring instantly and spun like a coin dropped on the floor, slowly coming to rest again on the tray as if nothing had happened. He did this again and again, it melted before his eyes into a puddle and flipped back to it's solid state.

In the molten form he tried moving his finger towards it. Slowly, as he got closer the molten liquid started to move towards the faint light on his finger. It was like it was magnetised, and his finger was the magnet. He moved his finger away very slowly and the liquid followed until he got too far and it stopped again. He watched as the liquid then started to move towards the keys. It curiously went under the key ring and around it as if it was being very cautious, like it had a mind of it's own.

George grabbed the side of his head, his legs suddenly felt like jelly. A buzzing noise filled his ears and he thought he heard a voice.
"Baarra...."
Trying to focus, he could barely see the symbol on

his screen. Then all of a sudden, he blacked out, falling to the floor. As he did so the liquid sprang back into it's ring form for the last time, the sleeves released from George's wrists and the screen went bright for a split second, then it went blank. The lights around the back section had stopped flowing, it was just a very faint constant glow.

As George fell, he knocked over a pile of things on the desk, not knowing where the ring part had gone. He was out cold, covered in paper and items from the room. His arms stretched out in front of him with the being's objects loose and unlit around his wrists.

The sense of cold and the taste of dust from the room's concrete floor, started to bring George round. How long have I been out? He pulled his watch out of his pocket, but was unable to see the face of it, as things were still a bit blurry. Noticing the wrist sections were loose now, he pulled them off after he rolled over onto his back. He could taste blood along with the dust now, his mouth and lips were dry and cracked, like a dried-up river bed. The buzzing had passed, but it had left him with the worst headache ever! Slowly sitting up, checking himself, George looked at his watch again, the time had stopped at 4:48, he had no idea what time it was now. Shaking it, he checked it again, I don't know what I thought that would do!

He managed to steady himself as he stood up, using the trolley for support. Once up he placed the sleeves back on the top of the tray and looked for the being's object.
It had gone! Disappeared!

Picking his keys up from the tray, he slipped them into his pocket to get them out of the way whilst he looked for the object. He then locked the wrist and back sections away in their secure cabinet. He checked the tray and drawer to make sure he hadn't put them away before he passed out. The only things left in the drawer were the objects from within the ears, he even looked all over the floor, but the ring was nowhere to be seen. He was starting to get very anxious now. Why had the lights stopped flowing on the back section, what have I done? He thought.

George searched and searched but he couldn't find it anywhere. He finally closed the drawer and locked it, hoping nobody else went in there for a while. Being one of the only people with clearance, he was lucky. Pulling the door shut behind him he turned the key in the lock and slipped his large bunch of keys back into his pocket.

....

On return to his desk he started to write up the report of their findings for the day, the wall clock in the lab said 5:37. That's ok thought George, he'd not been unconscious for that long. He started to write everything that had happened in the craft with the parts, the planets and the other craft designs. He left out the bit where he lost a vital piece of evidence from Roswell. He thought it best not to say anything about that.

George finished his report, his head still pounding from earlier, the clock on the wall of the lab now said 7. Closing the brown card file, he tied the string around the cardboard button on the front, just under the large red words saying, 'TOP SECRET'. George then placed the file into a secure cabinet, on top of all the other reports he'd written for this investigation. There were hundreds of files in this cabinet, I can't remember half of these, he thought. Click, he locked it with a key from his fob, then sorted everything out ready to leave for the night.

Suddenly the door of the lab opened! It was Tom. "What are you still doing here? You scared the hell out of me!" shouted George, holding his chest.
"What do you mean George?"
"I thought you'd be home by now. You left hours ago."
"Ermmmm, ok George! Have you been here all night?" asked Tom.
"What do you mean, all night? It's 7pm!"
"Ok, George, stop fooling around buddy, it's 7am George. Everyone is arriving, some of the team came down with me in the elevator, they'll be here in a moment." Laughed Tom. "You're going mad George."
Just as Tom had said that Henry walked into the lab.
"What time is it Henry?" asked George.
"Morning! It's ten after seven. Why?"
George sat down again on the chair he'd just left to go home. What's happening here? He thought to himself.
"What's that on your head?" Henry pointed at a mark, he reached out and wiped some dried blood away from the side of George's temple, "Have you hit your head?"

"Are you ok George?"

"I fell over last night, I must have knocked myself out!" announced George, as he rubbed the side of his head. "I thought it was seven at night? Don't tell anyone about this it's not a problem, I'm fine. Let's just get on with things." He added.

Tom and Henry frowned at each other and Tom encouraged George to go and get some attention, but he wouldn't, he didn't want anybody to find out the object was missing from the drawer. He cleaned himself up before the rest of the team arrived.

There were always people around down here, more people than you would think, all doing other things, working on different projects so you were never alone and sometimes you wouldn't know what time of day it was if you didn't have a watch on, and George's had stopped a long time ago. George had noticed there wasn't anybody around last night as he made his way back to the lab. He called a meeting with Tom and they went through what had happened the day before in the craft.

"We can't say anything about our findings yet Tom," Stressed George.

"Why? Don't you think we should tell the Chief?"

"No! Not yet, we have to make sure what we saw in the craft stays between you and me for the time being. I'll know when to tell them Tom, we need to do further tests first." George insisted, expressing how keeping their findings secret was vital to the investigation.

The day drew to an end, it had flown over even though George had lost fourteen hours or so of his life somewhere. Unclipping his truck keys from his security keys, he then placed his security keys into the safe. He was the only person with access. On leaving he locked the lab door and clipped his truck keys back onto his trouser belt loop and walked into the hangar, hopefully making it out tonight.

George left via the elevator, where he was decontaminated, then he went through a security check as he did every time he or anybody left Area 51. He changed out of his research clothing into his dark blue boiler suit with added oil stains for detail. He opened a door to the rear of the security check, this door opened into a small corridor which had the words 'Security Office, No Unauthorised Personnel' written on the front. It was just as bad in the large elevator, that just looked like another large room to anybody with untrained eyes. There were two large hangars inside, but it only looked like one, they were exactly the same on top of each other, this hangar was supposedly never used.
'NO UNAUTHORISED PERSONNEL' clearly stamped on every door.

When one elevator went down the other came into place as the elevator descended into the bowels of the earth. When it came up, the top hangar was pushed upwards out of view and nobody knew it was there. The rooms were empty, like a large storage area but massive, big enough to lower trucks and even planes into. All this happened under the canopy of one of the few hangars in Area 51.

George walked out of the building in his boiler suit, towards his truck. He drove a 1945 Dodge Power Wagon, it had seen some mileage since he got it. A beaten up grey colour when clean, but under the camouflage of the desert dust it looked a light beige in colour. It took George ages to drive home from Area 51, living at Indian Springs which was approx 66 miles away.

....

   Picking up the phone, the Chief bellowed, "Hello!"
He just listened. Not saying a word, the colour drained from his face and his smouldering cigar burned away in between his fingers. The large over-hanging ash breaking free in slow motion and landing on the desk next to him, exploding into a grey dust cloud before settling back down onto the wooden surface. What was to come next had shocked the chief and chilled him to the bone. As he put the phone down his only words were;
"I completely understand, there will be no loose ends, consider it done!"
There were no names mentioned in this conversation and the phone line went dead.

Chapter 14

As soon as George arrived that morning he was called to the Chief's office. He had just arrived at Area 51 that morning, after his five days leave he was feeling ready to get these findings investigated. He had gone through security so the chief knew he was there, even though he hadn't even gone down in the elevator yet.

"We were finally starting to make some headway here George!" explained the chief.

"Yes, Sir what do you mean. We're starting to make some headway? We have had some significant breakthroughs over the last couple of weeks and we hoped to have some more in the near future sir!" replied George.

"Close the door George, I have something to tell you!"

George glanced at the open doorway, then closed the door with a curious look on his face.

"The project is getting moved!"

"What! Where?" George asked with a stunned look on his face.

"The whole project. The craft and the parts from the being are going to be transported from Area 51 over to Area 49! I know this will come as a big shock George, you've been a part of it for so long now. This is a massive operation of a highly top secret nature. You are the only other person that knows about this, other than myself and SIS cleared agents! You have that clearance and you need to know what is happening now. The being will stay here at Area 51 in its cryogenic state until further notice." Explained the Chief, "And you will be heading to Area 49!"

"What? I'm confused! You mean I'll be going to Area 49? But Chief…" George was cut short.

"You will be going to Area 49 George! I'm not asking you, I'm telling you the state of play as it is now! They have requested all personnel from the original team, follow the craft. That only applies to you and Tom. The others have all been re-assigned and moved elsewhere!" The Chief explained.

"What! Where? Where's Henry gone? And the others! When are they going Sir?" questioned George, "Except for John, Sir, who had that terrible accident while driving home from work last year!"

"Yes, that was nasty. God rest his soul. But that aside, you and your family will be catered for, you will be moved, as part of your job to a new house and a new life in Titusville near Area 49 in the state of Florida! I will see to it personally that you get everything you need George, you have been a great asset on this project and you will be sadly missed! Don't forget you work for the S.I.S. you can be moved at anytime, anywhere! As for when the others are going? I have the unfortunate news that that's already happened."

"Already happened? When?"

"You have been off for five days, a lot can happen down here in five days George."

"I know Sir, it's just a shock, that's all. When is the

move happening Sir?" he asked.

The Chief looked at his watch and pondered for a second before saying anything.

"Well, that's the thing George! It already has!"

"Wha..."

George was cut short.

"The craft should be about two-thirds of the way there by now."

"Man, you don't waste any time do you?"

"This decision came from high up, really high up!" he exclaimed. "All your things, your reports, your files, the objects, the plans, and anything else from this investigation have also gone with the craft over to Area 49."

"Everything? The objects as well?"

"Of Course! Everything except the being. That stays here until further notice. Is that ok George?" asked the Chief. "Why were you worried about the objects going?" the Chief said with a deep frown across his forehead."

"No, no Sir, nothing wrong with the objects going at all Sir. I would have presumed they'd go. I'm just wondering how I'm going to tell Linda all this Sir. That's all!" he said trying to throw the Chief off thinking about the objects.

   I wonder if anybody has realised about the missing object yet? George must have had this question written all over his face.

"Can I ask, when do I go Sir?"

"Tomorrow, you go tomorrow George!" came the chief's reply.

"But how? We haven't packed, we haven't got any plans, how?" stressed George.

"It's ok, it's all in place. A removal truck should be arriving at yours in about, oh, in about an hour George, by the time on my watch." The Chief said as he quickly glanced and shook his wrist to make sure his timepiece was still working. "You'd better get your skates on George. You can just about make it back if you put your foot down in that truck of yours. Then you'll be able to tell Linda you're getting re-located!" laughed the Chief.

"But Chief!"

"Call me Bob, George. Please, I'll see you at Area 49. Now go, your personal belongings are in the changing room next to your locker. There is a pack inside containing your new post and your new housing details and everything you'll need when you get to Florida. I'm sure you will be pleased when you read it all. Just remember to put your house keys inside the mailbox when you leave. If you hurry you can make it back," smiled Bob. "Oh and by the way! Here is a map, George, the route has been planned for you so you don't bump into the convey of trucks taking the craft etc. You know the score! I'll see you there. And one more thing George, we've sent another convoy of trucks to the Wright-Patterson Air-force Base, just to throw the press off the scent of anything going on, they have been on this story like a rash since that craft crashed at Roswell!" added Bob.

"Why? What's at the Wright-Patterson Air Force Base?"

"Another Top Secret Area! Now, you'd better get a move on George, or Linda will be wondering what's going on."

"Ermmmm, right, ok I'll see you there Bob."
George said, as he couldn't help thinking there was
more to this than the Chief, or should he say Bob
was saying…

Chapter 15

Four days earlier…

The new team had been working really hard to
gather all the data and parts together ready for the
mammoth task that lay ahead of them. The logistics
of moving an unidentified flying object across the
United States of America without anybody seeing or
getting suspicious wasn't the easiest task in the
world, added to which it all had to be done before
George returned from his leave.

Tom had already been reassigned to Area 49
before George came back, he had already started to
make his way across to Florida with the given route
from Bob.

The trucks were down in the underground
chamber ready to be loaded with the craft and all of
the other parts. Everything had been checked and
rechecked a hundred times to make sure nothing
had been left at Area 51. The being was still in its
preserved state and would remain there for the
foreseeable future. A crate had been built around
the craft in the room where it had been stored for
the last four and a bit years. This was so it could be
completely covered. The only problem they faced
was the same as when they brought the craft here, it
was longer than the truck carrying it and because it
was a doughnut shape, the diameter was as wide as

the length, a lot wider than the truck's trailer. This meant it had to be carried on its side, making it very tall so its route had to be planned very carefully to ensure there were no tunnels or low bridges in its path. The distance from Area 51 to Area 49 was about 4,345 kilometres and would take about four to five days to cover, with stops at a number of unnamed places on the way.

The night before the move, everything was in place and the craft was securely loaded onto the truck. With it's massive width and length, the truck needed an escort all the way to Area 49. The mission had been made to look like a military operation, the escorting trucks were going to be full of armed personnel and they were heading out in the morning. There was a large convoy of trucks going, so it was easy to hide what was really happening. The personnel in most of the trucks didn't have clue as to what was going on or what they were taking, they all just thought the operations from Area 51 were moving...

The day before the move!

George nearly broke the land speed record getting home that day. Breaking the news to Linda didn't make him too popular at first, telling her that they had to move over to Florida and worse of all they were going tomorrow. She was furious with George, but they didn't have time to argue about it as the removal van pulled up on the front of the house, not long after George had returned home. He tried to explain the situation, saying that the department he worked for was being re-posted there and it was out of his hands.

The team of removal-men descended on their home, armed with big crates ready to pack everything they could get their hands on. Linda frantically rushed around the house trying to gather the things that they would need on the journey over to Florida.

"This is happening all to quickly George!" declared Linda.

"I'm sorry, but what can I do?" sighed George.

They had to make sure their son, who was nearly four years old now, was going to be ok. The pack that George had been given from the agency had made sure that the family were well catered for. George had been given a promotion and was to lead the new mission plans in Area 49. They had seen the pictures of their new house, which wasn't far from George's new post, so it would be easier and closer for George to commute to work. As far as Linda knew George was still doing work on the military planes but she knew there was more to it than George was letting on, she had had her suspicions for a while now.

As George started to pack some of his things upstairs he had another dizzy spell, he didn't dare tell Linda this time. He'd continued to have these dizzy episodes and they were getting more and more frequent now. Linda kept asking him to go to the doctors to see about the first one, but he wouldn't, he kept saying he was all right and she wasn't to worry.

From what George could gather, Tom had been sent to the Area 49 a few days earlier to make sure everything was in place ready for George and the arrival of the craft. He needed to be there for the beings that were still in their pods, in their suspended state. Tom's house in Indian Springs had already been cleared. Tom lived a few streets away from George in Indian Springs but George had to drive past his house to get to his own. He had seen a large truck there at his place a few days ago, he just thought he must have been getting something delivered.

Tom didn't have any family to worry about, there was only himself. He drove a Ford F-3, it was a very rugged truck and lots of people used that type around the desert because of the harsh terrain. George thought he hadn't seen his truck when he'd got to work or at his house.

The last few things from around George's house were placed into boxes to either take with them or to be taken by the removal company. Their entire house had packed away into the back of a truck in a matter of hours. Their sons toys, the plates, cups and all the things they would need first when they got to Florida. Linda had a pile by the front door waiting to be packed into the truck when George had finished looking around the house, to see if anything had been left. She kept looking at the pile and thinking that it wasn't going to fit in their truck and imagined George going through it all saying we don't need that and we don't need that, which put a smile on her face.

They had their supper that night sitting on the floor of their empty house. After they had all finished, George was playing with Raymond on the porch with his toy cars when Linda mentioned about starting to pack the truck. George smiled at his son and ruffled his hair as he got up, his son continued to make car noises and smash the cars into each other making a massive pile-up, then he would start with the "nee nor nee nor" of the emergency services coming to help out. George watched for a moment and smiled at Linda, as he walked towards the pile of things to pack into the truck, saying, "Bless him!"

George finished sorting through the pile of packing, just like Linda had thought. Finally he got the truck all packed nicely with just a few things left for the morning. He'd packed the loading bay of his truck low so he could see out of the rear view window. If it doesn't fit, it doesn't come! He thought to himself.

Linda had put their son to bed while George had been doing the truck, he wiped his brow and said to himself, time for a beer I think!

George and Linda sat on the kitchen floor leaning against the dresser, with a completely bare house. Everything was now either on its way in boxes or in the truck, except for the things they needed in the morning, before they left for their new life in Florida. On the side were two coffee cups, three plates and some things for breakfast and that was it. "How weird is this?" George said.

"I know, it feels just like when we moved in and we hadn't unpacked!" replied Linda with a hint of emotion on her face.

"Don't be sad honey! We will have just as nice a place in Florida!"

"I know George, we just have so many happy memories here!" she said with a tear rolling down her cheek.

"Here, don't cry baby!" he said as he wiped the rolling tear from her beautiful face.

It was getting late, George swigged the last few drops from his beer bottle and whilst placing it on the floor next to him, he said,

"Well, my dear, I think it's time for bed! We have a very early start in the morning!"

Linda finished her drink and followed George out of the room, turning the lights off as she passed the switch.

George woke up suddenly at 3:27am that morning. Or at least that's what his watch said, which he didn't know was working properly. He couldn't get back to sleep, it didn't help that they were all sleeping on the floor in the same room. So he went to sit on the front porch of his house, staring out into space. It was about the time just before dawn when everything is waiting patiently for the imminent arrival of the sun to blanket the Earth's surface. It was eerily quiet, very still and amazingly clear. Every star you could possibly see was out in the sky. He gazed into space wondering if, for the last four years, someone, somewhere was looking for their friends or their craft that had crashed on our beautiful planet. Had they been here before? Were they on their way back to find them?

Linda was still fast asleep unaware that George wasn't beside her for most of the night. She woke with the smell of fresh coffee at 5:30am and walked downstairs to see through the fly screen that the door was open and George was sitting on the porch swing outside. He turned round when he heard Linda at the doorway, he could just make her out through the mesh on the fly screen door.
"Are you ok George?" asked Linda.
  George didn't say anything and just held out his hand beckoning her to come and hold it, to take in the last moments of their time here. She opened the screen then walked towards him, as she got close enough her hand reached forward to hold George's. He grasped it with a loving squeeze and pulled Linda around to sit on his knee. George had a glazed look in his eyes and a tear slowly traced the last wet line like a drop of rain rolling off a leaf. With a loving hug Linda whispered into George's ear,
"What's wrong darling?"
George's gaze was transfixed on a point on the horizon, gazing into the unknown. He replied after a few moments of silence,
"I love you Linda! No matter what happens in the future, please know I love you and our son with all my heart!"
"Stop! What's wrong George? Why are you talking like this? We love you too! You know that!" Linda said as she hugged him even tighter.
  In the back of George's mind he was very worried about the future, not just for him but for the future of mankind. They had been dealing with something

so out of the ordinary for such along-time, it had become ordinary to him. Linda and most of humanity didn't have a clue. He had thought for a while now, that it was only a matter of time before all this got out and then everyone would be scared for the safety of the planet.

George pulled himself together and finished his coffee, as he started to pack the last few things into the car, ready for the long trip to Florida. Linda had woken up their son to give him some breakfast before they set off, she was quite looking forward to living in Florida now and couldn't wait to get out of Indian Springs and see the ocean and their son would love growing up in Florida.

The time had come to set off, their Dodge's open back was packed full, a tarp pulled tight over the top. They had a long journey ahead and needed to get on their way. Making sure they hadn't forgotten anything, they all got into the truck, said their farewells to Indian Springs, placed their house keys into the mail box, as requested and hit the road at 7am. George and Linda were taking the route they had been given, Highway 95 then picking up Highway 93, straight down till they reached Phoenix, Arizona. Then they would take Highway 10 towards San Antonio head through Houston and along the coast. Eventually heading towards Jacksonville and down to their new home in Titusville, Florida. The convoy had taken Highway 40 all the way to Memphis, then they would pick up Route 78 and head towards Jacksonville then straight down to Cape Canaveral (Area 49). So George was lead to believe...

Chapter 16

George and Linda made it a long way down Highway 93. It was a hot, sunny day and it had taken them nearly four hours so far, only stopping for fuel. They had covered nearly 155 miles already, it was just coming up to 12 midday. Raymond was getting restless, so they decided to stop for a break and stretch their legs. They pulled off at a diner on the side of the highway, ice cold Cokes were calling, an ice cold chocolate milkshake for their son with a quick bite to eat for all, then back on the road again. Next they were heading for Phoenix which was about another 190 miles away on the long winding roads through the valleys and canyons of the desert. In the distance they could just make out the buzzards circling their next meal. Another four hours drive, they were planning on staying there over night and starting the journey again in the morning.

Their first day of travelling had come to an end. They knew it was going to be hard work with their son, they were all hot and tired and ready for a good night's sleep in a nice comfy bed. They found a lovely motel in Phoenix and had something to eat, then it was straight to bed ready for the same again tomorrow.

They were heading down towards a place called Fort Hancock just past Ciudad Juarez. George had looked at the planned route and it showed the possibility of plenty of stops on the way. This part of the journey was about 490 miles and was going to take about nine to ten hours in their truck. He made sure they had a full tank of gas and a couple of Jerry cans full, just incase. George made sure everyone had a good breakfast before they headed out on to the road again.

They had been driving for what seemed like ages, only stopping to refuel every time they saw a gas-station. They plodded on along the long deserted roads, something seemed very strange to Linda, it was deserted, they hadn't passed many other vehicles on the road at all. She mentioned this to George but he had said he hadn't noticed. After a lunch break, they kept going through the heat of the day. Linda and their son had closed their eyes while George was driving. She was next to the wound down window, letting the cool rushing air blast her face and flow through her hair, cooling her down. The sun was beating down on the truck, slowly cooking them like they were going to be the buzzard's next roast dinner. All George was focusing on was the heat haze on the road ahead. It looked like a shimmering lake, like someone had stolen the ground ahead and replaced it with a vast, fizzing, mirrored ocean of emptiness. It played tricks on George's mind over the miles and miles of barren desert, inhabited by only the toughest of tough animals and reptiles, who prayed on the few that didn't and couldn't survive the heat of the day and the cold of the night.

George was dripping wet with sweat, it was rolling down his face and landing on his shirt covered chest. He kept wiping his brow with his handkerchief but that made no difference because it was soaked already from all the sweat he'd mopped up. He opened a few buttons on his shirt, he thought this might help! But it didn't, not one bit, the heat was intense. George carried on driving along the road, he thought his mind was playing tricks on him. Every time he saw something in the distance he thought it might be another vehicle emerging from the shimmering ocean-less void miles ahead, but then nothing would pass.

It happened again, only this time he was sure there was something driving towards him. He used his soaking wet handkerchief to wipe his eyes, taking a few big blinks to clear his salty blurred vision, he finally focused on an object in the distance. Out of the hypnotic heat haze just ahead of them, something stretched right across both sides of the highway. He saw two large military vehicles, with a few military personnel standing, armed and looking like they meant business.

As George got closer, he could see that there was a jeep as well, with a long flexible aerial bent over and fixed to the front of the vehicle. George tapped Linda on the arm to try and wake her, she just brushed her arm, the automatic response to usher away the ever annoying fly or bug. He tried again saying, "Linda wake up, Linda wake up!"
She finally stirred and looked towards George stretching her arms above her head, pressing her forearms and hands on the roof of the truck, giving out an enormous yawn.
"What's wrong George? I was just about to dip my

feet in the cool waters off the coast of Florida!" she said whilst finishing her yawn.

George was transfixed on the road ahead, he lifted a hand up and just pointed out of the front window. Linda looked and immediately pulled her arms down and shuffled in her seat wondering what was going on.

"What's happening George, should I wake…"

"No!" he interrupted, "Let's see what's happening!" Their son was laid across the middle of the seats, with his legs pointing towards his Father and his head on his Mom's lap, fast asleep, his lips looking cracked and dry from the heat in the cab. Linda's brow was dappled with beads of sweat and a few had become too heavy to stay fixed in place. They collected together and the weight of their accumulation got too heavy and slowly followed the contours of her brow and trickled down, leaving a droplet on his forehead. George started to slow down the truck as he approached the road block.

………

"Operation Clean Sweep! The light grey coloured dodge has been spotted and the road block is in place Sir. Over!" Were the words spoken into the field radio in the cabin of a military jeep.

"Continue with the diversion plans and mission 'Clean Sweep! Over!" Came the crackled reply.

"Roger that! Over and out!"

………

The two military trucks, one on each side of the highway, were parked with the backs of the trucks pointing at each other. The military personnel waved and pointed at George to pull over at the side of the road. He pulled over next to a sign saying 'diversion' with an arrow under it pointing towards a dirt road on the other side of the highway. The ranking officer placed something back in the jeep and started walking over to George's truck.

There were no cars on the road at all, they'd been driving for ages and not seen another vehicle. George thought it best not to say where he worked to the military man in command as he walked towards his open truck window. He turned his truck and came to a stop facing the dirt road and asked what the problem was.

The military man kept his distance from the truck, told them that there had been a massive landslide up ahead and all traffic was being diverted this way. They could take the road or they could turn round and go back to the nearest town and wait for it to be cleared, which wouldn't be until tomorrow or even the next day. Then, he turned to face the road again as if he was waiting for the next vehicle to arrive. From where the officer was he could only see George and Linda in the vehicle as their son was still laid down asleep.

"Where does this lead to?" asked George, "We need to get to…"

George wasn't given the chance to finish, with the soldier's eyes looking into the distance his only words were,

"Just follow the diversions that have been clearly placed please, they will take you round the incident!"

"Are you expecting trouble?" George pointed at the armed military men.

The man just stood his ground and didn't say a word. George frowned and drove across the other side of the highway and onto the dirt road, leaving a dust trail in his wake as he sped off into the distance.

"It's going to be dark in a few hours!" George pointed out, "I hope we make it before the sun goes down, I don't fancy being out in the middle of nowhere over night!"

"It's ok George, there must be somewhere on this road we can stop!" Linda reassured him, trying to unfold the map. George had a funny feeling that something wasn't right, a road block with a high military presence in the middle of nowhere. Something didn't add up.

The officer walked back to his jeep.

"Targets acquired. Operation Clean Sweep in motion. Over!" The officer awaited a response.

"Roger over and out!" came the crackled reply as the radio contact went dead…

Chapter 17

About 20 kilometres down the dirt road they finally came to a cross roads. The diversion signs had disappeared, there were no more. They hadn't seen any other signs since the one on the main road. George stopped the truck. The bumpy dirt road had woken their son up back down the track. George got out and stood in the middle of the crossroads, turning in each direction, kicking the dirt.
"Which way now?" he shouted, adding a big; "Aaaaaaaarrrrrrggghh!" on the end.
"Calm down George, you won't do yourself any good screaming like that." Linda said as she opened her door to the truck.

George walked back to the truck kicking the dirt in the road and mumbling something to himself. Suddenly he stopped and started to sway, falling to his knees.
"George!" Linda cried, grabbing a bottle of water as she rushed towards him closing the truck door, shouting to her son, "Stay in the truck!"

George was there on his knees slumped over, arms out-stretched and hands flat on the floor in the dirt. Linda knelt down beside him and placed her arm around his back for support. "Are you all right George?"

He sat back and tried to focus on her face, he could see her lips moving but he couldn't make out what she was saying. It sounded like she was miles away. He had a ringing noise in his ears that drowned out the tone of her voice. After a few minutes had passed, things started to sound clearer, she came back into focus again. He could hear her voice saying, "Here take a drink George, you must be dehydrated."

He grabbed the bottle and had a swig of the water that had been slowly boiling in the cabin of the truck on their journey. He gasped for air, then poured some of the water over his head, this didn't have the desired effect of cooling him down, it felt like all the pores, all over his body were boiling.
"I'm ok Linda, I think the heat just got to me,"
"Here, grab my arm and I'll help you up, honey!"
Linda linked her arm through his and slowly stood up, helping him to his feet again.
As George brushed down his dusty jeans and got his balance again he said, "Where's Raymond?"
"It's ok, I told him to stay in the truck when I closed my door, but my door is open!"
George couldn't see him through the windshield and quickly rushed over to the open truck door to look in. He shut the door spinning round quickly on the balls of his feet shouting, "Raymond!!!"
The colour drained from Linda's face,
"No, no, no!" she said racing over to the truck to look in through the open window.

Raymond wasn't in the truck. The toy car he had been clutching all journey was parked on the seat where he had been sitting. The bag with all his other things, like a change of clothes, snacks, drinks and toys for the trip, was open on the floor. Linda too, span round shouting his name.

"Raymond, Raymond!"
Their voices in unison disappeared over the vast
desert that stretched out in all directions.

They both started looking frantically around the
truck, there was no sign of him. There was no sign
of anything in fact. Just desert, a few rocks and the
mountains in the distance.
"Where could he be?" cried Linda.
"Just keep looking!" replied George, "He has to be
here somewhere, there's nowhere for him to go!"

Just then, a head popped round a big rock about
twenty yards away from where the truck was
facing.
"Pee pee!" Raymond smiled running back into the
arms of his terrified mother.
"Don't ever do that again Raymond! I told you to
stay in the truck." Linda said whilst she squeezed
the life out of him. A tear slowly rolled down her
cheek leaving a track in the dusty foundation she
was wearing.
"How did you get past us without us seeing,
Raymond?"
George walked over and hugged them both, smiling
he said, "Thank god!"
"I needed a pee!"
George and Linda burst out laughing and smiled at
Raymond as they walked back to the truck.
Raymond jumped in and grabbed his toy car
oblivious to the drama he had just created.

George grabbed the map out of the truck and
spread it out on the side of the hood, he studied it
for a while, tracing his finger along the highway
they had been on before the diversion. He got to

where he thought they had been diverted, but he couldn't find any roads. There was nothing on the map along that stretch of highway. He scratched his head and looked again. Linda could see there was something wrong.

"Are we lost, George?"

"No, I just don't seem to be able to find this road on the map!" he said whilst turning it over to make sure he was looking at the right side.

"What's that there?" Linda was pointing at a dust covered rectangular shape on the floor, near the other side of the crossroads. It looked like it must have been there for years.

George walked over to it, he bent down and flipped it over with his fingers, awaking a tiny gecko that had been shielding itself from the scorching desert heat. Once the dust had settled he could make out some writing on it. It wasn't a diversion sign.

"White Sands Missile Range" George read slowly. The sign had an arrow under the writing, but which way had it been pointing? They didn't want to end up in the middle of a missile range.

"What does it say George?"

"Nothing! Don't worry."

"George! What does it say?"

He blew the rest of the dust off and held the sign up for Linda to read as he walked back over to the truck. Her hand covered her mouth and she just stared at George, then looked back at the sign. He walked over to the rock that Raymond had taken a pee behind and leaned the sign on it for all to see. He followed his son's lead and after he finished having a pee himself, he slowly walked back doing the buttons up on his jeans, he opened the truck door and they both just sat there looking at the sign through the windshield.

George broke the fear-stricken silence; "Which way then? Should we toss a coin?"
They both smiled at each other and shook their heads. The way George had placed the sign made it point into the middle of the desert with no road to follow.

The road straight ahead looked like it stretched onwards into the flat desert plains. The road to the left would take them to some mountains that looked miles away, George thought that would just head them back parallel to the way they had come. This meant there was only one way left. This way headed into a mountain range, which didn't look very far away. They both looked at each other and said; "That way it is then!"

George rubbed his forehead, let out a big sigh and turned the key in the truck, it rumbled back to life in the heat of the day and they headed towards the mountains, not knowing where they were going. As they drove off, a desert wind sent a dust storm from down the road behind them. A dust devil formed out of the cloud and crossed the road knocking off the sign George had placed on the rock. It fell face down in the dusty desert again, waiting for the next lost travellers to discover it, left scratching their heads as to which way it had been pointing. The dust devil seemed to stall, as if the noise had distracted it, then it headed off down the road into the desert, looking like it knew where it was going.

Which was more than George did. Raymond was kneeling, looking out of the rear window of the truck. He watched as this unknown entity spiralled off down the road, he smiled and waved his new friend off on it's journey.

....

With one hand on a field radio and the other on a pair of binoculars a voice broke the silence of the airwaves;
"Clean Sweep, target passing. Over!"
A deadly silence filled the air once more, then;
"Clean Sweep in place. Over and out!"
The radio fell silent.

....

It was about 5pm now, they had been driving along the dirt road for miles and they hadn't seen anyone. They were in between two mountain ranges, the road had taken them up and through some really tough terrain, they were on their way down into a valley. All they could see ahead was more desert with the dirt road stretching out in-between the two mountain ranges. They could feel it was starting to cool down now, but time was against them to find somewhere to stay for the night, or get back onto the main highway again. George noticed in the distance there was what appeared to be a gas station. He could make out the tall sign with Texaco written on it. Was this another mirage? he thought.
"There!" George pointed into the distance, "Am I seeing things or is that what I think it is?"

"Thank god for that!" sighed Linda.

As they approached the gas station, their jubilation was rapidly stolen, their faces dropped at the sight of an old derelict building. George pulled up on the forecourt, his wheels driving over the old air chime that sounded a bell in the office. Nobody came running anymore. The windows that were still intact were covered in dust and sand, some old curtains hanging out of the broken pains, laid dormant in the stagnant air of the desert, slowly being bleached by the red hot sun. The once shiny gas pumps on the deserted forecourt were now dressed in flaking paint and covered with rust spots. They looked like they hadn't been used for years, sandblasted by the desert winds. A lizard scurried over the pump and stopped on the top looking at the truck, giving George an evil stare, it then leapt off and rushed out of view.

George turned the truck off and asked Linda to stay put until he'd had a look around. Getting out of the truck he walked towards the gas station's entrance. There was an old spinning Coke sign next to the door, it was on top of an old dispensing machine that read 5 cents a bottle. He spun the sign with his hand, it squeaked! Like it hadn't spun in years, he then checked the rejected coin slot, just in case. George opened the door shouting, "Hello!" as he did.

No answer.

He shouted again, "Hello!"

Still no answer.

He walked in and looked around, it was clear that nobody had been here for a while. There was dust and sand everywhere, probably a very busy gas station before the highway opened, he thought to himself. There was still merchandise on the shelves, he picked up an old chocolate bar, it had 'Hershey's' written on the front. George stared hungrily at it and then unwrapped it. The chocolate had turned white, I think not, he said to himself. Continuing to look around he saw an old Texaco baseball cap, laid covered in dust and cobwebs on the counter near the till. The till door was wide open with nothing but dust lining the compartments. He picked up the baseball cap and jumped as a large hairy spider ran across the counter, wondering who had removed his temporary resting place. George slapped the cap against his thigh, to make sure there wasn't anything else hiding inside. He placed it on his head chuckling to himself as he did so. There was a notice board behind the counter, a letter had been stuck to it with what looked like a big knife. He walked close enough to read it:

......

Dear Sir,

Notice to occupants:

A compulsory purchase order has taken place on White Sands Texaco Station.

We have stopped all gas deliveries to this re-fuelling station as of the 1st of July.

The US Military, plans to turn this area into a missile range. A testing ground for the development of weapons.

This is a notice to evacuate the premises of White Sands Texaco Gas Station before: 9th July 1945.

Thank you for your cooperation.
Military Department USA.

......

My God! George thought to himself, we are in the middle of a testing facility. He looked around to see if there were signs of anybody living there. But by the looks of it, that wasn't the case. He tried to open a door to the rear of the room, it was locked or jammed shut. From the outside it looked like a workshop, maybe where they did servicing he thought. Giving up on the door he tried a few other doors in the gas station. He jumped out of his skin as he opened one of them and the bell that warned the attendant of a customer suddenly went crazy. He closed the door and looked out of the window, there was Raymond, jumping on the cable that lay on the dirt. Linda was next to him trying to grab his hand to pull him off it. This was a great game for Raymond. George opened the door and walked out wearing the new baseball cap he'd acquired.

"What's that George?" Linda laughed, "You're mad, put it back!"

Flicking the peak of the cap, George said, "It's mine now!"

Linda went back to trying to stop Raymond jumping on the cable, it was too much fun for him to stop he was running around the pumps making it chime.

"Oh, I give up! Well, what are we going to do now George?" Linda said as she placed her hands on her hips.

"The sun will be down soon, it looks like we might have to stay here over night!" George shrugged.

"What! Are you serious?" replied Linda.

They pulled the truck up close to the gas station and made a makeshift bed for Raymond across it's seats. George and Linda were going to sleep on top of their boxes in the back of the truck. There was an old dusty sheet he'd noticed in one of the rooms inside the gas station. He went back in and brought it out, walking just to the side of the gas station to give it a good shake. Something grabbed his attention as he shook the sheet, out of the corner of his eye he saw a flash. The sun was low but it was still on the mountain side they were heading towards. He stared at the place he thought he'd seen the flash. His mind must be playing tricks on him, he thought. But then just as he was going to turn and head back, it happened again! A flash like the sunlight was reflecting off something high up on the side of the mountain. He rubbed his chin and watched again. Nothing! He headed back to where Linda and Raymond were, placing the sheet on the back of the truck he gave Linda a big hug and ruffled Raymond's hair, as he always did. As they put Raymond down for the night in the cab of the truck, George locked the doors, but left the windows open slightly. He was a light sleeper, so he would hear if Raymond was needing to be out.

After Raymond had fallen asleep, Linda and George stayed up talking about the drive. They were sitting on the wooden porch area of the gas station, around an old gas lamp George had found inside. He had placed it on an old upturned Coke crate that had been used to fill the dispensing machine. There were a couple of old chairs inside that he brought out for them to sit on. George pulled 5 cents out of his pocket and slipped it into the Coke machine next to where they were sitting, nothing happened! George frowned and thumped the worn company name in frustration. He turned his back on it, opening and closing his hand after hurting it on the steel.

"That'll teach you!" giggled Linda.

"It was worth a try honey."

Then just as he sat down two bottles of Coke fell from the dispenser, clattering together as they did so. George and Linda just laughed, he opened one on the handy built-in bottle-opener. It fizzed over drenching his hand in warm brown bubbles.

"You're not going to drink that, are you George?"

"It seems ok to me, just a bit warm!" he replied as he took a swig from the bottle. Which in-turn came straight back out onto the sandy porch, quickly being guzzled up by the ever thirsty desert floor.

George was left with an awful warm fizzing sensation in his mouth, so he tried eating some of the food Linda had bought back in Phoenix for the journey. He offered the unopened bottle to Linda.

"No thanks honey! I think I'll give that one a miss, but thanks away!"

They couldn't believe they were in the middle of nowhere, lost. George hadn't let on that he knew they were in the middle of a missile range, he thought it was best not to. Linda would only get stressed out and they couldn't go anywhere else that night. Saving some food for breakfast they quietly placed the basket back in the cabin with Raymond, so no animals could get to it and climbed onto the back of the truck, covering themselves with the dusty blanket.

The temperature could fall very low in the desert

at night, so he and Linda snuggled together to try and keep warm. The noises of the animals in the distance kept Linda awake for awhile, but George was asleep in no time. The howling of a pack of wolves could be heard in the mountains, but they didn't sound like they were too near. She finally drifted off to sleep in the early hours of the morning, wondering what lay ahead of them in their search for humanity tomorrow...

Chapter 18

Smoke started to rise slowly from under the truck, a thick dense white cloud engulfed George's vehicle. Two rings with pins attached bounced off the toecaps of a highly polished pair of boots and came to rest in the moonlit dirt. Suddenly from all around the gas station, ghostly shadows moved using the cover of the night, causing turbulence in the cloud of white smoke that eclipsed the truck, making it swirl as the glimpse of a dark figure emerged from within. A gas mask flashed past a gap in the thick man-made fog. An odd light show started from within the haunting cloud. Shadow after shadow came into view, until the truck was surrounded by the invisible army. Beams of lights could be seen cutting through the smoke, like the eerie sight of headlights on a foggy winter's night. Coughing could be heard through the thick smoke but nobody was stirring. The clouded army suddenly stood still, waiting for silence.

The limp, lifeless body of a person was carried by a masked man from within the cloud into the gas station, shortly followed by another, causing the smoke to be disturbed, it gently followed in the wake of the body disappearing into the building. "Clear!" came the muffled voice from within the cloud.

As quickly as the invisible army had arrived, they faded back into the night, disappearing like a ghostly apparition. Apart from two of them!

The remaining two came out from within the gas station. One of the masked men looked through the window of the door as he closed it. He could see two bodies curled up on the floor, hands tied behind their backs, ankles tied together with a rope joining the two. They calmly stood on the porch where George and Linda had sat, just hours earlier. The masked man had removed all the items from his victim's pockets. They had tape around their head covering the mouth, their eyes were taped tightly closed. Unaware of their fate, they carried on with their night's sleep.

Suddenly, the awakening of a loud engine filled the silence of the night. The two big doors of the workshop swung open. A hidden army had been in there the whole time, silently waiting for the dead of night to strike their prey. The doors were locked from the inside stopping the snooping of any lost passer by. A massive military vehicle disguised as a garage recovery truck rumbled out from the building, it had the words 'Bob's Servicing and Recovery', written on each side and across the two big doors to the rear. It manoeuvred so the back was placed in front of George's vehicle. The masked men followed the truck round and pulled out two long ramps from the rear, they fixed them to the back. One of the men walked up a ramp to the back of the vehicle and slowly emerged with a large hook, this was attached to a long steel cable. He walked back down the ramp and fixed it to the front of George's truck, the cab was still full of smoke from George leaving the windows open slightly. Another masked man tried the door. It was locked!

"Here!" came the muffled shout from another masked man, who had just closed the door to the gas station.

He tossed a bunch of keys at the masked assassin. They flew through the air, but the shout came too late as the man calmly used the butt of his rifle to smash the driver's window. The rush of air going in caused some of the smoke to flow out of the opening. As this happened the keys that were heading his way flew straight through the now open window, they vanished into the dense rush of exiting smoke. Not realising what had just happened the masked man reached his arm through the window and released the brake near the steering wheel. The smoke levelled off at the height of the smashed window so he hadn't noticed Raymond lying across the seats or the place where the keys had landed.

"Oh well, he won't be needing those anymore!"

The undercover military vehicle revved and the cable started to tighten. George's truck started to move forward with the masked man standing on the foot plate, his arm still through the window steering it up the ramp. When it reached the top, the wheels were guided by rails inside the larger truck. The man jumped off and walked towards the front of this disguised military vehicle. George's Dodge was slowly swallowed up by the size of this immense cargo bay until the last of it disappeared into the darkness. The doors at the rear of the truck were locked shut.

"No traces are to be left!"

The soldier opened his door and grabbed a bundle of clothing off the seat, as he pulled off his silhouetted military clothing he quickly changed into an oil stained boiler suit with the imaginary company logo stitched on the front.

As he climbed into his cab, the man banged his arm on the side of the vehicle shouting!

"Let's roll out."

The remaining men did a sweep of the area with their torches and disappeared into the building again. Another engine started up and a smaller truck emerged out of the building, this one had all the other men inside. They had all changed into civilian clothing, although still wearing their gas masks just for safety. The smaller military truck they were in had also been disguised with the words, 'Bob's Servicing and Recovery' written on the doors. They headed off into the night with the larger vehicle following.

"Operation Clean Sweep complete...Over!" was the message sent across the airwaves.

"Roger. The birds have taken flight...Over and out!" replied the crackling speaker.

"Let's get out of here quickly before the birds arrive!" he said whilst taking his gas mask off and breathing in a huge lung full of fresh air, "I don't want to be around when they arrive."

"Roger! This is Bird One, we are 10 clicks from target...Over!" the pilot said looking at the radar screen.

"Roger, Bird One, start descent...Over!" replied the tower.

"This is Bird One, we have visual on target...Over!"
The pilot awaited his orders.
"Roger, the bird is good to go. Repeat, the bird is good to go...Over!"
The order arrived over the pilot's radio headset.
"Roger! Beginning first run...Over!" the pilot said whilst flipping the red top of a switch in the cockpit.

The B-45 Tornado went into a dive between the two mountain ranges closely followed by his wingman. The target was coming up, fast. The two planes screeched through the breaking dawn sky, silhouetted against the feint light of the rising sun on the horizon. The planes were nearing the target at a rapid rate, there was no turning back now. They thought they were on a test bombing exercise, according to their briefing. The pilot flicked the switch under the red cap and pulled up into the sky. Two large bombs were released from under the plane. They toppled through the air without a hint of sound. The silent assassins lit up the target area on impact. The second plane followed directly behind, flicking his switch, just as the first bombs hit. They sent a cloud of flames and dust high into the air. The bombs hit moments after the first ones just to make sure of total annihilation. Bird Two flew out of the cloud and soared up into the dawn sky.
"Yee-haa! That was close Bird One...Over!" Bird Two said as he got back into formation.
"This is Bird One, the package has been delivered... Over!"
"Roger, Bird One, continue with fly by to check

target was hit…Over!" replied the tower.
"Roger! Starting return fly by…Over!"

The Tornadoes started their turn, they had to go round the mountain range so the dust could settle before they started their second run.

The trucks had driven off down the dirt road towards the next mountain range. They had no sooner driven 2 kilometres, when they could hear the faint echo of the massive engine of the B-45 Tornado, carrying a devastating payload ready to be deployed. There was a blinding flash of light that lit up the whole sky and then a few seconds later they felt the impact from the bomb exploding. The ground shook beneath the truck, making it hard for the driver to keep control. The shock wave was so great, it had caught them up in no time. The explosions had formed a large mushroom in the dawn's pale blue and orange sky, back in the direction they had just come from. They could still hear the faint crackling noise of the Tornadoes' engines breaking through the air, as they headed back round the mountain. The driver could hear the communications between the pilot and the tower.
"This is Bird One, beginning second run on target… Over!"
"Roger, Bird One, standing by…Over!"

Bird One's flight around the mountain had taken just enough time for most of the dust to settle. Some of it was lingering in the still morning air. The Tornado broke formation and started it's dive into the residual dust cloud, hovering stagnant around the destroyed target area.
"Tower, this is Bird One, target destroyed. Testing

complete...Over!"
"Roger Bird One, return to base...Over and out!"
The airwaves fell silent.

The breaking dawn's silence shattered once more as Bird One pulled up and headed back to base, they could be heard roaring through the sky, cutting the air with their massive jet engines, like two fire breathing dragons returning to their lair.

The disguised military vehicle carrying George's Dodge drove up through the mountains and found it's way back to the highway, carrying an unexpected passenger.

The officer picked up the field radio to check in: "Operation Clean Sweep...Over!" The officer waited for a reply.
It was a few moments before the crackle of the radio broke into life and the eerie silence was destroyed.
"Operation Clean Sweep, secure line come in... Over!"
"Test bombing by Birds complete. Followed by Clean Sweep of the area, targets destroyed no loose ends...Over!" replied the officer.
"Roger! Proceed to rendezvous point with package...Over!" replied the invisible voice.
"Roger...Over and out!"

The plan was to make the Dodge disappear, they couldn't leave the truck at the gas station incase somebody found the wreck. They had agreed on a secure location for the dismantling and melting of the vehicle, they just had to get it there without anybody seeing it.
"Listen! Did you hear something?" asked the soldier in his disguise.

"What's wrong soldier?" asked the officer.

"I can hear something, is the Dodge fastened down securely?"

"I hope so soldier!"

They pulled the truck over into a parking area and listened. The vehicle that was following pulled in behind and parked close, sitting, armed ready for action if needed. The officer walked over and told them that they had heard noises from the back and were checking it out.

"There! Did you hear that?" he said walking back to the truck.

There was a dull thud and a funny noise, like a whimper, a cry coming from the back of the truck.

"I thought the back was clear soldier!" replied the officer.

"It was Sir, I checked it myself Sir, it was empty!" stressed the soldier.

"Well, what's that noise? Did they have a dog? It's coming from the back of the truck. We need the back opening, now!" urged the officer.

They unlocked the back of the truck and swung open one of the doors. It was pitch black inside. A haze hung in the air, making the soldiers torch-beam look like a spotlight on a misty night. As he leaned in to see what the noise was, he inhaled a mouth full of the residual sleeping gas, he pulled his head out quickly coughing and retching. He took a large breath in to clear his throat.

"Give me that torch!" the officer instructed whilst holding his hand out waiting for it to be placed in his palm.

He turned the torch on and shone it into the back,

he thought he had seen something in the rear window of the Dodge, like a head bobbing down when it had been spotted by the beam of light. "Did you see that?" he asked, pointing at the rear window of the truck inside.

The thudding noise had stopped but a faint whimpering could still be heard. He calmly climbed into the back, using the rear bumper as a step to help him whilst shining the torch under the truck on his way in to see if he could see anything. Once in he also started coughing, he placed his hand over his mouth to stop the deadly mist from being inhaled.

Slowly side stepping down the length of the Dodge, there was just enough room around the vehicle to do this, he pulled his hand away from his mouth and reached for his side arm. His back pressed up against the side of their truck. Edging his way down one step at a time, shining the torch and pointing his gun in the same direction, but always going back to the rear view window. He was nearly there.

"Can you see anything yet sir?" a voice shouted. This startled him slightly.

"Shhhhh!" he replied from the darkness whilst trying to compose himself again.

He crept up to the smashed window, pointing the torch and gun inside as he stepped along quickly so he could see in. There was nothing on the seats, the faint aroma of the sleeping gas irritated his nostrils again, which made him waggle his nose and cough. Shining the torch around he could see a sheet moving on the floor, it was shaking in time with the whimpering.

With the gun trained on the sheet he said, "Hello? Who's there? Show yourself?"

There was no answer, he tried the door handle, it was locked. He didn't know which item to put down, the torch or the gun? He placed his gun back in it's holster and reached into the vehicle through the smashed window, the jagged edges of the remaining glass shards cutting into his side. His finger tips tickled the top of the sheet, not quite being able to reach it, he stretched a bit further, the glass cut in deeper and deeper with each movement. Finally he made one last attempt to reach it, saying, "Hello, is there anybody there?"

He grasped the sheet between two of his fingers and leaned back pulling it with him, saving his side from further torture, trying to keep the torch aimed at the quivering lump under the sheet as he did so. The sheet came off and exposed a shaking mound on the floor of George's truck.

It was Raymond!

He had woken hours later, when the sleeping gas had worn off, unaware of the awful events of the night. He didn't have a clue what had happened to his Mom and Dad. He hadn't realised that his protective layer had been removed, he continued to whimper, curled up in a tight ball on the floor. It sounded louder now the sheet wasn't there to muffle it.

"Hello, who do we have here then? It's ok, you're safe now." The officer tried to convince the child he was ok.

"Hey, it's ok, come on, look up, you're safe now."

Raymond stopped shaking and slowly lifted his head from the floor of his dad's truck.

"That's it, it's ok."

As the officer held out his hand, he noticed there was glass everywhere inside the cab, the light from his torch picking up the glistening shards. Raymond's face had a deep cut on the cheek and looked like it had been bleeding, the blood was dry now and smeared towards his nose. Raymond looked startled, like a rabbit caught in a car's head-lights, he was trying to get used to the beam from the torch and couldn't make out the person holding it. He lifted a hand up and wiped his eyes, a mixture of blood, sweat and tears filled the corners, making it even harder for him to see.

"Daddy? Daddy?" Raymond shouted.

"It's ok, it's ok!" The officer said whilst his eyes started to well up, "Come here. Give me your hand."

"Daddy? Daddy?" He was starting to get anxious now.

Raymond screamed for his daddy and his cries of panic grew louder, the officer pointed the torch away from the boy so he could see better.

"Mind the glass and come towards me!" he said in a soft friendly voice.

Raymond found comfort in the man's voice and started to calm down slightly. Still looking scared he tried to move one of his hands, a big piece of glass was right in front of him.

"Mind that glass, come on you can do it!" the voice softening even more.

Raymond knelt up and tried to feel his way back

onto the seat again, the officer then brushed the glass onto the floor with his hand, so he didn't get it in his knees. Raymond finally made it to the window and the officer wrapped the sheet, he still had, around him and lifted him through the window, minding his legs as he did so. Raymond lent back through the window as the officer started to side step back down the truck, he started to squirm and shout, reaching out for something so the officer nearly dropped him.

"Careful! What's up, what do you want?" he asked.

"Car, I want my car! Bag! Bag! Bag! I want my nummy!" Raymond yelled.

"You mean you want your mommy?"

"No, no, nummy, nummy!"

The officer looked back through the window and there on the floor was a open shoulder bag with some things in it, some clothes, a tattered old muslin-cloth and a few toy cars from what he could see. He couldn't reach it with Raymond in his arms so he continued to walk back down the truck. He passed Raymond down to one of the soldiers saying,

"Take him into the front cab ASAP we don't want anybody seeing him, it might jeopardise the mission."

He carried the child round to the front cab whilst the officer went back to the cab to collect the bag. He leaned back through the window grabbing the strap on the bag and pulling it through the slivers of broken glass. His side felt damp, he couldn't tell if it was sweat or blood from the glass cutting into him, as he'd reached in for the kid.

He shone his torch around in the cab once more, nothing but a few empty water bottles could be seen. The back of the truck was still packed with all the belongings George and Linda were taking with them. A tear slowly rolled down and dripped off the cheek of the officer and landed on the seat, it was quickly soaked up by the residual powder created by the sleeping gas that coated the interior of the truck. He wiped his eyes, composed himself and walked back checking around with the torch as he did so, just to make sure there was nobody else in there.

He jumped off the back of the truck and landed with a thud, his big boots creating a small puff of dust as he landed which quickly dispersed into the air. He turned to the soldier who had checked the vehicle, asking him why he hadn't seen the kid in there when he had loaded the truck into theirs. The soldier told him that the cab was full of smoke and he still had his gas mask on, when the smoke cleared enough to see, it was still up to the open window height, the kid must have been laid down, or in the footwell.

The officer leaned towards him and whispered, "I want a full report on my desk, ASAP when this mission is complete!"

They swung the door shut again, locked it and walked back to the front cab. The officer got in first next to the child, then the driver returned to his seat. The other soldier got in the vehicle that had been following them. The officer just stared at the kid and then looked at the driver saying,

"What's gone wrong here, they told us there were

two they didn't mention a kid!"

"You'll have to call it in Sir!" said the driver.

"No, we'll maintain radio silence as requested, we'll deal with it at the rendezvous point, it's their problem, not mine, we ain't killing no kid!" voiced the officer.

Raymond sat on the seat next to the officer, shaking and looking terrified, as he grabbed his tattered piece of muslin he called his nummy, from the bag now beside him. The officer quickly realising, this was his comfort blanket. The man then grabbed a cloth to clean Raymond's face, he soaked it with some of the water from his canteen before bringing it towards the cut on his cheek. Raymond moved his head away.

"It's ok, I'll help you."

The officer smiled at Raymond as he mimicked doing it to himself. This time Raymond let him come closer and wipe the blood from his cheek, he did it again with a clean cloth and wiped all of his face this time. The boy looked completely different now he wasn't covered in dust and blood or anything else. The officer offered Raymond the water, he took it, drinking like he'd never had water before in his life. He'd stopped shaking as much now and was calming down, who could blame him with all these strangers around?

"What's your name?" questioned the officer.

There was no answer from Raymond, his pupils looked wide, he seemed disorientated and unaware of what was happening. They thought it was an effect from the sleeping gas wearing off, after all he was only small and the gas got trapped in the cabin of the truck. The kid just looked at the officer and took another drink. The driver reached into his box and pulled out a candy bar, he handed it to the kid. Raymond sheepishly lifted his hand and took the bar from the driver, the officer helped him open it and Raymond sat there eating it while the driver started the truck again and signalled to the vehicle behind to roll out.

The convoy carrying the craft had made it safely to Area 49 without any suspicion. An area had been constructed under the swamp land called Pepper Flats, close to where the planned space launches were going to take place in the near future. The craft had been placed in it's crate inside the specially constructed holding room until the time came that it was needed. All the parts had been shipped in the same convoy but not in the same vehicle, they were to be kept apart until the new team had more knowledge and a greater understanding of the technology they had found. The rooms were locked and the operation would remain highly classified for the foreseeable future.

Tom hadn't made it to Area 49, he had just vanished without a trace as did a few of the others who were involved with the original findings. The only one who was left, was the Chief who followed the craft to Area 49. He was continuing to work on the top secret project, he'd been in on things from the beginning and knew what was going to happen.

Raymond was brought to the rendezvous point where the officer explained what had happened.

They weren't expecting a kid to be one of the targets. No loose ends, that's what they'd been told, Operation Clean Sweep was to have no traces of any survivors. He explained that the operation had gone to plan and the kid wasn't part of it! Clean Sweep was a success and that's all that mattered.

The military had been left with no choice but to concoct some cock-n-bull story about a horrific crash and put the child up for adoption, hoping he was going to be too young to remember anything about the events. All Raymond had left was the bag he had come with, containing his toys, a nummy and some clothes. He hadn't spoken a word since the ordeal in the back of the truck.

It wasn't long before the government adoption agency had found a lovely home for Raymond with a loving couple who couldn't have children of their own, he would be well cared for and would be given every opportunity he could wish for, his new family were very wealthy indeed and in a very odd way they looked very similar to his real Mom and Dad!

Chapter 19

August 4th 1968.

   After delivering the bad news that they hadn't found the object in Scott's apartment, the edgy agent left the Chief's office, his steps caused an echo in the marble hallway, it sounded like he was in a cave. Nobody else stirred as he walked towards the elevator. All alone, apart from a large man sitting at a small desk on a swivel chair, dressed in a black suit, white shirt and a black tie. The rolls due to the size of his neck hung over the top of his shirt collar. He made the agent walking towards him feel very uncomfortable as he watched him closely, his gaze fixed on the agent's eyes like he was guarding the gates of Hell. His desk had a phone on his right and a small screen on his left which he used to watch the surveillance camera in the elevator. He slowly turned a pad with his left hand that laid in-front of him, pointing at an area on the pad, without moving his gaze from the agent's eyes.

"Sign out please," ordered the man as he finally moved his eyes to check the agent's name badge.

   The large security man was tapping his finger just above the space on his pad for the agent to sign, picking up the pen, the agent signed it. He handed the pen back to the security man, who just slowly turned the pad back around and moved his gaze to face the monitor once more. The agent was left holding the pen for a few seconds before he placed it back down.

Raising his eyebrows he continued towards the elevator, placing his hand on a screen by the doors. A thin light that stretched across the screen moved down from the top to the bottom, a light beside the door went from red to green and the elevator door opened. Inserting his key in the keyhole, he turned it once. All the lights flashed and he pushed the zero button, then the doors closed. He stood in the middle of the square box held up by only a few steel cables. The ascent from what seemed like the bowels of the earth was slow. There weren't any other stops on the way, it went from zero to four up, and zero to nowhere down. He stood there, feeling very uncomfortable, sensing the security guard's eyes watching, burning into his soul from the gates of Hell below…

The words the security guard had said echoed around Scott's head,
"Things happen to people who ask questions around here."

The man who parked near to him wasn't at work that day and his parking spot had been used by another car. Scott noticed this out of his office window as he watched more and more trucks passing outside the security fence, emerging from a warehouse in the distance. What is going on? He said to himself. He had to find out.

That day on his way home he noticed the black car following him again. He needed to be sure this time. He went home and knocked on Karl's door. Karl answered, looking like he'd just woken up, rubbing his eyes and letting out a big yawn.

"You up to much Karl?" Scott asked.

"Not now," he said as he finished yawning again, "Why?"

"Just come for a ride with me in the car." Scott said.

"Now hey, I'm not into……"

Scott didn't let him finish.

"Please Karl," asked Scott, appearing to be stressed.

"Ok, calm down, what's up Scott?" questioned Karl.

"Remember that car I told you about? It followed me home. I swear I'm not imagining it. Just come with me for a drive. Ten minutes. That's all I ask. Please." Scott pleaded.

"Ok, no probs, just calm down, I'm sure it's nothing Scott." Karl replied.

Karl locked his apartment and they headed down the stairs.

Before they went out to the Scott's Stingray he told Karl where to look for the black Sedan that had followed him. As they got outside Karl didn't make it obvious but he had a quick glance in the direction that Scott had said. There it was, the black car, windows half way down and the faint puff of bluish, white smoke could be seen exiting the opening. Karl followed Scott to his Corvette. They got in and drove off past the suspicious black Sedan. They were laughing and talking as they passed it, so not to let them know they were onto them. Karl had moved the wing mirror slightly so he could see. The black Sedan pulled out a few cars behind Scott.

"There! You see. I'm not going mad. There is

something going on here. It's following me." Scott stressed.

"It does seem like it, but why would they be following you?" Karl questioned Scott.

"I have no idea." Scott replied.

"Have you done something at work? Is it about Kimberly?" Karl asked.

"I have no idea." Scott repeated.

They drove around for a while, to nowhere in particular, just taking lots of different streets to see if the car followed them. It did.

Scott finally pulled up at a diner and they went in for a coffee to throw them off the trail. The black Sedan parked for a while in the parking-lot and then disappeared. It drove past the back of Scott's Corvette, really slowly, as if they were having a good look at it.

"I'm sure they have been in my apartment too!" exclaimed Scott.

"What? When?" Karl asked.

Scott told Karl about the other night when he came home and the balcony door was open and there was the faint smell of cigarette smoke lingering in the air.

"Have you seen or heard anything suspicious when you've been in?" Scott questioned Karl.

"No! Nothing! Well, no nothing really," he stopped to think.

"What do you mean, no nothing really?" Scott asked.

"Well, the other day I went out to put my trash in the garbage can and a man in a suit was walking from our area where the trash cans are. I gave him a funny look and asked if I could help him. But he just kept on walking and didn't say a-word. I didn't think anything of it until I got to the trash and the lids were off each can! I hadn't given it another thought until just now." Karl told Scott.

"Would you be able to recognise him again?" asked Scott.

"Not sure, I didn't really see his face, he had passed me. He did have black sunglasses on though." Karl responded.

"Well, that narrows it down a bit." Scott frowned.

They finished their coffees and headed back to the apartment. Scott was worried about what was going on. He didn't have a clue why anybody would want to follow him. He hadn't done anything wrong in his entire life.

"I'll keep an eye out around the apartment for anything suspicious bud." Karl said.

"Thanks Karl, I'd appreciate that!" replied Scott.

Scott went for a surf early the next morning, he loved the early morning rip. The sun had only just come up on the horizon, casting a hypnotic, rippling orange glow across the ocean towards him as he sat on his longboard waiting for the waves. He hadn't seen the black car that morning, this had relaxed him slightly but he was still worried. He didn't know whether to say anything at work, all he kept remembering was what the security guard had said…

The surf was great, it was easy to forget everything out there, just him and the waves. Finishing his surf he decided to head back. Walking out of the ocean, he placed his longboard at his feet and undid his wetsuit, he left the top half hanging around his waist, exposing his finely tuned body to the morning sun. Leaving his legs encased he headed back to his apartment for a shower with his board under his arm.

Scott finished getting ready, grabbed his keys and headed out of the door. He always kept his keys in a very safe place, an old empty tin can in his food cupboard, so nobody would find them if they broke into his apartment. He didn't want his car stolen and since the other night he didn't know who had been in his apartment. He jumped into his car and headed off to work.

On arrival he noticed that the man's parking bay had the new car in it again, he shook his head and carried on into work. Kimberly had phoned him that morning, she was back now and wanted to know if he would like to meet for lunch today. He thought the idea was great and couldn't wait for lunchtime to arrive. The morning went by really quickly, in fact the time got away with Scott and it wasn't until there was a knock at his door, he looked at his watch.

"Come in!" Scott shouted.

It was Kimberly. She popped her head around the door.

"I thought I'd call on my way down for lunch." Kimberly said.

"Gee, you're a sight for sore eyes, it's a good job you came by, I didn't have a clue what time it was. I'd gotten carried away with this project." Scott replied.

Kimberly walked slowly over to Scott as he stood up, grabbed his tie and pulled him towards her until their lips touched ever so lightly. She pushed him back into his chair and hitched her skirt up and sat straddled across him, pressing her lips on his she gave him a hard loving kiss.

Kimberly got up and calmly said, "Well, are you coming for lunch or what?"
Scott was caught off guard, his tie was all over the place. The knot had gone really small. He sat there wide eyed with lipstick on the corner of his mouth. He stood up to compose himself and looked in his mirror on the way over to the door where Kimberly was waiting.
"Hang on, you missed a bit." Kimberly said in a sexy voice.
She used a cotton handkerchief from her purse to gently wipe the corner of his mouth, before folding it back up and putting it away. Scott felt all flushed, he'd lost his cool but he didn't care one bit, it was worth it.
"I've missed you." Kimberly said over her shoulder as she opened the door.
Scott just smiled and followed her aromatic scent out of his office like he was in some kind of trance.

Scott tried to ask Kimberly about Section XX, she couldn't tell him anything. She was signed to the government secret's act and her job would be in jeopardy if she ever spoke to anyone about it.
"Surely you can tell me something Kimberly?" pressed Scott.
"We can't let my job interfere with us, if we both just do what we are here to do, it's not a problem,"

replied Kimberly.

"Ok, I won't ask again, I promise!" smiled Scott. He wasn't going to tell her about the key or the car. He thought best to keep her out of it if this place was as bad as the security guard had made out. I'll not compromise Kimberly's position, but I will find out one way or another what is going on here... thought Scott as they headed for lunch.

Chapter 20

The black car sat motionless outside Scott's apartment. The two men inside were waiting for the coast to clear. As Karl left at about 2pm to go surfing, he walked across the road with his longboard tucked under his arm and headed down towards the beach, oblivious to the black Sedan parked up the street.

The coast was clear!

The two agents got out of the car with a black bag and walked towards Scott's apartment. They entered by picking the lock through the main door, at the side of the building, passing the mail boxes and into the stairwell. They headed up the stairs to Scott's floor. Their suit jackets flapped open, revealing a glimpse of a pistol handle as they turned the corner towards his door. One man stood guard while the other crouched down near Scott's door handle. It was as if he had a key, the speed at which he picked the lock was unbelievable. They were in and the door was closed in the blink of an eye. As quiet as mice they searched the apartment for the second time. They had to find something this time, they couldn't go back empty handed again. Anything that had been moved was put back exactly as it was found. Both of the agents had gloves on so they didn't leave fingerprints, there couldn't be any suspicion.

Agent 1 reached into the black bag and pulled out

what looked like a box with a handle on it. He held it up by the handle and squeezed a trigger. There was a screen facing him, he watched as he pointed the device around the room, an outline of everything in the room appeared on the screen. He did this in each area of Scott's apartment. Nothing.

They searched everywhere, even opening the doors to the kitchen units, the outline of all Scott's food showing on the screen. Everything except the object they came for. Where could it be?

The box was placed back into the bag and the two men left empty handed once more.
"We're in for it now!" One of the agents said. The two men managed to get out of the apartment without anybody seeing them and headed back to Sector XX, ready for the onslaught.

Scott was working late again that night, he needed to get on top of things with this program. He'd been down to the test site but something was wrong. The program wasn't responding, the remote module wasn't communicating with Capcom from a test site miles away but still on earth.

Capcom was the central operations room in NASA. Scott thought if it didn't work here then they would be stuffed if it got all the way to the moon and didn't work. It needed re-programming so he had his work cut out and it was back to the drawing board. When Scott was over at the testing facility, he had been shown the Apollo rocket parts for the first time. It was massive, far bigger than he'd imagined. How could something like that ever lift off the ground?

It wasn't long before Apollo 11 would head off on a mission that would change the course of history.

Scott returned to his office, as he walked in he got a whiff of stale tobacco smoke, the same smell that he had noticed in his apartment, it lingered in the air. He had a look around but nothing had been moved. Gazing out of his window, Scott was transfixed on the falling dusky sky, wondering what the hell was going on, as he subliminally witnessed the darkness of night blanket his view.

Kimberly had phoned his office while he was out at the test facility, she left a message wondering if he wanted to meet that night in Mickey's bar again. He couldn't, he had too much to do. He tried phoning her back but there was no answer. It was well after the time she had called, he was glad he'd told her earlier that he would be working late that night. It was approaching 8pm and he'd started to rub his eyes, they were getting blurry with the glare from his large computer screen. Saving his work he turned off the device and grabbed his jacket once more, pulling it on he heard his keys rattle as he swung it over his shoulder.

As Scott made his way towards the elevator, the buzzing noise from the floor cleaner burst into action behind him, nearly making him jump out of his skin. Scott spun round to see what it was, he saw the cleaner holding both handles of the machine looking at him as if he was mad. Arriving at the elevator Scott pushed the call button and stood waiting again, he was getting used to the time it took to arrive. Scott placed his hand into his jacket pocket, absent-mindedly fiddling with his keys. When the doors opened, he was greeted by the sound of tranquil music. The elevator was empty. Turning to face the panel he went to push the 0 button, the empty keyhole below catching his eye. Hmmm, I wonder, he thought to himself, as he pulled out the bunch of keys from his pocket and flicked through them. Car key, apartment key, building key, mail box key, office key and… hmmm? He held the key in his fingers, moving it slowly towards the hole, his hand started to shake.

The key reached the hole and he slotted it in. It fit like a glove. With all his other keys on the fob, he tried to turn the key. It clicked to the left and all the lights flashed, the button near the keyhole lit up. Scott hesitated as he went to push the button, he glanced around the elevator once more, then he pushed it and stepped back into the middle of the elevator as it started to move. Suddenly having second thoughts as he descended to an unknown fate. Why did I push it? Frantically, he pushed a few buttons to stop it and take him back up. Nothing happened. It just kept going down and down, he tried to withdraw the key from the keyhole, but it wouldn't come out. When he'd inserted the key and pushed the button, the security camera had been activated.
He was being watched!

Thump. The elevator came to rest at the bottom, as it did the key that he'd been trying to get out turned freely and popped out along with the rest of his keys, he quickly tried to place the key back into the keyhole so he could go back up but it was no use, he placed them back into his pocket and waited, looking at his distorted reflection in the steel door of the elevator.

Where was he? What had he done?

An eternity seemed to go by whilst he was waiting for the doors to open, but in reality it was only a few seconds. Suddenly the doors began to slide. There were three people standing in front of him with their backs to the elevator. Scott slowly lifted his arm and tried to push the button on the panel one last time, it was no good. The agents standing there slowly turned round to face Scott.

He couldn't believe his eyes. There, in the middle, was Kimberly! With an agent each side of her, she smiled at Scott as she raised her arm and pointed something at him. He frowned and tried to shout her name as she mouthed; "I'm sorry!" whilst pulling the trigger of whatever she was holding. There was a bright flash of light, no sound just a bright flash. His body went into spasms as he crumbled under his own weight, he landed in a heap on the floor of the elevator still jerking from the effects of what had just hit him. He watched Kimberly turn and walk off, her slow sexy walk imprinted on his mind as he faded away into unconsciousness.

The two agents grabbed an arm each and pulled Scott's limp lifeless body down the white marble corridor. They had walked quite some distance to a door that had 'ISO ONE' written on the front.

Kimberly had disappeared into the room next door, she watched as the agents pulled Scott into the room. They pulled him up onto an odd looking chair in the centre of the room, the chair was the same colour as the floor, everything was bright white. Scott's ankles were strapped to the legs of the chair and his arms were handcuffed, with a chain going under the seat. A large strap was placed around the back of the chair and his chest to keep him upright.

In front of Scott's paralysed body was a large mirror, the room was all white marble, it looked very clinical. The two agents walked out of the room and closed the door behind them. As the door shut it seemed to blend in with the surrounding room. The agents joined Kimberly in the room next door, looking through the two-way mirror they waited for Scott to regain consciousness. The agents were the same two men who had been following Scott in the black car. They had the black bag in the room with them as they waited. One of the agents reached into the bag again and pulled out the box with the screen and handle on. He pointed it at the mirror, towards Scott.

"Give me some good news agent."

"Object secure Chief!" The agent said.

"About time agent," replied Kimberly as she let out a huge sigh, "Operation Smoke Screen is active."

Chapter 21

Scott started to stir. His head slumped over onto his chest. As he came round he was dazed and confused. Looking down, blurry eyed, he could see his hands were handcuffed to a chair somehow and his legs were strapped to the chair legs, something around his chest held him up.

Had he seen right?

Had he seen Kimberly fire something at him?

He couldn't remember.

It was when he tried to move that he realised he hadn't dreamt his predicament, he couldn't move. He was strapped to a chair, but why?

Scott tried to focus on the room around him, he was squinting, the only thing he could make out was a swirling reflection of himself. Looking down and back at the reflection, his vision started to return, allowing him to see how he was tied to a chair. He tried moving his arms again but it was no use he was fastened in tight.

"Why? What's going on? What do you want with me?" Shouted Scott.

There was no answer. He sat there for a while, listening and looking around now his eyes were back in focus. He couldn't see a door, the whole room was just white and echoey, apart from the mirror on the wall. Scott noticed in the mirror, high up in the corner of the room behind him just out of his view, there was a surveillance camera, he couldn't turn his head round that far, but he could see it in the mirror behind him. A red light on the front moving with the lens of the camera.

He shouted again, "What do you want with me?"

A door opened in the corner, Scott couldn't make out who had entered the room, the bright lights from the corridor silhouetted the figure walking towards him. He tried to look over his shoulder but couldn't see, they were just out of view.

"Kimberly?" he called, as he heard what he thought were the sound of her footsteps walking towards him from behind.

Still no answer.

Scott closed his eyes trying to adjust to the blinding light. Then he felt the very light touch of a finger stroking the back of his neck around to under his chin. He slowly opened his eyes as Kimberly walked round into view, this was when he realised he had seen her and he hadn't been dreaming.

"What's going on Kimberly? Are you all mad? It's me Scott!" he shouted.

"You have something we need Scott, we have been searching for it for years." Kimberly replied.

"What could I possibly have that is yours?" he asked.

"The key…"

Scott butted in and didn't let her finish, "But I only just got the key the other day, it appeared in my pocket when I was at work. I didn't have a clue where it came from. Honest, I'm telling the truth." He was getting flustered now, all the thoughts coming out at once.

"It's not the key Scott. The key was planted on you

to lead you down here! You have been holding
something for a long time. Maybe you knew about
it, maybe you didn't. That's not the problem here
we just need it back!" Kimberly said.

"Anything! You can have anything. Just untie me
and I'll try and find what you want. Please
Kimberly, I thought we had something special."
Scott stopped talking.

"We did. We do. It will all be ok. Don't worry
Scott. You have been in our sights for a long time
now. Longer than you could possibly think of. The
car that has been following you, you know about
the car Scott, don't you? It has been tailing you for a
long time. But you have only realised recently
haven't you?" Kimberly said.

"Yes, the black Sedan!" Scott replied.

"That's the one Scott, what if I told you that that car
has been following you for years. Those two men in
that car know more about you than you know about
yourself Scott. Remember Prof. Jefferson at Harvard
university?" Kimberly asked.

"Y-y-yes." He frowned as he answered her
question, "What's he got to do with anything?"

"Well, Prof. Jefferson gave you everything you need
to know for your future, the classes on particle
physics and all the technical courses, speed of light
theories, space travel, planets etc etc etc. That was
all for our benefit, and yours of course. Your job
here at the space centre, it's all been planned for
years. We just needed to know that you were ready
before we train you up for your real mission."
Kimberly said.

"Mission! What mission?" Scott looked shocked,

"I have a mission? I'm writing the program for the module."

"Well, that's true, in a sense. You were the only person who was able to develop this. You were gifted with something from a very early age and it seems to have enabled you to excel in this field. The program you have been writing is for a module, but not what you think…" Kimberly was cut short by another voice in the room.

"That's enough agent. You've told him too much as it is!" a deep, gruff voice echoed in the marbled room.

The thundering steps of a large muscular man in a black suit echoed into the room through the doorway and stood before Scott, his suit only just fitting his huge body.

"Well…Well…It is remarkable. You look more like him in person than the photos I've seen of you. You have his eyes!" The man said staring at Scott, making him feel uncomfortable.

"What are you talking about? Who the hell are you? What am I doing here? Who do I look like?" Scott fired lots of questions at the man.

"Calm down! All will become clear very soon Scott!" the man said as he leaned forward and looked into Scott's eyes. He walked off saying, "It's remarkable, I hope this works." As he closed the door behind him and Kimberly.

Scott was all alone in the room again, he was starting to sweat. He could see in his reflection his brow was glistening, the bright lights bouncing off all the white walls enhanced his fearful look as he gazed around the room. Scott sat wondering what the hell was happening. He thought back to his time at Harvard, remembering Prof. Jefferson gave him special attention in his class. He'd often wondered why things just fell into place all the time. He started to question his very existence. What were they all talking about?

Who do I look like?

Why am I here?

What do I have?

He had a million questions floating around his brain, but he couldn't find an answer for any of them. Scott knew he was adopted and didn't know who his real parents were and he didn't look anything like his adoptive father.

Who were they talking about?

"I WANT SOME ANSWERS!" Scott shouted at the top of his voice, "NOW!"

He heard the door open again and the sound of footsteps graced the marble floor once more. Another man came into view. Without saying a word he held up another object and pointed it at Scott. Scott closed his eyes and his head sunk into his shoulders ready for another blast of whatever they hit him with before, he was like a turtle hiding from a vicious predator.

"Don't worry Scott, I'm not doing anything that will harm you." The man's voice calmly reassured him.

Peering out of the corner of his eye, Scott looked at the man, he had in his hand what looked like a box with a handle on it. Intently looking at a screen on the front, the man pointed the box at Scott and moved it up and down very slowly, whilst walking around him.

"Just stay still for a moment please Scott!" asked the agent.

"What are you doing?" questioned Scott.

There was silence from the man until he finished, he looked at the mirror and gave the thumbs up. He then left the room and the door closed once more.

I'm getting sick of this, Scott said to himself. He started to shake his hands in the cuffs to see if he could loosen them. It was no good. They were far too tight, he was locked up like a criminal.

What am I going to do? I shouldn't have used the key in the elevator then this wouldn't have happened! He thought to himself whilst losing the battle to break free. Staring into the mirror he looked to see if he could see any movement behind it, but he couldn't, all he could see was himself looking straight back. He saw the door open again. When it was shut you couldn't tell where it was at all. Kimberly walked back into the room and slowly wondered around him with her sweet, sultry, sexy steps. She stopped in front of him and leaned forward. Scott's eyes were still drawn to look down her gaping blouse even though he was tied to a chair. He let out a huge sigh. Kimberly lifted her hand up and onto Scott's shoulder. She then traced her finger down his muscular chest and onto his arm. She was biting her bottom lip as she did this, gazing into Scott's eyes. Her hand had slipped into Scott's jacket pocket without him realising. She stepped back and dangled the keys in front of him.

"Hey! They are my car keys and apartment keys, what do you want with them?" He asked.

Kimberly held them up and unclipped the apartment keys and his car key, she then placed these keys into her pocket. Holding his key fob that he'd had for years and the key he had found the other day, she walked back out of the room not saying a word.

In front of Scott there was a noise. The floor started to rise. A rectangular white section of the floor came up from the ground on a central tubular pillar, it stopped at table height. Then it span round so Scott's legs were under it, just as if he was sat at a table. Another section came up at the base of the pillar and formed a new floor.

Someone else opened the door and walked into the room, it was the large man again. There came another noise and a section flipped up on the floor, and then a box rose from the ground creating another seat opposite Scott. The section that had flipped up made a back rest, the man sat down facing him. Scott hadn't seen anything like this before in real-life, maybe only in the movies. He thought he'd been taken into the future. The man put his hands on the table, cupping something in his right hand he then lifted it away, leaving behind Scott's key fob.

"What is this?" the man questioned.

"Ermmmm my key fob!" Scott said sarcastically.

"Don't get clever with me Scott!" the man said as he pushed the fob into the centre of the table.

"Do you know how long we have been looking for this?" he asked.

The man raised his arm and pointed at the fob on the table. He then motioned to the mirror and

pointed at Scott. The door opened and the man who previously had the box walked in.
"Release his arms!" were his only words to the man. He did this and walked out again in silence. Scott rubbed his wrists where the cuffs had been tightened, he had a red mark all the way round his wrists.
"That looks sore Scott!" said the man.

Scott just looked at him and continued to rub his wrists. Finally he broke the silence and asked what he was doing here and if he was been detained for something, he wanted a lawyer.
"You are not being held, as of this moment, you now work for us!" stated the man.
"I do not! I work for NASA." Scott replied.
"No. You now work for us! I'm not asking you I'm telling you!" barked the man.

Scott didn't like where this conversation was going. He placed his elbows on the table and rubbed his hands on his face as if he was washing it without water.
"This isn't happening!" Scott shouted.
"Oh, it's happening alright Scott and I think you'll want to be part of it when you find out exactly what it is!" replied the big man.

Chapter 22

"Stop! Don't move a muscle, don't even breathe, I heard something!" said the agent with his finger up to his mouth.

Karl arrived back to his apartment that evening, he gave Scott a knock to see if he fancied joining him for a beer down on the beach. No answer. It was all silent. He tried again. Still nothing!

He thought he heard some movement as he walked off to his apartment. Looking back at Scott's door it was all silent. Karl grabbed a pack of beers and wrote a quick note saying, "Heading off to the beach for a beer if you fancy it? I'll be there for a while, come over." He slipped it under Scott's door and hurried off. As Karl walked out of his apartment building through the mail box area, he noticed a letter sticking out of Scott's mailbox. He can't be home yet he thought to himself. As he left the building he noticed that Scott's car wasn't there, he hadn't paid any attention on his way in. Maybe he's still at work, the mad bugger, on a night like this, Karl said to himself. Heading over to the beach with his pack of beers to sit and watch the breakers coming in, he couldn't think of anything more relaxing in the world.

Inside Scott's apartment there had been a noise when Karl had knocked, the two men were in there again. They had been there for a while. They had to clear his apartment with no suspicion. All Scott's

belongings were being boxed up ready to be
cleared, this had to be done to look for any clues,
any signs that he might have known he'd had this
object in his possession. One of the agents picked
up the letter that Karl had slipped under the door.
"Well, I doubt he'll be needing this!" he said as he
laughed to the other agent and crumpled it up into a
ball, tossing it into the trash can.
"Let's just concentrate on the job at hand agent, this
isn't a laughing matter!" the other agent said with a
stern look on his face, "and try and keep it quiet
please!" he added.
"Yes Sir!" came the sarcastic reply whilst saluting
the other agent behind his back.
"I saw that."
   The furniture was to be left, that came with the
apartment when Scott had rented it, but all the other
belongings were being put into storage. The agent
was keeping an eye out from the window looking
towards the beach. He saw Karl walk across the
road and down the path towards the beach with his
beer. I wish I could do that, the agent thought.
"All clear Sir," said the agent at the window.
The other agent picked up his walkie talkie and
pushed the button on the side to open the channel.
"All clear, over!" he said and released the button.
"Copy that, over and out!" came the reply.
   The two agents could hear the rumbling of a
heavy truck, it had been waiting just round the
corner. The words 'BOB'S REMOVAL SERVICE'
were stamped on the side, with a telephone number
underneath. It backed into the space where Scott
normally parked his Stingray. The two doors

opened at the rear of the truck and a ramp slid out. A team of removal men dressed in blue overalls, with the company name printed on the back, walked down the ramp and into the building. One after the other they went in and then emerged with box after box of Scott's belongings. An operation executed with fine military precision. It took them a matter of minutes to completely clear Scott's apartment of his belongings. One last look around and they left the room, wiping the handle and locking the door behind them.

On the way out of the building the agent calmly picked the lock on the mail box and removed the letters, then shut and locked it again. He emptied the trash can in the dumpster at the side of the building and then threw the trash can in the back of the truck. As he closed the door he banged on the side to tell them to roll out. The truck started it's engine and drove off. The whole operation couldn't have taken more than twenty minutes. The two agents returned to their black car, they both lit up a smoke and drove off.

Karl returned from the beach later that night after finishing his beers, except for the one which seemed glued to his hand as he walked home. He threw the empties in the trash can as he left the beach, smashing a few in the process. When he entered his building he noticed that the letters that had been sticking out of Scott's mail box had gone. He must have been home Karl thought to himself. As he walked up the stairs to his apartment, there was the faint aroma of stale cigarette smoke in the air. When he reached the floor of his and Scott's apartments he noticed the note he pushed under the door was gone too, he could tell this as he had left the corner sticking out because it wouldn't push in any further. Karl didn't know but he'd been trying to push the note against the shiny black shoe of the agent, who was waiting by the door after he heard the knocking. Outside Scott's apartment Karl noticed a cigarette butt, it can't have been put out properly on the concrete floor, as there was a long ash trail that had burnt right up to the filter leaving a scorched trail in it's wake. Karl bent down and placed his Bud on the floor, he picked up the but with his finger tips, the long ash trail broke off and laid on the singed cold floor, he waved his hand above it and it disappeared into the air, leaving a dusty residue falling back to the concrete. He held up the butt and looked at it, like a detective investigating the scene of a murder looking for clues. He had always thought of himself as bit of a detective ever since he was a child, that's all he wanted to be, the Eliot Ness of Coco Beach.

As Karl stood up he grabbed his Bud and walked to his apartment. Cigarette butt in one hand and a Bud in the other, he tried to find his keys by hitting each pocket with the base of his bottle. Clank! They were in the right pocket. He put the bottle in his mouth and clamped his lips shut like an oyster hiding a precious pearl. He fished around in his pocket for his key to unlock the door. As Karl entered his lounge he grabbed the trash can by the door, it had been overflowing for a day or two now. I'd better get this emptied I think, he said to himself. He took one last close look at the cigarette butt and

put it on the top, squashing all the trash down as he did. Picking up the trash can he walked back downstairs and out to the dumpster. As Karl lifted up the dumpster lid he noticed on the top was a crumpled up piece of paper. That's odd, he thought, that looks just like the note paper I'd written the note to Scott on. The bright yellow piece of paper rolled slightly as Karl disturbed the trash. He put his trash can down and picked the ball of paper up, he de-crumpled it and turned it over.
It was his note!
But why was it in there?
What's up with Scott?

Something doesn't add up here he thought to himself. Karl folded the note he had written and put it in his pocket. He then dumped his trash and walked back into the apartment. He didn't knock again because Scott's car still wasn't back, Karl went straight into his own apartment.

Chapter 23

Scott had been left alone for a while, when the door opened suddenly, it made him jump. He had been wondering what was going on and what was going to happen to him. The table and chair were still in front of him. A man wheeled a trolley in and left it next to the table, he then left the room again. Scott studied the trolley and looked at what was on top of it. The trolley was like a white cabinet on wheels, it had a handle for pushing and two doors on the front. He could see what was on top of the trolley but not what was inside it. On the top were two brown files, one about two inches thick and the other looked like it only had a few pages in, the one on the top had some writing on the front of it. Scott tried to read what it said, he tilted his head to the side so he could see it more clearly. He couldn't work out all the words, but he could make out some, that were stamped on a diagonal right across the front in red; 'TOP SECRET CONFIDENTIAL'. It had a string on the side that wound around a button on the top to keep it shut. Scott raised his eyebrows and tried to focus on the other writing, 'Rosw... Inc... 194...' The writing was faded on the front cover and he couldn't make it all out very well. Beside this was a pen, a glass of water and a burger. Scott's mouth started to water looking at the drink, he was thirsty but not that hungry. The trolley had been placed just out of Scott's reach. He was still strapped to the chair around his chest. He tried leaning forwards to reach but it was no good he couldn't move, the chair and his fingers were just missing the handle at his furthest stretch. He tried a few times but he just couldn't reach it and gave up putting his arms back on the table.

A short while later the door opened, Scott noticed in the reflection in the mirror the gruff voiced man walked in again. He sat in the chair, that had formed from the floor, and looked at Scott.

"I think it's about time you knew what's happening here and who you really are. My name is Bob," the man said.

"Well Bob, it's about time!" replied Scott.

Bob picked up the files from the trolley, he slapped them down onto the table, Scott was sure he saw dust fly off them.

"What you are about to hear will change everything you know about humanity and our very existence!" he stressed, "You have to keep a clear and open mind from now on!"

"Ok!" frowned Scott.

Bob started to talk to Scott, asking him if he knew the stories about The Roswell Incident. Scott nodded and said that everyone knew about the Roswell stories and how it was all a big mistake and that it was in fact a high altitude weather balloon.

"That's right isn't it?" Scott asked.

"Well, in a fashion, part of that is right!" Bob replied.

"Part of it, which part?" questioned Scott.

"There was a weather balloon involved, but something brought the weather balloon down.

Something not of this world, and we have it…" Bob was interrupted.

"Hang on a minute, you're trying to tell me you have an unidentified flying object, pull the other one!"

Bob smiled and replied, "Well, to put it bluntly, yes we do! We have had this craft for twenty one years now…"

"What! You've had a space craft for twenty one years and nobody knows abou…" Scott was cut short.

"Will you shut up and just listen to what I'm going to tell you. It's going to take a while and you are going to have to listen to me carefully. Have I got your full attention? This isn't a laughing matter! Thank you. On the 7th July 1947 an incident took place on a ranch in Roswell involving an unidentified flying object not from this planet. We recovered the craft and its occupants…" Bob was stopped again.

"What, you have aliens as well?" Scott asked.

A red mist descended over Bob's face.

"Will you just listen! We recovered the craft and it's occupants. They were taken to a research facility in Nevada, New Mexico, called Area 51. You'll also have heard the stories about how that place doesn't exist, no doubt. Well, to make it clear, it definitely does exist. I worked there from 1947 to 1951 when the craft was brought here to Area 49 and yes, before you butt in, we do have lots of areas around America, fifty one to be precise. We have had numerous people work on the craft over the years, but nobody has been able to make it work or get any further than your father did!" Bob knew that would be a conversation stopper.

"You knew my father? What, my real father?" Scott said as his face turned the same shade of white as the walls in the room.

Scott fell silent and looked completely shocked. He didn't know what was coming next, he felt like he'd been hit by a steam train.

"Yes, I knew your father, I worked alongside him at Area 51. He was a great man." Bob said as he pulled the bottom file out and placed it on table top in front of him. Scott saw this just had, 'Confidential' stamped on the front.

"Was?" Scott tried to think. "What happened to him?"

This was the bit Bob wasn't looking forward to. He had to lie to Scott.

"We're not sure Scott, all we know is that they were relocated over to Area 49 along with the craft and the rest of the team. They were meant to pick the keys up for their new place at Titusville on a certain day and they didn't turn up! Their abandoned truck was found in the middle of nowhere and recovered by the military. You were asleep in the front seat, dehydrated and starved. Unfortunately we have no idea what happened to your parents. They had just vanished. The truck had nothing left in it, the only thing you had with you was a bag, which included a few toys and some clothes with your name written inside. Raymond Wilkinson." Bob stopped talking so Scott could take a few moments to let it all sink in.

After a few minutes Scott hesitated and asked,

"What was my mother's name?"

"Linda, she was called Linda," Bob answered, "I wish I could tell you more Scott. He truly was a great scientific mind, but because of the nature of our work at Area 51 he wasn't allowed to tell anyone what he did there, not even your mother. She thought he was an aircraft mechanic working on military planes. The only two pictures we have of him are this one on his file for his name badge, and this one that was taken off the security camera the day before he left for Area 49."

Bob showed Scott a picture of George, his father. He couldn't remember him. A tear formed in the corner of Scott's eye and slowly rolled down his cheek, finally dripping onto his lap.

"And my mother? Do you have a picture of her?"

"No, unfortunately we don't Scott, or would you like to be called Raymond?" asked Bob.

"My name is Scott, it has always been Scott to me and it will stay that way. So where do I fit into all this now?" he said whilst wiping the next rolling tear from his face.

"Are you sure you can handle all this Scott? I'm not sure you can."

"Carry on, I want to know everything you have to tell me."

Scott found his inner strength and shook off the new information.

"Well Scott, you were placed into an orphanage but it wasn't long before Mr and Mrs Salvador found you and gave you the best life you could possibly have wanted. Until that God forsaken accident which killed them both," Bob started saying.

"You know about that too?" Scott said.

"Yes, when we realised we were missing something that should have come from Area 51 to Area 49, a crucial piece of the puzzle, we searched and searched until the only place we hadn't looked was with you. We had to track you down and we managed this when you were eleven, when you flagged up on a government test at school as being highly intelligent. Since then you had the best of the best teaching available to you, your adoptive parents were very cooperative with us. It seems that even the wealthy have a price too. Sorry Scott! Can you not remember how everything was set out for you growing up? You achieved full marks and had the best tuition along the way. They have all been teaching you. Getting you ready for some very special tasks. Tasks that only you can recall. Things you will need to know, they were implanted in your education." Bob explained to Scott.

"What things? And what is this part you are talking about? I don't have anything from my real parents!" Scott told Bob.

"You do and you don't even know it. Remember the fob, you have your car keys on. Nice car by the way! Do you know what this part is?" Bob placed the fob back on the table and pointed at a ring on the fob.

"Eh part of the fob? I got that from my adoptive father when he passed away, it was left to me with all their belongings. He used it for his keys and it reminded me of him." Scott replied.

"That's where you're wrong. It was actually your real father's key fob. All we can think of is that it must have been mixed up in the bag with all your toys and clothes when you were found. We think the keys must have gone missing when you were driving over and your father wasn't able to start the truck, he must have gone for help. When he hadn't returned your mother must have followed in search of him."

Bob painted this made up story for Scott so he wouldn't question the wrong doings of years ago. It was all a big cover up.

"If you look at the two pictures closely, the first picture shows George, your father, with his keys clipped onto his belt, here, and the last picture of him, here, shows the keys clipped onto his belt in the same place but look, look closely."

Bob pointed at a part on the fob with the tip of the pen he'd picked up from the trolley.

"Here! And here!" He said while he got out two close up copies of the picture, just of the area he was focusing on.

Scott could clearly see that the key fob was the same as the one he had. The one on the first picture showed a key fob with what he thought was his father's truck keys and maybe a house key. The second picture showed the same key fob with another ring attached to it. This ring was on Scott's key fob. What was it? Scott thought to himself.

"Now we've all got familiarised with one another, can I have these straps and cuffs removed, please?" Scott asked.

Bob thought for a moment, "I don't see why not." He said as he held his hand up like before. It wasn't long before someone had entered the room and unlocked the straps and cuffs from his chest and ankles. Scott stood up to stretch and the man who had unlocked him reached for his side-arm under his jacket.

"At ease man, he's not going anywhere!" said Bob. Scott looked round to see what had happened. "I'm going to show you something now that you probably won't believe, you have to watch closely and keep an open mind," Bob said excitedly.

He opened the doors of the trolley and reached into it. He pulled out two things that looked like long sleeves, made from a funny looking material. He placed them over his hands and up his arms, they tightened to fit his forearms and some vein-like tubes appeared to grow down the back of Bob's hands. This created a chrome glove-like structure around his fingers. Just like it had done all those years ago with Scott's father. He left the back section in the trolley. Bob brought one hand over to the screen on the other arm. Scott was looking more surprised by the second, as the screen lit up and showed some weird symbols on it. Then the tips of the fingers started to glow with some unusual lights. Bob moved his hand towards the screen and touched a ring like symbol. Scott's fob melted instantly and turned from its solid state into a molten liquid, the same colour but just like a little puddle of shiny metal. He then moved the finger he used to touch the symbol towards the melted key fob. Scott was shocked at what happened next. He always wondered what the thing was for on his fob and what kind of metal it was, because it never dulled or tarnished over time, it always looked shiny and unmarked even though he had his keys on it.

What happened next would make Scott realise that Bob wasn't joking about any of it.

The puddle of liquid was under the keys on the fob, it was moving around the keys. Just the same as what had happened to George all those years ago, but when it reformed, it had done so around his key fob and George had put them into his pocket with his keys, not realising he'd taken the object.

Bob reached a finger towards the molten object and the chrome coloured liquid moved towards his finger. As it got closer, an arc of light connected from his finger tip to the object, the arc caressed it, jumping around on the surface like a streak of lightning touching the earth. Finally, once the molten object was clear from the key fob, Bob touched the symbol again and the object flipped up and reformed into the exact same shape on the table.

"Wow! Metal with a memory! I've heard of this stuff, just didn't think it was real!" exclaimed Scott in shock, "This day just gets weirder by the second."

"I thought you'd like that. We have two other sections that act like this, so we had hoped this would do the same," said Bob.

"What do you mean? You didn't know?" asked Scott.

"Not really Scott, we had a good idea it would from the research your father had done, but we didn't know for sure until just then!" replied Bob.

Bob picked up the object and started to explain

where they had found that particular piece. How when they had pressed these symbols on the screen weird things happened. The object that Scott used as his key fob, he'd been carrying it around for years and his adoptive father before that, it was from the throat area of an alien being. The piece literally was from out of this world. These pieces were stored at Area 51, they only realised that this piece was missing once all the items had been transported to Area 49. When they began work on the project again, looking back through the reports it mentioned there were three items extracted from the being but they could only ever find two of them.

"What else do you have up your sleeves Bob?" asked Scott.

"Patience Scott, patience!" Bob exclaimed.

Bob slotted the newly formed ring back in its rightful place, which had been empty for the last eighteen years, next to the other items from the being's body.

"Make it happen again with one of the other items," Scott said excitedly.

"All in good time Scott, you will know all you need to know in good time." Bob gathered together the tray with the items on and placed it back in the trolley.

"Your life will never be the same ever again, from this day forward Scott!" said Bob.

"What do you mean Bob?" Scott asked.

Bob stood up from his chair and made for the door, lifting his arm up to summon somebody to open it for him. As he did so his chair folded up on itself and vanished into the floor. You couldn't tell where it had come from. The agent who had wheeled the trolley in to begin with, walked back into the room. Bob held the door open and the man wheeled the trolley out again.

Scott found himself alone in the bright white room once more. He started to get frustrated, he wanted his questions answered.

"How about a restroom break?" he shouted, towards the mirror on the wall in front of him. The table that had risen out of the floor span ninety degrees and descended, becoming the floor again. The floor looked like it had a borders outlining different rectangles and squares, these were still white so didn't stand out much unless you looked closely. Scott stood up from the chair he had been locked to for what seemed like an eternity. He walked around the room to stretch his legs, running his hands over the wall where he thought the door had opened, it was hard to tell. The walls had faint lines on them where the sections had been butted up together. He found the seam he thought was the door and tried to get his finger nails in to open it, but it was no good he just lost his grip and he stumbled backwards. He walked back to the middle of the room and stood looking at the mirror.

There was a faint noise, a rumble. Then in the corner next to the mirror, a section rose up from the floor. Scott stood watching, a section of about four feet square, looked like it was levitating straight up from the ground. Scott couldn't see under the square, it had a curtain of bright blue light following it as it rose to about eight feet. Scott started to take small slow steps backwards, until his back hit the wall where he had tried to find the door. Once it had risen, it just stopped. Nothing happened. He waited a while. Scott squinted at the bright light until his eyes got used to it. Curiosity finally got the better of him again, and he slowly walked towards this unusual object. He stood looking closely at the light. Lifting his arm towards the illuminated curtain he pushed his finger into it. The blue light was coming from below, he could tell this as the beam was cut at finger width right to the top. He moved his head to the side and tried to look inside the curtain of light. Scott was surprised at what he saw, it was a little room, a bathroom. He could see a toilet which slightly resembled the seat that Bob had sat on earlier. Scott pulled his finger out of the light and then put it back in again, looking once more. He could see the beam of light was very thin on his finger. As thin as a laser-beam. He then tried his whole hand through the light, he couldn't feel anything when he did this. Scott followed his hand with his arm and stepped in sideways, as if he had to go through the beam the thinnest way. His body then followed his arm until he was fully encapsulated by the curtain of bright, cloudy blue light.

When Scott was inside this tiny room he turned, trying to look out. It was amazing he couldn't see into the room at all. He placed his hand through the beam and looked back, with curiosity, into the room he had just left. Scott couldn't believe it! He brought his hand back in and chuckled to himself, shaking his head. There was a white tube behind the toilet, it looked telescopic, it even had a small circular sink, this too had a white tube coming from the floor, the same width as the sink, it just looked like a white tube with a bowl in the top. Great, all this technology and they forgot the taps, he laughed to himself. Scott turned to use the toilet. He looked down, great no water in the can, he thought to himself again. "I think you need to rethink these new products," he shouted to nobody.

Scott turned to the toilet and started to pee, as he did this he noticed it was passing straight through a blanket of light again. It passed through and disappeared below. A dark square rose from the back of the toilet whilst Scott was peeing. A tiny screen appeared on the front, a small green cursor beeped and flashed in the top righthand corner. The cursor started to move leaving letters behind it.

The first words read: Urine analysis.
"What the fu..!" Scott stopped himself from finishing. "What's all this?" he said to himself. The toilet was analysing his urine as he was peeing. "I'd hate to take a dump in this can!" he laughed. The cursor continued typing:

PH..............normal
Protein.........normal
Glucose........normal
Minerals.......normal

Scott was finding things really weird at the moment. He finished and the screen typed. 'Urine test complete, have a nice day.' He turned to the sink to wash his hands, what was going to happen here? Scott wondered. There was a mirror above the sink, this too had a cursor flashing in the corner where a dark screen had appeared. He could just make it out, the cursor was also bright green. It started typing: 'Place hands into bowl, lift slowly. Scott hesitated then placed his hands into the bowl. His hand disappeared under a cloudy white light. He thought this was the bottom of the sink, as his hands broke the light a jet of flat water squirted from right around the sink and just above this there was a high pressure air blower. As he raised his hands the sink was washing and then drying them at the same time. He finished raising his hands, the sink stopped blowing air the second his finger tips left the bowl. Scott's hands were perfectly clean and dry. He looked at the mirror once more, the typing said, 'Complete.'

Turning to face the same way he walked in, Scott stepped out sideways from the light screened room back into the area he had left. The weird square bathroom descended into the floor as if nothing had happened. Scott looked around the empty area again.

What's next?

Who was watching me from behind that mirror?

What did they want?

Why was the rest of my life never going to be the same?

He had all these thoughts and questions, but no answers.

Scott walked towards the mirror. He shielded his eyes and tried to look through the mirrored glass, he couldn't see a thing apart from his own eyes staring back. He moved back slightly and knocked on the mirror, it didn't sound like glass, it sounded thick and dull. Scott let out a yawn, he didn't have a clue what time it was. All he could remember was that the clock in his office said eight pm when he left that night, before all this weird stuff happened. "What's happening?" Scott shouted, "Can I at least have a glass of water?" he added.

The door opened again, in walked a man holding a glass of water. Drinking it down in one go Scott handed the man the glass back. "Thank you!" he shouted as the door closed shut behind the man.

Then he heard another noise. This time from the edge of the wall. A section started to fold out from the top. The bottom stayed fixed to the wall and it continued until it was flat, stopping about twenty inches from the floor. He stood looking at this large rectangular thing slowly falling towards him, it was a bed. The bed was fully made up with fluffy sheets, lovely plump pillows with a pair of shorts on the end.

"I can see why they need someone like Kimberly down here!" he said out loud.

Just as he finished saying that, the lights went out, leaving it pitch black. Scott didn't move a muscle. "Ok, I take it back. Sorry Kimberly!" he shouted. As he did, an outline of light encased the rectangular bed, all around the underside, giving Scott just enough light to see what he was doing. You've got to be kidding, he thought to himself. "I could do with a shower, or maybe not!" he laughed, Scott felt stupid shouting into the empty room.

Another rectangular panel started to rise from the ground in the opposite corner, just like the bathroom had done, screened with a bright blue light. He walked over to it and placed his hand into the light, the room only had a few things in it that Scott could see. There was an oval tube section, quite large on part of the floor panel. Two brightly lit oblong impressions could be seen inside the oval, there was another oval part mirroring the base section. The oval section above was attached to the white tube that held up the rectangular top, similar to the one in the bathroom. Away from this area there were a few flat trays that hung down on silver chains, Scott presumed this area was for hanging his clothes on. Scott walked into the area through the sheet of light and started to remove his clothes. He walked over to the lit imprints on the floor, they were slightly apart from each other. Placing his feet onto these parts they sank and disappeared beneath the brightly lit impressions. Another screen in front of him said, 'Reach arms up above head, keep them straight.'

Scott could see up into the section above him now. He could see it had the bright cloudy white light again, he thought it looked a little bit like a light fitting. He closed his eyes for a moment wondering what was going to happen.

The oval tube started to descend. As the object moved down, his fingertips broke the light covering the base of the oval, he was covered with water. Just like the sink it blasted out from all the way around the oval tube. As the jet met in the middle it caused a turbulent torrent of mashed up water. It hit Scott on the top of his head, causing him to take a deep breath as the water was cold to begin with then slowly got warmer. The oval section slowly moved down, reaching the top of Scott's head, he could feel the force and the warmth of the flat water jet ruffling his hair. As in the sink, the water was followed by a blast of luke warm air, very high powered all around the oval. He could feel the air warming and cooling him all at the same time, regulating to his body temperature. The section continued to move down his finely tuned torso, he just stood there with his arms in the air getting showered.

"This feels great!" he shouted out into the empty room.

As the section neared the end of it's journey Scott felt fantastic. It stopped and the screen had a new note written on it, "Complete, step out please." Scott stepped from the area, completely dry from his drenching. He smelt great, it must have something in the water he said to himself. He couldn't believe it, I could get used to this. Just then he realised he'd left the shorts on the end of the bed in the room. You idiot! He said to himself, what are you going to do now?

He quickly ran out to the bed and grabbed the shorts, slipping as he turned to go back into the shower area, he noticed it had started to return back into the floor.

"No...No...No!" he shouted, as he was performing a frantic dance to try and get into the shorts they had provided him with. After managing to steady himself again, he walked back to the bed. Scott sat on the edge and leaned forward putting his head into his hands, he watched the area descending into the floor.

"My clothes, my clothes!" he jumped up and threw himself, sliding across the floor, the sound of freshly cleaned skin screeching to a halt echoed around the room, just as the rectangle finished its descent, turning into the floor once more. He laid on the floor and thought for a while and then stood up. He walked around to his usual side of the bed and climbed in.

"It won't be long now Sir, the drugs will take effect soon!" The agent calmly said to Bob behind the mirror.

Scott's eyes closed as he laid there gazing into thin air, thinking about the weird events of the day, slowly and unaware he had been drugged, he drifted off into his drug induced sleep.

Chapter 24

Karl awoke the next morning to the sound of his alarm clock. He usually woke when Scott started his Stingray up and wheel spun it out of the parking area of their apartment block, but this didn't happen today. It was 6:30am, Karl didn't have anywhere to be that morning, apart from hitting the surf again. He rolled out of his bed and threw on the nearest T-shirt he could find from the bedroom floor. He took a swig of the dregs left in the bottom of the bottle of Bud he'd returned from the beach with last night, nearly choking on a drunk fly that couldn't resist the temptation. Karl walked into his bathroom and spat the decomposing remains of the fly into the sink, he brushed his teeth and swilled out his mouth. Coffee, I need a coffee! He said to himself. He pulled on his jeans and headed out of his apartment to walk to the nearest coffee place. As he left he noticed that Scott's parking space was still empty. Karl walked off down the street, wondering where he could be and what had happened to Scott.

....

Scott woke the next morning to the sound and smell of a rich dark coffee being poured into a cup beside his bed. His eyes slowly adjusted to the ambient glow of the white room once more. At first he thought it must have been a nightmare, but then, he realised that it wasn't, it was real. He laid there, motionless for a moment, before he looked to see who was pouring the coffee. It was Kimberly. She sat down on the edge of the bed, the harsh, hard demeanour of the Kimberly that Scott had witnessed yesterday seemed to have melted away. Kimberly turned to Scott as he laid in the fluffy white sheets, saying in her soft angelic voice. "Sorry Scott, I'm so sorry, I had to, it was my job." "So you should be, I shouldn't even be talking to you!" Scott was still annoyed with her, "You shot me with something! What the hell was that thing anyway? What's going on?" Kimberly just twisted her mouth to one side and placed a hand on the coffee cup, as she passed it to Scott she said, "I can't say anything Scott, not yet! But you'll find out more today!"

Scott sat up and took a sip from his coffee, it was far too hot. He noticed a small puncture wound on his forearm, it ached when he tried to bend it. "What's happened here? Have you been sticking needles in me? Never-mind, I need some clothes, mine disappeared when the shower went back down last night." He pointed to the area on the floor that had eaten his clothes.
Kimberly lent forward and pulled out his clothes from under the trolley she'd brought the coffee in on.
"There you go Scott," she said with a heart warming smile, "I am sorry Scott, I hope you can forgive me, but I had to do it. One thing you need to know is, I meant all I ever said to you. Let me see your arm."
Scott just wanted some answers. Still!

Kimberly stretched open Scott's arm to take a look then stood up and headed out of the door. As she left she turned to look at Scott, staring straight into his eyes, Scott could feel the agonising pain of her guilt as she turned and left the room.

The bathroom rose from the floor as it had done the day before, somehow it hadn't shocked Scott as much this time. He finished his coffee and placed the empty cup on the tray which sat on the top of the trolley. Grabbing his neatly folded clothes, he vanished through the curtain of light into the futuristic room again, emerging once he had finished getting dressed. The bathroom disappeared and the bed folded away. He stood in the emptiness, all alone in the bright white room, waiting.

After what seemed like ages, the door opened and in walked Bob and Kimberly.

"Morning Scott, I hope you had a pleasant night's sleep?" Bob asked.

"Well, under the circumstances, it wasn't too bad, probably had something to do with the zap you gave me!" Scott exclaimed.

"I doubt it." Replied Bob.

Kimberly stood silently in the room next to Bob, she knew what was happening. Bob looked at Scott wondering if he was up to what lay ahead.

"Are you ready for the rest of your life?" asked Bob.

"Maybe, if someone is going to tell me what the hell is going on!" Scott said.

"Remember, I told you about your real father yesterday? Well, he and his team were working on something that could change our understanding of our very existence!" Bob told Scott, "It's time you saw something. By the way, you will not be able to get out from down here so please don't try." He added.

Kimberly held the door open as Scott followed Bob out of the room into a long white corridor, their footsteps echoing in unison as they walked. Scott noticed they were passing door after door along the long corridor. Each door looked the same as the last, the only difference being the number on the front. At the end of the corridor were two frosted glass blast doors and a room to the right. The room had a large window facing the corridor with a glass door beside it. Inside the room was a security guard sitting at a white desk, he had watched them walk down the hallway on a screen in front of him. He looked up and walked to the door, Bob turned and gave him a nod before putting a key into a hole then he placed his hand on a screen next to it, a light traced down the palm on his hand and the doors started to open. Bob walked through with Scott close behind, turning to look at Kimberly who had stopped on the other side of the frosted door.
"You not coming Kimberly?" Scott asked.
"No! This is where my clearance stops I'm afraid, Bob will take you from here. See you soon, hopefully Scott." She replied with a guarded smile spreading across her face.
Scott looked slightly worried as the thick glass doors started to close leaving Kimberly in the corridor.

Once the blast doors had closed, they seemed to be in an empty void about a metre deep and twenty metres high, Scott could only just make out the ragged rock face of the old cavern walls towering above his head. They were faced with another large, towering door. Bob repeated the procedure to open it. This door was thicker! About a foot thick, from what Scott could see and made out of steel. It had a circular port hole window in the centre. You couldn't see through though it was slightly frosted, just like the first doors.

"Man, you don't want anything getting in here do you?" Scott pointed out.

"Or anything getting out!" Bob exclaimed.

Scott gave Bob a quick glance.

"What do you mean?" Scott questioned.

"All will be clear soon Scott." Bob said.

   The massive steel door started to move, it rolled to one side. Scott's eyes opened wide. He couldn't believe what he was seeing before him. They had entered into a large chamber, like an aircraft hangar. The size was immense, like two football fields wide and just as high. There were people walking around all donned in white lab jackets, some carrying clipboards and others sitting at desks working. Around the edge of the hangar were glass rooms each with its own door. There were people working in them too. Scott could see about twenty people in total.

   As the door had opened most of the people who were in there had stopped what they were doing, glanced in Scott and Bob's direction, they then carried on with their work. Scott saw a few familiar faces in the room, he saw Colin and Fiona who he'd met in the canteen before, they didn't mention they had clearance for down here. They had their lab coats on and looked extremely busy, they gave Scott a quick acknowledgement, well at least Fiona did. Colin just looked at Scott, pushed his glasses up and looked back down at his work. What a funny man, Scott thought as he followed Bob into the hangar.

In the centre of this vast arena was something that left Scott gobsmacked, he just stood and stared at it. Held up by a wooden frame was a really shiny unusual object, something that Scott had never seen before, something that he was guessing not many people had seen before.

"Erm, Bob! What is that? Is it what I think it is?" enquired Scott.

"What do you think it is?" asked Bob.

"Is that what my father was working on?"

"Yes, this is the craft that we recovered from Roswell in 1947, we had it brought here to NASA, Florida, or as we like to call it, Area 49, years ago. It was brought here to see if we could gain knowledge and further the work your late father had started. He was a fantastic scientist, your father, he helped us find the blueprints we are working on now." Bob added.

"A blueprint!" Scott queried.

"It's easier if I show you than try and explain things. Follow me." Bob said.

Walking off towards the craft Bob looked round to make sure Scott was following, he was transfixed on the object.

"Come on, we haven't got all day Scott, we'll get to that part in a minute!" exclaimed Bob.

Scott started to walk slowly towards Bob, he caught

him up and they started walking together towards the craft. Bob was telling Scott about the work his father had started as they walked, but Scott wasn't listening. Bob's mouth was working but Scott couldn't hear a thing. They stopped just in front of the craft and Bob finished his sentence,
"So that's where we got up to. Are you listening Scott?" Bob asked.
"What? Erm, yes, course I am, could you just go over that part again!" Scott frowned and tried to focus, he stretched out his arm to touch the craft. His fingers brushed the soft yet shiny material, it felt like cold hard skin.

A technician started to walk towards Bob and Scott. He was pushing a similar looking trolley that had been wheeled into the white room where Scott had spent the night. He stopped the trolley in front of Bob and opened the two doors on the front, he reached in and pulled out the two arm sleeves. Placing them on the top of the trolley before Bob, he then reached inside again and pulled out an object that Scott hadn't seen before, a weird looking object. Scott thought it looked like a brain split in half and spread out. It had some flowing lights moving around the grooves on the surface. The technician held it up and Bob turned round so he could place it on his back. It seemed to have two straps that came out and locked over Bob's shoulders holding it in place. Picking up the arm sleeves he pulled them onto his forearms, the straps tightening around his arms just like yesterday.
"Follow me," Bob said as he stood in front of Scott wearing these weird objects on top of his crisp white

shirt and tie.

"What? Where?" Asked Scott.

"In here of course, where else?"

"You've got to be kidding!" laughed Scott.

Bob placed his hands on some makeshift steps that had been assembled to gain access, this also lead onto a platform that circled the entire craft. He walked up them and disappeared into an opening on the side. Scott was a little hesitant to follow, but he did. Slowly he climbed the steps and walked into the opening. I can't take much more of this, he thought to himself.

"What do you make of all this?" Bob asked with his arms outstretched, his silhouette glowing from the flowing lights encircling his body.

"Well, I don't quite know what to make of it all. I'm just waiting to wake up, to tell you the truth!" Scott exclaimed.

"Believe me you couldn't be more awake if you tried Scott!" replied Bob.

Scott looked around inside the craft, it was mainly a vast empty room apart from a spinning ball of light in the middle and these tube like things that…

"Oh my God! Are they?" Scott pointed at some pod-like things, just noticing that there was something inside.

"Erm is that an Alien?"

"You better believe it!" exclaimed Bob.

There were four in total, circling this unusual ball of light. Scott noticed the empty one.

"And this one?"

"Well Scott, you don't need to worry about that one. It died in the crash, we don't know exactly what happened, the pod was all smashed up with this gooey substance all over the being and the floor. It has been stored, intact may I add, at Area 51."

He walked over to the pods to take a look, he gasped and placed a hand over his mouth when he saw what was inside. The large black eyes were staring straight back at him through the pod's opaque membrane.

"Are they awake?" Scott asked.

"I hope not, they haven't moved in twenty-one years. These lights on the side, we believe are monitoring the beings, keeping them alive inside the pods." Bob said as he pointed to the lights with his glowing finger tips.

"What is going to happen to them?" asked Scott.

"Well, we have devised a plan, you will find out about it in good time Scott. This is what I want you to see…" replied Bob.

Bob walked past the centre of the craft, where the sphere of light was spinning, in between the entombed dormant beings encased in their pods and some moulded seat-like structures facing the beings, over to a long, slightly curved part of the craft that projected into the room. He started to touch symbols on the screens which he had done the day before, only this time he wasn't making solid metal melt. He made a display appear before Scott's eyes, the same display that Scott's father had shown to Tom all those years earlier. Wow, Scott stood looking at this apparition that Bob had created. Bob went through all the different parts of the display, the solar system, the craft designs and everything else.

Scott took a step back and asked Bob a question, "What do you need me for?"

"We can't make it fly!" Bob replied.

Scott looked at Bob as he was pressing the symbols. "What? And what do you expect me to do? I don't know anything about space craft, I've never seen one before!" he exclaimed.

"We've had this thing for twenty one years and we can't get the damn thing off the ground!" said Bob, "It's so annoying. We must be the only country that has a captured space craft and we can't make it work. We are hoping that you might be able to shed some light on it!" he added.

Scott raised his eyebrows and laughed, "And that's what you want me for, is it?"

Bob didn't say a word, he just looked at Scott, as he brought up a display showing the two solar systems with a line between them.

"What do you make of this display Scott?" Bob asked.

Scott looked intensely at the display, he studied it for a few moments and said,

"It looks like this could be their galaxy, in relation to ours. This line between the two could be the course of their journey. Do you know anything about this wavy line underneath?" Scott asked.

"No! Not really, we have come to a bit of a stand-still now. We've gathered that that must be where they came from, but where is it, and how have they made it here? We've had some of the best scientific minds in the S.I.S work on this and nobody has been able to make sense of it," explained Bob.

"Well, just a stab in the dark, but I would say that

they, the beings as you call them, have found the ability to travel great distances at great speed. These two galaxies are hundreds, if not thousands of light years away from each other, they would need the ability to travel close to or beyond the speed of light to make contact possible." Scott said.

"This wavy line with another straight line through it could be that they have developed a way of bending space." Scott added.

"Well, that's a new one, go on, I'm intrigued!" Bob said.

"Well, look at it this way. I studied a lot of theories on space travel at college, anyway if you can create a ripple, or a portal, connected to another portal, and so on, say in the vast vacuum of space, then theoretically you could pull yourself through, making your journey time and speed far greater than anything we could ever imagine. It's never been proven, its just a theory," Scott said, "come outside and I'll show you what I mean."

They left the craft and walked back down the steps and over to the trolley.

"Hand me your pen and a piece of paper Bob." Scott said.

He drew a line and wrote the letter 'A' at the start and the letter 'B' at the end.

"Right, at the moment we have one way of getting from 'A' to 'B' a straight line, which is a fixed distance, yeah? We can go round things, over things or through things as long as we follow the line. Well, if I draw a line like this…" Scott started to draw the same length line but in a wave.

"Get it?"

"Nope, you lost me!" Bob said, confused.

Scott tried to think of another way to explain his theory.

"Right, look at it this way then, I'll fold this paper, then again and again and again."

Scott did this until he had folded the paper right up, making it look like it was concertinaed, he wrote A and B again at the top and bottom of the folded paper. He then unfolded the paper showing Bob the distance between one and the other.

"Now, if I fold the paper together again making it wavy, I reduce the distance between the two points, see?" Scott said, "Then if I do this..." Scott then took the pen and pushed it through the middle of the paper creating a hole, "The distance is next to nothing!"

"Ok, I get it." Bob said as he placed his hand on his chin, pondering.

"We have had some of the best minds working on this and not one of them could come up with what you have just said! This is why we need you!" Bob exclaimed, "We need you to carry on where your father left off. Would you do that?"

"What about my life?" Scott said.

"The way I see it Scott, you have two options here. One: You say you'll do it, or two: We'll tell you you'll do it! I don't want to sound too harsh, but they are your options, the way I see it!" Bob said.

"Well, when you put it that way. I guess I'll do it, I don't seem to have any other option, do I?" Scott replied.

"Good choice Scott, it's better this way." Bob replied. "You will be given everything you require, all you need to do is ask."

"I have one request!" Scott said.

"That was quick. What's that then Scott?" questioned Bob.

"I want Kimberly as my assistant helping me, or I don't do anything!" Scott stated.

"I was afraid you were going to say that Scott! I'll see what I can do." Bob said.

"No, don't see what you can do, just do!" Scott said with a serious face. "And I need everything that has been documented about the craft, the recovery at Roswell, the beings, absolutely everything."

"It's all been taken care of, everything you need is in that room over there." Bob pointed to a glass door with the word, 'Roswell' written on it.

"What about my apartment and all my belongings, my car?" Scott questioned.

"All taken care of as well." Bob said calmly as he pointed to another room, "You'll find all your belongings in there."

"What!" Scott said as he rushed over and opened the door. There to Scott's surprise was all his life in a room. Still boxed up and stamped with, 'Bob's Removals' on the side. Scott shook his head in disbelief. His cherished Corvette Stingray was in there too and all his things from his office. How the hell did they do this, how did they get my car down here? I'm not cut out for all this espionage. He thought to himself.

"I know this must be a shock to you but you have a chance here to make history. If you can help us with what we are planning then we could all make history and blow every evolutionary theory out of

the water." Bob said as he walked towards Scott.
Scott thought for a moment. "Ok, when do we
start?"

"How does 'Right Now' sound?" replied Bob, "If
you open that door, it will take you to your room."

   Scott opened the door and saw a room very
similar to the one he spent last night in. The only
difference was this room had some of his clothes
hung up in what looked like a wardrobe. The doors
had been left open so he could see where it was in
the bright white light of the room. The rest was the
same as the other room.

"Everything is voice activated, so all you have to do
is ask." Bob said.

"Ok, but I do have one question for you. What were
all the trucks doing that were loaded with soil?
Where is it all coming from? I noticed them when I
was sitting at my desk. If I've noticed it then so has
everyone else." Scott explained.

"Well, all in good time Scott, all in good time." Bob
replied.

   Scott closed the door shaking his head, what have
I gotten myself into here? If only I hadn't tried that
key in the elevator.

   As Scott walked over and opened the door with,
'Roswell' written on the front he saw a mountain of
files and boxes. Oh well, no time like the present,
he thought as he picked up the first box with,
'Roswell Incident' written on the front. He started
to read.

   A few hours passed as he looked through file after
file, transfixed on the information about the Roswell
incident, then a knock on the door startled him.

"Come in." Scott shouted.

The door opened and in walked Kimberly.

"I didn't think I'd see you again!" Kimberly said as she closed the door behind her.

"You haven't got anymore zappy things have you?" Scott asked as he held his hands up, surrendering.

"No, relax, I'm not going to do anything." Kimberly said walking towards Scott.

She didn't stop as she got closer, she just grabbed his hands above his head and kissed him with a passionate 'I'm sorry' kiss.

"Hey, cool it! I haven't even forgiven you yet!" Scott said as he broke free but then went in for more of the same.

"So, you need me to help you do you Scott?" Kimberly asked.

"I need somebody to help me go through all this info, I can't do it all by myself and try to work out the craft." Scott replied.

"Let's get started then!" She smiled.

They spent hours that day just reading all they could from the boxes and the files, trying to piece together the incidents from the last twenty one years. As the day drew to an end Kimberly told Scott again how sorry she was for what she had done. Scott didn't know if he could trust her again, but he didn't know anybody else down there. For now she was his only way out!

As everyone, including Kimberly, left for the night, Scott found himself alone in the hangar, he walked around the vast place trying doors. They were all locked. The only places he had access to were the hangar, his rooms and the Roswell room.

As he stood looking at the craft there was a loud clank and part of the hangar fell into darkness, then another area fell into darkness and another. The lights were slowly shutting off, until all that was left was a light over the top of the craft, slightly illuminating it from above. Scott was near his door standing at a distance, he admired the outlined beauty of the craft that had been forged on another planet, a work of art. Whoever they were and wherever they came from, they were far more advanced than we were, Scott thought. There was one last clank and the hangar was in complete darkness, all that Scott could see was the faint eerie glow coming from the top and inside of the craft.

Scott went back into his room, as he walked in he said, "Bed. Shower."
Slowly just like the night before a bed started to fall from the wall and the shower area rose from the floor. He showered and got ready for bed. Was this it? Was this how things were going to be from now on? He had always been a bit of a loner, very comfortable with his own company, he'd always known he had a purpose in life. Was this it? He lay in his new bed drifting slowly off to sleep.

Chapter 25

The new day started with another knock at his door, Scott rubbed his eyes and sat up in bed wondering if he had dreamt the noise. No, there it was again. Knock, knock, knock. He looked around to make sure this wasn't one big nightmare again, then said, "Lights on." As he slid out of bed and walked to the door, the lights grew stronger. He had no clue as to what time it was, it had been pitch black in his room. Unlike the other room he had been kept in, this one had a door handle. He turned the handle and pulled the door towards himself.

"Good morning Sir!" Said a happy employee whilst walking past him with a tray, "Where would you like it?" he said.

"Like what?" Scott replied mid yawn.

"Your breakfast Sir, coffee and pancakes Sir. Where would you like it?" The question came again.

"Ermmmm, anywhere I suppose, and stop calling me Sir. My name is Scott." He said.

"Ok Sir, I mean Scott. Table." The employee said as he stood with the tray full of food and coffee, "Scott you have to say; table, the voice command is only programmed for your voice Sir."

"Table." Scott said as he gave the employee a funny look.

Just then a small table formed from the floor right in front of the man, he placed the tray down and turned round; "Enjoy!" He said as he closed the door to the room.

"Wait! What time…" Scott shouted but it was too late, the door had closed and the employee, he hadn't heard. Oh well, Scott thought, it must be time to get up. Scott grabbed a gooey maple syrup soaked pancake and took a bite. These are great, I could get used to this, he thought as he slurped the hot coffee whilst trying to say, "Bathroom." He felt really weird having to say the parts of the room he wanted to use. The bathroom rose from the floor and he entered it to get ready for the day. This room was slightly different as the toilet and the shower were all in one room. He walked through the bright light as he knew what it contained this time, there were his clothes nicely pressed, folded and waiting for him. Beside them, hanging up was a white lab coat, he could see there was a name tag with a photo of him on the pocket. It was the same photo they had used for his NASA ID badge, he never liked that photo, he thought it made him look like a geeky serial killer. He giggled to himself whilst having a shower in readiness to don his new lab coat and see what the day ahead would bring.

Finishing the last of his luke warm coffee and really soggy pancakes, he opened the door. The hangar was as busy as yesterday, he hadn't heard a thing from his room. Scott asked the first person he came to what time it was, they completely ignored him and carried on with their job. He could see Bob standing at a desk around the edge of the hangar, not far from where Scott was standing. He walked over to him and tapped him on the shoulder.

"Morning Scott, or should I say afternoon!" Bob

said.

"What! What time is it?" Scott asked, "I can't get a friggin answer out of anyone round here." He added.

"Only toying with you boy, it's 0 six hundred hours Scott. That's six am to you newbies!" Bob said sarcastically.

"I know what 0 six hundred hours is Bob, thanks." He said whilst yawning again.

"Coffee!" shouted Bob.

"No, I'm ok thanks, I've just had one." Scott replied, "and you don't have to shout I'm only here!"

"Not for you boy, for me, me! I need coffee down here, it keeps me going." Bob said as he patted at his chest.

Bob had said all this without raising his head from the table to look up. Scott peered over Bob's shoulder to see what he was looking at. He had the folded up piece of paper that Scott had demonstrated with yesterday, he was opening it up and shutting it. It looked like he was playing the accordion.

"What are you doing Bob?" asked Scott?

"Thinking Scott! Thinking!" Came the reply.

"Don't you have some work to do Scott? There is somebody waiting for you in the Roswell room. Then I would like to see you in the briefing room at ten hundred hours. That's…" Bob was cut short.

"I know ten am." sighed Scott.

"A fast learner, that's what we need around here!" Bob said as he patted Scott on his shoulder and walked off.

"But how am I suppose to know what time it is? I don't seem to be able to find my watch!" Scott said as Bob walked off.

"Use the sun!" Bob laughed as he kept walking.

Use the sun, very funny, Scott said to himself as he looked up imagining he would see the sun rising on the horizon. I wonder if I'll ever see the sun rising on the horizon again? Scott headed over to the room with 'Roswell' written on the door. You couldn't see into the rooms that were around the edge of the hangar, they all had a frosted glass front. He opened the door looking forward to seeing Kimberly again. There she was sitting at the same part of the desk as last night, intently reading from a pile of files in front of her. She hadn't heard Scott open the door, he crept up behind her and put his hands over her eyes.

"Morning." He whispered in her ear.

Scott felt her cheek move up his hand, he could tell she was smiling. Her eyelashes were fluttering on the inside of his fingers as she tried to contain her excitement.

"Good morning Scott." She replied in a low sexy voice. Scott moved his hands and Kimberly spun round to face him on the office chair where she was sitting. Scott leaned forwards and kissed her on the cheek, then spun her chair back round to face the table.

"Some of this stuff is fascinating Scott. We don't know the half of what's going on in the world, they keep everything locked away, hidden from everyone." Kimberly said.

"I imagine it's for the good of our world, don't

you?" asked Scott, "There are things here that would send the world into chaos."

"You're right Scott. Thank you for asking me to help you by the way." Kimberly said with a big smile on her face, "I've been wondering what happens behind those other doors for years now."

"I have a meeting with Bob at ten am, how am I suppose to find out what time it's is down here? I haven't seen anybody with a watch on." Scott said.

"That's weird, I hadn't noticed," replied Kimberly, "I'll go and find out for you and I'll grab us some coffee on the way."

With that Kimberly went to ask someone. Scott grabbed a file from the pile he had been going through the day before and started to flick through the pages. The front cover had; 'Initial findings' written on it. He opened the file and saw the first page. This report had been written by his father more than twenty years ago. A tear filled the corner of his eye, he wiped it away and began to read. This was the report from when his father and Tom had experimented with the things that Bob had put on yesterday. It must have been so fascinating to have been the ones to first work on this find, Scott thought. He studied the files so intently, making sure he didn't miss anything his father had written down.

His father and Tom had worked on the project for years, but never managed to find out how the craft actually worked. I will continue my father's work and find out what it will take to get this craft flying again, Scott said to himself.

Kimberly walked back into the room saying, "It's

seven thirty am now. If you need to find out the time there is one clock at the end of the hangar, it's locked inside a glass cabinet. Somehow the craft stops watches and clocks from working properly in the room. The clock is bright yellow and looks like the sun, you can't miss it!" Kimberly exclaimed as she placed a cup of coffee in front of Scott.

Scott laughed, use the sun! That's what he meant by that.

"What are you laughing at Scott?" Kimberly asked.

"Nothing, don't worry about it." Scott said as his laughter faded away, "We have a mountain of files to read still, so we best crack on." He added.

Scott and Kimberly were fascinated with what they were reading.

"The government sure does like cover a lot of things up that they find!" Scott said.

"You're right there, and this is only one part of it! Imagine what else is being covered up as we speak Scott."

As the time ticked on, Scott and Kimberly had read file after file of scientific data. Scott had been making his own notes from the findings all those years ago. He'd had a slight glimpse as to how clever his father really was, his knowledge and understanding of this craft and the beings would far exceed Scott's in all directions. But hopefully Scott could put his field of work to good use now. He was more technically trained and his skills in computers were far advanced than anybody's who had worked on the craft in the past. They continued reading the files, gaining knowledge from what other people had found out. Coming across a file filled with photos Scott opened it and gasped, putting his hand over his mouth. These were the photos of the being, as they had found it and as they had revealed it all these years ago. Step by step evidence of what had actually happened, right up to the being's preserved state as of now.

Scott needed to take a short breather and went for a walk into the hangar to make sense of all the files. He walked towards the craft, thinking, day dreaming about his father working on it. As Scott got closer to the craft he stopped and froze, staring, imagining everyone in the past walking around it, trying to get some understanding, his father looking into the craft and waving for someone to come and have a look. Then the old movie he'd been playing in his mind faded away, back to reality. He stood there for a while until in the distance his daydreaming trance was disturbed by somebody calling his name.

"Scott! Scott! Are you ok Scott?" Kimberly came into his view, he could make out the words coming from her mouth before he could hear them, as they became clearer he said, "What! Erm, yes."

"You were miles away then Scott, I've been calling you for ages. It's 10 am." She said.

"What!" Scott said as he hastily walked off to Bob's office leaving Kimberly standing there in front of the craft.

．．．．．．．．．

"Close the door Scott!" came the voice from behind a high backed swivel chair that looked like it was on

fire, as a puff of thick grey cigar smoke filled the air.
"Well, have you got to grips with it?" Bob asked.
"Early days yet Sir, but I'm sure in time we can..."
Scott was stopped short.
"Time is what we don't have Scott, we need
headway on this project now. We have eleven
months to..." Bob stopped himself from saying
anything else.
There was a long pause before Scott spoke, "Eleven
months before...what Sir?"
"You'll find out Scott, you don't need to know that
right now."
"Sir, if you want me to make headway I'm going to
have to be in on everything. What's happening in
eleven months?" demanded Scott.
"I can't tell you yet Scott, but when the time comes
you'll be the first to know, believe me, you'll be the
first to know. How's your co-worker?" Bob
changed the subject.
"She's fine Sir, I have a question. I am going to be
allowed to leave here, aren't I?"
Bob just looked at Scott and stubbed his big fat cigar
out in the overflowing ash tray on his desk.
Breaking his silence by saying, "Do you think you
can make it fly? I think you had better keep
working, we have a long road ahead."
   With that Scott turned and left the office, closing
the door behind him, he thought to himself, I hope I
see the real sun once more. With his head low he
walked back across to where Kimberly was
standing, on top of the steps looking into the craft
through the open doorway. The sphere of light
spinning in the centre of the craft dappled her face

with a rainbow of colours. I hope this is all worth it? He thought to himself.

As Scott walked up the steps behind Kimberly he gave her a fright, she jumped and nearly lost her balance. Scott put his arm on her back to stop her from falling.

"What's wrong Scott?" She asked.

"Nothing, I'm in the dark again."

"What do you mean?"

"Nothing!" He added, "Don't worry."

The coloured lights were still flowing to all the different areas of the craft through the vein-like tubes under the floor and in the walls. The beings that were left in their pods laying there, were eerily gazing upwards, into the craft, the light bouncing off their grey suits through the clear jellylike substance they were surrounded by.

"Will we ever fathom it, or them, out?" He asked as they both turned and walked down the steps. Scott asked for the back section and other objects to be brought to the room where they were reading the files.

A short time later there was a knock on the door, and the technician wheeled the trolley in containing the parts. Scott had read in one of the files about how strong the magnetic pull was when these parts where on the being after they had discovered the craft. They didn't seem to have the same effect with just the back section and the arm pieces on. Were they losing their power? Or did they all have to be worn to create the magnetic field, if it even was a magnetic field. There were so many unanswered questions it was baffling.

Scott and Kimberly studied the objects intensely, reading about where the head and throat pieces came from and how they had just flowed out of the being, then re-formed on the table, was just amazing and somewhat unbelievable. Why did his father have this ring section on his keys? If only he didn't, then I wouldn't be in this mess now. He thought to himself.

Scott gazed out of the open doorway into the hangar from where they had been reading the files. He could see the team of white lab coats continuing with their tasks, still trying, years later to work everything out. They had built scale models of all the craft designs, they had photos from every angle, inside and out, taped up on boards around the hangar, it looked like a crime scene. But they had not been successful in their quest yet. Maybe this was my calling in life, he thought.

Chapter 26

Karl was starting to worry about Scott now, it had been days since he had seen him. Where could he be? This wasn't like Scott at all, thought Karl. Even though Karl had only known Scott a short while they had formed a good friendship. Karl had tried knocking on Scott's door each day he had passed, but there was no answer, he hadn't even seen Kimberly when he went to check out Mickey's bar. Who were the men in the car following Scott? He wondered. Karl had so many questions floating around in his head with nobody to answer them.

The two men were still assigned to watch Karl. They were a bit more discrete this time though, Karl had no idea they were following him. They needed to know Karl wasn't stirring up trouble, trying to find Scott. They reported in, telling the S.I.S that Karl had been asking around about Scott. To try and throw Karl off the scent, Kimberly had told Scott to write a letter to his friend. She said that he would be getting worried about him. She was right. She told him they would send the letter upstate and then get them to post it to him, explaining that you had to leave because you had been moved urgently to a new area, she explained. Scott thought that this was all getting too weird for his liking, but he set about writing the letter anyway. He must have been missing for well over a week now, Karl would be wondering what had happened especially with the black Sedan following him.

Dear Karl,

Sorry I didn't get a chance to say goodbye my friend, everything happened very quickly. There was a problem at one of NASA's facilities and I was re-posted to a new area. It's nowhere near the coast so can you keep my long board safe, use it when you like. All my mail has been re-directed here and the apartment cleared. I hope you get a great new neighbour.

Take care my friend; and hopefully our paths will cross once again soon.

Your friend,

Scott.

Kimberly read the letter and said, "Great he should get that in a few days time." As she placed it into an envelope and took it out to the security guard beyond the large hangar door.

"This all seems to me like it's happened before." said Scott.

As Kimberly came back from handing over the letter she had bumped into Bob in the hangar, he'd been busy explaining to someone where he wanted photos taking of the craft.

"Kimberly!" Bob called her over, "Where's Scott?"

"Erm, in the Roswell room. Why?" she replied with a puzzled look on her face.

"Get him out here, I've had a great idea."

"Ok!" said Kimberly as she headed back towards the room.

Kimberly opened the door to be bombarded by a barrage of questions from Scott, "Why was the craft moved here? And why was the alien being kept at Area 51?"

"I'm not sure Scott, Bob wants u…" She was cut short, as Scott fired another question her way, "How could a weather balloon bring down something as technical as that craft?"

"Scott, Scott, stop!"

"Sorry, I'm rambling on, aren't I? What is it?"

"Bob wants us out there, now!"

With that Scott stopped asking questions and followed her out into the hangar. They walked over to where Bob was standing. He was gazing into the reflection of himself on the craft, it made him look funny. With it's shiny chrome mirrored finish it reflected a distorted image of anything around it.

Bob looked like a short fat dwarf. Scott stood beside Bob and couldn't hold in a slight giggle as he looked at the three of them standing side by side on the surface of the craft. Just as he'd managed to calm down, Kimberly joined in with a slight chuckle to herself.

"Ok! Ok! So it's not my best picture." Bob said with a grin on his face, "This is what I've brought you here for, a photo, to mark a new beginning, a new hope of finding out anything about this craft. Where's he gone?" Bob said as he looked for the photographer. "Hey we're here, we're ready man we haven't got all day you know!"

The photographer hurried over to where the three of them were standing. He got himself in position and shouted, "Smile."

Just as he did the flash from the top of the camera blinded all three at the same time, causing a moment of blindness making them all rub their eyes. The man took one more and said, "Thanks," as he walked over to the dark-room to process the film.

"Everything is done in-house here at Area 49, there is no outside involvement at all." Stressed Bob. "That keeps everything as secure as possible. Well that's it folks, back to work, we need some answers, and quick." He added, whilst he turned to look at his fairground image once more.

Scott and Kimberly walked back over to the Roswell room to continue with the project they'd been allocated. They closed the door to try and make head-way with the mammoth task that lay before them.

Chapter 27

Scott awoke suddenly, sitting bolt upright in the fold down bed, pearls of sweat running down his chest. It was as if someone or something had planted an idea in his head whilst he was sleeping, so vivid, so real. He quickly got up, something was telling him, feeding him with the urge to go to the room were the body sections were kept. This area was his at night, he was all alone. The only light in the hangar was that from the faint multi-coloured glow emitting from the open doorway to the craft and in the distance through the porthole in the large steel door. The small bright red dots on the cameras set up around the hangar didn't give off any light at all. He could see these moving from side to side, as the cameras panned around the hangar. Watching them for a while he timed his run to the room when they weren't looking. Half way there he tripped on something and clattered into a desk, knocking the swivel chair, making it spin. He stayed still for a minute. He could see the light from the porthole window had been disturbed, a shadow from the security guard beyond the door passing the glass. A distorted beam from a torch was trying to shine through the porthole, filtered slightly from the frosting in the glass. The security guard could go through the blast doors but he didn't have clearance to come into the main hangar. His view was restricted, he was unable to see Scott.

Something must have alerted the guard. The chair Scott had banged into, just stopped spinning as one of the security cameras focused in on that area once more. Sitting with his back against the desk he waited with baited breath for the camera to pass. Finally, he could make his way to the room, his eyes adjusting more and more to the darkness with each second. He tried the door handle, it was open, he could just make out the trolley with the pieces in. Slowly he wheeled it to the door, waiting for his moment to get back across the hangar to his room. Still dressed only in his shorts he set off, stopping halfway to wait for a camera to pass by, crouching behind the trolley until it passed. He'd made it. Wiping the sweat from his brow he closed the door to his room, poured himself a glass of water from a tray next to the door and sat down on the end of his bed taking a slow drink, staring intensely at the trolley in front of him.

Scott finally walked over to it. As he crouched down he could see a faint glow coming from within, illuminating the gaps around the cabinets doors. Clenching his fists then rubbing his face, he wondered if the idea, the vivid dream that had awoken him in the middle of the night, would work or not. Doubting himself he walked back empty handed and sat down again on the edge of the bed, thinking. It's gotta be worth a try, he said to himself. The glow from the lights around the base of the bed was just enough for him to see everything, casting a glistening reflection over his sweat covered torso. Scott paced the floor. Forwards and backwards, his gaze never leaving the motionless cabinet sitting in the middle of his room. "I have to try!" he said to himself as he opened the doors to Pandora's box.

Slowly, one by one, he placed the pieces on the top of the trolley. First, the back section which had faint lights flowing around the deep grooves. Then, each arm sleeve, followed by the belt and finally the parts from inside the being. Standing in front of them he looked for a moment. Which one first? How am I going to get that section onto my back?

Looking slightly bewildered he placed this odd looking piece onto the bed and slowly laid back onto it. It moulded to his back, straps seemed to form around his shoulders and it blended into his body. Just like that then, he thought. He picked up the arm sleeves and slipped them over each wrist, the chrome coloured glove sections tightened around his hands, he could still move as normal, it didn't feel cold or hard. Now, what did the file say about the belt? The being was naked when the belt was removed. I hope nobody walks in now, he thought as he slipped his shorts down and kicked them to the side. Picking up the belt he passed it around his back and clicked it together at the front, the finger imprints glowed as the belt tightened to fit his waist. There was no record of any experiments to see what the belt could do. The only pieces left now, were the sections that came out of the being's body.

"This could go terribly wrong," Scott thought out loud, "What do I do here?"

From what Scott had read in the report these parts just flowed out and laid beside the being.

"How can I get them in? Should I even be doing this?"

The symbol above each screen was glowing, the trace of a faint blue light was moving round in a circle chasing it's faded tail. Scott moved his hand to each symbol, touching them both. The screens lit up on each arm, the bright blue light formed a line across the screen and moved each way to reveal a body. Was the screen showing his body or did it think he was the being? There were lots of symbols around the body with lines pointing to the various areas and sections on the image. Scott pressed the symbol that was next to the belt and waited. Nothing happened.

He noticed that two of the imprints on the side of the belt were glowing, more like a pulsating light. Then two of his finger tips started to glow. Placing the two fingers from each hand in the imprints, the belt seemed to melt and formed around Scott's groin, making him look like he had a pair of shiny chrome pants on. Nice! He thought whilst breaking into a worrying smile. The pants seemed flexible, just like cloth, when Scott touched them. Raising his eyebrows he looked at the screen once more.

As Scott touched the screen, he found when he moved his finger around, the image of the body moved too, he could look at it from all angles, turning it with his finger. He stopped when the body showed the back section. Placing his finger on the image, Scott was surprised at what happened next. Vein like tubes moved around his body, down the sides of his body and up the sides of his neck, they seemed to mould into him, having a life of their own. They had the same faint light in them, the same multi-coloured lights that flowed around the craft. He touched the chest area on the screen and just like before with the belt, the chrome coloured material seemed to ooze across his body, forming over the muscle areas, coating him, armouring him, protecting him. Scott did this again with the other areas, until he only had a few visible bits of skin left, the coloured amour had protected every muscle and organ in his body, but he could still move freely. The material was alive, it knew exactly where to form, a living, organic armoured skin that protects its host.

He slowly moved over to the large mirror in his room, as he came into view the image that stood before him wasn't like anything Scott had ever seen before. Like a knight in shining armour. What is this? Why has nobody tried this since they found the craft? He thought.

....

The smoke covered the back of the mirror as Bob exhaled the last draw before stubbing yet another cigar out beside him.
"I knew it wouldn't be long before you tried something like this, I can read you like a book," Bob said to himself as he watched Scott transform through the two way mirror. "All that you need to do now Scott is make those pieces melt into your body."
Bob had been notified when Scott thought he'd dodged all the cameras in the hangar. He hadn't.

Scott looked down at his hands covered in this material, his finger tips pulsating with lights. He tried to turn round and looked at his back in the mirror, it was hard to see, but it looked like he had a split brain moulded onto his shoulder-blades. The eerie grooved lights illuminating it as he looked. Scott walked back over to the trolley shaking his head in disbelief, picking up the ring that he'd carried around for years not knowing what it was. He looked at it closely in the palm of his hand, then he clenched his fist around it before closing his eyes and placing it in his mouth.

"Well done," Bob said to himself as he watched Scott.

Scott brought his hand over to the screen, his finger hesitated over the symbol from the throat area.

"Go on, press it!" said Bob in the other room. Scott touched the symbol, his head arched backwards, as he felt the hard ring shape on his tongue melt. It seemed to slip down his throat, he tried to straighten his neck but it wouldn't move. His eyes straining, his veins popping to the surface of his skin, unable to breath, his hands clawed at his own throat.

Bob leaned forward in his chair, holding his breath, a concerned look drowned his face. All of a sudden Scott learned forward again and took a deep breath in, like he'd been under water for a long time. He couldn't feel the part anymore. Then, he started to cough. Scratching at his neck with his gloved hands, he tried to feel the object but he couldn't. He could swallow fine but he was still coughing. Bob sat back in his chair once more and sighed a huge sigh of relief, as Scott started to breath once more.

Scott thought it was too late to turn back now, so he picked up the parts he had read about that came from the ears of the being. How can I do this? He thought once more. He placed them back onto the top of the trolley.

"You can do this Scott," Bob said with his cigar tinged breath.

Scott remembered what Bob had done when he showed him the part on his keys, he touched the symbol on the screen and the parts melted on the top. He brought his hands down towards the two molten puddles on the trolley, as his finger tips got closer, the two molten sections moved towards his fingers. He moved them away, they stopped moving once more. He did it again but this time he let his finger tips touch them. The puddles seemed to be sucked into the glove like parts of his new hands. He then saw the molten liquid flow up the light carrying veins which had been created from the back section, it moved up his arms, over his shoulders and up each side of his neck. The new veins stopped just below his ears, this is where the liquid flows out of and disappears into each ear. His head shook violently from side to side, then Scott fell to his knees. Crouching like a dog, his head shaking, still coughing, he tried to shout but nothing came out, not a sound. He tried again and again, but nothing. Scott fell to the floor, his head finally calming down and he was motionless curled up in a ball, covered in this shiny material, staring into thin air. Bob stood up, his hand resting on the reverse of the thick glass. He gazed at Scott, motionless and tentatively waited for something to happen.

It was nearly twenty minutes before Scott moved again, he rolled back onto his hands and knees, then tried to stand up. He felt stiff, like all his muscles were in cramp.

"What have I done? Why?" He swayed a bit and steadied himself, looking down at the screens on his arms. He wanted the sections out! He had changed his mind, a moment of madness, what was he thinking? The symbols for the parts had disappeared, he fumbled with the screen trying to find them again, they weren't there. Where were they? Where had they gone? Now what was he going to do now?

Whilst Scott was trying to see where the symbols had gone, he had touched one of the parts of the body and before he knew it more of the light flowing veins had formed around the back of his head, then criss-crossed over the top of his scalp. This was closely followed by the same chrome coloured material, encasing over the top of the veins, shaping his new head, slightly bulbous to the top. It didn't stop there, this was soon followed by something flowing around in front of his mouth and over his nose. He felt a pipe go down into his throat and into each nostril, making him gag as it happened. The veins criss-crossing, covering his nose and mouth totally, finally being covered with the amour. His face transformed into a thing not of this world. The areas around his eyes were left uncovered. At least he could still see.

Scott tried to breath again. He could, but only just, it felt like he was being suffocated. Then he felt a cool flow of air hit the back of his throat, he also felt it up his nose. Was this helping him to breath? With each breath he took he could feel this cool air, what was it? It had a funny taste to it, he thought. He didn't have any control over what was happening, all he could feel was a slight bit of pressure on his back as he breathed in and out. "Is this back section helping me breath? It must be!" Scott realised, "All I've been doing is pushing the symbols on the screen, I haven't got a clue what would happen."

Bob was still standing there at the back of the mirror, watching Scott do what nobody had been willing to or been able to do, until they had this part Scott had unknowingly kept safe for years.

Scott looked down at his body, he then looked into the mirror again. I hope I can get out of this mess, he thought. Looking down he noticed that all the finger imprints on his sides were glowing now, so were all the finger tips of each hand. He lowered his finger to the imprints and made the connection. As he neared the imprints he saw little arcs of light go from the ends of each finger tips, like little streaks of lightning. The fingers were pulled into position on his side, he shook, his arms straightened and his body glowed from the coloured veins of light. Just as he had read in the file about the skin disintegrating, he saw a strong orange glow spread over the back pack. As he tried to look in the mirror he could see it was creeping around his sides radiating from this pack. He looked back at his reflection and all of a sudden his vision disappeared, like he had been instantly blinded.

Bob couldn't believe his eyes, he was witnessing Scott turn into the being from years ago.

Slowly, Scott started to make out the edge of something, things were outlined in a blue light, he could see the edge of the mirror, he turned and he could see the bed and the trolley. All edged in this bright blue light, his vision had started to return. Turning back to the mirror, he realised that his eyes were covered with black oval lenses, they covered the whole area of his eye sockets up to his eye brows and down to his cheek bones. He gasped and raised a hand to them, feeling around them, he saw the bright orange edge of light moving over the top of his head, leaving a grey smooth material in its wake. It seamlessly moulded around the lenses totally encasing his body. Looking down he watched the last of it cover his feet, it had stopped.

There, standing right in front of Bob was Scott, covered in the protective suit the being had arrived in twenty years ago. A stereo typical alien, just like those sightings from people who were deemed as mad.

Scott didn't know what to think, as he looked at his arms he could still see the screens, like they weren't even covered with anything. That's weird he thought. He could see that there were symbols and what looked like writing on the inside of the lenses, information being put onto it somehow. Like a computer screen, with lots of blue symbols and writing. As he was looking at the symbols he could still see himself in the mirror, but that's not all he could see. Scott saw a glowing red mark on the mirror, like a heat print, it was a hand print! Scott tilted his head to one side as if he was trying to look through the mirror. Bob stepped back taking his hand from the back of the glass, he had the feeling Scott was looking straight at him. The hand print slowly disappeared from the glass leaving Scott baffled, he knocked on the mirror and placed his ear to the glass to see if he could hear anything. It was silent.

Unknown to Scott, and Bob who was watching from behind the mirror, when Scott was fully equipped with the being's pieces, the craft had started to do funny things in the hangar. The security camera had picked up that the faint glow from the doorway to the craft had gone very intense. A beam of light came from the craft's doorway and lit up the hangar, a blast of light squeezed out through the porthole making the security guard turn round and look through the frosted glass, with the light blinding him. Then suddenly all the security cameras started playing up. They showed some interference on the TV screen then a bright light. Then nothing!

The guard looked through the glass of the towering steel doors, he couldn't see much past the bright light, shielding his eyes, he tried again to look through the frosted porthole into the hangar. "I need to get out of this stuff before someone sees me," Scott said. He touched a few of the symbols again and the grey suit started to disintegrate, just as quickly as it had appeared. He went back through all the symbols in reverse order. Scott managed to have everything off before anybody saw him, the only thing he couldn't do was remove the parts that had melted into his body. Where were those symbols now? What were they doing in his body? How could he get them out, now the symbols had gone?

As the section fell to the floor from Scott's back, the light coming from the craft dimmed once more, back to its faint flowing glow. The guard was still trying to look through the frosted glass when this happened, he turned away from the blinding light, rubbing his eyes, he couldn't see, it was no use. Most of the things made from metal in the room were hovering above the ground. As the light stopped, they all fell back down to the floor leaving everything scattered everywhere, like an earthquake had hit. Scott heard the noise from his room and wondered if the team had arrived to start work again. But no, it was still too early. The security guard picked up his phone to contact someone, but it was dead, he pressed the top of the phone to try and make a connection, nothing! He then rattled the button in frustration trying to make the phone work, still nothing, it was no use the phone was dead.

Quickly removing the parts off his body Scott placed them back in the trolley and closed the doors. He quickly grabbed his shorts and pulled them back on. Turning back to face the mirror after being startled by the noise in the hangar, he wondered what it was, he also wondered what he'd seen on the mirror. Scott tried to work out what he had seen on the glass, tried to see it again, but there was nothing there this time. He walked back over to it and stood, staring, waiting for a noise or a sign to prove he wasn't going mad. Maybe I am going mad, he thought to himself as he turned away from the mirror to finish getting dressed.

Scott managed to get the trolley back to the store room before anybody had arrived that morning, dodging the cameras just like before. He hadn't really noticed that the place was a mess because it was so dark. The only thing he was worried about was the fact that three things were missing, the mouth and ear sections. Scott wondered how long it would be before someone discovered they were missing.

Chapter 28

When everyone arrived for work the next morning, Scott came out from his room. He was a bit sheepish, and a bit nervous to say the least. He wondered if he should tell someone what he had done. Without Scott knowing, Bob already knew exactly what he had done.

"What's happened out here?" asked Scott as he entered the hangar, "It looks like a tornado hit the place." He added as he tried to hide the fact he knew exactly what had happened.

Most of the mess had been cleared up before Scott had walked in, but he started to help by picking up an office chair which had been thrown twenty feet away from its desk. As he did so, he noticed Kimberly walk into the hangar and head straight for the Roswell room. He hastily put the chair back on its wheels and kicked it towards the desk, before following her into the room. Kimberly looked upset,

"Hey, what's up?" asked Scott, "Is everything ok?"

"Yeah I've just got a lot on my mind at the moment. Let's just crack-on with this pile of files."

They continued to read up on the pages and pages of reports from years ago, trying to make a breakthrough.

"I don't know what we are going to find out, when it's taken years for the others to get nowhere." Kimberly said.

"You're right there!" Scott replied.

Scott walked out of the room to try clear his head, which was full of facts and figures, after reading so much, he walked towards the craft. All of a sudden his head started to pound, he raised his hands to the sides of his head and winced in agony. Scott fell to his knees. He was in reach of a desk and managed to grab a corner. The lab technician shouted for some help. Kimberly heard this and rushed out of the room to see what was going on, she saw Scott on his knees holding the front of his head.

"Scott!" Kimberly shouted.

She ran over to where he was slumped, "What's happened?" She shouted at the technician.

"I don't know, he just grabbed his head and fell to his knees." He replied.

"I'm ok, stop fussing everyone." Scott said as he tried to clamber to his feet again.

"Don't move, just wait." Kimberly said as she placed her arm under Scott's elbow to steady him.

"Look, I'm ok, please just stop fussing, I'll be fine." He replied.

"What happened?" she asked.

"I'm not sure, I was walking towards the craft and I suddenly got these pains, right here." Scott pointed to just behind each ear.

"I'm ok now, it's gone, I feel fine, like nothing had happened," he added. Not really, it still hurt like hell, but he worried that if he said anything they would have him in the infirmary in a flash.

"Just sit down a minute!" came Bob's deep voice. Scott hadn't noticed that Bob was standing right behind him. He jumped round in surprise, he moves with such stealth for a big man, he thought.

"Did I startle you Scott?" Bob asked.

"Just a bit Sir!" Scott replied.

"Ok everyone, back to work! Nothing to see here. What happened Scott?"

"Not sure sir, I'm ok tho…" His sentence was cut short again, I hate him doing that, thought Scott.

"My office! Now!"

Scott stood up and followed Bob to his office, closing the door once he had got through.

"What happened in the hangar last night?" Bob asked.

"What, what do you mean? I was in my room all night sleeping. I don't know what happened Sir."

"Why did it look like a bomb had gone off in here this morning?"

"Sir, I don't know Sir."

Bob rubbed his eyes and sat down in his big chair, he spun round and said, "That'll be all then Scott!" as he lit up one of his big cigars and blew a ring into the air above his head.

Scott was so confused, did he know what had happened? He went very pale and walked back over to Kimberly, taking some deep breaths as he did.

"What did he say?" asked Kimberly.

"He wanted to know what had happened in here last night," replied Scott.

"Well? What did happen?"

"Don't you start!" Scott said as he walked off.

The pains in his head weren't so bad when he was away from the craft, so he tried to walk towards it again. Getting to about the same place, he could feel the pain starting again. Somehow he felt drawn towards it, like something was pulling him. Some kind of invisible force, beckoning him. Scott stood still to see if the pain would ease, he closed his eyes. "What did you say Kimberly?" Scott asked as he turned round only to find Kimberly was over at the other side of the hangar talking to Bob. He thought she was right behind him, Scott thought she had asked him something.

Again, he heard a voice, this time it was a whisper, not clear but a definite voice. He leaned forward, trying to concentrate, trying to listen. Silence.

He looked over towards Kimberly and Bob, they were both looking at him in a peculiar way. What are they talking about? He wondered.

The pain was still there but it was bearable, Scott tried to get closer to the craft. He must have looked stupid walking slowly towards the craft, after he had been in it the day before. The pains didn't get any worse so he tried going up the steps into the craft, once inside he had disappeared from view to all in the hangar. He heard the whisper again, this time it made him jump, as clear as if someone had spoken right next to him.

"What?" Scott said.

The noise, whisper sound came again, Scott couldn't understand. It sounded like a voice but he couldn't be sure, then again. It was a voice, but a language Scott had never heard before.

"I can't understand you." Scott said in a low voice.

"Du.ESAPSU," the whisper came again.

"I can't understand you." He said again.

Scott listened. Nothing! Standing there in the craft

he looked round for a while, but the voice didn't come again. Maybe I was hearing things, he said to himself and walked out and down the steps of the craft.

As Scott walked back over to the room where he had been reading the files, he noticed that Kimberly was still talking to Bob. What could they still be talking about? Scott wondered. He was starting to become a bit paranoid.

I wonder if anybody heard me talking to myself, they'll think I'm going mad.

He still wasn't feeling too good and started to worry that it might have something to do with the objects inside his body. Pulling his chair round he sat down and reached for a pen on the desk, as his hand got close to it, the pen rolled away, as if he'd pushed it, but he hadn't touched it. He tried again, when his hand was nearing the pen, the pen rolled again. Moving his hand quickly he grabbed it.

"What is happening to me? What have I done?" Scott whispered to himself, letting go of the pen and watching it fall to the desk with a thud. The metal pen stayed there motionless.

Scott tried to pick up a paper clip that had fallen out of one of the files, he couldn't, it didn't move, why? That was metal, how strange he thought. As he was looking at the paper clip, Kimberly walked into the room and saw Scott studying it. "Are you all right Scott?" Asked Kimberly.

"Yeah, I'm fine, why?"

"Oh nothing, just the way you're looking at that paperclip, you sure you're ok? You scared me out there in the hangar when you fell. Bob's worried too!" she added.

"I'm fine, I just think things are getting to me a bit, it's been a surreal few weeks. I don't know how much more of this I can take. There is a space craft out there and everyone just accepts it, it's not strange to them. What do you make of it all?" Scott asked.

"I'm not sure really, I'm used to dealing with weird stuff here, not this weird I know but there are plenty of weird things that happen around here, believe me!" Kimberly answered.

"Yeah I'm sure."

That night once everybody had left, Scott went to the parts room again. The sudden urge to get these things out of his body had entered his mind, but how could he do it? He dodged the cameras again just like the night before. Entering the room, he could see a bright light coming from the cracks around the doors on the cabinet. It got brighter as he walked towards it. Scott wheeled the trolley back to his room. Placing the sections on his body once more, he hoped he could get the foreign objects out. This time he seemed to fit the parts to his body easier than the night before.

Bob had anticipated Scott's move that night and was already in the room, watching from behind the mirror. He was fascinated with what Scott had done in such little time, nobody else had thought of or dared to wear the objects as the being had worn them.

When Scott had the full skin on again he still couldn't find the symbols for the objects in his body, they just weren't there. All of a sudden Scott could hear a loud screeching noise, he grabbed his head like earlier that day in the hangar and fell to his knees.

"Nooooo!" Scott shouted. Then it stopped!

There was line after line of writing appearing on the inside of the lenses, symbols and letters, he couldn't understand them. He was on his knees staring straight ahead at the mirror trying to make sense of it all. The images looked as if they were being projected in the distance even though they were on the screen. This technology was more advanced than we could ever imagine. Then he saw a picture he recognised, it was the Earth. Everything else stopped flashing up, and the only thing he could see in the lenses, was the Earth with the Moon revolving around it, spinning there right in front of him, just like the projection in the craft. He reached out for it, but it looked like his hands just went right through it. It was our planet, Earth.

He looked at the screens on his arms, they were blank. Then he focused back on the projection, a symbol appeared above the planet, then another and another until there were five of them. ShuGi.

A line under the symbols flashed like on a computer, then each symbol started to spin, like it was spinning through hundreds of different symbols. Finally, the first letter appeared, then the next, until it spelt, E.A.R.T.H. Then the image shrank into a tiny bright blue dot in the centre of the lens, until it disappeared from view.

Scott stood up in his room, slowly turning away from the mirror where he was being watched. Bob didn't have a clue what Scott had just seen inside the lens of the suit, but he watched intently on the edge of his seat as Scott headed for the door into the hangar.

Leaving his room, Scott walked into the corridor towards the hangar, as he opened the next door he was greeted by a bright light coming from the entrance to the craft, it lit the whole of the hangar. Then it suddenly went dark, the only light coming from the craft was the faint multi coloured light again. Scott could make out the doorway in the distance. Then just like the night before everything got a bright blue edge to it, he could see everything, like he had some kind of night vision goggles on. He could make out the craft and all the desks, he could even see the security cameras, that weren't moving anymore. He noticed something near the craft, something moving. He walked towards it. A faint rumbling noise could be heard from behind him, turning round Scott noticed that some of the office chairs used in the lab had decided to follow him as he'd walked past them, there was a screech from a desk as it too had decided to join in.

Reaching the object that was spinning in the air, he realised it was a pen, like the one he held and mysteriously pushed earlier that day. It was floating in mid air, just tumbling over and over, round and round near the doorway to the craft. Scott reached out his hand, which was now covered with the grey suit, he pointed his faintly glowing index finger slowly towards the pen, the light intensified, he didn't get a chance to touch it. As he got closer the pen just moved slightly further away and started to spin quicker. He raised both his arms

up and positioned them at each side of the pen and slowly moved them closer, trying to catch it. As his hands moved in, the finger tips of each hand started to glow again and the pen stopped spinning instantly. Scott found that he could control the pen, when he moved his hands the pen followed. Slowly closing his hands together, the pen crumpled up into a little ball. The ink from within slowly dripped from this small squashed object floating in mid air. Scott moved his hand towards it and grabbed what was left of the pen, he studied it for a second and then threw it towards a trash can, he thought he'd missed, but the crumpled remnants went straight through the side of the trash can and bounced along the floor, coming to rest oozing ink onto the concrete surface of the hangar. The office chairs had stopped following him when he'd been studying the pen, they had all been fighting for a place in the line behind him, the traffic jam of seats had squashed in between a row of desks. Scott looked down at his hands and then back up at the row of chairs. "I wonder…"
He threw his hands towards the chairs, they squealed along the floor bashing into desks and rolling over and over, until it all went quiet once more. Scott looked down at his hands, shaking his head in disbelief.

Bob had been alerted to the security cameras failing in the hangar, he knew why and ordered that nobody was to enter until he gave the all clear. As the phone went dead he placed the heavy receiver down in its cradle and sparked up another long Cuban cigar, awaiting Scott's return, he knew he was in for a long wait.

Chapter 29

Standing there staring at this thing, this unimaginable object, Scott was in complete awe. He was motionless, transfixed, lost in thought. The size, the shape, the seamless body with its mirrored chrome colour, was just fascinating. He reached out to touch the body of the dormant, unknown object. His finger glowed again when he was within inches of the craft, streaks of lightning reached from his finger tips and caressed along the outer skin, making an electrifying crackling noise. Instantly he was distracted by a symbol which had suddenly appeared in the corner of the lens.

The screen lit up on his arm. Looking down, Scott studied it for a moment, he could see the shape of the craft. But there was a difference, it had steps leading up to the doorway. The symbol was still in his vision on the lens, then another one appeared. Not knowing what to do Scott pressed the image of the craft on his arm, and waited.

Suddenly, the underside of the craft seemed to melt, just like when the objects had melted and flowed into Scott's ears and mouth. It looked like a rippling pond, after a stone had been thrown in. The wooden steps that had been placed in front of the craft were suddenly shattered into hundreds of pieces as the molten material formed some new ones. Still being supported by the wooden stands underneath the craft and the walkway around the craft, it now had these new floating steps that didn't quite touch the floor and didn't seem attached to the craft, it looked like it was hovering just in front of the open doorway. Scott kicked some of the broken wood to the side so he could see the steps better. Very odd, he thought to himself. Glancing at the screen on his arm, he noticed that it had gone blank.

Scott tried one of the new steps, noticing that the underside of his foot had a faint glow, he didn't know whether it was the material on the sole of his foot or the craft that was glowing. As he lifted it, he realised it was both. The place where his foot had just rested was awash with multi coloured flowing lights, just like the ones inside the craft. The lights faded on the step as he moved his foot away, as did the ones on the soles of his feet. It was like the suit he was wearing, was alive, it somehow connected with the skin of the craft. Taking a step up towards the craft, Scott noticed the same thing happening after each footstep, he left a swirling multi-coloured light in his wake. Continuing up the steps, leaving each foot-print to fade, his soles stayed glowing as he passed through the open doorway into the craft. Somehow he was connected to the craft. Moving around the craft he noticed the light would gain in strength where he was standing, like all the flowing lights were following him. Scott made his way over to the spinning ball of light inside the craft and stood there waiting. He looked at the screen once more, it was still blank.

As Scott walked over to where he thought the control panel was, he watched the skin of the craft melt away, turning into a shimmering haze, then dissolving, allowing Scott to look out into the hangar. He wondered if it was some-kind of glass. He reached out to touch it and just like before when he touched the surface outside arcs of lightning stretched from each finger as they glowed, caressing the transparent skin, making an electrifying crackling noise, a kind of static. Something on the sloped area caught Scott's eye, he looked down and saw that the area was glowing with different symbols, all lighting up, blues, reds and greens, all the same colours that were flowing around the craft. There were circles, inside circles with flashing lights and symbols, lines with different coloured sliders all made out of lights on the surface, under this weird skin. To the side there were the different shapes of craft outlined in a bright blue light. What did it all mean?

On Scott's other side, there were four long tube like images, they looked like the pods the beings were in. Each one had a different symbol above it. Scott touched one of the symbols. The image changed from the tube to the same display as on the front of the pods, the vital signs of the being inside. There was a red line that went up and then slowly came down, this had another symbol above it. "I wish I knew what all these symbols meant," Scott said. He touched all the symbols above the images and brought up all the vital signs for the other beings. How were they being kept alive, if they were alive? All the red lines seemed to be beating at the same rhythm. Scott walked away from the control panel and headed over to the pods, he stood looking down at the beings, one at a time. He touched the cover to see if he could feel the temperature, but he couldn't. When Scott had moved away from the panel his finger tips had stopped glowing, they only seemed to glow when he reached out to touch something or when he was in contact with the surface.

Scott had lost track of time whilst he had been inside the craft, if anybody was to walk in on him now, he thought, that would be it. They would think one of the beings had escaped. Walking back over to the control panel, Scott wanted to see if he could make any sense of it, but it was no use, it would take a lifetime and they still wouldn't be any closer to fathoming it out. As his fingers caressed the panel of lights, he must have touched one of the symbols by accident. The lights changed on the panel, an image appeared before Scott, the same one as in the lens earlier in his room. The Sun, Earth and the Moon, our solar system in graphic detail. But there was something different this time, Scott noticed a tiny red dot flashing on our planet, on the Earth.

Scott reached his hand forward and positioned his fingers on the panel, he picked out the image just of the Earth, like he had control of how big the image was in between his hands. He enlarged it so he could see clearly. The image of the Earth was still spinning in front of Scott's eyes, he placed his finger on the Earth and it stopped spinning instantly. He moved the Earth round with his finger to find the flashing red dot. There it was. He looked closely at the image, it looked like it was coming from an area surrounded by the ocean. He expanded the image again, so he could see exactly where on earth it was coming from. It looked to Scott like it was coming from off the coast of Ireland, near the UK.

"Why there?" he wondered, "What was there?"

Manoeuvring the Earth back into the display Scott pressed a symbol under our planet and the image changed. Something he recognised, numbers and code, it was the program he'd been writing. The one that would allow the module to communicate with Earth, a tracking program, it was his program! But how? How was it in the craft's memory, or was it from his memory? The program finished and a red light started to flash on the panel beside him. The words 'Ū.P.Ł.Õ.Å.D...Ç.Õ.M.P.Ł.Ę.T.Ę' appeared in front of him then slowly melted away, leaving on the screen a series of 0s and 1s. Line after line scrolled down the panel in front of Scott.

"Now what?"

Then Scott was distracted by a sound coming from inside the hangar. A sound like an electronic typewriter. The wall of large printers had fired up in the hangar. They all burst into action, ingesting ream after ream of printer paper. The paper was spewing out of the machines and folding back up on the floor, each piece still attached by the perforations joining them together. The numbers flowed down the screen as Scott walked through the craft to the doorway to see what was happening. He stood looking into the hangar with his new alien view, through the lenses of his new skin. All the objects and furniture were outlined in this bright blue colour, just like in his room the night before. He was motionless, watching the printers working on their own. Finally, Scott turned and walked back into the craft to see what the screen was doing now, it was still going through the sequence of numbers. "What does all this mean? How can I stop it?" Scott wondered.

Scott was standing back in front of the control panel, he was fascinated by the screen and all the flashing numbers. We'll have to see if anybody can decode this in the morning, he thought. With that his gaze went back over to where the beings rested in their pods. He walked around them and the spinning ball of light. I wonder if they can be brought out of this sleeping state? He thought as he stroked the clear material covering the surface of one of the pods. His finger tips lit up and letting out the streaks of lightning once more as he touched this odd material, it didn't feel like glass to Scott, more like a skin, hard but soft at the same time, like a membrane. He'd touched the pods when he came in with Bob, but they didn't feel the same as this with his uncovered hands.

"What is this stuff? Was the craft like a living organism? Did it fuel itself? The craft had never been without power for the twenty plus years it had been on Earth. Where could the beings have been heading?" Scott had all these questions, but nobody to answer them. His mind flashed back to in his room when the symbols had changed to English, could the rest change to English? He walked back to the control panel again, the numbers were still computing on the screen.

The control panel was big, it flowed all round where Scott was standing, there were also images on the walls, even on the glass where he could see into the hangar. A series of symbols was just at his eye level, he pressed one. A faint red line created an outline on the glass in front of Scott, he was surprised at what happened next. Inside this outlined area something started to happen, like a television, a picture started to move. It showed a garbled, scrambled picture, a bit hazy to begin with then becoming clearer, explosions after explosions, funny TV clips from old shows like 'Howdy Doody' the oceans, tornadoes and very high waves, land covered with ice and snow, rockets blasting off into space, a view from space towards Earth, what was all this? It was mesmerising, the pictures and films kept coming. People coming down a large ramp onto sand and walking off into the distance. Scott couldn't take his eyes off the screen. They were walking out of a dark opening, rubbing their eyes and pointing, the picture started to pan out, it was some kind of structure. Scott noticed some symbols next to the opening; 'A.R.K.U//II' as the view zoomed out it left on the screen a monstrous thing shining, motionless, half in water, the other half laying on some sand where the people were walking off. Scott noticed that this object was the same shape and colour as the craft he was standing in. A light was glowing pulsating from it's middle, it was a doughnut shape, but the size of city. Smaller objects were hovering in the distance, they seemed to float around this larger dormant structure. These images were moving fast yet this particular one seemed to stay the longest. Then the last segment of images were of Scott, his hand placing the key into the hole in the elevator, a view of Scott strapped in the chair and lastly him walking down the corridor with Bob. Then as quickly as it had started it came to an instant end. The screen cleared, the pictures ended yet the outline was still there. Scott stood there, not sure what had just happened, his mind was going all over the place. He hadn't really taken in that the last part of the film was of him, it took him a few minutes to realise this, but how?

"How am I on the screen? What were all those film clips? A.R.K.U//II what does that mean?" Scott wondered. "They must have been able to pick up our broadcasts, we have been broadcasting for years now, all the world's events. But there were things on there that were before TV was invented, things that couldn't have been broadcast, things that nobody would have seen unless they were here!" Then he paused, his own eyes widened under his new disguise. "Had they been here before???"

   Silence fell, the printers had stopped in the hangar, their job was done, what had they printed out? Would anybody be able to work out what these numbers meant?

"Scott! Scott! Are you in there Scott?" Came Bob's deep voice.

"Shit! What do I do now?" Scott said. "How am I going to explain this?"

"Scott! I know you're in there Scott. I watched the whole thing last night and tonight. "Scott!"

How could he have watched the whole thing? Scott thought, then his mind flashed back to the imprint on the mirror! He was behind the mirror, Bob had seen everything...

Walking to the doorway of the craft in the being's alien skin, he looked at Bob. Scott could see him clearly, but to Bob, Scott looked silhouetted in the doorway to the craft. His hand quickly covered his mouth as he took a shocked gasp. The vision of the alien Scott stood before him, it was out of this world.

"What have you done Scott?" asked Bob, "You couldn't help yourself, could you?"

Bob was surrounded by multi coloured, swirling orbs, these entities seemed to flow all around his body, passing in and through his flesh, as if he wasn't even there. This wasn't the first time Scott had seen something like this, he use to think of himself as a bit of a freak when he was younger, he'd seen this happen before when he was in high-school. He'd seen the doctor about it and they couldn't shed any light on the matter. Unknown to Scott it had been documented on his record and Fiona knew all about it.

Scott opened his mouth to speak from within the alien shroud, then stopped himself realising he wouldn't be able to talk his way out of this one, he opened the palms of his hands outward and shrugged his shoulders, leaving his glowing footprints, he walked down the new steps of the craft, onto the hangar floor where Bob was standing about twenty yards away. As he opened his palms his finger tips glowed and the screen lit up on his arm, casting a light enabling Bob to see him. The symbols for one of the pods was flashing, spinning and glowing brightly. Scott reached over to his arm to touch the symbol.

"No Scott don….."

It was too late, Scott had pressed the symbol, the pack on Scott's back started to glow brighter, the lights inside the grooves flowed faster. His feet left the ground and he felt off balance, his arms started to grab at the air around him, trying to get hold of an invisible object. He looked like he was swimming in the air, his legs and arms scrambling to get grounded once more. He reached out to where Bob was standing, but he was too far away. Bob took a step forward as if he was coming to help, then stopped as he watched Scott turning in the air, he was being mysteriously pulled back up the steps into the craft. He tried to hold onto the edge on the doorway but he couldn't get a grip on anything. "Help!!!" Shouted Scott as he disappeared into the abyss of the craft.

His glowing finger tips slipped, creating a crackle of lightening as they scraped along the craft's silky surface, this was the last thing Bob saw of Scott as his hand disappeared into the craft. The pull was too great for Scott to fight, his feet couldn't touch the ground. As he entered the craft he could see an impression on the backside of the empty pod, it was glowing intensely, it had the same lights swirling around it that were flowing around Scott's back section. He was turned round and round by the invisible force and sucked backwards into the pod. The back section slotting into place in the pod. Scott's arms and legs were still grappling in mid air, fighting to get himself free.

Bob started to walk forwards to see what was

happening. A very intense light blasted out of the doorway, Bob shielded his eyes and felt his face suddenly get hot. Turning and crouching to hide from the heat he waited for it to stop. It did, the light disappeared. Bob got up and walked towards the open doorway, he kicked something with his foot and looked down, his eyes still blinded by the light. There were broken pieces of wood strewn everywhere. Then he noticed the new steps leading up to the doorway of the craft, his eyes were just getting used to seeing in the darkness again. He was moving very cautiously, he stepped up the first step and shouted; "Scott!"

There was no answer. He continued up and looked through the doorway into the dappled multi coloured light being cast from the craft's veins. He saw Scott with his back in the pod. His arms and legs struggling and thrashing around, trying to break free. The body shape in the back of the pod had the same veins of light flowing around, Bob could see that the impression of the previous being was far too big for Scott.

Just as Bob tried to enter the craft, he saw Scott's legs get pulled into the pod, as if they had been sucked down against the pod's base, the impression changed shape, forming around his legs, fitting him perfectly. A platform lit up beneath his feet and started to move, the soles of his feet started to glow until they made contact with this plate. Then his arms seemed to be pulled into the impressions of the pod and again the pod changed shape to fit his arms. The finger tips started to glow as his arms were being pulled in. Hand prints inside the pod had the same glow and his finger tips were guided into place. As soon as they made contact the glow faded and his fingers seemed to be locked in place. Scott was still struggling, his body squirming but unable to move, fighting as long as possible to get free. His neck was stretching forward trying to prolong the inevitable. His head finally whipped backwards into the pod and the veins of light seemed to mould up the sides and around the back of his head. Bob stood there helpless and silent, in shock at what had just happened.

Scott could see Bob watching at the doorway, as he battled to get himself free from the invisible force of the craft. He couldn't move. His body was locked in, forming part of the craft now. The only sound was from the beating of his own heart, echoing around his fear-stricken head. The veins of multi-coloured lights had moulded around the sides of his body, just like the other beings who'd laid dormant for years. Then Scott felt something. Something inside his suit. Creeping up each side of his chest. He felt it stop in the middle of his chest, just below his rib cage. Then it started again, moving up his chest towards his neck. His breathing felt shallow, each lung getting tighter by the second. Whatever it was continued, inching its way up his torso, then Scott felt it separate again and go either side of his neck, moving slowly towards each ear, another split! This time into four, two each side. Scott let out a chilling scream, this pain was the single worst thing he'd ever felt. Something had squeezed into his ears. Then the pain stopped. This agony had distracted him from the other thing moving towards his mouth. Then he felt it, his eyes trying to look down inside the lenses, straining his vision. This too separated into three. He could feel it under the breathing apparatus around his mouth, feeling it's way like the antennae of hungry insect looking for its prey. It found it!

Scott felt something go up each nostril and into his mouth. Making him gag as he felt something at the back of his throat, he thought this was it, his time was up. These things continued down his throat, it was cold, like steel. Sliding down for what seemed like forever, every second the fear that he'd met his end came close. He could feel the back of his throat burning like he'd swallowed acid. That's when he felt whatever it was that had gone up his nostrils, it had met the other tube at the back of his throat. He couldn't breath. He couldn't scream. He was terrified.

Bob didn't know what was happening inside Scott's alien suit, all he could see was his lifeless body flinching as it laid there. For all Bob knew, that was it. Scott had gone.

Scott's eyes looked up again, trying to focus after straining looking down. Motionless, he felt like he was drowning. Clutching and holding onto his last breaths for as long as he possibly could, his vision blurred as he tried to focus on Bob, standing in the doorway, trying to stay awake, he drifted in and out of consciousness, grasping at his last few moments of life.

Bob watched and waited for a movement, a sign to tell him that Scott was all right. Nothing happened, he was sure that was it for Scott.

"What have I done? I've stood here and let Scott be taken into this craft. Why didn't I help him?" Bob said to himself. His head bowed in embarrassment, his complexion of guilt made his skin crawl.

"Why? I didn't expect this I had other plans for you Scott, it wasn't meant to be like this." Bob said out loud into the craft.

The base of the pod started to glow, a thin bright orange light encircled the perimeter of Scott's body, all around the pod. It started to move up creating a cover similar to the other pods. A gooey jellylike liquid filled the inside, with a solid skin forming on the outside, like a crust. It looked very similar to when the alien suit formed over Scott's body, it was uneven in its formation around Scott. The liquid didn't spill out, it looked like the orange light was creating a wall, a kind of rock-hard membrane on the outside to protect the being inside. Just like the others in their pods, Bob thought.

As Scott regained consciousness once more, he could see the light moving up his body out of the corner of his eyes. A voice in his mind was telling him to stay awake, his eyes transfixed on the glowing edges. He could see ripples inside the light but he couldn't feel anything against his body. The orange glow was level with his sight now and he watched it go past his eyes. The orange light only seemed to be around the top edge as it made the pod's crust. As it passed over his face, he could see out once more. I'm still breathing, Why am I not drowning? The voice in his head echoed. He could just make out Bob standing there as he strained his eyes to look over, Scott felt like he was trying to see

underwater, Bob was all blurred. This thick liquid
had encased Scott's body from head to foot.

Scott was falling unconscious again for what
seemed to be the hundredth time, then all of a
sudden he felt his lungs go cold and he felt his chest
inflate then again. He slowly came round and his
vision started to come back, though he still couldn't
see out clearly through the pod's wall of liquid. He
was breathing again. The veins of light that had
invaded his body were feeding his lungs with air,
very cold air. Scott could feel a sensation of
pressure on his chest from the outside, like someone
was pushing down on him. It felt like waves of
motion like the liquid was pulsating around the pod
very fast, in time with Scott's heart beat. Then he
felt his body tighten up, as if the liquid was
hardening, not completely but enough to put
pressure all over.

Bob ventured into the craft, looking around as he
did so. More weary with each footstep, he walked
over and stood in front of Scott. He reached out to
touch the pod's new skin that was encasing Scott.
As he touched it it gave him an electric shock, a
small streak of lightning shot from the surface of the
membrane and made a crackling noise as Bob's
hand flew backwards. He looked at his fingers and
shook his hand, what was that?
Bob shouted Scott's name over and over; "Scott,
Scott. Can you here hear me Scott? Just make a sign
to let me know you're ok."
Nothing.
Scott could see Bob standing right there, just in front
of him. He could see his mouth moving, but he

couldn't hear a thing encased in his fluid-filled tomb. He couldn't move. He could hardly breathe. Then Scott felt a sudden rush, a new sensation, like he was being filled with something. The tubes which had gone down his throat, were pumping liquid into his lungs. Holding his breath once more, too scared to breathe, he fought to stay conscious again, until he started to feel dizzy, his eyes were popping out of their sockets under his alien mask.

The panel on the side of the pod erupted into life. A blue light starting as a dot in the centre, turned into a line across the screen and moved each way. The image of a body was formed on the screen. Outlined in blue with all the organs shown, symbols lit up beside the image and a line underneath started to flow across the screen, a heart trace with the beat forming, just like in a hospital. Then the image of the body disappeared, left in it's place was the same image that was on the screens for the other pods.

Scott was alive!

Chapter 30

Bob sighed a huge sigh of relief, knowing Scott was still alive inside his alien tomb. Staring at Scott inside, he touched the panel on the side, but it was no use, there was nothing he could do. All the objects that had been retrieved from the dead being all those years ago were now part of Scott.
"We have no way of getting to them and no way of continuing our research now," said Bob to himself, "what are we going to do? It's like having a large broken toy, that nobody knows how to fix!"

Bob sat down on the craft's floor and leaned his back against the side of the craft. He stared into space looking at the ball of spinning light in the centre of the craft, surrounded by the four filled pods. He rested his elbows on his knees and put his head into his hands. "What are we going to do now?"

Scattered images filled Scott's mind, messages flashed up on the inside of the lenses. He read them out loud in his head, this doesn't make sense, I can't speak, how the hell am I gonna tell him that. Scott thought.

Bob noticed a light out of the corner of his eye, a screen on the sloped area to the front of the craft. He battled against his large force of gravity to pull himself up from the floor and walked over to where he'd seen the light. A symbol was flashing on the panel, he'd never seen anything on this area before.

"I wonder what this is?"

A symbol, like the one that was on the pieces they had retrieved from the being. It was flashing on the shiny sloped surface, like it was being projected somehow. But it wasn't, it was inside the panel. He watched. Then the symbol flashed quickly, like it was going through a million different symbols in a split second, trying to find the right one. Then it stopped, and went blank. But not for long.

…H…î……B….Õ….B…

The letters appeared before Bob's eyes. He was stunned and scared, yet freakishly excited. He didn't know what to do.

"Ermmmm. Hello. Who are you?" he said, as he looked around in the craft.

A few seconds passed, then.

…î..M…..Õ..K, came the reply on the panel.

"Who's ok?" Bob asked.

…î..T.Š….Š…Ç..Õ..T…T.

Bob stumbled backwards, he placed his hand over his mouth.

"But… How…? Where are you? I've just seen you get eaten up by this thing, I thought you were a gonna."

…Ñ..Õ…T…..Ŷ..Ę.T.

The letters seemed to be getting better at forming on the panel.

"How are you doing this?" asked Bob.

.Î.M…NÕ.T…Š.ŪR.Ę…TH.Ę…ÇR.ÅFT…ÎŠ… ŠÕM..HÕ.Ŵ…ÅBŁ.Ę…TÕ…R.Ę.Å.D…MŶ……… TH..ÕŪ.GH.TŠ…

Bob was in shock, "What can I do? Can I get you out?"

…Ñ.Õ…

"There must be something I, we can do? Something
to help?"

…Ñ.Õ…

"Who are the beings? Where do they come from?
Can you communicate with them or the craft?"
asked Bob.

….Î.M…TR.Ŷ.ÎÑG…TH.Ę…MĘŠŠ.ÅG.Ę…
RĘ.ÅDŠ…..Ç.RÅ.FT…ÑĘĘD.Š…TÕ…BĘ…ÎÑ…
ŽĘRÕ…GRÅV.ÎTŶ……..MÅ..Ñ.ĘTÎ.Ç…PŪŁŠĘ…
FÎĘŁ….ÑÕT…
FŪÑÇTÎ.ÕÑÎÑG…..ÑĘĘD..DÅRK…….MÅTTĘ……
………….

"What the hell does that mean Scott?" asked Bob.
Bob stared at the blank response on the panel, he
waited and asked the same question again.

"What the hell does that mean? What the hell is the
Manetic pulse fiel?"

The panel remained blank for a while, until…

…ÇRÅ.T…R˜NNING..TRAÇKING…
PROG..AM….NEE..S……Š.P.ÅÇĘ….

"What? What does that mean? Space!"

…ÇRÅFT…ÑĘĘDŠ…TÕ…BĘ…ÎÑ….Š.P.ÅÇĘ……
ŁÕŠÎÑG…ÇÕM..M.ŪÑ..Î..ÇÅT.ÎÕ.Ñ..
….Ŷ.Õ..Ū…..Ñ..ĘĘ..D…T.Õ…………ĘVÅ.ÇŪ.Å..
ŠPÅÇĘ………ŠPÅÇĘ……ŠPÅÇ…..

With that partial last word, the symbol flashed and
disappeared. Scott's strained eyes closed and this
last image, seen through the alien lenses in his
liquid capsule, faded into his darkened memory.
Bob's face started to fade away until he could fight
his fate no more. Scott finally fell unconscious,
destined for an uncertain life within the craft. His

new home, but for how long?

Total shutdown, only the craft or the pod were able to sustain Scott's life for the near future. There was nothing, not even a memory stirred in Scott's dormant mind.

"What does that mean Scott? Evacua…"
The panel lit up once more and the symbols were replaced by a countdown, 10…9…8
"Scott! Scott!"
No response!
"What the hell did that mean?" Bob wondered.
"Evacua…"
7…6…

Oh hell! Evacuate! Bob finally realised what Scott had tried to say, he turned and ran towards the open doorway. He could see the craft's surface had started to change, it had a shimmering look to it around the doorway, a bit like a heat haze on a road. As Bob got to the opening he jumped out, landing in a pile of broken timber, the remnants of the old steps that had been destroyed. Turning to face the doorway, Bob looked at the new steps to the craft, suspended in the air. Then before his eyes, they melted and seemed to run up the craft, like a waterfall in reverse. Electrifying streaks of lightning danced around the surface of the craft and reached out to the sides of the hangar, caressing the room with its deadly elegance. The steps reformed into a seamless new door to the craft. Bob picked himself up and bounded towards the craft shouting, "No!" as the last parts of the surface crackled with the dancing sparks.

Bob could just about reach the craft and jumped to

where the new door had formed. There was a bright flash of light and a deep reverberating resonance that echoed inside his head and throughout the hangar. It was like he'd been hit by a bolt of lightning, making him fly back across the hangar and into a desk about twenty yards away. The same residual sparks of lightning caressing his hands, trying to work their way up his arms. He laid there motionless, in the collapsed debris of the desk. The craft still had the same lightning wrapping around it from where Bob had tried to touch it, the fingers of electricity crackled off its mirrored surface, showing the invisible shield that must now be protecting the craft.

Kimberly was the first to arrive the following morning. She was stopped by the security guard outside the hangar. He told her there had been some strange lights coming through the porthole in the blast-door last night, but didn't see anything. His security camera didn't pick anything up in that sector because he didn't have the clearance. Kimberly went through the security checks and entered the hangar as normal, on her own. As she entered, the massive overhead lights powered up one by one, from where she was at the door first, then continuing down the hangar. As the lights came on near the craft she could see all the debris scattered across the floor.

"What's happened in here?" she said to herself. She ran over to Scott's quarters and knocked on his door. No answer, she tried a few times, still no answer. Kimberly tried the door, it was locked. "What's going on? Where is everyone?" Kimberly thought out loud whilst walking further into the hangar. In the distance she could see a lifeless hand poking out from the side of a desk, she ran towards it thinking it was Scott.

"Scott! Scott!" she shouted as she ran. She stopped just before the desk to peer over the top fearing the worst, it was only then that she realised it wasn't Scott and it was in fact Bob. She walked sheepishly around the desk wondering if he was still alive. He didn't look it.

"Bob! Bob!"

No response! No movement! Kimberly crouched down beside him and pulled away the debris from around his lifeless body. Bob's face was cut and burnt, his hands looked burnt too, kind-of scalded. Kimberly grabbed one of his hands and tried to feel for a pulse.

Bob was still alive!

Another lab worker arrived.

"Over here, quickly!" Kimberly shouted.

The lab worker ran as he saw Kimberly's hand waving in the distance near the craft.

"What's wrong?" he asked as he came nearer.

"I don't know, I've just found him like this, he's still alive. Bob! Bob!" she shouted as she tapped his cheek with her hand. Bob started to come round, he moaned, then slowly started to open his eyes. He was very shaken.

"Quick, get him a glass of water!" she said.

The lab assistant ran off to get one, it didn't take him long. As he did this Kimberly was trying to keep Bob awake. Trying to sit him up, he was a dead weight, she propped him against the drawers of the desk, or what was left of the drawers of the desk.

"What happened Bob?" she asked.

"Ermmmm! I, I don't know!" came his stuttered response.

"Can you remember anything?"

"I, I, no, not really." he said in his weakened state.

"Try, try Bob. Where's Scott? Have you seen Scott? He's not answering his door. Have you seen him? Bob, focus, have you seen Scott?" Kimberly was frantic for an answer.

"Scott, Scott! Oh no, Scott! The craft!" Bob suddenly had a moment of realisation. His eyes widening, as if they were about to pop out of his head. He pointed at the craft, as if he'd witnessed something terrible.

"What about the craft?" Asked Kimberly.

Bob closed his eyes tightly and a tear slowly formed in the corner, as if he'd closed them too tight and one had squeezed out. It slowly rolled down his cheek until it hit a congealed bloody scratch on his face. The tear dissolved the blood in its path, leaving a diluted red tinged salty track down his colourless face.

"What's happened? What's happened to Scott? What have you done to him?" Kimberly asked.

"I didn't do anything, he did it to himself, he…" Bob wasn't allowed to finish before Kimberly butted in again;

"What? What do you mean, he did it to himself?"

"The…the parts…the parts we recovered out of the being. He knew, somehow he knew what to do. He found out how to get the parts into himself, he's connected with the craft. The pod…he's in the…in the…in the craft." Bob started to struggle with his words.

"What happened last night? Please tell me the truth Bob"

"I…I am telling the truth. He's in the craft, inside the pod." Bob said.

Kimberly looked round at the craft.

"Where's the door? Where's the door gone Bob?" Kimberly ran towards the craft.

"No! No! Grab her. Don't touch it!" shouted Bob. Stopping just before she reached it.

"Why? Scott's in there! Can we get him out?"

"No, no, I don't think so. That's why I'm laid here, because I tried to get back in. The craft has some kind of protection field," explained Bob. "Help me up and into my office."

In Bob's office he tried to tell Kimberly about everything that had happened, from the previous night's events to that night when Scott had been swallowed up by the pod inside the craft.

"This mission has just taken on a new direction." stated Bob.

Bob wrote down the things he could remember, from the time before he was knocked unconscious by the mysterious bolt of lightning as he touched the craft.

Space!

Manetic Pulse Fiel!

What did it all mean? How are we going to find these things out now? Especially with the one person who could help, locked inside the craft, Bob thought to himself.

"We need to call a meeting." Bob said to Kimberly
"About what?"
"About the mission! I know you didn't know
anything about the mission, neither did Scott really.
He was brought in to get the craft to work again, but
now things have taken a turn for the worst. Get me
the head of each department from inside Area 49,
everyone who has clearance for this sector. Have
them meet me in my office in one hour."
With that he sat back in his chair, flipped his Zippo's
lid and sparked up another rather large Cuban
cigar.
"They'll be the death of you!" Kimberly said, as a
large tear rolled down her cheek.

Chapter 31

As the heads of each department entered Bob's office, Kimberly was last to walk in. "Please wait outside Kimberly." Bob ordered.
"But, bu…"
"Please wait outside, your clearance doesn't allow you to be here for this." Bob told her.
Kimberly turned and walked out of the door, slamming it shut behind her.
"Why can't I be in there?" she whispered to herself, "I need to know as much as anybody in there what is going to happen."
The area around the craft had been cordoned off, so nobody could get hurt like Bob had. They even had armed guards in the hangar now, not letting anyone near the craft. Kimberly walked over to try and get some clues as to what had happened that night in the hangar. Broken step debris was strewn everywhere still, nobody had touched a thing. She walked all around the craft, keeping a safe distance, wondering what had happened and what was happening to Scott inside, was he alive still? Or had he come to an untimely death at the hands of technology they knew nothing about. The craft was still being supported by the wooden posts, it still didn't work, and now there was no way of getting into it. Sealed shut, this chrome coloured mysterious thing entombed Scott.
Bob's office door opened and out walked the

heads of department, all looking baffled. They all walked over to the craft and started looking around it from a distance, just like Kimberly had done moments earlier. One of the heads was talking to Bob and pointing at the craft, Kimberly couldn't quite hear what they were saying, but she did pick up one thing that Bob said and that was;
"I'm sure it will fit, we'll know more by the end of the day."
"What will fit? Know what by the end of the day?" Kimberly said to herself, "What are they planning?"

There were a few of the lab technicians standing by the extremely large printing devices, holding up reams and reams of printer paper, all still attached by the perforations across the middle. One of the technicians was holding the paper up while the other was looking intensely at the printout, whilst trying to keep his glasses on his nose.
"Sir! Sir!"

The man reading tried to get Bob's attention, he'd shout Sir then look back at the printout, then back to Bob and then shout Sir again. All the time trying his very best to keep pushing his glasses up.
"What is it? Can't you see that we are in the middle of a crisis here Colin!" Bob shouted back at him.
"I know Sir, but your gonna want to see this Sir!" he replied.
"Just a minute please!" Bob said to the man he was talking to, as he made his way over to see what all the fuss was about.
"What is it man?" Bob said as he neared the printers.
"Take a look at this, what do you make of it?

Bob grabbed the printout from the man and looked at the paper.

"It's a load of numbers. The printer has obviously gone mad like everything else around here!" Bob exclaimed.

"I don't think so Sir, this is a code Sir. I don't know what for but this is a code Sir," he said as he fidgeted around, pointing at different parts on the paper.

"A code? What on earth makes you think that Colin?"

"Well, I was brought in to try and break codes for the army Sir. Code breaking, that was my field, before I got into Area 49 Sir. I know it's a code from something. Not sure what, or where, but it is for sure. But yes it's definitely some kind of binary code Sir." Said Colin.

"Ok, ok just get onto it, let's see what you come up with man." Bob said frowning and shaking his head, as he walked back over to continue his conversation.

The technician gathered up all the printouts and walked hastily back over to a room and shut the door. Bob wasn't the nicest of men when it came to ordering them around. Kimberly was hovering around to see if she could overhear anything else, but the only other thing she heard and saw was Bob shaking the hand of a man she hadn't seen before as he said;

"Ok, you have a green light, let's get moving on this, you have less than a year to pull this off! And let's get this thing covered up somehow."

Something isn't right here, thought Kimberly.

A massive ring had been built around the craft, attached to this was a cover which encircled the whole craft, then lifted halfway up the hangar. That afternoon Kimberly noticed that people were going into the covered up area. Managing to poke her head in she noticed they were measuring all the dimensions of the craft, everything in fine detail. What were they planning on doing? She wondered.

Kimberly was scared that she'd have her clearance taken now that Scott wasn't there. She was an asset to Bob in her previous role, finding people who had the knowledge that was required for Area 49's work. She never knew what went on behind the doors to the hangar, she didn't really need to know. "Had I become too attached to Scott? Was that a problem for Bob and my position? Surely he couldn't let me go, not now, I know too much." She said.

Bob called for Kimberly to come to his office later that day.

"I can't be accountable for what might happen to you, if you breathe a word of what you have seen down here over the last few days." Stated Bob.

"I won't, I swear Bob, nobody would believe me even if did tell them. You know me Bob, I've always done everything you've asked of me. I've never told anybody who I work for, everyone just thinks I work at NASA." Replied Kimberly, as she feared for herself.

"Well, I've been told to let you know about our future mission," he said with a cheeky grin on his face. "You'll be part of what we are planning and not a word can be spoken of it outside of these walls. Is that clear?" Bob said.

"Yes Sir! What's going on? What's the mission?" questioned Kimberly.

"Sit down, this might take a while." Bob said.

"And don't forget! I'm counting on you not to say a word to anyone Kimberly."

As Kimberly closed the door to Bob's office, she looked shocked and stunned. How the hell is that even going to work, she thought whilst looking at the craft and what about Scott? He's not... She stopped herself from thinking such a thought by shaking her head and walking towards Scott's room.

Chapter 32

May 2nd 1969

The space race was in full swing. The Apollo project had seen a great achievement in the development of new space craft. NASA had gained so much knowledge and new technology from the Roswell crash, it had all helped to forge the new Saturn V rocket. Most of this new technology was still a secret to the public.

The USA was on schedule for launching their first manned mission to the Moon. The Saturn V rocket had been designed by top scientists from all over the world who had been brought to America with operation Paperclip in the late 1940s, this included the renowned scientist Von Braun. They had all been helping design and structure the space program for the future. The best scientific minds of all.

They had all been part of or had a part in the Roswell incident at some point in their career. Some had even helped develop the Saturn V rocket, which had now undergone a major redesign, ready for the lunar mission.

....

A deafening rumble stopped everyone in their

tracks… the earth started to shake, trembling could be felt throughout the hangar. A water dispenser in the corner gave a loud glug, as a large air bubble was vibrated free from the tubes below.

None of the lab workers knew what was happening, they looked at each other in confusion, then back at the area the noise was coming from. They took a few steps back as the noises got louder and louder, it was coming from behind two huge steel blast doors. Nobody could see what was going on, as the doors remained sealed shut. Dust started to fall from the roof, vibrated free by the demonic tremors.

Behind the enormous steel doors, the point of a massive circling cone with spinning teeth poked through the wall. Dust and smoke plumed out into the void left between the blast doors and the underground wall. The cone toothed monster continued to spiral through the wall, until the last few boulders and rocks bounced off the machine and fell to the floor. The headlights cut into the dusty air like two spotlights leading the way on a foggy night.

A burrowing machine, controlled by an invisible operator, had broken through the wall and had formed a huge opening. Rocks and debris fell against the blast doors from the solid inner wall, sending a dull resonating echo down the tunnel from where the monster had arisen, this drowned out the grinding noise coming from the machine. The blast-doors shook as the large pieces of rubble fell against them as it broke through. Dark shadows of the men who were following, disturbed and swirled the thick air with their movement, their ghostly silhouettes clambered over the fallen rocks like they had just escaped from Satan's lair. Their head torches performed a spectacular light show in the dense atmosphere, as they stood in the wake of destruction caused by the man made monster. They came to a standstill, posing on the rocks, waiting for the stagnant dust cloud to settle, and the machine to stop.

Silence.

The monster stopped. All that could be heard was the odd rock still tumbling into place on the ground. They stood and waited. A low frequency vibration could be heard in the distance, it grew louder and louder then all of a sudden a cyclonic wind passed the men. They all crouched down,shielding themselves where they perched, holding the jagged four and a half billion-year-old rocks for support, looking up through their goggles and bandanas covering their mouths, they could see this almighty wind had turned the stagnant dust cloud into a vortex of spinning particles. A tornado of dust that seemed to reach up into the cavernous void behind the huge steel doors and the heavens above.

The tornado disappeared above their heads, a shaft of broken light bounced of the sharp cave like walls, casting an ambient light down into the void. The team of men started to rise from clutching the rocks. They walked further into the opening, coming face to face with the two huge towering blast doors. The word 'AREA' written on one door and '49' on the other in huge flaky white paint, looked like it had been on there for years. The men looked up, the void went straight to the surface. Far above their heads they could see a faint movement, a shadow from a mammoth fan, used to ventilate the shaft they stood in below. The cavern's sharp jagged rocks were jutting out and glistening with moisture, as the tunnel cast light down onto the rubble below. Drips from the cave walls could be heard in the distance as silence descended once more.

This was how they had been able to get the craft down into Area 49, well below the marshland surrounding Cape Canaveral. A secret operations base used for the development and containment of unknown projects.

"What is this place? What are these doors doing here?" One of the men said in shock.

Once the dust had dispersed, they started to make the opening larger, clearing the debris caused by the machine. The tunnel could be seen beyond the workers, it was lit like a mineshaft. A festoon of lights attached to the tunnel's walls, lit the way to where they came. It went on and on into the distance.

Just behind the mechanical mole was a truck. It had a conveyor belt leading up to the top spilling the ground-up rocks into the back as the mole was progressing forward. A man jumped from the truck's cabin and walked through the opening into the void, wearing a ragged old NASA baseball cap. He put one foot onto a pile of rocks and looked around. He spat a big lump of black tobacco, which splattered the rocks and looked like thick black tar oozing over the surface.

"Let's get this mess cleaned up! Our job here is finally done thank God!" he said before turning around and walking back to his cab.

After the truck had been filled to the brim once more, its engine rumbled into life and he drove off down the tunnel into the distance. Once everything had been cleaned up and the tunnel entrance made secure, the men who had created the tunnel were picked up in a canvas sided army truck and driven out. Not knowing what they had come across.

The secured phone rang in Bob's office, he walked over and picked up the receiver,
"Hello?" said Bob.
"The package will arrive in due course, wait for the doors to be opened."
"O…" The line went dead before Bob could say; Ok! He raised his eyebrows and said; "Well there's no going back now. God help us…!"

Bob collected himself together and walked into the hangar, his palms sweating, his brow dampened with glistening droplets of fear.
"Can I see everyone in the briefing room in ten minutes please?" he shouted, seeming to make the blast doors rattle again.
"What's going on?" said Colin, as he came out of his room where he was trying to decipher the printouts. Murmurs could be heard throughout the hangar, whispers about the noises coming from behind the blast doors, nobody knew what was going on.

As everyone stopped doing what they were doing, they all started to make their way to the briefing room.
"Please sit down, what you are about to hear is of a

highly top secret nature. You are not permitted to speak of this outside this area. Do I make myself clear?" Bob said sternly.

Nobody answered.

"Do I make myself clear?"

"Yes, Sir!" They all responded.

"As you all know there was an incident here in Area 49 last night. We've had this craft since 1947. I have worked on it for the last twenty-one years and we still didn't know who they are, why they came to Earth or how to use this craft. Its technology is far more advanced than we could ever imagine. After this meeting, you will all be a lot clearer on what is going to happen and what has happened." Bob said as he walked around the back of everyone sitting in the briefing room.

"Where is Scott? Shouldn't you wait till he gets here?" questioned one of the lab workers.

Returning to his chair, Bob turned it round to face everyone and sat down. As he lit a big Cuban cigar, he started to explain things through his cloud of toxic smoke.

"Last night, here in the lab we lost Scott..."

"What!" Came a voice.

"Well, not really lost him, he's still here, but he's not here! If that makes sense?"

"Ermmmm... No not really Sir."

"Let me explain!" said Bob.

A tear started to form in the corner of Kimberly's eye, her head bowed down as if mourning a loved one. Closing her eyes allowed the tear to lose its grip on her lashes which were keeping it in place. It dripped onto her skirt, closely followed by a cascade of others. Fiona placed her hand on Kimberly's shoulder, trying to offer her some kind of comfort. Kimberly slowly looked up, wiping the remaining tears from around her eyes. It took all her strength to smile at Fiona.

"Are we all ok? Can I continue with this? Please hold it together Kimberly or I'll be forced to have you removed from the meeting." Bob had no compassion, he was like a rock.

Bob continued to tell them about all the events that had happened the night before in Area 49. Everyone was shocked and horrified, they found it quite hard to believe that something like this could have happened, and why Scott? He told them that Scott had been involved with this mission for years, without knowing a thing. Bob explained about George, Scott's father and how he was the head of the department in Area 51, when the crashed object was found and taken there for investigation. Scott had been under surveillance for years, they were told how he was placed into a home where he would want for nothing and have the best possible education. Scott had had a connection with this craft for years, ever since he was born without knowing a thing.

"This day had been Scott's destiny!" Bob explained. "Things have changed slightly from the previous mission, not drastically but they have changed all the same. The same plan we had for the craft will still go ahead. Scott has just gone into the craft unwillingly, and we didn't have time to train or convince him otherwise. Our new mission will proceed as planned from this point forward, do not breath wind of what has happened to another living soul beyond this room. I will not be responsible for anyone who breaks the secrecy code." These words were said with conviction, striking fear into the hearts of all listening.

"The mission has already started, as of the moment you all walked into this room. I'm assuming you were all wondering what all the noise was coming from the chamber behind the blast doors? Well, you will soon find out in the next few days. The package will be arriving soon, just as planned and we don't have long to get things into place. We owe it to Scott to make this work. It might be the only lifeline he has!"

Chapter 33

Colin had been working on the printouts for a few days now. He wasn't getting very far and feared that he wouldn't be able to decipher the code in time. There was still no sign of the package arriving, everyone was walking on eggshells waiting to fit everything into place. Then that morning, out of the blue, there was another rumble beyond the blast-doors, a red light above them started to flash. Everyone stopped and focused their attention towards the rumbling.

The noise got louder and louder, then it stopped. The doors vibrated, just like a few days ago. Only this time they started to open! There was a deafening screech as the doors slowly began to pull apart along the track at each side, they hadn't been opened since the craft was brought down the ventilation shaft and into the chamber. The doors inched open, until the airtight seal was breached. Then there was a loud hiss and a blast of cold damp air which filled the lab, it blew some paperwork off the desks in the distance.

They watched in anticipation, waiting to start on the new project that could change the history of evolution as we know it!

As the doors came to a stop, they were fully open. In front of everyone was a long flat platform. Hundreds of wheels spanned the length of the base along each side. On the back of the trailer was an enormous covered object. From where they were all standing, they could see straight through it. A massive empty cylinder, they had all seen objects like this before working at NASA, but somehow this just looked different. The sheer size of it, this close, was daunting to everyone. The blast doors were twelve meters square and the cylinder on the trailer, only just made it through with inches to spare at the top and the sides.

The trailer slowly crept along, the men making sure the object didn't hit the sides on the doors. It seemed to take forever to get into the hangar. Once in place, the trailer came to a stop. Everyone stood looking at this mammoth object.

"Well, stop staring at it! Let's get this thing uncovered and get to work." Said Bob.

The large blast doors started to close. The workers in Area 49 watched the men going back down the long tunnel as the doors closed, leaving them travelling off into the distance, the festoon of lights turning off section by section as they drove away.

With a loud echoing BOOM! The doors finally closed, seeming to make the room shake. Bob was standing next to the object watching the lab technicians undoing the cover that was draped over it. When they had finished, they all grabbed a part of the cover and slowly walked away, pulling the large tarp off the object. It finally got to the point where gravity took over and the cover fell to the ground, unveiling a white body with the words 'UNITED STATES' written in red down the sides.

"It's a lot bigger in reality than I thought it was going to be!" said Bob.

"Wow!" came another response.

"Well, this is the stage two section of the Saturn V. This rocket will be our first manned mission to the moon. This is the final part to the briefing you have all been waiting for. You have all been working on a mission, a mission that will change the way we think about evolution as we know it. Everyone here at Area 49 has been working with this craft for years now, we don't have the ability or the technology to fly the craft. The time has come to send it home. We don't know if this will work but we have the perfect cover for this mission. The Saturn V has been modified to fit the craft inside."

Everyone looked shocked and stunned to hear this.

"But what about Scott?" asked Kimberly.

"Well, this was always the plan Kimberly. Scott has been preparing for this journey all his life, he just hasn't known about it." Replied Bob.

"We are sending the craft, with Scott in it, back into space? What will happen?" a voice from behind Bob asked.

"We aren't quite sure yet, we…" Bob was cut short.

"You're not quite sure yet! Are you kidding?"

"No, we just don't know what will happen. You have all been working on this craft for years now and we haven't made any progress what so ever in making it fly. Yes, we have been able to take some of the technology from the craft and develop some amazing things, but we can't find out how to fly it. This kind of technology would change every form of transport in the world. You've all been inside the craft, it's too advanced for us to work on. The things I witnessed here in this hangar, were not of this world. The instrument panel that works through the mind of the host. It's just something we can't understand. This craft came from somewhere in the universe that is hundreds if not thousands maybe even millions of years more advanced than we are. We are pretty sure that they have been coming here to Earth for some time, it's documented throughout history, that people have witnessed strange flying objects and spotted weird alien looking beings. We found that craft in Roswell with just that on board. The way we see it, this mission couldn't have happened if we didn't find the part that Scott had unknowingly been carrying around for years. We were going to ask Scott to do this, but he took it upon himself to try all the parts on. The internal parts went missing a few days ago, I knew where they were because I'd seen everything whilst Scott was being monitored. Once the parts were in his body they wouldn't come out again, I came to the conclusion that they needed to be inside a living host. Scott was the perfect candidate, wasn't he Fiona?"

"I wanted to get him ready for this trip before all this happened, it's too late now. His future is out of our hands. I just hope he gets to where he's going!" said Fiona sadly.

"A team of highly trained engineers will be here shortly to start making plans to fit the craft into the modified stage two of the rocket. We don't have long to get this done and we are the privileged ones that will help with this mission."

"What are you expecting to happen?" asked Kimberly.

"Well, we are hoping that the craft will kick-start its flight path home once it's in zero gravity, or space."

"How do you think that's going to happen, when there isn't anybody flying it?" Kimberly questioned again.

"We don't know. Before I jumped out of the craft, Scott sent a message through the craft, it appeared on the panel in front of me. It read 'craft needs to be in space losing communication'. He also mentioned something about a 'Manetic Pulse Fiel not working! We presume this had meant to say, 'Magnetic Pulse Field'. We just don't know what we are working with. Scott is entombed in that craft, sitting right there and we can't get to him or get him out. I wish we could, but this might be our only chance of sending someone on a mission they could only dream of. A mission that could change everything we know, everything we've believed in for years. The history of the human race, whether we did really evolve from apes or whether we came from somewhere else and were put here to colonise this planet. This could change everything. Do you understand that?"

"Yes I understand, but he…"

"Look his vital signs on the side of the pod seemed ok, I think he was in the same state as the other beings that had been in there for years."

   Kimberly walked off towards the Roswell room where she and Scott had been working together. They had this planned all along, she thought to herself.

Returning to the room Kimberly sat in the office chair wondering if she would ever see Scott again.

First thing the next morning a team of people arrived to start fitting the craft into the stage two section of the Saturn V. This wasn't going to be easy. For this to work the section had been modified, made longer to accommodate the craft. A partition had been fabricated to separate the fuel from the craft. This had to be welded in place, sealed and insulated so no flammable liquid could get through. This would provide a great cover for the mission, nobody would know the craft was in there. On top of this section there had to be a kind of booster, something to jettison the craft from the fuel stage before it floated off into space. This was going to happen by using explosive charges at the base of the craft. It would propel the craft forward, out of the spinning fuel section and out of sight from the crew of the Apollo 11's mission and deep into space.

Before the craft could be fitted into the rocket section, they had to coat the whole inside of the fuel stage with insulation. Then the craft would fit like a glove, no-one would know it was there. Overhead heavy lifting gear would help manoeuvre the craft into place. The craft would be lifted by one end, whilst it was still sitting on the wooden platform, then it would be butted up to the Saturn section and a massive electro magnet placed on the side, just like the ones used to bring the craft down the ventilation shaft. They just hoped they could get near it with these things without its shield stopping it. If they couldn't it would be back to the drawing board to find an alternative way, maybe place the craft into some kind of synthetic skin to help lift it. They just didn't know really how they were going to get it in there, but hopefully they could. The first plan was lift it and suspended it in the air, like the large doughnut above Krusty Creams, then it would be pushed into the rocket and covered with another heavily insulated cover sealing it in, making sure that any electrical connections were still accessible. This too was coated in insulation which will shatter off as the craft was blasted out of the rocket and into the sub-zero temperatures of outer space. All this work was going to take them to the wire, they will be pushed for time to get finished before the Apollo 11 mission blasts off for the moon. Once in space, Scott was on his own, no-one knew what was about to happen he would be on his own from then on.

Chapter 34

May 1969.
Launch date, T-Minus 70 days and counting!

The day had arrived, Bob gathered everyone together in the lab. They were finally finished. You couldn't tell that inside the enormous cylinder, a craft from another world was at rest, being housed ready for its planned journey home. The craft still contained the remote camera, it was useless without its power, the delayed live feed was gone.

Down in Area 49 the operation room was up and running, a whole wall of data reels, computer monitors and TV feeds. Everything was being recorded. The SIS had also placed a set of backup controls and a monitor station at Houston's Mission Control Centre, just incase. This was a large stand alone section that butted up to the existing stations, it had been made to look inconspicuous against the other monitoring equipment. It was a duplicate of the computer that was running Scott's program, to track and monitor the lunar module whilst it was on the Moon's surface. They couldn't have planned things better, from what Bob had witnessed, the craft was also running this program, it had been the plan they had in mind all along, he'd been working on it before he was acquired by the SIS to work in Area 49. SIS had employed him before he knew it, he thought NASA was signing his pay-cheques. They hoped to use this program to try and track the craft after it had been jettisoned from Apollo 11, Scott had done them a favour by being pulled into the craft that night months ago. They weren't to know that the craft was going to read Scott's mind and up-load the program for them. That was Scott's hidden real objective and the fact that he would have had to be onboard the craft as well.

Fiona had played a big part in Scott's life without him even knowing it, having been responsible for his wellbeing since high school. She was involved with Scott's high school doctor, this made it possible for her to keep an eye on him throughout his school days. Even though Scott didn't need to see the high-school doctor very often, whenever he did she would report to Fiona about why he'd been in. She had been monitoring his days at NASA and Area 49 since he arrived. All the samples and tests that Scott had provided, knowingly and unknowingly through his new toilet system and in the covert night time blood tests. Fiona had analysed the lot, making sure his diet had been kept right and he was ready for space travel. Most of which Scott knew nothing about.

The stage was now set for the imminent launch of the Apollo 11 mission, the only thing left to do was to get the section of Saturn V back to the assembly building. They knew they were pushing it with the speed the crawler took to get back down the tunnel.

"Stand back!" shouted Bob.

The blast doors started to open once more. They hadn't been opened since the package had arrived months ago. They screeched open along the metal track, sending a deafening high pitch frequency through every human's ears. Once the doors had come to a complete stop the trailer, which had brought the section of the Saturn rocket, was hooked back up to the truck and it started to move. This section of the rocket was still strapped on, it hadn't left the back of the crawler since it had arrived. They placed the cover back over the large cylinder for it's journey back down the tunnel, then once it arrived back at the Vehicle Assembly Building nobody there would know or could tell it housed an alien craft. All they had been told was there had been a delay on the design and manufacture of the S-II second stage, some problem at the North American Aviation company who was building this section. They needed an insulated bulkhead at one end to stop any fuel reaching the astronauts, incase of an explosion. They'd all bought it and set to work putting all the sections in-place at the Vehicle Assembly Building. The Saturn V was put together on the Mobile Launcher Platform, this was known as the MLP to everyone that worked at NASA. The MLP will then travel from the VAB to Launch complex 39A where the Apollo 11 mission was due to launch from.

T-Minus 57 days and counting!

The MVP started to move, very slowly with the Saturn V Apollo 11 mission resting on its back, carrying a very special payload. It would take approximately five hours for the MLP to travel from the VAB (vehicle assembly building).

Bob looked on in disbelief that the day was nearly here. The day so many had been working towards for years now. He watched the Crawler-Transporter as it headed off on its slow journey towards Launch Pad 39A. It was 57 days until the Apollo 11 mission was set to launch, 7-16-69 was the date that had been scheduled. Before then they had to do some vital checks, the first being a flight readiness test, then a countdown demonstration test and then the launch date. Making sure that everything went to plan, Bob was overseeing the involvement of operations from the SIS. Most of mission control would be based at Houston, Texas. But some operations involving the lunar module were still going to be monitored from the Kennedy Space Centre in Florida.

The crew had been in place for months, their names and positions were as follows;

Commander....................Neil Armstrong
Command Module Pilot....Michael Collins
Lunar Module Pilot..........Edwin 'Buzz' E Aldrin Jr

These men had been carefully picked, selected through a rigorous process. They had all been involved with the Apollo Missions for some time, Michael Collins had even designed the insignia that was to be displayed on the planned mission to the Moon. None of these men knew the real mission they were playing a major role in, a cover up beyond all cover ups.

T-Minus 30 days and counting!

Everything was in place, the checks and final tests on the Saturn V rocket were all going to plan. Scott was somewhere in there, somewhere within the vast structure about to be blasted off into space in the near future. Bob had been keeping an eye on things, overseeing the security and plans for the lunar mission, making sure nobody was getting suspicious. Kimberly was helping him with this, he'd been keeping a close eye on her because of the involvement with Scott he didn't want her to let anything slip. Kimberly knew what Bob was doing, she wasn't stupid, it was only a matter of time before Bob didn't need her anymore.
"Then what's going to happen to me?" she wondered, "It's not as if I can disappear. I know just how Scott felt now, a prisoner! Why did I agree

to all this. Hopefully one day I'll see Scott again."
She'd thought the same things every day, but her
thoughts were always shattered by the reality that
Scott would probably never come back!

Chapter 35

Launch Day

"All systems cleared for launch! Repeat. All systems cleared for launch!" came a voice over the airways as Bob listened to the man at mission control.

"Positions please! We're all ears Jack." Ordered Bob. "Let's wish him, I mean them! A safe journey and a speedy return home!" he added.

Deadly silence filled the room as they stood watching the launch pad from a safe distance, Kimberly stood to the side of Bob. She gave him a quick glance when he'd made the slip up. Her eyes widened, making him realise he'd said something wrong.

"God Speed!" Bob said under his breath as Jack King at Mission Control took over the airwaves.

Live from Mission Control
(NASA Apollo 11 transcript)

"Firing command coming in now, we are on the automatic sequence. We are approaching the three minute mark on the count."

"T-Minus three minutes and counting, T-Minus

three we are go with all elements of the mission at this time. We are on an automatic sequence says the master computer, which supervises hundreds of events occurring over these last few minutes."

"T-Minus two minutes and forty-five seconds and counting. The members of the launch team here in the control centre, monitoring a number of what we call 'Red-line values' these are tolerances we don't want to go above and below in temperatures and pressures. They're standing by to call out any deviation from our plans."

"Two minutes, thirty seconds and counting, we are still go on Apollo 11 at this time. The vehicle's starting to pressurise as far as the repellant tanks are concerned and all is still go as we monitor our status for it."

"Two minutes, ten seconds and counting. The target for the Apollo 11 astronauts, the Moon at lift-off will be at a distance of two hundred and eighteen thousand and ninety-six miles away. We've just passed the two minute marker on the count-down."

"T-Minus one minute, fifty-four seconds and counting. Our status board indicates that the oxidiser tanks in the second and third stage now have pressurised. We continue to build up pressure in all three stages here at the last minute to prepare it for lift-off."

"T-Minus one minute, thirty-five seconds. On the Apollo mission the flight to land the first men on the Moon. All indications coming in to the control centre at this time indicate that we are go."

"One minute, twenty-five seconds and counting, our status board indicates the third stage completely pressurised. Eighty second mark has now been past, we'll go on full internal power at the fifty second mark in the count down. Guidance system goes on internal at seventeen seconds, leading up-to the ignition sequence at eight point nine seconds. We're approaching the sixty second mark on the Apollo 11 mission."

"T-Minus sixty seconds and counting, we've past T-Minus sixty."

"Fifty-five seconds and counting. Neil Armstrong just reported back, it's been a real smooth count-down. We've past the fifty second mark, power transfer is complete, we are on internal power with the launch vehicle at this time."

"Forty seconds away from the Apollo 11 lift-off, all the second stage tanks are now pressurised."

"Thirty-five seconds and counting we are still go with Apollo 11."

"Thirty seconds and counting! Astronauts report it feels good."

"T-Minus twenty-five seconds."

"Twenty seconds and counting."

"T-Minus fifteen seconds, guidance is internal."

"Twelve, eleven, ten, nine, ignition sequence start, six, five, four, three, two, one, zero. All engine running! LIFT-OFF, we have a LIFT-OFF, thirty-two minutes past the hour. Lift-off on Apollo 11."

"Tower cleared!"

"We're gonna roll program," came the distorted voice of Neil Armstrong amidst the roar from the deafening engines.

"Neil Armstrong reporting their roll and pitch program, which puts Apollo 11 on a proper heading."

"Thank God for that!" Bob said whilst wiping the sweat from his brow.

"Plus thirty seconds."

"Roll complete… and has finished its program," was the update from Neil Armstrong just after thirty seconds of flight, adding, "One bravo," to the end.

"One bravo is an abort control mode!" added Mission Control.

"Altitude two miles" Beep.

"Apollo 11...Houston...You're good at one minute." Beep.

"Roger." Came the response from the Apollo crew.

"Down range one mile, altitude three....four miles now. Velocity two thousand, one hundred and ninety-five feet per second."

"Start model, pressure red line is lit... I don't... No it doesn't make a difference, no difference. Ok, let's punch them out. Everything is go, Jack." Said Neil from Apollo 11.

"We're through the region of maximum dynamic pressure now." Responded Jack.

"Yeah everything looks good here."

....

"Well, so far so good." Bob said as he turned to look at Kimberly.

Kimberly could hardly watch the launch, she was sure that something was going to go wrong. Her anxiety showed, as she peeped through her fingers to watch the screen for a split second. Repeating to herself, "It'll be fine! It'll be fine! He'll make it, I just know he will!"

"Will you relax Kimberly, you're making me nervous." Bob whispered into her ear as he reached for his hankie to wipe his wet brow.

"I'm ok, sorry Sir."

Bob walked to the back of the room and lifted the receiver on a large red telephone, pushing a few button as he did so. Kimberly could see his mouth moving but she couldn't make out what he was saying. Who was he talking too? She wondered. Placing the phone back onto the cradle, he walked back over to Kimberly with a content smile spreading across his face.

"What are you so happy about?"asked Kimberly.

"Everything is going according to the plan so far." Bob replied.

"What everything?"

"Yes, everything! All systems are working fine, reports from Area 49 are confirmed as going to plan!"

"Thank god for that!" Kimberly said as she let out a huge sigh of relief. "But you knew it would! Right?" She added.

"Yeah course I did," came his cocky reply. "We're not out of the woods yet though, there's still a rough ride ahead and the next few hours will be crucial in seeing if the plan really will work."

The live feed from the Capcom speaker burst into life once more, making Kimberly nearly jump out of her skin.

....

"Staging is complete and ignition…" Says Apollo.

"Apollo 11, this is Houston, thrust is go on all engines, you're looking good." Beep.

"Roger, we hear you loud and clear Houston." Beep.

"Houston be advised that visual is go today." Beep.

"This is Houston, Roger that."

....

As the Apollo mission headed on its path to the moon, nobody had a clue about its real mission. Could the SIS get away with sending a UFO back into space under the cover of this other mission?

Kimberly couldn't help but wonder if the astronauts would really make it to the Moon, or if they were really in that massive tube of highly flammable liquid? Would Scott get through this alive and return home one day? She had no answers to her questions.

Nobody could tell for sure what would happen when the section containing the craft was jettisoned. There was no trial run here like there had been for the Apollo 11 Mission, when they sent Apollo 10 into space a few months earlier just to make sure it could be done. A few people in NASA and the SIS hoped nobody could tell that the section in between stage two and stage three of the Apollo 11 rocket was slightly more bulbous than the same section on the Apollo 10 mission's rocket. This was the part that had been altered, re-designed for the craft to fit in. They seemed to have got away with it! So far!

Chapter 36

Three minutes and twelve seconds into the flight, the second section was successfully jettisoned. Bob and Kimberly waited with bated breath, hoping that nothing terrible would happen. All they wanted was confirmation from Area 49 that everything was going to plan. Bob was praying for the real mission, not the fact that we were about to achieve the greatest moment in human history. His mind was on the mission to return the craft home, whilst Kimberly was just hoping Scott was ok in the craft.

Nobody knew if he was still alive or if he'd died whilst being entombed in the craft months earlier, there was just no way of knowing. They hadn't been able to gain access into the craft before it was encased in the second section of the Saturn V rocket, ready for the Apollo 11 mission.

"Second stage jettison complete!" came the voice from Mission Control in Houston.

Just as the voice had stopped speaking, the secure phone rang, the one that Bob had used earlier to call Area 49. Bob answered in his deep voice. "Hello!" Holding the receiver to his ear, he just listened, then calmly placed it down again without saying another word.

"Well?" said Kimberly as he walked back towards her.

Nothing, he said nothing, not even sharing a content little smile this time.

"What's going on?" she whispered when he'd arrived back at her side.

His gaze never left the screen in front of him. They were intently watching the live feed from the remote cameras on the Saturn V, listening for anything that could jeopardise their mission. Approximately ten seconds after the second stage had Jettisoned, the explosive charges should have fired, propelling the craft deep into space. There was no way of knowing if this had happened without alerting someone to the other mission. They just had to wait for the call from Area 49.

The feed from the Saturn V was delayed slightly before it got to them, it was being diverted through Area 49 first before going anywhere else, for example the news crews and TV channels. The SIS were monitoring the feed so the public and NASA wouldn't see anything they shouldn't. Their feed suddenly went blank, just a black screen on the control panel in front of them. About ten to fifteen seconds passed with nothing, Kimberly feared the worst had happened, but then a flicker and another, a partial unfocused image flashed up and then again, this time the picture stayed on the screen. Bringing her hand up to her mouth and taking a large breath in, she waited, holding her breath, not moving a muscle. All the colour drained from her face in an instant, looking like she'd seen a ghost. To her relief the distorted, hazy image slowly came back into focus on the screen in front of her eyes and the voice from Mission Control started to speak once more. She let out the breath she'd been holding onto for what seemed an eternity, sighing a deep sigh of relief.

"We're sorry about the loss of communication there folks, we'll try our best not to lose it again."

"I don't know if I can take any more of this!" she said to Bob. "Please tell me what was said. Is everything ok?"
"Everything is fine."
 Bob continued to watch the screen. He hadn't seen anything that resembled the craft pass by. Thank God, he thought. That would have been it, all hell would have broken out if the cameras had shown that.
"Now we just wait." he said as he lit up one of his huge Cuban cigars, blowing the smoke high into the air above his head, which hovered lazily like a swirling cloud just beneath the ceiling.
 Things must be ok if he's lighting one of those up now, thought Kimberly as she nearly choked on the toxic fumes hanging in the atmosphere.
 A grainy black and white picture was all they were receiving from the remote cameras, they had been installed in each stage, pointed back towards the Earth, giving a birds eye view of everything that was happening miles above their heads. That's all they could do now. Wait!
 It wasn't long before their minds were put to rest, as the phone rang once again. Bob answered the call and listened, this time his look said it all. A smile, a content expression spread across his face.

Looking at Kimberly he grinned and she was reassured that all had gone ok. But how does he know that Scott was ok, she wondered. He didn't, all he knew was the mission was going to plan.

The message from the SIS at Area 49 said; "The explosive charges had fired and the craft was free from the second stage. The tracking signal wasn't responding as yet, but who knows when this would begin, it might not start until NASA have dispatched the Lunar Module on the surface." Scott had designed the program and he wasn't around to ask. He was on his way to the unknown. "How will we know if everything goes to plan Bob?" asked Kimberly.

Pulling Kimberly to the side in the monitoring room, Bob leaned over to her and whispered, "Keep your voice down, we can't afford any slip-ups here. If anybody hears you, that would be it. Not just for you and I, but for Scott too. They would pull the plug on all of this, and that's not what we want. Is it?"

Turning slightly away, her stomach was churning with the view of Bob's discoloured teeth and the stench from his Cigar tainted breath, it was making her retch.

"Ok, you're right. I'm sorry Bob, but I'm just so worried about Sc…"

Bob didn't let her finish before he butted in with a comment that sent spine chilling shivers through Kimberly's body.

"I would try and forget about Scott if I was you! You won't be seeing him any time soon, if at all! If he does ever return I'll be long gone by then!" With that Bob walked back over to the monitor and continued to watch the delayed feed from miles above their heads.

He will be back, one day, he will be back. Kimberly thought to herself.

BANG! BANG! BANG! The door flew open and in walked a soldier, stopping and standing to attention as he was confronted by Bob.

"At ease soldier."

Handing the Chief a piece of folded paper, then taking a step back, he awaited a response from Bob as he carefully opened and read the message. Calmly he folded it back up, placing it into his jacket pocket once he'd finished. Asking the soldier to lead the way, he followed the man out and closed the door without saying a word to the others in the room. This had Kimberly fearing the worst.

"Where are you g…" Kimberly shouted as the door closed, cutting off her last words. Shocked and stunned she froze for a minute before opening the door to see were Bob had gone. Kimberly looked left and then right down the long corridor, glimpsing Bob's jacket as he'd just turned the corner at the end. He was heading out! But where and what was going on? Hurrying down the long empty corridor, her high heels echoed as her steps speeded up, not the best for being discreet. She came to the corner and peered around it. "No!" The elevator doors had just closed. Running into an empty room where she could see outside to the front of the building, Kimberly saw Bob get into the back of a black Sedan and the car drove away at speed!

"No! Where is he going? What has gone wrong? I'll never catch them now!" she screamed.

The nightmare had begun in her mind, fuelled by nothing but her own wandering imagination, feeding her the worst kind of thoughts imaginable, a horror story was starting to unfold and she was the author.

Chapter 37

The black Sedan pulled-up outside another building, a smaller building in the middle of nowhere, 'Maintenance' was written above the door. Secretly this was where the SIS were delaying the live feed to the TV and news crews around the world.

Just inside the door a man was sitting at a desk, dressed in a boiler suit with a NASA logo on the breast pocket, surrounded by brooms, buckets, spades and all kinds of maintenance items. He was intently watching the Apollo 11 launch on a small TV screen, when the door opened, the man quickly stood to attention when he saw it was Bob who'd come in.

"At ease soldier." said Bob.

Bob showed his ID to the maintenance man. He took the badge, looked at it, then looked back at Bob, before turning a key on a drawer next to where he was sitting. A panel slid open beside where Bob was standing, revealing a flat screen, Bob placed his hand on it and waited for clearance as he looked around the room. The screen turned green and the room, from where the desk was situated, moved backwards, everything seemed to be moving, it looked like the room was extending. The walls with the brooms on and everything around him seemed to move away from where Bob was standing. A concealed entrance was slowly being uncovered in front of where he stood.

As the room came to a stop a light switched on revealing a staircase leading down into the floor. Bob casually walked down the secret staircase, breathing in the damp stale air as the floor slowly closed over his head when he was clear, placing the desk and all the items back into their original place in the room whilst the maintenance man carried on watching the launch on TV as if nothing had happened.

All alone, Bob found himself walking around a warren of tunnels, all slowly descending further into the ground. Bob finally opened a door which had the words, 'No Unauthorised Access' written in big red letters on the front. This was a smaller room with an unmanned desk, a bookcase and a water-machine, these were the only things that donned the walls. Covered in sweat, he loosened the collar of his shirt to try and allow some air down to cool him off, it was wet and tacky to the touch. He removed his jacket, as he did so he was hit by his own musky body odour, his armpits were drenched, it was no use, nothing was helping to cool him down so far. Pulling a cup from the water-dispenser he pressed the lever ready to drown his thirst and re-hydrate his body. There was a glug, then another but nothing came out. He tried again, then suddenly a jet of water hit the bottom of the cup, a build-up of pressure in the system must have released a plug of green slimy algae allowing the liquid to flow once more.

"I think I'll give that a miss," he said to himself as he placed the plastic cup on the desk leaving the green entity floating around in its very own pond.

Bob walked over to the bookcase and pulled on the top corner of a certain book, 'The Catcher in the Rye' this always made Bob smile. The bookcase released from the wall, making the same noise as if he'd opened a bottle of fizzy pop. A few pages of an open book on the desk fluttered in the residual breeze created by the sealed entrance. As the bookcase was pulled forward it revealed another long corridor. Stepping inside he took a deep breath in as a rush of cold air hit his sweat soaked shirt, freakishly relieving him of the humid conditions from where he had come.

Bang! The bookcase closed behind him. Bob had only used this entrance a few times but the door slamming behind him always startled him. The lights turned on as soon as the door slammed shut, illuminating his way, leading him off into the gloomy distance as he walked forwards. Faced with another door at the far-end, Bob placed his palm on a screen next to the door, just like the other security systems. The door slid open, only this time it opened into an elevator. Walking in, Bob stared at the far wall as he pushed the solitary glowing button on the panel next to him. No floors up on this one, just down!

Coming to rest with a bump, the wall Bob was staring at slid open and he stepped out into his office at Area 49. He watched the filing cabinet slide back into place behind him, concealing the secret doorway once more. This entrance had been created for whoever was in charge, to get out or get in quickly in case of an emergency. It certainly startled a few people when he showed up out of the blue.

Bob quickly changed his shirt for a freshly pressed one, which was hanging in his office, then ventured into the hangar. It looked very empty now that the craft wasn't in there. It won't be long before something else takes it's place, thought Bob as he walked out of his office and over to the monitoring room back in Area 49.

"We've picked something up Sir, I thought you'd better take a look!" said the man intently watching the live feed coming in from the camera. "If you just take a seat I'll have it up for you in a second Sir."

"We don't have seconds, hurry up man!" Bob's impatience was starting to show, his red face turning a deeper shade with every word.

The man started to rush and brought the live feed up on the screen in front of Bob.

"It's a bit grainy Sir, but this is what we caught on the remote camera. We cut it before anything was seen outside of these walls Sir."

Bob's face said it all, the plan had worked. There on the screen in front of Bob was the sequence of events as they'd happened in space only a short time ago. A brief glimpse of everything going to plan.

The second stage had jettisoned, then a few seconds later, a bright flash as the explosive charges propelled the craft into space away from the Saturn V rocket. The only problem Bob could see, was it had been propelled on a trajectory towards the Moon and not out into space like they'd hoped.

"Play that again please."
Bob must have watched the sequence fifty times, over and over again. He'd taken control of the machine in the end so the man could watch the feed as Apollo 11 ventured further into space.
"Amazing, just amazing!" Bob repeated.
"Who else has seen this recording?"
"Nobody Sir, just you, I, and the other team members down here Sir. Why?" Questioned the man.
"Why? Why? Oh nothing, it's just the most incredible cover-up in the course of history as we know it man. That's all!" stressed Bob. "Copy it and have it on my desk ASAP. Oh, and make sure nobody, I mean NOBODY sees this without my clearance. Have you got that?" he added.
"Yes Sir, right away Sir."
   Kimberly made her way back into the control-room where she had watched the launch with Bob. News and TV crews were littered everywhere outside the perimeter fence of the NASA complex. They looked like a plague of locusts, swarming around, all trying to get the best place to devour the unfolding events, spreading the news as quickly as they were receiving it.
   As soon as the Apollo 11 Mission was out of sight, the public who'd tried to get as close as they could to the launch, started to disperse, gridlocking the roads as they hurried home to continue watching the story on TV as it happened over the next few days.
"Why couldn't I go with Bob? What is going on?"
Kimberly sat down and tried to picture Scott

entombed in his new home, floating lifeless in space, surrounded by uncertainty. Struck by a fear of helplessness, Kimberly vacantly watched the screen in front of her, not knowing what to do.

Chapter 38

The chrome circular shape floated in space like a jellyfish in the ocean, its silky smooth surface soaking up the dark space around it, making it virtually invisible to the naked eye. The multi-coloured lights leaked out above and below the centre of the craft, casting a faint ghostly image in the dark emptiness as it headed on its new journey. They had no way of knowing what was happening, there were no cameras on, or pointing at the craft. Hope, was all they had now.

Hours went by without any word from Area 49, as the Apollo 11 mission travelled deeper into space with the craft slowly following. All eyes were on the cover-up mission to walk on the Moon, only a few people knew of the real mission going on in the background.

On the craft Scott lay dormant, in a state of hibernation, oblivious to everything that was happening. His body was alive. His mind? Nobody knew!

How would the craft be able to set its path home without anybody controlling it? He thought whilst looking down at himself lying in his pod. A glowing object passed the corner of his view, he turned round and saw something, someone. Someone stood at the front of the craft looking out, staring beyond the shell that protected them from the deadly vacuum of space.

"Space! Space? What the hell am I doing in space? What is happening, I should still be in the hangar at Area 49!" Scott looked around as his mind started to wander. There was another movement, then another. The glowing outlines of the beings were sitting up in their pods, whilst their bodies laid encased, motionless. Slowly, one by one, they walked over to where the first one stood. They all looked at one another making some kind of gesture or acknowledgement towards each other. Their hands passed through each other's as if they weren't real. They can't be, thought Scott as he stood beside himself, shaking his head to wake up. But he wasn't dreaming.

Scott looked up in disbelief, as he did so he tried to grab hold of something. He felt his legs turn to jelly, but then realised he couldn't actually feel them, a weird sensation flowed through his body, not weightlessness more of a scared, terrified feeling. The craft didn't seem to have a ceiling, all Scott could see were the stars, like he was looking up into the clear night sky back home.
"Ok, this thing is in space, when were they gonna tell me that part of the plan?" He thought.

One of the things walked up the wall and stood on the side of the craft looking out, like he was standing on the inside of a doughnut's edge. The others joined him, it was like the craft was moving sideways, travelling the flat way. The being lifted his hands up and used his glowing finger tips on some kind of instrument panel which had lit up in front of him, moving its fingers over the objects and lights, Scott could see everything from where he stood. One of the being's leaned its head backwards and looked in Scott's direction, staring straight at him through his jet-black alien eyes. Scott took a step back away from his pod, and looked around just incase the being wasn't looking at him. But it was. The being's head was at the same level as Scott's, only it wasn't standing on the same floor as Scott. It was standing on the wall, or was Scott on the wall, or wasn't there anything called a wall in this craft. He suddenly remembered that he'd been able to make things happen inside the craft with the weird glowing gloves he'd worn.

It looked back and out into space, leaving Scott standing where he was. The beings started walking around the craft at this level, it looked like they were walking around a tube, each doing different things on different panels in front of them which popped up out of thin air. They were doing all this whist their bodies laid lifeless in their pods. Including Scott's.

What were they doing? How was all this happening? Thought Scott.

Are they able to project a mind's image of themselves, a holographic projection?

But how?

I wonder if they know it's me in this skin and not the being who was found dead, who's body is still stored at Area 51 years after the event? He couldn't answer his questions, he had no-way of knowing.

Scott came to the conclusion that they were trying to make the craft work again, he remembered communicating with Bob through the craft. Maybe that's it! He thought. Maybe they become part of the craft through their minds when they are held within the pods and are able to make it work as if they were actually here. That way they could travel vast distances through space whilst their bodies lay dormant, maybe their bodies were just another form of vessel, another craft sculptured to carry their mind in and keep it safe. Scott had all these ideas flashing up in his mind, he didn't know what was real or unreal anymore, were these thoughts being planted into his mind? He didn't know.

They didn't seem to be phased by Scott presence, he just stood there watching everything the aliens were doing. One of the beings walked down from the wall and stood near to its pod. It created a fantastic image of the solar system using the screens on its forearms and its glowing finger tips to do so, flicking through different universes until it stopped and brought up an image that Scott hadn't seen before. A planet very similar to ours! A planet that looked like it had three Suns and two Moons nearby. The image started to turn, this allowed Scott to see it more clearly. Two of the Suns were joining together, one merging into the other, but they were different colours. One was yellow, like fire, like our Sun but the other one that was colliding into it, was blue, bright blue. It looked like the blue Sun was swallowing up the other one, large bursts of yellow and blue flames blasted off into the surrounding space as the two Suns devoured each other. The larger Sun sat in the middle of the image with the two smaller Suns merging together as they orbited around the planet like ours. Then in turn they all moved around the larger Sun, just like we did here on Earth, orbiting our Sun.

Two Moons were in between the Earth planet and the merging Suns. The larger Sun looked a long way away from the planet, but where the two Suns where circling the planet, there was a orangey brown colour on the surface, like it had been burnt or scorched from these two Suns, mixed with a blue colour that could only be described as the oceans of the planet. But as the image rotated further Scott noticed that one side of the Earth-like planet was white, covered in ice or snow. The image continued to spin, as the merging Suns moved slowly around it showed the ice side was when the blue Sun was facing the planet. As this happened it was in turn shielded from the large Sun causing one side of the planet to be in a permanent ice-age.

The being must have communicated with one of the others, as another one walked down off the wall right up to Scott, stopping inches away from his face, its eyes looking straight through Scott as if he wasn't there. Then it continued over to where the image was being shown. Scott took a deep breath in as the alien passed right through his soul, as if that would help him somehow. The being just walked on as if he wasn't there, its particles trying to catch up after the disturbance of Scott's imaginary body.

Scott could see them pointing at certain parts of the image, their glowing blue outlines looked horrifying in the low multi-coloured light coming from the veins around the craft, their entities connecting with each other somehow. Scott couldn't hear anything, which made him think he wasn't in tune with them, but why? He wondered.

As the being stood next to the other one he too brought up a holographic display showing another part of the universe. It was our Solar System this time. They both stared at the two images, pointing and moving planets as if they weren't there, then placing them back into position. Another image appeared on the screen, a line! What was that for? wondered Scott. Then he remembered the image Bob had shown him, the line that had the wavy line under it. The suspected route the craft had travelled to get to Earth.

Plotting their way home, that's what they are doing, thought Scott, they're plotting their way home. They're making the plans to set off back to where they came from.

Scott sat down on the edge of his pod, on top of his own legs. That's funny, he thought as he looked at the pod. I can sit on this as if it's really there! He reached out to touch the pod, his hand passed straight through the substance that had filled and encased him, like it wasn't there, but then his hand stopped as it hit the base, the part that was fixed to the craft by these veins of coloured light. He bent down and touched the floor, his fingers illuminating as they drew nearer to the craft. He could swirl the lights around on the floor like he was caressing the surface of a moonlit pond. The swirls of colours intermingling, then slowly reforming and continuing to flow just as they were. He moved his hand away. Fascinating! He thought. Looking back over to the ghostly apparitions who were looking all around the holographic image, he couldn't help but wonder, would he ever make it home to Earth one day?

One of the being's slowly turned around leaving the image visible, he stretched out his arms and formed another control panel along another section of the craft. They seemed to be able to do these things where they pleased, as if the craft was alive somehow, reading their thoughts, helping them in all ways possible. The material that the craft was made out of seemed to have a mind, or a memory of some kind. It could be pulled around and formed into many different shapes and sizes, moulding and changing as and when the beings instructed it to.

Scott noticed on the new control panel a message written across the surface somehow, it said;

'DARK MATTER FUSION REACTOR DRIVE'

This message was in English, then it all flipped and spun round forming some new symbols and letters. That must say the same in their language, thought Scott.

Dark matter fusion reactor drive! What the hell could that be? Scott asked himself.

"Zero gravity! Of course," he said. "Need to be in space! That was the message from the craft, or was it from one of the being's trying to communicate with him? That's it," he suddenly realised, "the craft needs Dark Matter as fuel. They must have found a way to contain this phenomenon, it's only a theory on Earth that this stuff really exists. It must do!"

Scott's mind was gaining knowledge by the

second but he didn't have anyone to share it all with. Standing up he plucked-up the courage to try and walk onto the edge of the craft. It must be easy with this rounded shape inside the craft, he thought, as he placed one foot onto the slope and then the other, jumping as he did so. He held his arms out to his side trying to help him balance, so he didn't float off into space.

"This is amazing," he said to himself as he looked out into the far reaches of space. There, far in the distance he could see the faint glow from the after-burners, coming from the back of the Apollo 11 mission as it headed towards the Moon. The craft was following directly behind, on the same course.

At the front of the craft, Scott could see something happening. The spinning sphere of light in the centre of the craft had intensified, the speed of the ball became faster and faster with every second that passed. Small streaks of electricity, like forks of lightning reached out from the front of the craft. Looking like some kind of tentacles from an alien jellyfish hunting its pray, feeling for something in the darkness beyond its reach. They danced in the vacuum of space, creating a spectacular light show for all in the craft to witness. There were four in total, all searching, all knowing exactly what to look for.

Then one stopped, then another and another until finally the fourth streak of lightning came over to where the others had stopped. It formed a shield, creating an electrifying globe around absolutely nothing, no bigger than a tennis ball. The lightning started to retract back towards the spinning ball of light in the centre of the craft. Protecting their find, the forks of lightning wrapped all around the invisible bounty from space.

As the tentacles neared the alien jellyfish, they turned around ready to feed their find to the gluttonous sphere at the heart of the mysterious craft. Hesitating at the entrance to the ball they waited and waited. Then, the sphere slowly turned red, then bright red, until it passed the spectrum and returned to a bright white light. The deep misty coloured clouds contained within the heart of the craft dispersed and the sphere was empty, it was ready. Ready to be refuelled with the enigma that is Dark Matter. The veins of light running throughout the craft slowly followed in-suit, draining the colour from within, leaving the inside bathed in an eerie white glow.

Slowly the forks of lightning continued to feed their invisible find into the Dark Matter Fusion Reactor, placing it in the dead centre of the core, inside the Fusion Engine. Scott walked down from where he'd watched this live show and headed towards the centre of the craft, his eyes were nearly popping out behind his holographic alien mask, his mind was blank, lost for words as to what had just happened. He could only imagine what lay in store for him, as his journey had only just begun.

Chapter 39

Bang! Bang! Bang!

Kimberly nearly jumped through the roof as she was lost deep in thought, daydreaming about what was happening to Scott up there in the realms of space. A soldier walked into the room, the same soldier that had come for Bob, asking for her to accompany him. Without hesitation she followed the soldier out of the room, down the corridor and into the elevator, they walked out of the building and got into the back of the same black Sedan that had picked Bob up earlier. The driver started the car as soon as the soldier sat down beside Kimberly on the back seat. The car was stiflingly hot, all the windows were wound up and there wasn't a breath of fresh air coming in on the hot launch day.

Kimberly was driven around to the building she normally entered in and was asked to report to her area. On leaving the car she took a huge breath in as the dry air in the car had nearly suffocated her. I could have walked here, it would have been much better than been stuck in the back of that car. She thought to herself.

On entering the building she had to show her ID badge to the security guard on the main desk. A large sweaty man, dressed in a guards uniform looked like he'd just got out of a swimming-pool, he was so wet, it was running off his brow and dripping onto his chest. She handed over the ID, he looked at it and asked Kimberly a question;

"I hope all's going to plan out there today?"

"What! Erm… What do you mean?" replied Kimberly, not knowing how to respond to his question, she immediately turned defensive.

"Ok, keep your shirt on!" said the man, as he sat back down in front of his fan, which he'd placed on his desk to try and keep him cool.

Clearly that doesn't work! Kimberly thought, as she hurried off down the corridor trying to clip her ID badge back onto the top of her skirt, dropping it once or twice as she did so, this got the guards attention, not because she'd dropped it but because he'd noticed her bending down to pick it up again. He let out a quiet wolf whistle in harmony with a squeal from his chair as it took the strain from his large sweaty body once more. Kimberly looked round to see what had made the unusual noise, only to catch a glimpse of the man as he went out of view. She slowed her speeding foot-steps down to a walk and made her way to the elevator.

When it arrived the doors opened, like a jewellery box filled with music only to reveal an empty shell. Thank God for that! Kimberly thought as she placed her key into the special keyhole. "I'm a nervous wreck!" She said whilst pushing the button surrounded by faint music. "I hate these things!" She said as she started her descent to Area 49.

As the elevator came to a stop she retrieved her key and waited for the doors to open. They didn't! She pushed the button again and still nothing, she tried the alarm button. Still nothing, as she waited and waited her fear was growing by the second that something was wrong. The temperature was getting warmer and warmer inside the steel box dangling on the end of a long wire. A phobia had troubled Kimberly since childhood, it starting to show it's menacing face again. The fear of being stuck in a confined space, she was extremely claustrophobic, it terrified her. It all started when her big brother pushed her into an old bomb shelter in their back yard, he blocked the door shut for ages until her dad found her hours later curled up in a tiny ball, shivering with fear.

Sitting down in the corner of the box with only a faint light and the annoying music as company, Kimberly placed her arms around the tops of her legs and curled up into the very same tight ball she'd done all those years ago. Her back pressed into the elevator wall as she remembered the chilling incident, the memory of which had been stirred up from the past. Fearing the worst, her mind began to wander. "Why today? Why now? What's going on?"
"HELP! HELP!" She screamed over and over again at the top of her voice.

Kimberly looked up and saw the red light coming from the security camera which monitored the elevator. She'd had an idea! Standing up, she jumped, trying to get the attention of whoever was watching it, trying to alert them that someone was trapped in there. Shouting as she did so over and over, "HELP! HELP!"

This all seemed too surreal for Kimberly, being so stressed, shouting for help, yet listening to the soft tunes piped in from somewhere. Trapped in this box she'd used for years. It was no use, nobody came to her rescue or raised the alarm. Placing her key back into the keyhole, she tried the button once more. This time something happened, something she wasn't expecting. The moment she pressed the button, the elevator plunged into darkness. Every light except the faint glow from the tiny red dot on the camera, went out, leaving her blind and trapped, but the music played on.

A few minutes went by until the emergency lighting switched on inside and cast a haunting red glow around the walls of the steel box. Her mind played tricks on her as she managed to see things that just weren't there. Kimberly curled back into her ball against the wall and closed her eyes returning to the noisy darkness once more, wondering if it was just her mind playing tricks. This didn't last long, only a split second, then her eyes opened wide, wider than ever. A faint sssssss, like a burst water pipe or worse still a gas-leak muffled the sound of the music in the background.

Kimberly looked around, she couldn't see anything at first. Then there in the gloomy red light a cloud of mist tumbled through the air towards her, like a raging storm front moving in off the calm tranquil ocean. She clambered to her feet, using the walls of the elevator to help. The mist slowly devoured each of her shoes and then it started to rise, filling the steel box, eating all the available oxygen inside it. It wasn't long until the dense mist had engulfed most of Kimberly's body, she couldn't see her legs or her waist now as it continued to fill up around her.

A two foot air gap was all that was left above Kimberly's head as the mysterious cloud swallowed the rest of her body. Jumping up she gasped for air, or what was left of it. But it was no good, her movements made the gas swirl, causing a turbulent storm of toxic chaos. Holding onto her last breath, as there was no air left anywhere, she fought until the bitter end, until she couldn't hold out any longer. Her drowning breath came as she took a long oxygen starved lung full of the unknown cloud. The elevator vibrated as Kimberly's unconscious body hit the deck. Her crumpled figure laid face down on the cold steel floor of the suspended box. Still and lifeless, yet somehow the music played on, finding its way through the dense cloud as if nothing had happened.

There was a flash from the lights on the roof of the elevator, then another, until they filled with life again illuminating the residual cloudy air contained inside Kimberly's steel tomb. As the doors slid open the thick toxic smoke oozed out, dancing along to the faint disturbing music, spilling into the bright white corridor of Area 49. There was a quick glimpse of a gas mask, then another, disturbing the air as Kimberly's motionless body was turned onto her back and pulled along the cold floor, the back of her head bumping over the threshold of the sliding door to the elevator.

"Be careful!" came a deep bellowing voice. "She's not dead!"

Kimberly's body was dragged off into the distance, along the shiny marbled surface, leaving the cloud of smoke hanging in the air around the open doorway. The two men held one leg each as they pulled her lifeless body down the corridor before turning into a room and closing the door behind them.

Knock, knock, knock.

"Come in!" shouted Bob.

An agent dressed in a black suit opened the door and walked inside the room where Bob was watching the recording of the Apollo mission, closing the door before coming over to were Bob was bent over next to the screen. He lent forwards and whispered into the chief's ear, "Agent acquired Sir, should we proceed with or without you?"

Bob stood up and said to the man recording the live feed, "Remember what I said! Nobody sees that, NOBODY!"

With that Bob motioned to the agent to lead the way, he followed closely behind, mumbling, "I have to see her, I owe her that much at least."

Kimberly's body was lifted onto a surgical trolley, her arms and legs were strapped down and a needle was inserted into her arm ready to be hooked to a drip. A few men dressed in operating gowns stood around the room watching as one of them pumped a clear fluid into the soft skin on her arm. A few moments later Kimberly's body twitched, she took a deep breath in as she opened her eyes like a startled animal. Dazed and confused, she looked around the room trying to work out if she was still alive or dead. Struggling with the reality of her surroundings, she tried to move but was unable to lift her arms or legs. She couldn't understand why at first, then as she looked down she could see why. The straps that held her in place were cutting into her skin, it was as if once she'd seen the problem the pain arrived. Kimberly let out a loud scream as she tried to break free. It was no use, the more she struggled the worse the pain became.

"It's no good Kimberly, you won't get out of those straps." Bob said as he came into view over the top of Kimberly's head.

"Why? Why Bob? What are you going to do to me?"

"Your job is done now, you're not needed anymore Kimberly. When we're done here you won't remember a thing about where you came from or what you used to do here. It'll all be wiped from your memory. You became too close to Scott and we can't have a liability on the mission, it could jeopardise everything."

"No Bob you don't have to do this, I'm ok! I won't say anything to anyone. I can still help, I can." Kimberly said as she pleaded for her life.

"It's no use Kimberly, my orders are to leave No loose ends. Anywhere!"

Kimberly's eyes gently closed, fearing the worst.

"Where am I going? What are you going to do with me?"

"It doesn't matter Kimberly, I could tell you but it won't make things any different."

"Is this what you were going to do with Scott? It is, then you were going to send him off into space, weren't you?"

"That's right Kimberly, but he made it easier for us. He did it all by himself, we couldn't have done it any better. At least this way he still knows who he is."

One of the men dressed in a surgical gown held a syringe up and squirted a few drops into the air, just to make sure there weren't any bubbles in it. He then stuck the needle into the end of the cannula on Kimberly's arm then depressed the plunger until all the fluid had been pumped into her system, leaving the body's own blood flow to carry the fluid to her brain. It didn't take long for the serum to take effect. Kimberly's eyes closed and her body fell lifeless once more.

"You know what to do with her now, make sure nothing goes wrong." Bob said as he left the room and headed back towards mission control.

Chapter 40

As the Dark Matter sat dormant in the dead centre of the reactor, the fusion drive awaited its next instruction. The tentacles of lightning slowly retracted into the craft, disappearing as if they hadn't been there at all. The small ball of electricity protected the precious dark energy, waiting patiently for the reactor to do its job.

The beings calmly walked around the inside of the craft, opening screens and pressing objects that appeared out of nowhere, making all kinds of things happen around the craft. One of the beings walked over to one of the seats facing a pod and sat down. The chrome chair moulded around the figure of the being and then reclined backwards allowing the alien to look out into space. Bringing up its forearm the alien looked at the screen and pressed something. The tips of the fingers started to glow as the being spread out its hands. Two chrome coloured tubes rose from the floor either side of where the projected image of the being had sat down, stopping beneath each hand and turning into two large spheres with a flat section facing the ghostly alien.

As the being tried to make contact with the screens, tiny fingers of static electricity crackled off the surface until the connection was finally made. Its fingers speedily working the symbols on the screen. A projected three dimensional image appeared in the air in front of the being, it was outlined in a bright blue light. One of the others walked over and stood beside the seated alien, staring at the display. It then started manipulating the image with its glowing hands, pulling parts here and there, flicking sections off the image that it didn't need.

Scott was still sitting on the edge of his pod watching the beings work with fascination, he didn't have a clue what they were doing but he was transfixed with their speed and capabilities. Just then an image of Earth showed up on the holographic display, the being beside it reached into the three dimensional image and turned the planet around. A red dot flashed, it looked like it was the same red light that Scott had seen when he'd looked at the image in the craft.

It was flashing in the ocean just off the coast of Ireland. What could that be? Could it be some kind of Earth beacon? Something that they used to locate our planet, a homing signal? Thought Scott.

Just then the other two beings in the craft returned to their seats and sat down, as with the first being, the chair moulded around the image of the being and reclined backwards so they were all looking out of the top of the craft, or was it the front? Scott was so confused now as to what the hell was happening, he just continued to watch in amazement.

The other beings sat down and brought up their own displays in front of them, slightly different to the first ones, these controls had a hand print on them. They all stopped and glanced over in Scott's direction. He looked at them, each one in turn, not knowing what to do. If they'd been saying anything to him he couldn't hear them, as he allowed his gaze to bounce from one to another.

"What? What?" Scott said over and over in his mind.

One of the beings looked at Scott then looked at the empty seat in front of the pod he was sitting on. They can see me! He thought, as he cautiously stood up and moved over to the seat. He stood in front of the chrome coloured thing that resembled a large chair, he just looked at it, the beautiful flowing veins of light could be seen moving just under its chrome coloured skin. Scott tilted his head and placed a hand on his chin, wondering what would happen if he actually sat down in it. He looked back at the being who'd ushered him towards his seat. Stopping what it was doing to gaze over in Scott's direction again, the being stretched out its arm inviting him to sit down.

Scott turned around and slowly bent his knees allowing his body to make contact with the chrome material of the seat. As Scott was only a projection of himself, he had no feelings at all, he couldn't sense if it was cold or hot, painful or comfortable. Scott felt small as he climbed onto the seat, though he was tall he was still short for the size of this chair. It moulded around his image and encased the projection of his body, it did all this as it reclined and faced Scott the same way as the others in the craft.

The screen on Scott's arm lit up and his finger tips had started to glow, he brought it over and held it up in front of his face to see what had happened. There in the middle of the display was a flashing symbol, he brought his other hand over and pushed it. He didn't realise this symbol was for the two tubes either side of his seat, they raised up from out of the craft, it was amazing to watch, like the craft was alive, everything the beings needed was there at the touch of a symbol on their screens. This craft must have a memory or is it alive! Somehow they can control everything, he thought.

Scott reached out towards the two hand prints on the control spheres that perched on the top of the tubes. Scott had watched these grow as the seats had reclined backwards, the two tubes now looked like the eyes from a weird looking snail, protruding and bending over with two handprints as pupils looking towards the beings in the chairs. The handprints burst into life with a multitude of bright colours contained within the indentation of the shape. He didn't have to do anything, apart from place his hands onto the glowing imprint that lay before him. Scott hesitated as he inched his hands ever closer, sending fireworks of static around his hands until they were pulled in to make contact. The being who'd sat down first was working the screen on his controls, he did it faster than Scott's eyes could track its finger movements, they just looked like a blur, the speed they were moving.

Just then Scott saw something moving above his head, he strained his eyes upwards to see what had caught his attention, he noticed another tube, this time something was being formed from the top of the seats they were in. The tube was about one foot in diameter, as it extended, it bent over the top of Scott, as if it was looking at him. The same thing was happening above each of the other beings, all in unison. Then the tubes thinned down, the chrome colour was being sucked away by the veins of coloured material, leaving a very recognisable object hanging in the air.

Left dangling from a thin strand of the light filled chrome material was something that glistened in the glow cast by the craft. Scott was shocked at what he could see, his gaze not leaving the object that hovered above his head. A clear yet cloudy crystal skull held on by a tiny vein slowly descended into the projection of Scott as he laid down looking out into space. There was nothing he could do, it was like he was mesmerised, being hypnotised by the beauty of the lights dancing around inside the crystal skull. The skull lowered into Scott's head, sitting perfectly, taking its place inside his projected alien image. As it lowered he saw what looked like a suction cup of soft flowing lights sucking, holding the skull in place, the same thing happened to each of the beings, a crystal skull was placed inside their heads as they laid looking out into space. The being's bright blue outline intensified as the connection was made, one by one they glowed like a beacon at sea, as the skulls were positioned in place.

The thin vein of chrome light stayed attached to the skull, holding it right between the eyes with this weird kind of suction on the end. As the crystal skull connected with Scott his outline intensified too, he glowed bright blue, then as his projection calmed down again, he noticed the other beings. Scott could see their crystal skulls through their outlined image, only this time it wasn't very clear, becoming more cloudy. The skulls had changed, as if something was happening inside them.

Scott's thoughts started to get scrambled, like he was picking up mixed messages from somewhere. From the position Scott was sitting, he could see his body lying in the pod, the monitors checking his vital signs on the side were going mad, they were fluctuating all over the place. His body was doing something inside the pod. A projected image of the skull that was now controlling his mind was displayed in front of him, it slowly rotated around showing in detail every contour, every colour in all its glory.

I wonder if I'm meant to be doing something now? He thought to himself.

"No! Leave it to me."

Startled Scott tried to look around, making the glowing vein move whilst holding the crystal skull in its place. "Who said that?" Scott thought.

"I did."

An image of one of the beings came into Scott's mind, he didn't know if it was in his imagination or whether it was real. The voice echoed in his head, somehow he didn't hear it but it seemed to have been projected into his mind somehow.

"Who are you? Are you real?" thought Scott.

"Yes, I'm very real. I'm sitting to your left." Came the projected mind voice again.

Scott looked over, once again making the vein move to keep the skull in place.

"Hello." The being motioned its hand towards Scott as it stared his way.

How can I hear the being's voice, this can't be happening. He thought to himself as he continued to look at the being staring back at him. There were a few moments of silence before the being's voice could be heard again. Not knowing what to do, Scott slowly brought his gaze back looking out into space. Then the voice started again in Scott's mind. As he looked back towards the being he thought was speaking, Scott noticed a bright red pulsating colour, deep inside its crystal skull. It was kind of cloudy in appearance and intensified with each word Scott could hear, then calming down in between. Scott listened to everything the being had to say.

"The crystal skulls allow us to communicate with any species, we can talk and you will hear what we say in your native language. These skulls are our life line, they help us to navigate around the universe, our interstellar communication gateway. We have them placed all over, they are held on planets that we visit, planets that our ancestors have visited for millions of years. Usually they are hidden but sometimes species can uncover them. Earth has done just that! But they don't know what powers they have. They can open up gateways in time and space. We use them to find pathways and communicate between distant galaxies."

"But how? How can you travel those distances in your lifetime? It's just not possible. Is it? asked Scott.

"Yes, it's been possible for millions of years, but

what you call years some other species might not. Your galaxy is still quite young and you have a lot to learn. We keep giving you a hand every now and then, just to help out. But we can't do too much."

"How?"

"All will be revealed Scott, all will be revealed in good time, but for now just lie back and enjoy the view."

"But, but... I have lots more questions."

The voice in his head fell silent, not another sound crossed his mind. How is this all possible? He thought again and again, running through everything that had been said by the being lying beside him.

Crystal skulls? What are they all about? He'd heard of some being found dotted around on Earth, nobody had a clue they were from an alien race who'd visited us in the past. The ones Scott had heard about were deemed as fake nineteenth century sculptures, carved with modern tools. Maybe they were carved with modern tools, just not our modern tools? He thought.

Scott's thoughts were suddenly scattered, as his hands held onto the two weird looking objects either side of his seat, they somehow felt fixed there, he couldn't move them one bit. Just then from the back of each came a streak of lightning, it reached out towards the sphere housing the dark energy, extending from each control sphere beside the beings, eight in total. They wrapped around and caressed the translucent ball that was connected to the craft in its centre.

The sphere started to glow from within, a dance of

creation, particles of matter bounced all over inside the clear globe. Patterns of colour erupted right before their eyes, the creation of pure energy had begun, encapsulated in the reactor. The particles were trying to gain access to the Dark Matter, attracted somehow, breaking down the walls of the electrified prison with their bombardment of positive energy.

Then, slowly at first, the encasing electrified wall gradually succumbed, allowing a particle through to meet with the Dark Matter. The coming together of their entities caused them to collapse, creating an implosion within the sphere. Utter chaos unfolded within. Then after the positive matter had raged war against the Dark Matter all that was left in the controlled reactor was a glimmer of hope, a flicker of creation, energy in its most pure form.

Just then a tiny dot of unimaginable power lit the clear sphere, the brightest pin-prick of light Scott had ever seen. It broke into life becoming brighter by the second, until the light engulfed the ball. The streaks of lightning coming from all their controls stopped instantly, their slightly tilted head position made them able to watch the unfolding events inside the sphere at the centre of the craft.

Suddenly an intense flash of light, like an atomic bomb going off shattered the now tranquil demeanour of the inside of the craft. Its power resonated out and into the surrounding space, like an imaginary rock had been dropped into the stillest of still ponds, casting an invisible ripple out into the realms of space. Scott imagined it like a star silently exploding in unknown regions of space, sending a shockwave of inconceivable power, off into infinity.

Clouds of flashes like an electric storm filled the sphere, lights strobed into the craft making it hard to see even through Scott's projected lenses. The clouds of flashing lightning slowly tumbled around inside the globe, until a slight hint of colour broke the mist. It was bright under the thunderous clouds in the sphere. Cracks started to appear all over the surface of the turbulent storm, transcending into a multitude of beautiful colours. Once more the calmness of pure energy flowed and filled the heart of the craft awaiting its orders.

Chapter 41

"Be careful!" shouted the man who'd just hooked up the drip attached to Kimberly's arm. "She is still alive, she's still human, for God's sake have some respect man."

"Sorry!" replied the man who'd just allowed Kimberly's head to drop onto the hard surface of the wheeled operating trolley, as they prepared her to be moved out of Area 49.

Waiting outside of a secure entrance was an ambulance, its engine running, ready to take Kimberly away. The men pushed her lifeless body back along the corridor towards the elevator. The doors had remained open since Kimberly had been gassed, to allow any remaining sleeping agent to disperse, leaving the air looking slightly murky. A faint tune from the elevator music could be heard through the mist in the distance as the men slowly wheeled the trolley down the marbled corridor.

Just before the men entered the mist, they stopped the trolley, one of them bent down and reached under the sheet that covered her beautiful body, he pulled out two gas masks and handed one of them over to the other man. They pulled them on and headed through the toxic remains into the steel box. The wheels bounced over the threshold and the attached drip holder waggled in the air as they stopped the trolley once more. As the men stood each side of Kimberly they both looked up towards the security camera, then at the same time they both gave a nod. The doors started to close, trapping them inside with the tranquil annoying music as the elevator began its ascent to the surface.

As the men were standing in the steel box a low suction noise started above their heads, slightly drowning the deathly boring sounds coming from the hidden speaker. It was clearing out any remains of the gas before they reached the top, expelling them into the chamber, then out into the air above the NASA building.

The image of the two masked men standing either side of Kimberly's covered body must have been a haunting sight for anybody watching on the monitor. They hadn't moved a muscle all the way up, they just stood there looking forward listening to the medley of awful music. Then the elevator came to an abrupt stop, causing the men to judder slightly.

"Finally! We're here! That seemed to take forever." Came a muffled voice from behind one of the gas masks.

"You're right there man and that music doesn't help! I'll be glad when we're out of here and sipping on a nice cold one." Came the response.

Each man pulled off their gas mask and placed them under the trolley out of view. They then looked back up at the camera and nodded. The doors began to open and the men were greeted with a bunch of irate employees complaining about the elevator taking too long.

"Stand aside! Stand aside! Please. Coming through!"

They shut up when they saw the trolley being pulled out very quickly. The sheet draped over the human body was flapping in the turbulence cause by their speed, the fluid in the drip started to bubble as Kimberly was whisked away. The two men headed down the corridor and around a corner, towards the emergency exit at the back of the NASA building.

"That was close!" said one of the men as he opened the exit door.

"It certainly was!" came the reply from the man squeezing the bag on the drip holder, as he tried to reduce the amount of bubbles.

   Swinging open the emergency door, the two men were greeted by some flashing blue, white and red lights that donned the roof of the ambulance that was waiting to take Kimberly. The back doors were open and two ambulance men stood there ready. They had to transfer Kimberly onto another trolley that was out and waiting. One man unclipped the drip bag and replaced it onto their holder, then they slid Kimberly's body over on the spinal board she was laid on. The two medics then placed a strap around her body and wheeled it towards the opening of the ambulance, banging the front of it into the vehicle, this caused the trolley to collapse underneath. It folded up as they continued to wheel it forward until it was in its place. One man jumped inside with Kimberly whilst the other medic closed the doors, then without a word he jumped into the drivers seat and sped off at high speed with the siren blazing.

"That could well be the last we see of her!" said one

of the agents.

"Where do you think they'll take her?" questioned his colleague.

"Your guess is as good as mine bud." Came his reply. "Speaking of Bud, how about it? Fancy a cold one?" he added.

"That's the best thing I've heard all day, our job is complete for the time being. That is until they decide to do away with someone else!"

"I hope it's not any time soon, I hate this part of things. She's been part of this Area for years now, working alongside everyone without any problems. It's just awful when people are no longer needed or just know too much that this has to happen to them."

"Yeah, your right. Let's just hope it's not one of us next time eh?"

"Shoot! I hadn't even thought of that!!!"

"Come on, let's go and get that cold one, there's nothing we can do about it anyway, we both know far too much as it is."

   With that thought in mind they both headed off towards their shiny black Sedan which was parked just around the corner of the building. All this was happening under the smoke screen of the first manned mission to the Moon. There were people rushing everywhere, technicians, commanders, security, you name it and they where there on this historic day. Some spectators still standing squinting up into the sun drenched sky, were trying to watch the last little vapour trail coming from the Apollo rocket, as it headed of into the infinite deep blue void of space.

Deep down in the depths of Area 49, Bob had returned to his office. He sat in his large swivel chair facing a photo he had on his desk, the same photo that been taken just after Scott had joined the team and Kimberly was working alongside him. It was placed next to some other pictures of Bob's late wife and his son's graduation photo. It showed Kimberly standing beside Bob, along with Scott at the other side, they each had a cheeky grin from laughing at Bob's squashed image on the surface of the craft. All three were positioned just in front of the craft as it waited to be sent on its return journey into the unknown.

Plagued with guilt, he stared into the eyes of Kimberly and Scott, trying to find some kind of solitude or forgiveness for his actions, but he couldn't. He was following orders. Again! "What have we done? These things can't be right, it's like we are living on another planet sometimes!" He said to himself as he picked the photo up. Giving it one last look, before slowly opening his desk drawer, placing the frame inside and finally closing it.

"How many more good people are going to be lost trying to find the answers we all gravely seek?"

Bob's hard shell had melted away for an instant as he started to have flash backs to George and Linda, Scott's parents, "If only they had the same drug that had just been used on Kimberly back then, there wouldn't have been any need for them to go missing the way they did."

Bob's sensitive side hadn't been seen by many he had to remain cool, calm and disciplined in his role at Area 49, if he didn't he wouldn't be able to cope with things like this. Taking a deep lung-full of air, Bob tried his hardest to brush off the events that were unfolding so quickly before him.

"I have to get on with things, we still have work to do and Scott is still up there somewhere, God only knows where, but hopefully he's still alive."

Bob pulled himself together and headed out of his office and back towards the monitoring room to check on the progress of the craft and the Apollo mission.

It was now three hours into the mission, everything had gone to plan so far, well so they all presumed. As Bob entered the room filled with TV screens and computer monitors, he asked the lead controller what was going on. That meant; give me some damn good news, in Bob's language.

"Everything is still on schedule with the mission as far as we know Sir."

"That's good to hear. Finally some good news, let's all hope and pray this works."

Bob sat down in a chair and pulled out one of his large fat cigars, he bit the end off and flicked open his Zippo lighter, all in one swift motion, it was opened and lit, ready to fire up the Stogie. The end flared bright orange as he took a deep relaxing lungful of his meaning of the word fresh air. His eyes closed and he laid back in the seat, soaking up the comfort he found in the addictive indulgence. Holding his breath for a while before blowing some Indian smoke signals into the air above his head. He watched as it dispersed, and the lazy smoke floated high up, hugging the ceiling, catching the drafts and slowly swirling as it faded into thin air, disappearing from sight just before another one took its place.

His cool, hard demeanour returned as he flopped forward in his chair and looked at the monitor in front of where he was sitting, through his dense cloud of tobacco smoke he began to ask some questions,

"Has anything happened? Have you seen anything of the craft since it jettisoned from the section of the Apollo rocket?"

"Nothing to report as yet Sir, the Apollo 11 mission is going to plan but…"

The man wasn't allowed to finish;

"I'm not bothered about the Apollo 11 mission man, has anything happened to our mission, the real mission!" he said with a kind-of frustrated calmness to his tone.

"No Sir, we haven't seen anything of the craft since it jettisoned from the section."

"Damn, I knew you were going to say that. How long has it been now? How far are they?"

"Not sure Sir, Capcom will be able to tell us that Sir."

"Well, don't just sit there man, try and find it out, we need to be on the ball here, if we slip up we'll all be up the creek without a paddle. Tell me when you find anything out, and I mean anything." Bob said as he studied the monitor intensely.

He watched and watched for anything that would give him a clue as to where Scott was. There was no sign or signal being picked up from the craft at that moment, they didn't have any idea where he could be or what was happening. They didn't even know if he was still alive! All they were picking up were the transmissions from the astronauts as they went through numerous checklists and data.

The time passed by in slow motion, only minutes had passed every time Bob looked at his watch, when he'd thought it had been hours, then the hours turned into days. Nothing! Not a thing, no sighting, no nothing! Bob was starting to fear the worst now and started to think the mission had failed,
"What does this mean for Scott? What does that mean for me and everyone else involved with the mission?" His thoughts were scattered all over the place as he continued to watch and wait for something. Something that would just give him a glimmer of hope, something to say that the mission was going to plan, something, anything.

He laid his arms on the desk in front of him and nestled his forehead onto his crisp white shirt sleeves, his actions were that of a worried man. He knew that they were in for a long wait, but just how long nobody knew.

That was until now…

Chapter 42

Two days and nearly two hundred thousand miles into the space flight, Area 49 intersected a confused message from the Apollo mission saying; "Houston, Houston! Do you have any idea where the S-IVB is in respect to us?" The voice of Buzz crackled over the silent airways from the now distant Apollo Spacecraft.

Bob's head shot up like he'd been stung by an angry scorpion. "Intercept that transmission NOW!" ordered Bob.

All the mission communications had been directed through Area 49 before going on to the main Capcom. They had to be the first ones to know if something had started to happen with their mission, they couldn't risk the mission been blown now.

"Roger, standby!" replied Area 49.

"Ha, what is it?" Buzz exclaimed.

"Can we have some explanation for that?" asked another voice from the Apollo Spacecraft's intercom.

"We have not, don't worry continue your program!" came the calm response from what they thought was Houston.

"Oh boy it's a, it's, it, it is really something, similar to, fantastic really! You, you could never imagine this!" was the confused garbled reply from Buzz.

"Roger, we know about that, could you go the other way, go back the other way!" Were the orders from

Bob to the man speaking into the microphone. They needed to see what the astronauts were seeing. "Well, it's kind of round yeah, pretty..spectacular....g..my.......what is that there?" Buzz said excitedly. "It's hollow, what the hell is that?..."

Area 49 didn't allow the astronaut to finish before saying, "Go Tango. Tango!" This was the call sign that told the astronauts to switch channels on their communications, it also meant the mission was still intact. If this was called out, the mission was still all systems go just in a covert manor, with no public or NASA broadcasts. The only people listening were in Area 49.

Bob was writing things down for the controller to say, it became very hectic all of a sudden, Bob was finding it hard to keep up with the messages that filled the airwaves. He was watching the grainy screen that was right in front of him, trying to see the object that the astronauts were talking about. He couldn't at first but then as the camera swung by it picked up the outline of something, something that resembled the craft, a large dark object floating in space near to the Apollo module. It was casting the odd shimmer on its surface, as it tumbled slowly beside them on their way to the Moon.

Suddenly, it burst into light, Bob knew what was coming next from the astronauts.

"Hey! There's a kind of light there now!" said Buzz. The man waited for a second for Bob to write down his next message. He was deep in thought, thinking out loud about what to do! "We need to get them onto the secure channel, why haven't they changed it yet?" This was just incase anybody, like the press, was monitoring the mission from outside the space centre. He quickly scribbled something down for the man to read.

"Get them to change channel... NOW!" shouted Bob, as a red mist spread across his face.

"Roger, we got it, we watched it, lose communication! Bravo Tango! Bravo Tango! Select Jezebel, Jezebel!" were the words Bob had written.

".....Yeah.....ha......but this is unbelievable!"

"We'll call you up. Bravo Tango! Bravo Tango!" said the man, who'd followed Bob's orders as he breathed his cigar breath all over him.

With that the airwaves fell silent for a few seconds while the astronauts proceeded to change the channel. Even though Area 49 were intercepting the transmission, they couldn't be too careful as to who was listening, at least if they changed to this channel they knew it was secure.

"Apollo 11, this is Mission Control."

They heard nothing...then after a few seconds the response from the astronauts could be heard repeating themselves over and over again, as if they were losing communication.

"Roger, Houston this is Apollo 11, come in... Roger, Houston this is Apollo 11, come..."

"We read you Apollo 11, this is Houston...Over."

"Roger. Thought we'd lost you then Houston... Over."

"No, we hear you loud and clear, stay on this frequency, I repeat, stay on this frequency...Over."

"Roger, ok."

"Now Apollo, we need to know what you saw...

Over."

"Roger. I can't explain it Houston, it was kinda round, shiny but dark, like a mirror but a weird shape. It was quite far away to see for sure, but it looked hollow in the middle, like an inner-tube from a car tyre. It was glowing from the centre, casting a bright light all over the outer surface... Over."

"Roger Apollo 11. Can you see it now?...Over."

"Yes...Over."

"Where is it in respect to you?...Over."

"It's still there Houston, it's right there along side us, about one hundred miles from us...Over."

"Roger Apollo 11, we hear you. Stay calm, this is what we want you to do. Monitor any changes you see, colour, shape anything at all you tell us straight away...Over."

"Roger Houston, we'll do that. On a safety level, is the mission still a go? I repeat, is the mission still a go?..Over."

"That's affirmative Apollo 11, the mission is still good to go. God speed boys, await further instructions...Over."

"Roger."

The communication from the astronauts went quiet for a while. This gave Bob and the others time to think, time to reflect on their mission which was now kind of going to plan. Something was happening up there, something that was out of their hands, they just had to leave it to its own devices and see what happened.

It wasn't long before the Apollo 11 crew could be heard over the airwaves again, "Houston, come in

Houston, this is Apollo 11…Over."

"Roger Apollo, go ahead…Over."

"Roger Houston, you said to tell you when something happened sir…Over."

"Yes, Apollo what is it? What can you see?"

"Houston the craft is glowing Sir, we have just hit what we thought was a pocket of turbulence, but that's not possible, there isn't any turbulence in the vacuum of space. It shook us bad Sir, real bad. Then we lost all power for a few seconds before it all turned back on as if nothing had happened… Over."

"Roger Apollo 11, are you all ok? Is everything still working properly?…Over."

"Roger Houston, we've proceeded with a safety check and things seem to be working ok now… Over."

"Could this have been a sun burst Apollo?…Over."

"Hard to tell Sir, it's stopped now, all seems to be working fine…Over."

"That's good to hear Apollo. What is it doing now? …Over."

"It just seems to be floating there, deep in space, glowing brightly…Over."

"Roger. What is its course?…Over"

"It still seems to be heading the same way as us Sir…Over."

"Roger Apollo 11, repeat your system check…Over."

"Roger Houston, system check on-going…Over."

Apollo 11 were unaware they were talking to Area 49 through all of this, Bob had just heard that things were very hectic at Houston as they hadn't heard from Apollo for a good few minutes. Bob stood up and walked around the room, his coffee cup clasped tight in his hand for fear of losing the only thing that was keeping him awake through all of this.

"What do we do now Sir?" asked the intercom man who'd been relaying all the questions to the astronauts.

"We wait! That's all we do now. Wait." Replied Bob as he slurped the dregs from the bottom of his cup.

Bob headed out back to his office to refill his coffee and await further communication from the men on board the Apollo mission. They were his eyes in space waiting for the real mission to take place. Only then would Bob know that Scott was ok.

Chapter 43

Calm beautiful colours glided around the surface of the sphere once more, sending a strong flow of energy along the craft's veins of life that had been starved for many years. The whole interior glowed, a network of tubes taking power to where it was needed from the heart of the craft. Scott watched in awe as the phenomenon unfolded before his projected eyes, he hoped he would remember this when, or if, he ever woke up again.

The skull was resting in place, still attached by the thin vein-like structure which now flowed with all the colours imaginable. The colours were feeding the skulls with a fountain of information, a constant bombardment of data and knowledge which had been gathered from the minds of the beings held within these jelly filled pods. It was all being uploaded into the heart of the craft. The continuous stream of optical lights filled the tubes just beneath the skin, flowing down into the hub of the UFO where nobody has ever been able to gain access.

Suddenly, the screens of all three of the being's forearms lit up at once, along with Scott's. Lifting his blue outlined arm up, he looked at the screen, finding it very odd that he could virtually see right through it, and the rest of himself for that matter. Looking at the screen he noticed a symbol flashing, it was the symbol for the parts that he'd allowed into his body. He'd remembered that from in his room at Area 49, that was something he now wished he hadn't done. That moment of madness could have cost him his life.

Scott pressed the symbol at the same time as the other beings, waiting for something to happen, he hoped that the things would somehow be expelled from his body and he'd wake up back in his apartment at Coco Beach. That didn't happen! Instead his glowing outlined body showed the objects as they started to glow brightly from within his projected image. He could now see what was about to happen, a thought ran through his mind like he was watching a TV programme. He could see a world, nothing like he'd ever seen before. It was as if he was looking at it from above, he could see things flying, hovering yards above the ground. Buildings that had huge circular platforms above them containing what looked like plants. Most of the ground was mounds of green with holes in, which looked like windows. These all spread out from a central structure resembling the craft Scott was in, only larger, a lot larger and it had circular impressions all around the top, these looked the same size as the craft Scott was in. "I've seen this thing before," he said, "but where?" Then he remembered, it was when he was inside the craft and he'd been shown a slide-show or film of certain things, that structure was one of them. It had hundreds of people walking away from it. "What could it be?" He wondered.

As he studied the image closely he could see all kinds of weird things, things he had never seen before. The central chrome coloured structure looked like it sat on some kind of housing, which was the same shape, just slightly larger underneath. As Scott looked he noticed that in the impressions on the top, something moved! Something lifted away from the larger object below, it was the same kind of craft as he was in, there were hundreds of them around the larger one, some missing and some still in place. Maybe this was a kind of craft too, something just like what Scott was in, only the size of a city.

The green mounds spread out from around the chrome coloured object, some had the weird looking platforms above and some didn't. Scott could see in the centre of the platforms was a dark patch, like a landing pad, then he saw one of the flying objects heading for one, it landed. "Wow," he said, "What is going on? This place looks amazing, I must be dreaming, or dead." Scott whispered, as his mind slowly came back to reality again.

Scott could see the other being's, they were laid in their seats moving their arms around in the air, as if they were operating some kind of invisible control panel. The finger tips of each hand were glowing bright blue, leaving streaks in the air from the speed they were moving. Each finger was doing something that could only be seen by its host.

All of a sudden, they all stopped what they were doing. They looked at one other then went back to a fixed gaze looking at the sphere in the centre of the craft. Scott was transfixed on the beings, he waited with anticipation wondering what was about to happen, he had the feeling of being a kid again on Christmas morning, hoping that Santa had visited his house, he had butterflies trying to undo the knots in his stomach as he waited and waited. Until he had to wait no longer. Each of the beings placed their hands on the pads at each side of their body. The chrome coloured material of the craft flowed up and over their hands, encasing each hand inside. The being to Scott's right looked at him and nodded forwards, ushering him to do the same. Scott tentatively raised his hands up and placed them in the same position as the other beings had done. The same thing happened to Scott. His hands were now fixed in place beside his body.

As he looked towards the other beings, he noticed that the coloured light was now flowing up through their arms and into the objects at either side of their heads, turning them from a solid colour into an object filled with a rainbow of colours. It wasn't long before his and the other being's projected bodies were filled with the same lights that flowed everywhere around the craft, making them part of the structure.

They were all connected now. Scott was somehow connected to each of the other beings in the craft, they all served a purpose, Scott was still waiting to find out what part he would be playing in all of this. He didn't have to wait long. Each of the crystal skulls started to glow orange, faint at first, then getting brighter by the second, until it was hard to look at. Scott was fascinated that he could still use his body in this projected form as his real body laid there entombed in the pod which rested before him.

Just then there was a bright flash above each of the

beings. A fuzzy image was left hanging in the air
right in front of Scott's eyes, slowly turning, trying
to form into something, as if it was tuning in.
Hypnotised by the object, fascinated by the ghostly
entity.

"It's magical, whatever it is!"

The orb's astronomical rotating speed mesmerised
Scott as he laid watching it. Suddenly a shape
started to evolve within the blurred image. The
outline of something could be seen through the
distorted light show. Solid white lines, almost silver
in colour, were starting to form a three dimensional
structure. It was something that Scott had just been
introduced to. The image of a skull slowly rotated
in front of him, the edges were bright, but the object
was clear. It was another crystal skull!

It stopped spinning and faced him, the haunting
apparition floated in midair, completely see through
apart from the reflected view of the sphere in the
background. A red cloudy colour emerged deep
inside the brain cavity, filling every part of it. The
swirls around the outside hadn't finished, they
continued covering the skull with different layers.
Each section translucent in appearance. First a
human-like structure and then the outline of the
skin and eyes, then finally the same protective layer
that had covered Scott, with the protruding mouth
area and the slightly bulbous head, still allowing
you to see through every layer.

A voice started in Scott's mind, just like it had
before when the other being had projected his
thoughts into his mind. He could hear it in his
native language.

"What has been the delay in your mission?" Scott presumed the voice was coming from the apparition.

There was a short pause before one of the beings replied, "We hadn't realised there was anything wrong, that was until we'd returned to zero gravity."

"Your globalisation craft has been off the communication grid for twenty one earth years! We have accessed your craft's hub and gathered all the information since you have come back into the grid. They have been busy trying to gain entry and find out who you are or who they are! We are safe so far, they still have a millennia to progress."

"We have witnessed the data since returning to zero gravity. Everything is in order now, this planet has developed since our last visit. There weren't any weather balloons on our last visit here."

"Your Dark Matter Fusion Reactor is fully functional I take it?"

"Yes, we have gathered the particles ready for the Reactor."

"You have your co-ordinates programmed? Return to hyper-sleep ready for the Fusion Reactor to create the Gravitational Plasma Hole."

Gravitational Plasma Hole? Dark Matter Fusion Reactor? What the hell are they? Thought Scott.

"It's a hole in the fabric of space, we can open them at given points around the universe. Bouncing communications off our well placed infrastructure. By opening these holes, the distance we actually travel is far less, so making it easier and faster, they pull us through so we hit speeds unfathomable to you. Your planets theory of the fastest speed being that of light, is wrong. We can achieve speeds a hundred times that of light just using the Gravitational Plasma Holes, turning your light-year theory into earth-years. You have lots to learn Scott Salvador."

"The skulls?"

"You learn quickly Scott. You'll be here before you know it."

"Where?"

With that the apparition dissolved, leaving no trace of the being's head as the pixels of light evaporated into thin air.

Scott noticed something above him, something had floated out from the centre of the craft, like a small ball of electricity, growing in size as it drifted further away into space. The sides stretching and moving, almost wobbling, like when you blow some soapy liquid through a hole and create a beautiful bubble. It grew larger and larger, until it was slightly larger than the craft they were in. As Scott watched with fascination he could see another bubble, then another, then another all inside each another. It was like a tear in the fabric of space, a hole filled with another hole and another projecting through space like a magnifying glass. Scott noticed each of the bubbles seemed to be getting closer to the first one, squashing up. That's what that distance line meant on the control panel, they all come together, then the craft just passes through them using the gravitational pull of each one to gain speed. He thought as he watched the tiny fingers of plasma caressing the outer edges of each one, making an eerie tunnel into the unknown.

The sphere in the centre of the craft continued to spin even faster and glow even brighter, the once calm tranquil interior was now a turbulent storm of a magnitude unknown to any man, passing through all the colours of the spectrum, until it stopped on the brightest purple you've ever seen. The outer edges of the craft started to dance with lightning, it crept down the sides and Scott could only imagine that the same thing was happening underneath. Its whole exterior glistened with this spectacular light show. This field of energy tickled the silken surface of the alien craft, it caressed the clear skin above Scott's head, he could see the crackling of tiny electrical arcs making ripples on its shell, as it made contact with the invisible shield. Then a bright blue pulse of plasma, the same shape and circumference as the craft, flashed, then again, blasting a ring of light from around the outer surface. Then suddenly a beam of purple light emitted from the sphere out into space, cutting through the centre of the Gravitational Plasma Hole, disappearing off into infinity.

One by one the beings stood up from where they had been controlling the craft and walked over to their own pods, the crystal skulls still held in place where they lay. They sat down and slowly rested back into position on top of their own bodies, disappearing into the pods once more. Scott was left on his own, still reclined in the odd looking chair, staring out into space, he hadn't noticed the material covering his hands had been released. Their collective job was done, they were sending the craft on its way home.

Scott followed what the other beings had done and climbed back into his own body that laid dormant in the jelly within his pod. He took one last look around and then gazed out into space before slowly lowering his head back, as he did, he noticed the purple beam of light seemed to go into the hole but not come out. A hazy glow radiated around its edges as it penetrated the watery reflective surface of the Plasma Hole. The outer edges of it started to glow as bright as a star in the night sky, like a ball of fuzzy lightning. The purple light was the same size as the opening to the Dark Matter Reactor, just like a laser beam, its edges poker straight and its colour constant. It looked like it should have popped the bubble in space but it didn't, it blasted straight through and off into the unknown.

The craft started to glow with more intensity now, the streaks of lightning wrapping around the material on its outside. Then, along the purple laser, stretched more of the blue bands of light and as if they were on elastic bands, they projected out and sprang back past the edges of the craft and out into space below, this propelled the craft forwards at an almighty speed, just as Scott once more drifted unconscious, not knowing what lay ahead.

The Dark Matter Fusion Reactor had worked once more, sending the craft on its journey home. Nothing inside the craft moved, it was as if the lights were moving outside on their own and the craft was standing still, no G-force whatsoever. The edges of each bubble or hole, looked like they were electrified with pulses of lightning, inter-laced squashed circles of plasma. Within the pockets were streaks of light, like they were travelling past stars at a speed only felt by the debris from a supernova. Each plasma hole seemed to spring them forwards at great speed, making them accelerate faster each time, allowing them to achieve the speeds they'd said.

Scott was unaware of everything that was happening, his mind had been shut down and his body laid dormant. The journey of enlightenment had begun.

Chapter 44

"What the hell!" shouted the man as he nearly spilt his coffee all over the panel. "Go and find Bob, now! He needs to see this."

Just before the craft had disappeared, a red light flashed in tune with the sound of a beep. It lit up on the control panel in front of the man monitoring the communications on the Apollo 11 rocket.
Beep…Beep…Beep…

The tracking program Scott was working on, had started. It had been downloaded into the craft's memory after he'd allowed the objects into his body.
"This isn't meant to be happening!" said the agent wiping up the remains of his coffee from around the controls. "The lunar rover hasn't been deployed yet."

Just then Bob rushed into the monitoring room, he'd been waiting in his office for something to happen. He gave his intercom man the nod and sat down in his chair next to him. "What's going on?" asked Bob.
"We're not sure Sir, it's the beacon for the lunar module Sir, it's started!"
"But the module hasn't been deployed yet!"
"Exactly!"
"No, it can't be! Can it?"
"Can't be what Sir?"
"The programme! It's working, this is it! This is what we've been waiting for."

"But how? We haven't placed the transponder into the craft for it to work! It's still sat there in the hangar waiting to be fixed."

"Look the signal is coming from further away than the Apollo rocket. It's there on your radar man. This is why we have this unit set up away from the Capcom, so we can see if it works. Maybe we didn't have to fix something in it! Maybe Scott has done it for us somehow!"

"But how Sir? That's impossible!"

"Is it? Really? Think about everything we've witnessed lately. Now do you think it's impossible?"

"Maybe, I'm not sure Sir."

"It must have been imprinted into the craft somehow. It must have." Bob said as he tried to convince himself that's what had happened.

The signal continued for about a minute as Bob and the team looked for any signs of a malfunction. There weren't any. How could this be happening? Thought Bob.

Just then the silent airways broke into life.

. . . .

"Jezebel come in, Jezebel this is Apollo 11...Over!" Area 49 had intercepted the message on the secure command channel.

"Come in Jezebel, this is Apollo 11, do you read?... Over."

"Yes, Apollo 11, this is Jezebel go ahead...Over"

"Jezebel we tracked the object until moments ago, then it...it..it..just..just vanished Sir...Over"

"What do you mean it just vanished? It can't just vanish! Are you sure you haven't just lost track of it?" replied Bob as he pushed his cigar smelling face in front of the agent to speak.
Just as Bob had finished his sentence, the beep stopped and along with it, the light ceased to blink. "Now what!" asked Bob, "Apollo await further instructions."

Bob leaned back in his chair to think for a moment. What could have happened? Was it a malfunction of some kind? Could the programme that Scott was working on, have really worked? Had he finished it in time before he was entombed in the craft? How did he upload it to the craft? Question after question filled Bob's mind as he struggled to grasp what had just happened. Reaching forward Bob pressed the button to communicate with the astronauts, "Apollo come in?"

"Jezebel! Apollo here...Over." Replied one of the shaken astronauts.

"Apollo. Tell me exactly what you saw before the craft disappeared...Over"

There was a moments silence before the traumatised voice responded, "We tracked the object like you asked, it..it..just vanished Sir, just vanished. One minute it was there and the next it was gone Sir. The whole thing lit up like the Fourth of July Sir, then it just disappeared. A ball of blue light grew in front of the craft, like a giant sphere with lightning wrapping around its surface. Then all of a sudden the object glowed like star in a clear night's sky, radiating the purest white light out into space. Then a beam of the most beautiful purple you could ever imagine pierced the ball, rings of blue surrounded the craft and within a flash the object had vanished. A shock-wave resembling that of an exploding star flooded the space around where the craft was last seen, it resonated out in circles of the purest colours possible. It shook our rocket, that's how bad it was. That is what happened Jezebel...Over"

Silence...

"Jezebel...Jezebel...Come in Jezebel...Over"

"Apollo! Do you have an eyeball on anything? Any debris? Anything to say there was an explosion?... Over"

"That's a negative Jezebel! I repeat, negative! The object has gone. No signs of anything. Should we abort the mission?...Over"

"Apollo, that is not an option, proceed with the mission. I repeat proceed with the mission as planned...Over"

"Roger, Jezebel...Over and out."

The signal had stopped, the red light ceased and for a brief moment Bob had thought, hoped, that they would be able to track the craft to wherever it had come from. How do I explain this to the ones above? He thought.

"Continue to monitor, I think our job is done, but just in case, keep a close eye on that beacon and inform me straight away if anything changes." Bob said as he walked out of the comms room on a heading for his office.

Bob could hear the phone ringing in his office as he grew ever closer, the powers above him were wanting answers. They were wanting to know how things were going. What do I tell them? He thought as he opened the door to the deafening bell of the receiver. He held the handle to his door wondering if he should just disappear out of the secret entrance he'd used to come down in. The thought of them wiping his memory, like all the others before him, wasn't sitting too good. He imagined some of the people they'd taken away in the ambulance, the place where they had been kept, the institutions for the mentally insane, the cuckoo's nest. The perfect place to hide all the people who knew too much or didn't do as they were told, they'd be made to fit in.

   Bob picked up the phone and placed it to his ear, "Hello!" He said in his deep rough voice. He just listened to the person on the other end without saying a word at first, then just before he hung up his reply came, "This outcome couldn't have been predicted Sir, we planned for everything but this, we had no control over this. We don't know what's happened it's that simple, the craft has disappeared without a trace."

Bob's head fell, his chin brushed his now dampened collar, he closed his eyes and pulled his hand over his hair. He placed the receiver on the cradle as he sat down in his chair, he picked up a half smoked cigar from his ashtray. It was the one he'd left as he rushed out when the beacon had started, the cigar had continued to smoulder, leaving a long charred shape in the base like some molten rock from a once active volcano. The ash broke off as he lifted it up to his mouth, causing a slight dust cloud as it fell back into the tray. The soggy tobacco leaves squashed together as he grasped it between his teeth. A light brown residue leaked out from the gap where the cigar met his lips. He sucked it back in as he flicked the flint on his Zippo to ignite the leftover stub.

With a deep breath in, he leaned back in his chair and blew the smoke high into the air above his head. His gaze was that of a troubled man, there was no script for what they had just done, nor was there anything that could be done to change what had just happened. Scott was in the lap of the Gods, literally…

Turning around in his chair he lifted the telephone once more, pushing a button to connect to another department.

"Hello," said Bob.

"Capcom." came the reply.

Bob was connecting to the Capcom in Houston, the main communication station they had diverted everything from. The team had placed a back-up tracking device there, it was mixed in with the other control panels.

"Capcom, this is the General of Special Ops, SIS, please put me onto whoever is in charge there."

"Ok, please hold."

"Hello!" came the voice of the Commander at Capcom.

"Hi, this is the General of Special Ops, SIS, can you tell me if you had any glitches on the tracking signal?"

"Never heard of the SIS, who did you say you were again? General of what? No, we haven't had any problems here, the comms went down a few times but that's about all, oh and a red light started to flash and emit a beeping noise, but then it stopped so we thought it was just a test for the lunar module programme. Other than that everything is fine. Why do you ask? Hello! Hello!" said the Commander as he pulled the phone away from his ear and looked at the receiver.

Bob had hung up as soon as he'd heard that the red light and noise had been noticed, his brain was working overtime as he thought about it working at Houston too, what was going to happen to Scott? Was he even still alive? A blast as they had described could have killed him and vaporised anything around it. How would they ever know?

Chapter 45

The Eagle has landed.

"It's one small step for man, one giant leap for mankind…"

Neil Armstrong had the whole world in the palm of his hand, waiting in anticipation as he made the first human footprint in the delicate lunar dust, which had coated the floating ball of rock for billions of years. They had done it, the first country to send a manned mission to the surface of the moon. Neil was closely followed down the ladder by Buzz Aldrin.

....

The Apollo 11 mission was a success. It had also been a success in another way, they had hopefully managed to send Scott Salvador on a mission of a life time. A mission hidden from most. A mission to prove once and for all where we originated from, or to find out if we are not alone in this infinite entity we call space.

There were only a few people left in the SIS that

actually knew what had gone on behind the scenes. Since finding the craft, to this day it has been in the hands of the highest agency in America, an agency only known to a select few. It's been covered up with lie after lie to keep the human race safe. These are people who can keep the secrets hidden for years at a time or until they see fit to reveal them to the public.

The being that had died in the crash many years ago, was still preserved, encased inside a large glass tube. A specimen from another planet, this alone was proof that we came from somewhere else or that life exists in a similar form elsewhere in the universe. It has taken its place in the secure storage facility at Area 51, alongside the many other artifacts that have been found around the world.

Stubbing his cigar out in the ashtray on his desk, Bob took one final look at the photo of himself with Scott and Kimberly. He picked up the frame. A reflection of his worried face looked back, bouncing off the front of the glass, almost accusing him of the demise of another human being, finding him guilty without a jury. What have we done? This same thought passed through his mind, repeating over and over again. He gave himself a guilty smile before opening the back of the frame to remove the photo. Giving it one last look before folding it in half and slipping it into the pocket of his jacket as he grabbed it from the hook next to the door. The shattering of glass broke the silence as he dropped the picture frame into the metal waste bin. On opening the door he stopped to take one last look around his office, just in case he never made it back.

Bob headed back over to the monitoring room for one last update before he left for the evening. As he walked through the hangar, he thought it looked so bare without the craft taking pride of place in the middle of the room. The desks surrounding the hangar were also empty, most of the people had left for the day, some would be finished now that the craft was gone. He noticed Colin was still in the data room, he could see him through the glass window holding up the printer paper, he was still trying to decipher the coded message that had printed off from the craft's memory.

I wonder what's going to happen to this place now? I suppose something else will take its place in the near future. Who knows? There's never a dull day around here. Bob thought as he opened the door to the monitoring room.

"You're just in time Sir, your gonna want to hear this," said the man who hadn't left the control panel in days.

"Houston tracked something on their radar, I've just intercepted a coded message from them to someone in a very high position. They said that everything had gone to plan, except for a short period, which coincided with the alert signal we picked up for the lunar module. They had picked up a bogey travelling alongside the Apollo Rocket. The transmission lasted the same length of time as ours Sir, I've checked and re-checked. It was recorded on their data sheets. What do you want me to do about it Sir?" he asked as he slurped the dregs from his coffee cup.

"Nothing, deny all knowledge if anyone should ask

anything, they don't even know we have been monitoring things here, they don't even know we exist. How did the message end?"

"It ended with; Have the crew reported seeing anything unusual? Capcom said, no Sir they haven't reported anything. We lost communication for a while, but then everything seemed to be fine when they came back online."

"That's ok then, maybe they thought it was the S-IVB, just like the crew had. Continue monitoring, you'll be able to reach me on my secure line if anything should happen. I somehow don't think we'll be hearing a signal from the craft in the near future, I'm afraid."

With that Bob walked out of the room and back over to the large steel blast doors. He placed his hand over the screen to get clearance to leave the hangar. The large door opened and he found himself in the void before entering the white marble of Area 49. His footsteps echoed as his hard soles made contact with the highly polished surface. Acknowledging the security guard as he passed his window and continuing down the long corridor towards the elevator, he hoped to return to the surface in one piece. Passing door after door the journey seemed to take forever, the elevator never looked any closer. The retracting dark grey door looked tiny in the distance.

As he grew closer and closer with each footstep he noticed the door opening, as if it had been waiting for him. The faint sound of elevator music slowly flooded the echoey corridor as it bounced off the hard marbled surface, gradually finding its way into

Bob's ears. His breathing became heavy, his chest working overtime to help refill his lungs with the manufactured air that filled the pristine white tunnel. Sweat started to dapple his brow even though the area was chilled with air-conditioning, his adrenalin had kicked in, preparing him for the worst.

By the time he reached the opening, the music had been drowned out by the deafening sound of his own mind repeating the same words over and over again. Why me? Why me? Why me? Horrific scenes played in his mind, like vivid nightmares. He'd been witness to things that would make the toughest of people collapse in a quivering heap on the floor. Deep down he loved, but also hated, his job with a passion. His feet were dragging as he took the last few steps before coming to a standstill in front of the open elevator. Wiping his forehead and mustering up the last of his energy, he made the final steps inside, closing his eyes as he did so. His ears slowly adjusted to the calming music within. Was this it? Would this be the last thing he heard as the surreal events played out in his haunting demise?

Bob opened his eyes as he turned round to face the door, it started to close, cutting off the echoing music that filled the corridor, but the concert played on just for him. He looked up at the camera, the tiny red dot giving it away instantly. Suddenly the elevator started to move, it jolted and dropped slightly. Bob flung his arms out to grasp hold of nothing, his arms scrambling on the metal walls trying to get hold of something, anything. But there was nothing there! He backed himself into a corner using the sides for support, leaving his arms out stretched. Again, the elevator bounced, his fingers clawing into the steel box. Then it started to move!

The colour drained from Bob's skin, a look of terror spread across his face. The elevator was moving, but it wasn't going up! He was moving down! Bob didn't even know there was anywhere else for it to go below their floor. He looked up shouting, "Nooooo!" as he slowly descended into the unknown. There wasn't any gas filling the chamber, this only made Bob fear the worst. "Where are you taking me?" he yelled at the top of his voice!

There was no reply! The only thing he could hear, was the cheerful music being played in the background. Moving over to the control panel, he frantically pressed every button he could see. Nothing worked, he now knew what all the others most have been going through as they slowly lost their mind and drifted off to sleep.

Bump! The elevator finally came to rest! Bob waited, slowly clenching his fists ever tighter by the second, drawing blood as his fingernails dug into the palms of his hands, squeezing out between his fingers and dripped onto the floor, splattering the front of his highly polished black shoes. He was ready for battle, anticipating the worst, the sweat ran down his face and dripped onto his suit jacket. He could feel it running down the underside of his arm, slowly tracking the contours of his figure, mixing with the blood on his knuckles before cascading onto the floor.

The door started to open, he moved to the side where the control panel was housed, thinking he had the upper hand against whoever laid in wait for him. That wasn't the case, he stayed there for a moment and when nothing happened, he plucked up the courage to peer around the corner. For a split second he thought he must be dreaming, it looked exactly the same as the floor he'd come from, a bright white corridor leading off into the distance with door after door on each side. Making him question his own mind;
"I'm sure that thing moved!" He looked back into the elevator and then back out down the corridor again. He brought his hand up to his mouth as he studied the situation. It was then that he noticed his hands were covered in blood, holding them out before him he looked at where his fingernails had penetrated his palms. His fingers were stiff from clenching his fists so tight. He reached into his pocket for something to wipe the blood up with. After using his handkerchief to clean himself up, Bob pressed the buttons again, trying to will the elevator to move. It was no good, nothing was working.
What do I do now? He thought to himself.
He mustered up the courage to venture out into the corridor, taking what felt like his very first child steps again. As soon as his body had passed the threshold, the door began to close, he hadn't heard it until the music stopped, then the thud of the door hitting the seal made him turn around. There was no button here! That's when he realised he had moved! But to where?

"Hello! Hello...hello...hello..."
The echo bounced off the walls into distance down the long straight corridor. There was no reply, there wasn't a sound, you could have heard a pin drop at the other end, it was deadly silent. Too silent for Bob's liking, he knew only too well nothing good was coming of this situation.

His footsteps dragged his body in tow, as he wandered on auto-pilot trying each door as he came to them, only to find them locked. He frantically twisted the handle and shook the door, one after the other, rattling them in their frames. There was no way to get in. Have I been drugged in the elevator without knowing? Am I dreaming? Why have I ended up down here? Question after question rang through his distressed mind.

There was one last door to try before he reached the end of the corridor. The doorknob turned and the door opened, he immediately let go, leaving the door slightly ajar. He waited and listened for a moment before he eased it open with his bloodstained shoe. The room was as bright as the walls he'd passed to get there. He could see a long white table, with four men sitting behind it, all wearing black suits, white shirts with a black tie. Each person looking towards the wall straight in front of them. Bob peered around the door to see what they were looking at. There was a small TV screen on a stand, he looked closer, seeing himself peering though the open doorway. It was the image of the corridor he'd just walked down. There was a chair facing the table the men were sitting at.

They must have been monitoring me as I came

down here, he thought to himself.

"Come in and close the door!" One of the men said without looking up from the screen.

Bob closed the door and walked over to the chair, his legs felt heavier with each step he took. Grasping the arm of the chair he turned and sat down to face the men.

At first they didn't say a word, they just sat there staring at him, intimidating him, waiting for him to speak. He didn't, he'd had so much training for his role at Area 51 and Area 49 he knew when to keep his mouth shut and that time was now!

They were good, their tactics among some of the best Bob had ever seen. But there was a reason they hadn't said anything, they were waiting, waiting for someone else to join the party. Something caught Bob's attention out of the corner of his eye, he glanced around to the screen. He noticed two men walking down the corridor. One at either end of a hospital trolley, they approached the room he was in with the staggered time-lapse effect the camera was recording in, each flicker making them closer by the second, until!

Knock…knock…

"Come in," said the same man who'd asked Bob to sit down.

The door opened and the two men calmly walked in and rested the trolley against the wall just inside the door, Bob heard a haunting squeak coming from one of the wheels as it turned. Underneath was a syringe, lying on a tray, next to a bottle of green liquid and a folded up sheet. The two men who were also dressed in black suits, white shirts and black ties, they stood either end of the trolley with their backs against the wall. Bob's heart was trying to break free from the ribcage which was holding it in place, it pulsated faster and faster, he felt like his whole body was moving with every beat. Beads of sweat had run down from his brow into the corners of his eyes making them sting, like someone had thrown a handful of salt in each one. He raised his bloody hands to wipe them, only to smear the congealed stains from his fingers onto his cheeks in the process.

One of men spun a square box around on the table and flipped open the lid, he motioned towards the finest rolled tobacco leaves which had been presented before him, "Please, take one Bob, you deserve it."

Bob hesitated for a few moments before he gave into the temptation, he reached forwards taking one from the top. Lifting it up to his nose, he slowly allowed the aroma to caress his senses as he closed his stinging eyes before moving it from one end to the other.

With his eyes still closed, his daydream was rudely awakened by the spring of a Zippo closely followed by the sparks from the flint as it burst into life, creating the most perfect flame. The hand was holding the lighter as still as could be, with not a hint of nerves to tremble the flame. Bob reached into his pocket and pulled out his clipper, he cut the end off and grasped the cigar between his lips like a vice holding a piece of wood ready for carving. He hovered it just above the heat waiting for the combustion to fuel his present. It started to glow red, slowly turning a brighter shade of orange as he drew back a mouthful of the toxic smoke. He savoured it before exhaling it forward towards the men sitting at the table. The lazy swirling smoke tumbled towards their faces, like a warm breath on a cold winter's morning. It seemed to hang in the air around the men, each one taking his turn to waft it away, followed by a slight cough.

"Well, let's get down to business." said Bob as if he'd gained some kind of superpower from his cigar.

"You know we can't have any loose ends Bob!" exclaimed one of the men.

"I'm far from a loose end man, and you know it. I've been part of this mission from day one. Right from when the craft had been found in Roswell. I've seen good friends come and go through the years I've worked on this project. So I'm far from a loose end as you put it!" Bob's anger was starting to show.

"But how can we trust anybody with the knowledge and secrets that you know?"

"I've not said a word to anyone the whole time we've been working on this and you know it."

The men looked at one another, as if they were telepathic, beaming thoughts backwards and forwards about what to do with him. Their decisions could take someone out of the equation with the click of their fingers. Just like Kimberly. Bob had thought he was one of the highest people there at Area 49, but he wasn't, they were now showing him where his place was in the pecking order.

"You've been answering to us all along Bob, everything you've done, all those loose ends you've tied up, everyone who's gone missing, it's all come from higher up. We even answer to people who answer to people and so on, you get the picture…"

"Ok that's enough," one of the others butted in and stopped him in his tracks.

"We all know what has gone on here, the real mission hasn't gone to plan and we can't risk anything getting out about it."

"But what about the others on the project? The ones who've worked on the craft with me for all those years. Colin and Fiona, what will happen to them? And the man in the monitoring room? He's still there waiting and watching for something, anything to happen!" replied Bob.

"Don't you worry about anybody else, we have our ways, you of all people should know that Bob!"

One of the men who'd walked in with the trolley bent down and picked up the syringe and the bottle of green liquid. He plunged the needle through the rubber bung and sucked up the coloured fluid, raising it into the air after he'd finish. He tapped it with his finger then squirted some out to release the air bubbles. Bob watched him, fear spreading across his face, waiting for the inevitable. He was ready.

"So, that's it then, you're just going to do away with me, like all the others, send me off to a mental institution for the rest of my life. Having them believe I'm round the twist."

"What? What are you going on about Bob?"

The man holding the syringe had walked around

the back of the seated men, his gaze transfixed on Bob.

"The trolley, the injection, that's what you've got planned isn't it? Send me off to the loony bin and have them throw away the key!"

"You couldn't be further away from the plan if you tried Bob." With that the man raised his hand up.

"What, but I…" came the response from the man who'd first spoken, his head making a loud bang, as it bounced when it hit the table.

The man stayed in place holding the depressed plunger as the needle was extracted from the neck of the now motionless man as he fell onto the table top. Bob was speechless, he didn't know what to do, his gaze went from one to the other around the room.

"Don't you just hate it when someone you thought you could trust, stabs you in the back when you're least expecting it?"

The man stood up and calmly lifted the wrist of the slumped victim, he held the pressure point to feel for a pulse, looking into thin air as he did so, like he was listening for something. The wrist fell back to the table like a dead weight. Looking at the man holding the syringe, he gave him a quick nod of the head. He ushered the other man over and between the two of them they grabbed the slumped man under each arm and dragged him over to the trolley they'd brought in with them. After lifting his lifeless body onto it, they pulled the folded white sheet out and draped it over, covering him completely. Then one of the men opened the door and they wheeled it out into the echoey corridor.

Bob could hear the squeak of the wheel and the men whistling as they walked off into the distance just before the door closed tight, cutting off the sound completely. He looked at the screen again and saw them wheeling the body off as if nothing had happened. In his mind the squeak from the wheel and the eerie whistling played over and over, like a broken record.

"What happens now?" asked Bob.

"Well Bob, you have earned your place with us, over the last few years you have gone from strength to strength, you have shown us you are trustworthy and able to carry out orders without hesitation or questions. This is everything you need to be part of the SIS, you will be privy to more information than you can ever imagine in your new role at Area 49. This isn't just a job, it's explaining the unexplainable."

"Do you have any questions for us Bob?"

Chapter 46

………

Year : 2067

Date : July 3rd

Day : Sunday

Time : 16:16

………

Beep…Beep…Beep…Beep…Beep…Beep…

The dormant reels of memory tape spun into action once more, throwing over seventy years of dust particles, that had settled on the top of the vintage machine, into the air, before falling lazily back down in the stillness of the storage room, finally coming to rest on top of some already dusty large coloured lights, which suddenly burst into life on the old control panel. They started to blink in unison with the piercing sound of…

Beep…Beep…Beep…Beep…Beep…Beep…

……….

Bursting through the Gravitational Plasma Hole, the craft stopped instantly, floating motionless outside the translucent bubble-like structure it had just created, in the vacuum of space. The darkest side of the Moon was its present location, using it as a temporary shield from the Earth as it locked itself onto the slightest gravitational pull. Just as they'd done over one hundred years ago, right before it had ventured into the Earth's atmosphere, colliding with the weather balloon and finally crash-landing over Roswell, New Mexico. The craft waited, hoping its signal would be picked up, hoping someone was still monitoring and awaiting its return one day.

The craft had returned, the lunar programme was still operational, still being transmitted via the old radio waves, a form of communication that Earth had discarded over fifty years earlier. All that it could do was wait for some kind of contact, hoping the signal would be intercepted, before they made the final part of their journey.

The beings laid dormant in their pods, still in hyper-sleep from travelling through the Gravitational Plasma Hole. As the craft waited, it started uploading all the data it could, from the signals being sent via the communications on the planet Earth. Gathering vital information about what had been happening on this planet over the last hundred Earth years, so it was ready to share it with the beings when they awoke from their pods. They could connect with certain transmissions being sent on their home planet, but most of the information was out of date before it arrived through the Interstellar-Com-Pods which were placed throughout the universe.

Space exploration had come on greatly over the last century, but travelling at great speeds through the universe hadn't been achieved yet. There had been the development of manned outposts on the near side of the Moon and on Mars. These had been established to monitor any meteors or asteroids that might venture too close for comfort.

Things had changed on Earth, but they still hadn't found any evidence of any other habitable planets that could be reached. Religious wars had devastated the land all over, leaving it highly radioactive in parts. One thing the beings had noticed on past visits to Earth, was the Humans inability to live together on this unique planet. Earth had been chosen for its abundance of resources, and its ability to sustain life with little or no supplies. Planned for millions of years, it was nurtured and grown to support the habitation of the species the beings had named the Human race. A race very similar to the beings themselves, cloned from the perfect DNA of a race that could achieve anything.

The Planet had found one good way of disposing

of its waste, they had huge rolling platforms positioned over the most active volcanoes, allowing the rubbish to fall into the natural furnace of the planet, incinerating it instantly, the heat and smoke from this was used to run the monstrous turbines that fed the world's manufacturing industry its energy. Coal and natural gas had been depleted over forty Earth years earlier, this pushed lots of housing underground, especially in the war stricken areas, which were becoming uninhabitable.

The humans had utilised the vast area under the sea, building a network of offshore cities, deep down on the floor of the oceans. Submersible vehicles were the new mode of transport around these areas, it looked like they were on another planet.

After the most recent war which started in Eastern Europe, leaving parts of the world in nuclear turmoil, areas of division had split the countries up, leaving some in ruins. The larger countries were still intact, in some areas they'd even started to rebuild. Some cities in the USA were overgrown with contaminated vegetation, these were off limits and had been for years. Trees had taken root in the streets of the once thriving metropolises, buildings had been crushed under the force of the fallouts, old rusty cars and trucks were strewn around, discarded like pieces of rubbish. Vast areas of flood plains, where the seas had risen from the nuclear tsunamis, now dried up, the ground cracked like a bed of a drought stricken river waiting to feel the cool quench of the rain once more. The tall evacuated skyscrapers were now covered in dust and greenery, strands of ivy dangling off the architecture, blowing in the breeze, tentacles of life extending from place to place, regaining what was once their home.

The detailed maps of the currant terrain and airborne deployment were being uploaded into the craft's hub along with all the information about the planet. A certain point had been selected for the craft to land, giving the beings the best possible chance of arriving without a hostile greeting. This was the independent state of Florida, the location to which the craft would be heading, once the signal had been located.

The transmissions the craft was receiving from Earth showed things were calm at present, unlike when the beings came last time, at the end of the Second World War. The beings had been sent to help people throughout the course of history with inventions and religion, most of which had been misunderstood from day one, the beings were all sent to help us progress. The Human race had been pre-programmed with the need to believe in something, the need to think there's more to life than just living. That's why they are never content, they always need more, this is where the globalisation process fell apart. Unlike the theory of evolution, to civilise a planet, the beings wipe out any hostile hosts, leaving the workers to do the job of cultivating the land and building a world, just like an army of ants.

As the beings find planets that are suitable to sustain life forms, they then set about preparing a particular life form for that planet, the perfect alien to colonise and cultivate the new worlds they create. They then set going the production of habitation, usually these planets already have some forms of life on them, sometimes they are hostile creatures and sometimes they find them just at the right stage in their early formation, perfect for life straight away, without the need to genetically modify their near perfect blue-print of life. Unfortunately on Earth one race had dug in deep and lasted out the last ice-age, only surfacing again after the beings had brought their human colonisation project here, these were the Homo-Sapiens, cave dwelling Earthlings which were thought to be extinct along with the hostile animals. They were able to interbreed with the master race, giving them their fighting nature, their primitive throwback gene.

The manufactured ice-age left a virtual blank canvas for the process to work, it takes millions of years to colonise a new planet, and with well over two hundred years of travel in the globalisation crafts called the Ã.R.Çs, the process had already started before the beings noticed. It was too late when they did, they had to let it run its course and hope the two species would be compatible with each other. They were left to source the planets natural reserves and develop as far on their own as possible. Slowly the cracks started to appear in the new race. War, religion. War, land. War, fuel. War, food. War.

The beings will never let it get out of control though, as this is their World now and Humans just live here;

Beep…Beep…Beep…Beep…Beep…Beep…

The signal continued through the night and into the next day, the museum was closed for the night. Its doors opened again for the tourists the next morning, July the Fourth, the still celebrated Day of Independence.

. . . .

"Hi Stan! Happy Independence Day! It's another lovely day my friend!" said the security guard with the most cheerful smile on his face, greeting people into the Kennedy Space Centre, Florida, USA.
"Hey, it is that! How are you doing today?"
"Ok thanks. You ready for the rush of people as usual Stan?"
"You bet! Just don't send them in before I can get the bots in place to show them around. You know how temperamental your kind be this early in the morning."
"You got it, have a nice day!"
Stan was always fascinated with the Silica-h-Bot that worked on security, he was so life like in personality. It was 07:00am, Stan placed his eye in front of the encryption point retina scanner and the large illuminated glass door swished back and disappeared into its frame, sliding back into place as he passed and entered the old Space Mission Museum. Stan had worked there for over fifty years his first day was in the year 2014. He'd loved it so much when he'd come on holiday as a kid that he wanted to work there, preserving all the fine

antique machines. He was one of the few humans that worked there now, the Silica-h-Bot's were slowly replacing the real people, as Stan would call them, the first new upgraded Silica-h-Bot, came to the facility in 2021. A bit primitive back then though, now, they were far more advanced. Their employment didn't cost the facility any Global-Units (money), that's why they were the best deployed h-Bots around the USA and the rest of the world, maintained by the h-Bot development company. Stan wasn't too worried because he was leaving soon, he'd lasted long enough here, it was time for his rejuvenation program.

Every morning on Stan's way to the h-Bot's docking facility, he walked past this very old motor car from the nineteen sixties. A Corvette Stingray, the plaque on the front said it belonged to Neil Armstrong, the first man to walk on the moon! It was housed in the main hangar, contained within a glass case now because the old metal chassis was decaying. It was just below one of the sections of a rocket suspended from the ceiling, which had been put up there nearly a hundred years ago, to show what we used in the very early stages of the space race. Stan knew all the history of this place and the era of the rockets, he used to do all the tours before the h-Bot's came along. He entered the h-Bot docking facility via another retina security check and said, "Lights please."

All the lights above his head illuminated and he was faced with the assortment of h-Bot's all sitting in rows on snug moulded black reclining docks, with headrests that squashed up to their ears. He used to think they looked like they were watching an old fashioned movie, just like he'd used to as a kid. Stan would swear they moved over night sometimes, as he would frequently find one that he could have sworn wasn't where he'd left it. They were seated each night to reboot, their induction power bank could recharge once connected to the chair, this allowed a full bypass reboot. There wasn't just one big battery in these upgraded models, more of a flowing power source. It was very similar to a human being, only the h-Bot used an energy nano cell, contained within a blue gel, a similar consistency to our blood. The bypass was the heart of the h-Bot, it pumped the nano-cells around the body, charging them as they passed through the induction pump, this was called the bypass. It gave a continuous charging cycle to each and every unique microscopic nano-cell which powered the h-Bots for years and years. When the cells did come to the end of their life cycle or they became damaged, they were collected by the Discharged Cell Magnet, as each cell deactivates it turns magnetic allowing the cell to be disposed of. Then whilst the h-Bot is in the Reboot Dock it's hooked up to the Cell Management system, a small tube which connects via a socket on its side. The defunct cells are then replaced with the same amount of fresh ones, ensuring the h-Bots are never without enough power.

Each nano cell had its own purpose in the h-Bot. Some were programmed to power the head and the memory, others the limbs and so on. The upgraded ones were far more intelligent than the last ones, they used to take forever to recharge their single battery pack, plus they used to have a mind of their own and were always breaking down. The new ones are capable of much greater tasks, having a fully working and stronger internal titanium skeleton, covered with a Kevlar Silica Skin which is virtually impenetrable. Each limb has its own unique silica muscle, allowing the joints to move in a very similar way to a human. The long string like tendons moved the limbs through the internal structures, using a material that had memory, at rest the h-Bot would slump over with these tendons at full stretch, but when activated with the Electro Nano Charge they could contract and extend, giving them strength and mobility, far greater than that of a human. Each h-Bot has its very own sensory fingerprints unique to each and every one, they can pass information through the sensors which can be seen to glow just under the surface of the Silica-Skin. They can learn from their touch, every object that is manufactured has to be made with a special Electro Code implanted into it, which has the information of the product so the h-Bot instantly knows what it is holding or touching via Induction Data Streaming. This had also been designed for blind humans in the way of gloves, allowing them to read and know what they are holding. The h-Bot's face was a moulded Liquid Pixel Display, LPD for short. A smooth face shaped screen that resembled a shop mannequin, only soft to the touch, made from the same Kevlar-Silica, only this part was translucent and when activated, it showed that h-Bots unique face. Their eyes have Product-Code and face recognition technology allowing the data from anything containing the Electro Code implant to be seen, storing the information into its virtual brain, then up-streaming it for that individual h-Bot, into the Blue-Sky main frame. A simple Electro Code adhesive film had been designed for data sweeping the globe, allowing the h-Bots to learn quickly. Their virtual brains are preprogrammed with a multitude of manoeuvres and information and with the adhesive data films they can gather intelligence wherever they are. They can then upload everything straight into the Blue-Sky storage area, which was circling the Earth via a network of satellites that were constantly down-streaming everything they could see plus everything they said or heard, for that individual h-Bot, straight to the mainframe facility. There weren't many places on the planet that the h-Bots couldn't send information from. They were always connected to the Blue-Sky storage, so anything out of the ordinary was picked up and dealt with. Nothing went amiss anymore. The h-Bots were inactive whilst connected to their reboot docking stations. Each one had a display pad which extended on a very sleek curved stem which was moulded to the side of the reclining dock. This had all the information about that h-Bot; charge, bypass reboot status, memory capacity, and lots of other things. Every h-Bot had a specific role at the Kennedy Space Centre, some were tour guides, some were security, and others were maintenance, they performed lots of different tasks to keep the place functioning properly.

Stan walked over to the system check panel, a row

of screens on the back wall of the room. It contained the same information as the screens connected to the docks, highlighting any problems with any of the h-Bot's. Stan quickly scanned the screens to see if anything had been flagged up. Nothing had, he liked it when there were no problems, they could be a bit temperamental sometimes. One screen had an image of the rows of docks, each having its own number assigned to it. He started to touch the screen, each image started to flash, alternating between the image of the dock and the word; Initialising!

In turn the LPD faces on the h-Bots, illuminated, glowing in turn as they awoke from their overnight reboot, readying themselves for another day's work at the Kennedy Space Centre. Their individual faces gradually appeared on the screen, their eyes still closed tight inside the bulbous contours of the eye socket, the nostrils appeared under the shape for the nose, and the flat, smooth section where the mouth would be, was a pair of digital lips displayed on the screen under which, was a series of microscopic holes for the speech to resonate from. Their ears looked like a pair of human ears but also made from the Kevlar-Silica, they too had microscopic holes only these were used to allow the h-Bot to hear.

Each h-Bot went through this sequence until the last ones face appeared. Each face different from the other. They looked like rows of people waiting to for the movie to start. The flashing word changed from;

Initialising
to
Reboot Complete
Press to Activate

Stan activated each h-bot that was needed for the
day's tasks, some stayed behind, initialised but not
awake. As he pressed the touch screen, the faces of
each h-Bot awoke, blinking, and yawning, as if they
really had been asleep. Stan thought that part was a
bit too real, a bit too freaky for his liking. One of the
h-Bot's had got up from its dock and walked over
and stood just behind Stan, it leaned forward and
said; "Morning Stan!"
Stan nearly jumped through the roof, as he hadn't
finished activating some of them, he was deep in
thought about which ones to initiate.
"Don't do that to me h-016, you'll give me a heart
attack one of these days, I keep telling you that, it's
just not funny." He said as his heart rate peaked,
making the alarm on his connection monitor go off.
He turned his wrist over to see what the reading
was and pressed the screen to stop it. These comms
devices monitored the body and communicated
with everyone and everything, linked to the Blue-
Sky network. That's one thing the h-Bots didn't
have to worry about, their heart, when they needed
a new bypass pump the old one was just taken out
through a secure section in the back of the unit.
They didn't have to worry about anything wearing

out, they had been designed to fit any operating system going, ready for upgrades anytime, anywhere.

I wish I was like that! Thought Stan.

H-016 stared into Stan's eyes, it's freakishly displayed humanoid face, perfect in complexion smiled at Stan then turned around, heading for the door h-016 said, "Have a nice day Stan!" then started to whistle, blowing out a tuneful sound that filled the room as it walked off to start the day. One by one the rest of the h-Bots awoke and raised from their docks, all heading out of the door to take up position in the museum.

Finally! All done!

Stan made sure the rest of the h-Bots were still in reboot mode, then picked up his inner ear communication device, a small tube like design, hollow through the middle and very flexible. It had a circular speaker around the end which slotted it into his ear, each one individually moulded for a particular person. Stan then unpeeled a new voice patch, this was a sticky little microphone that adhered to his skin, just below the throat. After he'd established connection between the devices, he followed the h-Bots out of the door, which slid back behind him as he wandered off in the direction of the museum floor.

Chapter 47

"Eeeeerrrreerwww...St...Stan...eeeerreeww...
Stan..."
Stan's ear burst into life with a squeal, he lifted his
finger up to his ear and poked the ear piece,
"Bloody tech stuff!" he said.
"What? Stan, come in, do you read, over."
"Erm, sorry, yeah I'm here, keep your pants on.
What's all the fuss?" he asked.
"We're having an energy fluctuation on the
network, could just be a faulty breaker in the
Hydrogen Power Core. Whatever it is it's pulling
power from the storage facility. Could you check it
out please. Over!"
"You gotta be kidding, have you seen the time?
We'll be pushing it now man."
"You're the closest, Stan."
"Ok, I'm on it! I'll let you know what it is. Over-n-
out."
   If this didn't get fixed there wouldn't be any
visitors that day. The h-Bots had their uses but
when it came to certain things they still needed a
human around. Stan hated going down to power
core, it was deep under ground, past the storage
areas, out of signal range, that's why they don't
send the h-Bots, you have to manually plug into the
network to communicate with Blue-Sky. He looked
at his watch and turned around, heading back into
the room he'd just left, he grabbed his torch and

maintenance bag and headed for the Hydrogen Power Core. The corridor was spotless, the same old marbled tiles donned the floor, unchanged in over a hundred years. Stan used to take his time down here, he loved to look at all the past years from the space race, all the past and present astronauts covered the walls with all their great achievements. He neared the elevator and pushed the call symbol on his communication device, as he came close to the glass wall, the Retina screen appeared on the front of the glass. He leaned forward and opened his eye, the Encryption Point scanner picked out the unique features from Stan's retina and opened the frosted glass door. As he stepped into the elevator, an automated female voice welcomed him, "Good morning Mr Stanley Goldman!"

"Good morning, Freckle!" replied Stan.

"You know that is not my name, Mr Stanley Goldman! My name is…"

"I know it's h-241, calm down, I think you suit Freckle better."

"Ok Mr St…"

"Stop calling me Mr Stanley Goldman, please just call me Stan, for the millionth time."

"I'm not programmed to call you that Mr Stanley Goldman, where would you like to be taken today?"

"Hydrogen power core floor, please."

"Thank you Mr…"

"Mr Stanley Goldman!" he finished the name for her, with a hint of sarcasm.

"Would you like to listen to some music Mr Stanley Goldman?"

"No, not today, but thanks all the same."

"You're welcome."

Stan paused and waited for it…

"Mr Stanley Goldman."

He just shook his head and stood in the centre of the glass elevator, waiting to reach his floor, the journey didn't take that long, not like the olden days! It was the walk down the corridor that took the time, the Hydrogen Power Core was situated at the furthest part of the complex, just in case, it could be sealed off from the rest of the buildings.

The elevator reached the floor Stan required and the doors opened, he walked out and was faced with the endless corridor that stretched off into the distance. Its bright white walls bounced the lights around, blinding Stan for a couple of seconds until his eyes became accustomed. The corridor was only lit for about twenty yards, then it was pitch black, the lights came on in sections as Stan walked down. As he walked away from the doors to the elevator he looked back, the lights had gone out, apart from the area he was standing in. A black-hole at either side, an eerie sight from afar, trapped in limbo. He often thought of spinning around and around really fast to see if he could remember the way out.

Not today! He thought as he pulled out his torch and clicked the switch, pointing it the direction he was walking. The beam illuminated the corridor and ingested by the dark that lay ahead.

Walking off down the passageway, the tune h-016 had whistled was playing in his mind over and over again. He walked on with only his footsteps as company, every stride he took echoed and bounced off the walls, being swallowed up by the darkness that laid ahead. Stan felt like he was on a conveyor belt, it didn't look like he was moving! The lights continued to flicker on into the distance, whilst turning off behind him on the way. He'd made it to the Hydrogen Power Core and unlocked the door using the retina scanner. He took a look around but there was nothing amiss in there, everything seemed to be ok, running smoothly. Stan pulled a small cable from the side of his communication device and plugged it into a panel on the wall. He reported back to the headquarters saying, "Everything is ok! "

"Ok Stan, come on back it must just be a glitch in the system."

Taking one last look around he closed the door and started to turn to walk back towards the elevator, something made Stan stop dead in his tracks, he waited for his echoes to fade into the unknown, then he listened. Tilting his head to concentrate, he focused his ears to try and hear better. I must be going mad! He thought. Then just as he lifted a foot up to set off again, he heard it;

Beep…Beep…Beep…Beep…Beep…

Very faint at first, far off in the distance! As Stan's ears became tuned in to the sound, he could hear it over his quickened footsteps. It was coming from further up ahead. But where?

The sound started to become clearer and clearer,

the closer he got. Stan passed door after door on either side of the passageway, stopping as he did so to place his ear against it, checking to see if that was where the sound was resonating from. He was getting closer, the high pitched beep was louder now. He continued until the last light had turned on in the corridor, revealing a solid white wall, he couldn't remember being down this far before, his only port of call down here was to fix the breakers on the Power Core unit every now and then. He walked up to the wall and noticed a room through a window on his left, it was empty apart from an old dusty desk and a few scraps of paper. Stan backtracked his echoing footsteps until he stopped to look at a door. Lost for words. He was sure this was it, whatever was making that noise, it was behind this door! He walked up to it and tried the handle, it was locked, he rattled it just in case it was jammed, but it wasn't. Taking his master key from around his neck he wondered if it would fit the lock, it was a skeleton key designed to gain access to all areas so he slotted it into the keyhole. The shining white door was blank with no inclination of what lay ahead. He'd heard the rumours of the things that use to happen down here in the past, things being covered up before the last war.

Stan slowly rested his ear against the door, listening carefully, before he turned the key...

BEEP...BEEP...

Yep that's the door all right! He thought as he

stepped back, his hand still holding the key in the lock. Stan took a look at his communication device, no signal! Typical! He started to turn the key in the lock, after the first quarter turn there was a loud clunking noise as the barrel turned, a screen flickered on the front of the glossy white door, appearing right in front of Stan's face. He automatically placed his eye in front of the display, thinking it was a retina scanner, it wasn't! It was an old-style palm reader, so nothing happened. Stan stood back and thought for a minute, it was then that he had the thought of placing his hand on it, he hadn't used a palm reader in years. He lifted his left hand up, whilst still holding the key with his right fingers. The display flickered and a bright line traced down the screen, allowing the key to turn once more. The screen changed to a picture of Stan with his name and details written on the door, before dissolving, leaving the words;

Storage
Room
49
Access granted
Proceed Stanley Goldman

Click! The door opened slightly. The resounding beep flowed into the polished corridor, bouncing off the walls as it finally escaped its confined prison. Stan pushed it further, the door slowly eased open, all the time he was saying; "H...H...Hello...Hello... Is there anybody there?"

He slowly felt for his torch on his belt and pulled it up, pointing it forwards as he held the door with his foot, he clicked the button once more. The beam cut into the stagnant air, the dormant darkness quickly stolen by the brightness of the light. He shone the torch around, spotlighting different objects as it moved through the thick atmosphere, a dusty desk complete with a turned over chair, that lay discarded on the floor, some lockers and some boxes. He reached behind, feeling for the switch on the wall, he found it and flicked it on. A lonely light bulb erupted into life once more.

"I wonder how long it's been since that was turned on last?" he said as he turned his torch off.

There was nobody in the room, in fact there was very little in the room, it looked like it hadn't had any visitors for quite some time. The room was tall and long, it had shelves along the back wall filled with dusty old cardboard boxes and a collection of old lockers stood in the middle of the room. Stan tentatively walked into the room, the shadows from the objects were playing tricks on his mind, making him think there were things moving. He walked all around the room, with the Beep...Beep...Beep...still resonating throughout. There wasn't anything in there that could be making that noise, Stan looked puzzled as he scratched his head. He walked towards the shelves at the back, this was where the noise was at its loudest, he could hear something else, a kind of humming noise. He pulled a few boxes down and felt through the gap, his hand hit a hollow wall, he knocked a few more times. It was definitely hollow. Pulling at the boxes, Stan cleared them all away to the other side of the room, leaving only the empty metal shelves with their decades of dust being disturbed, creating clouds of particles which made the air gloomy, causing Stan to cough as he tried to pull the shelves away from the wall. As he moved them he noticed that it wasn't actually a wall, the part he'd been banging on was in fact the back of the towering unit, it fit so snugly onto the back, it made it look like the wall. As Stan tried to look through the small gap he'd created, he was hit with an unusual smell, a powerful stale musky cigar aroma hit him like a sledgehammer, making him cover his nose with his hand. He tried to look into the room, but couldn't see anything apart from the glow of some lights, they seemed to be flashing in unison with the Beep…Beep…Beep. Grabbing his torch again he tried to point it through the thin gap, into the room beyond. It was no good, he couldn't see anything! He pulled at the metal shelving again after he'd put his flashlight down, making an opening big enough for him to squeeze through. "I'm getting too old for this!" he said as he gave it one last mammoth pull.

The feet scraped across the floor with a deafening squeal, drowning out the humming and beeping noise. He'd done it, he'd pulled it far enough to get in! He squeezed through and stepped aside allowing the light from the room to enter, sending a shaft of light that cut through the dusty air like a beam of sunlight shattering through a broken cloudy sky. As the lights illuminated, they showed Stan what was making the noise - an antique Radar Command Panel. Stan knew all about these, he'd worked on one in the museum, keeping it in pristine condition, the only thing was, the one in the museum didn't work anymore, the cells had died years ago, it was now on show as an exhibit. He moved closer while his eyes became accustomed to the gloomy light, seeing the reels of tape spinning on the top of the machine, he knew this one was doing something.

"This must be the Power Core problem? It's draining the energy, what the hell is it doing?" said Stan as he stood captivated, staring at the old machine, wondering what to do next!

Finally Stan made a move, he looked around to check out the rest of the room, before reaching back into the other area, feeling for his torch on the dusty shelf. His fingers tickled the body of the flashlight and it rolled away, then rolled back hitting his hand, he didn't want to take his eyes off the flashing radar panel. After a few times he finally grasped it, bringing it into the mysterious hidden room. Stan turned it on and started to move the beam around, he could see this was once a manned room, two chairs were positioned in front of the panel, notepads and pens, scattered across the flat area below the Control Module, an ashtray sat on the top of the machine, overflowing with cigar butts.

"That explains that then!"

To the side of the machine was an old water dispenser, the green stained interior was evidence it had started its very own ecosystem within the container. Stan moved his light over the front, a tattered label was only just holding in place, he could see some faint writing under the decades of dust that was clinging on for dear life. The particles couldn't hold on any longer as Stan took a deep breath in and blew hard, causing a concentrated mini cyclone of dust to erupt in the room. As he uncovered his mouth, he wiped the label with the back of his hand. Stan took a step back, his face in shock, as he read the front;

Best before: 04:07:1969

"Oh, my, God! That's nearly a hundred years old! What the hell is all this stuff doing here?"

Stan couldn't believe what he'd found, as he continued to point his torch around the room. Next to the water dispenser, was a desk, similar to the one in the other room, it was facing the wall, an old telephone sat covered in the same amount of dust as the rest of the items in the room. He reached over and picked up the receiver with two fingers, like it was some kind of poisonous insect, he held it just far enough away from his ear to see if it worked. It didn't. He carefully placed it back down on the cradle, as he scanned the rest of the desk for clues, he felt like an archaeologist who'd just found the discovery of a lifetime. An old desk lamp, the type that you can position over your work, sat patiently waiting for someone to give it back its life. Stan tried the pull cord that hung from the side, it was dead, the lamp had given up waiting years ago. Old pens stored in a round container, and a paper pad in front of the gap where your legs would go, remnants of a world long ago. The writing had faded on the pad so much it was unreadable. Stan explored the rest of the desk and noticed there were two drawers either side. He opened the deep bottomed one and pointed his light in, it was empty. He tried the top one, it contained a few scraps of paper, some paperclips and some pencils. He then moved over to the other side, starting at the bottom drawer again, he slowly pulled it open, half expecting something to jump out. He shone his flashlight in and saw a brown wooden box, sitting on top of a pile of beige coloured folders. Lowering his arm into the drawer he picked up the wooden box and blew the light coating of dust off into the distance, uncovering some faded writing and a decorative emblem on the top;

LA CORONA

HABANA
PRIVADA

Stan was hit with a strong scent of Cigars again,

but this time the smell was fresh, not stale!
He noticed the box had a small lock on the side as
he placed it on top of the notepad on the dusty
desk, unsure whether to open it or wait to show his
findings, as he traced the outline of the words with
his finger. His curiosity got the better of him, as he
tried the lid to see if it was locked. It wasn't! Stan
gently eased open the lid, slowly revealing the
contents that had been hidden for decades. Folding
the lid right back, he noticed more writing on the
inside, the same emblem and words as the front.
His gaze quickly moved to the objects within, a
folded piece of paper covered the top. Stan picked
it up, but as he did, something slid out and floated
to the floor, hovering on the dust it skimmed off,
trying to escape Stan's grasp as he hastily bent
down to catch it in the dark gloomy room. He held
it up in the light from his torch resting on the desk;
it was a photograph!
  Three people were standing, smiling at the
camera. Whilst looking at the photo he reached out,
trying to grab hold of one of the chairs, his hand
missing a few times from his lack of concentration.
Finally he got it, pulling it over from in front of the
Radar Panel, leaving four drag marks on the dust
covered floor. His gaze never left the captured
moment in time, as he placed the chair at the front
of the desk. Stan sat down, hypnotised, staring at
the photo in his dirty hand. Nipping the corner
between his two fingers, his eyes widened as he
intently studied what was on the photo. The three
people faded into insignificance as Stan's eyes were
drawn to what lay in the background! An object

Stan had never seen in the museum before, in fact he'd never seen one full stop. A round domed shaped thing sitting on a frame in the middle of a large building, it was so shiny, it bounced the distorted reflections of the three people as they stood in the foreground.

Stan could only describe it as a UFO!

Two men and one woman were locked in time, a snapshot of history, distant memories of world long ago. Stan turned the photo over to see if anything was on the back, he could only just make something out, faded black ink scribbled on the white paper, he wiped it on his arm, to remove the dust it had picked up when it skidded along the floor. He read the names out loud;

"Bob, Kimberly, Scott."

Each name behind the person on the front. He turned it back over and placed the names to their faces;

"Hello Bob, Kimberly and Scott. What were you up to I wonder?"

He carefully placed the photo to the side and opened the folded piece of paper it had fallen out of. I wonder if this sheds any light on these things? he thought, as he began to read;

....

Dear ?

If someone is reading this, then what we'd hoped for years ago must have happened. Where do I begin? The year is 1975, this Radar Command Module has been hidden upon my orders. My name is Bob Monroe, I work for a covert Government Organisation called S.I.S. formed at the turn of the century to gather intelligence and study the existence of life from other planets. Yes, you did read that correctly, life from other planets. To cut a long story short, which will make more sense once you've read the file which was under this box, in 1947 we were called to an alleged crash of a UFO, at a place called Roswell, New Mexico. After we recovered the said craft, we began working on finding a way to make the craft work, it was no use. It was stored at a place called Area 51 to begin with and was later moved to Area 49, here at the Kennedy Space Centre, Florida. We also obtained one deceased being from the crash site, this too was taken to Area 51 but never brought here.

It wasn't until the 1960s when plans were drawn up to try and send the craft home, or back to wherever it had come from. Our technology at this time is hopeless, we haven't got a clue. In 1968 a young man was found to harbour a special interest in the craft and was brought into the S.I.S. program to try and help. You will be able to see what happens through the evidence in these documents. He was unfortunately sealed inside the craft before it was installed inside the Saturn V rocket, containing the Apollo 11 mission.

This mission was a cloak screen for the real mission that was underway behind the scenes, which only a few people here knew about. The mission was a success, as far as we thought, but after years of no contact, the mission was abandoned and mothballed.

This machine and the folder that is in the drawer, are the only things left of the program. The hangar has been sealed shut, maybe even demolished by the time somebody finds this. I had the radar unit repositioned here so I could keep a close personal eye on things. It has been hooked up to the internal power grid and has a battery back up just incase that fails. The craft was running a program which Scott had written, a dual purpose program that was originally for the Lunar Module to send and receive data from the surface of the Moon. It worked for a brief moment after the jettison of the stage the craft was installed in, we'd made contact, then

nothing! Nothing for years, no more signs,
no more contact.

   If you are reading this to the sound of a
Beep...Beep...Beep... and the reels of memory
tape are spinning around behind you, then
something is happening, something has
come back, someone has RETURNED.

B Monroe.

B Monroe

      Secret Intelligence Service.

         ....

The piece of paper fell from Stan's hand, looking like an explosion as it hit the dusty ground. He sat back in the chair, the back creaking from years of underuse.

What the hell has happened here? This is the news the planet has been searching for years now! And it's been here all the time, who'd have thought, right under our feet.

His gaze moved back to the box, under the folded piece of paper that now laid on the floor, was another finer sheet of paper, something had left an impression on the top where it had sagged in between. He carefully folded back the delicate paper, revealing some old cigars, still tucked up in their very own compartment. Stan closed the lid, preserving them once more, as he shifted his view to the folder in the bottom of the drawer. He leaned forwards and picked it up, noticing some writing on the front. The words looked like they had been printed on with a big red lettered stamp, diagonally from corner to corner, across the flap that allowed access into the folder, Stan could just about make out the words;

TOP SECRET!

Stan could see more writing on the file, in faint black words just under the access flap, he tried to read it;

NO UNAUTHORISED PERSONNEL!
Roswell findings 1947

So, that letter about those stories was true! Stan thought, as he quickly checked his comms device, still no service. Stan looked at the time 08:30am, he realised there was only thirty minutes till the museum opened. Do I have time? He wondered, as his fingers fiddled with the string seal on the folder.

Stan's ears had zoned out from the Beep..Beep..Beep, his mind was now concentrating on the folder that lay before him. He slowly tried to unwind the string, its structure too delicate for movement, turning into a fibrous powder at the slightest touch. The folder was thick, full of documents. As Stan pulled out the pile of paper, the top sheet grabbed his attention straight away!

S.I.S Government
image.png

~~~~~~~

…TOP SECRET…

~~~~~~~

Project Name:
THE RETURN

~~~~~~~

Confidential Report

~~~~~~~

Authorised Personnel Only

~~~~~~~

1968

~~~~~~~

Project Terminated

~~~~~~~

1974

~~~~~~~

Stan read the front cover, as he placed the pile of documents on top of the opened folder. Running his hand over the words on the paper, he tapped the top, waiting for his mind to tell him to read it. Slowly he turned the front cover over and started to read, as the reels of memory tape continued spinning behind him, along with the Beep…Beep… Beep, he started to read the first page.

He didn't have long, but he needed to know who Scott was and why had he been sent on this craft? He quickly scanned through a few pages, trying to find the name, finally, there it was; Scott Salvador, the man who'd made history that nobody knew about. But why? Stan had to get back and tell his findings to someone, someone in a high position.

He placed the documents back into the folder, along with the note and photo, back into the cigar box. Then he placed them both back in the drawer. He got up from the chair and grabbed his torch then rushed to the door. The corridor was pitch black now, he'd lost his bearings as he frantically shone his flashlight one way then the other, going over the way he'd turned into the room in his head, he made a guess. As soon as his movement was picked up by the lights they started to illuminate his way back, trying to push the call button on his comms device as he ran. Arriving at the elevator in record time, panting and gasping for breath he tried to hold steady whilst the retina scanner detected his eyeball before opening the door for him.

"Good morning Mr Stanley Goldman!"

"Goo…Good…Good morning!"

"You sound odd. Where would you like to go, Mr

Stanley Goldman?"

"Mu..Museum please, I'm ok, museum please."

"Thank you, would you like some music on, Mr Stanley Goldman?"

"No…No thanks."

"Thank you, Mr Stanley Goldman."

Stan was too out of breath to argue with the elevator-bot, so he concentrated on his breathing. As he neared his floor, he couldn't wait to find someone to tell about his findings. He was ready to run again, as soon as the doors opened he was off in the direction of the communication centre, looking for the head of the museum.

Brushing past one of the h-Bots he rounded a corner in full sprint, nearly knocking him flying, shouting sorry without slowing down. The h-Bots gyroscopic balancing system only just keeping it upright, as it scanned Stan from behind, "Please slow down Mr Stanley Goldman, you should know better!" The h-Bot said, as it continued about its work.

Stan frantically rushed around, through the maze of museum artifacts and offices, trying to find the person he needed to talk to. Finally! he thought as he arrived at the clear glass door.

Chapter 48

Bursting into the communication centre Stan, really out of breath now, tried to scan the room for the head of the Museum. This facility had nothing to do with NASA now, they had pulled out years ago, moving all their space exploration projects to somewhere out in the desert, Stan didn't know where. "Mr Peterson…Mr Peterson, where's Mr Peterson?"

"Calm down Stan I'm here, what's up man?" he asked, as he walked from his office inside the comms room.

"You have to come and see this Sir, you have to."

"Did you fix that power leakage problem down there Stan?"

"Forget the power leakage Mr Peterson, there's something you have to come and see, now! I think it has something to do with the power leak."

"But I've just got a fresh coffee before we get invaded with scores of people wanting to visit the old Museum."

"Believe me Sir, your gonna want to see this."

Stan had all the other people in the comms room in suspense.

"See what Stan?" asked one of the others, "What's down there?"

"I need to show Mr Peterson first. Come on. Now!"

"Ok, ok, I'm coming, but this better not just be

another malfunctioning h-Bot who's found its way down there like the last time you dragged me down."

"No Sir, I swear."

  With that Mr Peterson followed Stan back towards the elevator to see what the problem was. Stan quickened the pace, as he was eager to show Mr Peterson his findings.

"Slow down Stan, I can't keep up!"

"There's no time to delay Sir, we need to get down there."

Mr Peterson was wondering what could be the problem, he'd never seen Stan like this before and he'd worked with him for years. As they came closer to the elevator, Stan pressed the call button on his comms device once more, then placed his eye in front of the retina scanner.

"Good morning again Mr Stanley Goldman, good morning Mr Chuck Peterson. Which floor can I assist you with today?"

"The Hydrogen Power Core floor please!"

"Again Mr Stanley Goldman?"

"Yes please."

"Would you like to listen to some music, Mr Stanley Goldman?"

"Aargh! No thank you."

"Stan calm down man, what is going on?"

"You need to see for yourself Mr Peterson."

"Please Stan, will you call me Chuck. We've known each other long enough now."

"Ok sorry, Chuck."

  They arrived at the requested floor, Stan was waiting impatiently at the doorway, trying to hurry the doors up so they could get to the room quickly. "Follow me Chuck, it's down the end of the corridor."

Their quickened footsteps, breaking into a jog, echoed in unison, bouncing off the hard marbled floor, travelling into the distant darkness.

"What's that noise Stan?"

"You'll see Chuck, you'll see."

The automatic lighting could hardly keep up with them, they were running now, as they hovered on the edge of the black-hole in front of them. Stan was looking at the doors as he was running, trying to remember which one it was he'd discovered where the noise was coming from. Nearly at the end now, he slowed the pace down, skidding to a halt.

"Is this it? Are we there?"

The high pitched Beep…Beep…Beep…seemed louder now. Chuck frowned at Stan, as he opened the door, using the same security checks as before.

"I didn't even know there were rooms down this far Stan!"

Stan turned and looked at Chuck, giving him an unusual smile as he opened the door to the room.

They walked inside, closing the door behind them, the lonely light still switched on from when Stan was in there earlier.

"What the hell is that fowl smell, and where is that noise coming from Stan?" asked Chuck, as he covered his face with his hand, then walked around the lockers in the middle of the room, "What is in all these boxes?"

"Over here Chuck! Forget that stuff. What you

need to see is behind here!"

"Behind where?"

"These shelves." Stan replied, as he pointed to the gap he'd created in the corner of the room.

Chuck walked over to the corner and peered into the dark room, noticing the synchronisation between the noise and the glow from the illuminated buttons, as they cast an intermittent eerie glow over the antique machine.

"What the hell is that Stan?"

"It's a Radar Command Module, just like the one in the museum Chuck. Only ours doesn't work at all. This one is doing something! This is the power drain on the hydrogen core."

"What is it doing?"

"I was hoping you could tell me Chuck. That's not all, follow me."

Walking into the room Stan switched on his flashlight, as he did so, he showed Chuck around, with the beam cutting through the now dusty air, spotlighting the different objects inside. Chuck couldn't believe what he was seeing, he was speechless as he followed Stan further into the room. Stan walked over to the desk and asked Chuck to sit down.

"The machine isn't all I found in here Chuck, wait till you see this."

Stan opened the drawer once more and carefully picked out the Cigar box and the folder containing the revelations he'd read earlier. Placing them in front of Chuck, he opened the Cigar box, revealing the folded piece of paper with the photo he'd placed back inside. He handed it to Chuck, who now realised what that fowl smell was.

   Stan watched Chuck's face as he looked at the photo of the three people standing in front of the object from the past. Chuck placed the photo down after looking at Stan, then he started to read the note that had been left for someone, someday to find. Looking intrigued, he read the whole letter.
"Is this some kind of joke Stan?" asked Chuck.
"No Chuck! It's all real, as far as I know!" he replied.
Chuck took another look at the note, then looked back at Stan.
"That's not all Chuck, take a look at the rest of the findings. It gives the names of the three people in the photo, on the reverse. I found the name mentioned in the note, as I scanned through the documents. Somebody from this planet, was sent somewhere, on that Craft that's in that photo, nearly one hundred years ago. His name was Scott Salvador."
"So what is happening with the Radar Module?" questioned Chuck.
"Well! Now this is just a guess, but I'd say that it's picking up the signal from something? You need to read the documents, I think they'll tell you everything we'll need to know!"
"We need to tell somebody about this, somebody who will be able to shed some light on it. We need to tell the military!"
"Are you sure about that?" asked Stan.
"Who else is there?"
"You're right Chuck, but we need to act fast, who knows what's out there, or what's come back!"

"Are there anymore documents Stan? If there are can you grab them and follow me."

Stan picked the rest of the folders out of the drawer and followed Chuck out into the corridor, as they headed back towards the elevator.

"Happy Independence Day Stan!" Chuck said sarcastically, "We need to get the rest of that shelving moved and some lighting rigged up down there, so we can see what we're doing."

"Ok Chuck I'll activate a few h-Bots to lend a hand and get that done ASAP, after I've brought these files back to your office."

"No, give me the files, I'll take them, you get the h-Bot and get back down there! We need to keep this under wraps for the time being, we don't want to scare anybody, in the mean time, we need to close the museum for the day."

"But Chuck, it's the busiest day of the year! We are already late in opening! If we don't want to cause panic, shouldn't we open as usual and contain this until the authorities get here? It's going to be mayhem once they get here."

"You're right Stan. I'll find somewhere for these folders and have a look through them myself, then I'll get onto the military for their help. We might be at the forefront of making history here, and we're in the right place for it."

Stan handed the folders over to Chuck and headed back to the h-Bot's Docking Facility, whilst Chuck made his way back to his office with the folders. Passing the other workers, he tried to bypass the barrage of questions being fired at him. He made it to his room and shut the door, pressing the button to frost the clear glass windows, allowing him to look through the pile of documents Stan had uncovered.

It took Stan most of the morning to clear the shelves and move all the things in storage room 49. He'd linked a lighting circuit up to the power supply, which illuminated the rest of the room, showing exactly what was in there. He had a good look through the desk that held the secrets of many years ago, placing all his findings into an empty box from the other room. The reels of tape were still spinning, still recording, still working, waiting for some kind of contact from the Radar Module. Stan left the machine, apart from moving a sheet of paper leaning against it, which he carefully picked up and placed into the box, with everything else. Behind this sheet was a black screen, an old computer monitor just the same as the one on the museum floor. He left everything else, leaving all those years of dust sitting, he didn't want to disturb it. The screen was blank, no sign of anything happening, just a square black screen. To the side of it the lights continued to flash along with the sound of Beep... Beep...Beep... With the help of the h-Bot, Stan had managed to rig up a network connection via a mobile communication device they'd brought down with them, now at least they had contact with the comms room in the museum.

In his cool, minimalistic office, which had views out over the whole museum complex, Chuck finished reading one of the folders, the same one Stan had read earlier. He was speechless, left in a hypnotised state. He finally looked at his comms

device around his wrist. Pressing a few things on
the touch screen panel and activating his computer,
a flat thin clear screen started to rise out of his glass
desk. His comms device picked up the screen, then
a red outline of an illuminated keyboard appeared
on the top of his desk. He sat back in the black
rolled reclining chair, moulded around his body. He
started to ask his computer some questions,
"Operation; The Return?"
"No such reported operation listed."
"Scott Salvador?"
"No information listed."
"Bring up contacts in United States Space
Exploration Unit, please."
The computer brought up the names and photos of
possible contacts for the Space Exploration Unit run
by the Government. This is the authority that still
operates some of the Space Exploration, they have
manned units on the Moon and on Mars. Most of
the money to build these outposts came from rich
companies who profited from the wars around the
world, they were more advanced base-stations.
Companies had set up Lunar and Mars hotels,
taking the ones who could afford it on a holiday of a
lifetime. Mining companies had started exploring
Mars, finally seeing what the red planet had to offer.
   The first name that came up was;

Logan A. Franklin

~~~~~~~
Lieutenant General

Space Superiority Systems Wing
(SYSW)

~~~~~~~

Los Angeles AFB.
California

Chuck asked his computer to send a request informing Lt. Gen. Logan A. Franklin, to contact him ASAP, as it was a matter needing his or someone's urgent attention, regarding an unusual transmission received at the Kennedy Space Centre, Florida.

   Chuck could only wait now, and see if anybody contacted him within the next hour or so, as he got back to reading the pile of folders that now sat on his extremely neat desk. His comms device activated, his initial thoughts were; That was quick! But his excitement was quickly diluted as he saw Stan's face appear on his screen in front of him.
"Mr Peterson, I have moved things in the storage room, and sorted a visual comms device located inside, we could hook it up to the network without any proble…"
"No! No! Don't do that Stan, we don't want this breaking onto the Blue-Sky network. I've been thinking, if this had been picked up by any network, or by any surveillance equipment, we would have heard about it by now! So hang fast on setting that link up Stan."

"Ok Mr Peterson, have you had any headway on contacts?"

"I've requested communication from the Lt. Gen. at the Space Superiority Systems Wing, I'm awaiting his reply as we speak Stan. I'll keep you informed as to what they want us to do."

"Ok!"

With that the image on the screen shrank into a tiny dot in the middle, then in the blink of an eye, he disappeared.

Chuck was intrigued reading the information about this forgotten mission, that he hadn't noticed at first, his comms device was activating. The image of Lt. Gen. Logan Franklin's secretary was trying to communicate with him. Her translucent face was hovering inside the screen on his desk, "Sorry to interrupt Mr Peterson, I have been asked to contact you regarding your request for Lt. Gen. L. Franklin, to contact you as a matter of urgency."

"Erm, Erm, yeah, sorry, I was deep in concentration then. Sorry who am I speaking to?"

"Lt. Gen. L Franklin's personal secretary, Mr Peterson. Can you tell me more about this matter of urgency?"

"I will only talk to Lt. Gen. Logan Franklin, can you please ask him to contact me? ASAP, I repeat, I will only speak to him and him personally."

"Mr Peterson. As you can imagine Lt. Gen. Franklin, is a very busy man. So your urgent request can be best dealt with, could you please tell me some more about the nature of your request."

"I don't care what he's doing or where he is just get Lt. Gen. Franklin on the comms ASAP, tell him it's a matter of national security, and if he doesn't contact me ASAP, I will not be held responsible for what might happen."

With that the screen went onto a holding image, it was the symbol for the Space Surveillance Systems Wing.

"What is it?"

"Sir it's Mr Peterson."

"Who?"

"The man from the old Kennedy Space Centre, he would like to talk to you personally Sir!"

"Can he not leave a message, for crying out loud, doesn't he know how busy we are here!"

"He won't Sir, he seems quite adamant about talking to you personally Sir. He says it's a matter of national security Sir."

"A matter of national security? Ok! Patch him through."

"Mr Peterson, I'm patching you through straight away."

"Finally! Thank you!"

"Mr Peterson, this better be good! A matter of national security, you say? Well let me be the judge of that!" exclaimed Lt. Gen. Franklin.

"Sir! Yes, Sir! Please call me Chuck. Have you ever heard of an organisation called the S.I.S.?" asked chuck.

Lt. Gen. Franklin's face said it all.

"Await my secure transmission!" he said as the screen was terminated instantly.

Moments later Chuck's screen broke into life once more.

"Now, Mr Peterson, can you please repeat what you

have just said?"

"Yes Sir, have you ever heard of an organisation called the S.I.S.?"

"Why?"

"Well, Sir. We had a Hydrogen Power Core leak which was picked up this morning upon opening the old Kennedy Space Centre museum…"

"Is that old place still on the go? I haven't been there in years."

"Sir, this is urgent, you need to listen carefully. To cut a long story short, we have uncovered an intriguing discovery here Sir. As of this morning nobody knew anything about what was found. I have taken the liberty of looking into…"

"Is this the long story short, Mr Peterson?"

"Are you going to listen to me? This is a matter of national security, it requires your urgent attention. Please listen!"

"Ok, you have my full attention, carry on."

"Well, where was… Oh yeah, we found an old Radar Module hidden in one of the storage rooms here, it has somehow activated, all on its own. Nobody knew it was here Sir. There are folders with documents, lots of documents, Sir. Some referring to an organisation called the S.I.S. Does this mean anything to you? Have you heard of it before?"

"Well Mr Peters… I mean Chuck, the organisation you are referring to had been abolished years ago, from what I heard, deemed old-fashioned, whether it still exists is another matter, far out of my reach. What else can you tell me?"

"You really need to see this for yourself Sir. We are

picking up some form of transmission, from somewhere. You need to see the documents and the other information we've found. Is there anyway you can come here?"

"Ok Mr Peterson. This better be worth my time, it'll take me two hours to get there supersonic, so I'll be there as soon as I can."

Chuck's screen dissolved again and he could only hope Lt. Gen. Franklin had taken what he'd said, seriously. All he could do now was wait and pray that he got here quickly, the whole world knew nothing, but time would wait for nobody, and time is one thing Chuck didn't think they had much of.

"Stan, come in Stan!"

"Yes Sir!"

"The Lt. Gen. is on his way. He'll be here as soon as he can."

"Ok Sir, is there anything we should do in the meantime?"

"No, all I want you to do is monitor the situation from that room."

"But what about the museum Sir?"

"Don't you worry about the museum Stan, I'll take care of that, you have to monitor the room, you know what's going on."

"Ok Sir."

   Chuck disconnected the comms link from Stan, then set the safeguard museum tour in place. He continued skimming through the folders of documents, learning all about what had gone on many years ago. After he'd finished quickly going through everything he secured the folders inside the safe in his office.

On the flight from L.A. to Florida, Lt. Gen. Franklin had contacted what was once known as Area 51 in New Mexico, he needed to know if they could shed some light on this subject. They denied all knowledge, but that was to be expected. Nobody ever knew what went on there, it had been like that for over a hundred and fifty years now. There had been attempts to gain access, especially in the war, but nobody ever really found anything out. Even if they did they seemed to disappear.

Chuck was impatiently awaiting the arrival of the Lt. Gen. He paced the floor of his office, one look at his comms device and one look out of the window, down the road way into the distance. Then in the distance he could see a cloud of dust following a procession of hazy black vehicles, shimmering on the hot road like a mirage in the desert. Their speed said it all, they weren't tourists, Chuck knew that for sure.

Chapter 49

The entourage pulled up at the front of the Kennedy Space Centre entrance, the military driver rushed around and opened the door for who Chuck thought was the Lt. Gen. Franklin. Full of importance a tall mountain of a man climbed out of the back of the car, chaperoned by a cascade of military flamboyance. They made their way into the Space Centre, causing a stir as they did so. Chuck had already made it down to greet them upon entering the building.

"Good afternoon Lt. Gen."

Chuck knew this from the emblem on the cases some of the operatives were carrying, it was the same as the one on the hold screen.

"Mr Peterson I presume?"

"Yes Sir."

"Well, let's not beat around the bush Mr Peterson, let's get down to business. That's why I've flown over the entire USA isn't it?"

"Ok Sir, this way, we'll start with the documents in my office.

"After you! Please, lead the way."

Lt. Gen. Franklin followed Chuck, who in turn was followed by his entourage of associates, all brandishing large, hard metallic flight-cases on wheels, the contents of which, they only knew about. They were wearing black, all black, from boots to dark sunglasses, they looked like they were on a Special Ops Mission, in a way, they were. On clearance through security, Chuck led them away from the entrance, towards the staff elevator, not wanting to cause alarm to the visitors on the complex. He called for the elevator, then using his retina scanner, he opened the door. As they all entered, the Face-Recognition-Cam picked up everyone. The Cam is linked to the population data base, everyone is on there, their profile information is flagged up beside their photo I.D. at the elevator monitoring station, operated by an h-Bot. This information is instantly cross-checked and verified with the Blue-Sky network. It's never failed yet, to miss an identity, that was until today!

They all tried to squeeze into the confined area of the elevator, rolling flight-cases too, one by one the Cam picked up faces, without receiving any data. Their face profile picture came up, but without their name, age, number, occupation etc, they didn't exist according to the network. The only person that was recognised was Lt. Gen. Logan A. Franklin. Chuck's ear piece alerted him to this matter urgently, telling him he was travelling with seven ghosts, the code word for anybody without a profile I.D. Chuck hadn't heard the term whilst working here at the museum, he'd heard it plenty of times in his previous employment, working in the military setting up the h-Bot deployment equipment, drones and Bots which were the first line of defence these days. He'd taken this job at the Kennedy Space Centre, hoping for a more relaxed environment. It was! Until today, when all hell broke loose.

The team of men exited the elevator, following Chuck, who'd been made aware of his ghost companions. He headed for his office, walking straight past the people and h-Bots without saying a word, one by one the entourage of ghosts followed him in, wheeling their cases with them.

"Mr Peterson, we need an area to set up a command module with links to all available networks."

"You can do here or you can set up down in the storage room where we found the machine working."

"Where are the files?"

"Here in my office inside my locked safe!"

"Then here will be fine, as long as we have full control and access to the whole building! We'll take things from here on in. We don't know what we are dealing with Mr Peterson."

"Full control? This is a working museum, we have visitors all day!"

"We'll be as discreet as possible."

As the Lt. Gen. finished his sentence, one of his ghosts handed him the pile of folders from his securely locked safe.

"What the hell! How did you do that?" Exclaimed Chuck, as he looked over to his now unlocked and wide open safe.

"I did say we need full access to the whole building! Mr Peterson."

"Yeah but come on! You could just have asked for them!"

The team positioned all the cases side by side, a small circle glowed on the top of each one. The ghosts walked up to their individual cases and placed a thumb on the glowing circle, then stood back. The cases started to open, transforming from their neat metallic look, into something Chuck had never seen before, he was speechless, amazed at the technology starting to unravel right in front of his eyes. Sections were folding out from areas that didn't look like they could hold anything else, complete with a row of seating for the ghosts to sit at. A slightly rough texture, matte black colour, a material Chuck had never come across. The Lt. Gen. then stood in front of the Command Module and touched his comms device again. Chuck jumped back as a green laser fanned out towards the Lt. from an invisible hole. It scanned his face, making a three-dimensional image of himself hovering above the metallic matte black control panel. Then the whole Command Module burst into life, screens appeared from nowhere, lights flickered and displays lit up showing images from all over the world, flight plans, space launches, Lunar base-camps, Mars outposts, everything you could image had erupted onto this amazing piece of kit. Chuck stood still, his mouth wide open waiting for it to finish running its setup, waiting for the transformation to be complete. The Lt. Gen. turned to face Chuck, with a, 'how did you like that!' look on his face.

The ghosts sat down, none of them had spoken a word since arriving. Their chiseled stone faces showing no sign of emotion, just following protocol, with each one having a particular job to do. They all sat down on the seat which had inventively appeared from inside their cases, facing their control

panels, they set to work straight away, not a moment's rest, as their fingers worked at lightning pace. Chuck was notified on his comms device about a security breach, it was them! They'd already accessed their network, his Retina Encryption easily by passed by their advanced equipment and the superior hacking skills they'd acquired, gaining them full and unrestricted access to the whole of the Kennedy Space Centre.
"Now! Can I use your desk? So I can scan these folders."
"A please would be nice! Yes, help yourself."
   He placed his small silver briefcase on top of Chuck's desk, then doing a similar thing as the ghosts had done with their cases, he placed his thumb on the glowing circle. This too opened and transformed, unfolding into some kind of weird tech, with flashing lights and screens. One of the ghosts left his seat and began to feed the pieces of paper through a slotted area at the front, the documents were being scanned and transferred to audio, a perfect digital rendition also appearing on the screens on both his and the ghosts panels, allowing them full and unrestricted access to all the information from the past. Each audio file automatically lining up in order, ready to transmit to the Lt.'s earpiece, sharing every vital detail from the uncovered files. The Lt. sat down in Chuck's chair and span round, placing his hands behind his head, he lazily leaned back with his feet slowly elevating from the floor, gazing out through the floor to ceiling windows over and across the landscape littered with parts of old rockets from

past missions into space. He was ready to listen! Ready to find out everything, the ghost fed the hungry machine the information and the secrets that were no more, as the Lt. slowly closed his eyes concentrating on the stream of information being uploaded.

Chuck waited patiently in the background, waiting for something to happen, waiting for that moment of realisation that finally told him; we are not alone! The Lt. Gen.'s face didn't alter, not a flinch, not a twitch, nothing. Chuck was beginning to think he wasn't hearing anything. He looked at the ghosts working away at their stations, there was no indication of their findings either.

What were they? Do they not know what has been found here? This will change the world as we know it, it'll solve that age old question humans have wanted for centuries. Knowing what has been discovered made Stan and Chuck part of this discovery, they'd made history, finally some evidence of life elsewhere in the universe.

The Lt. stirred, he began to sit up as he turned back round in Chuck's chair, "I've heard enough for now! Keep uploading those files Chuck. Please can you take me to the room with the Radar equipment in, I need to see it, now!"
Chuck noticed that the calm demeanour of the Lt. had changed, his face looked excitedly worried. The Lt. stood up and walked over to one of the ghosts, whispering something into his ear, then walking over towards Chuck, the ghost got up and followed him, staying close as they headed for the door.

Stan was still sitting in the room down below, an h-Bot was standing outside the door motionless in the now dark corridor. Stan watched the machine, waiting for something else to happen, the sequence of lights hadn't altered, the reels hadn't stopped, still slowly turning, recording every piece of data the machine was receiving. Chuck had notified him they were on their way down to the room. The mobile comms unit was working fine, linked into the network it had full access to everything. The smell of the stale cigars still lingering in the cool stagnant air. The room looked a lot bigger now that the shelving had been moved away, opening it up into the other room. Stan got up and opened one of boxes that they'd moved, it was full of old papers, he couldn't see anything about the hidden room, just dusty old files stored for safe keeping.

The murmur of voices could be heard echoing down the corridor, bouncing around finding their way into the room where Stanley was waiting. They were coming, their footsteps slowly becoming clearer, as they neared the doorway. This was Stan's cue to stop rummaging around in the boxes and sit back down.

"Hello Mr Chuck Peterson. Hello Lt. Gen. Logan A. Franklin. Hello..." The h-Bot fell silent as he wasn't presented with any information about the ghost following.

"Hello." They both replied in unison to the h-Bot waiting outside.

As they walked into the room, Stan was back sitting in the chair, watching the machine.

"Hi Stan, this is Lt. Gen. Logan A. Franklin."

"Hello Lt. and you are?" Stan asked the ghost standing behind him.

His look said it all, no need for words, his carved, perfectly sculptured face looked past Stan towards the machine, he was ready, ready to get to work.

"What have we got here then?" questioned the Lt.

"Correct me if I'm wrong, I think this is an old Radar Module, they were used a long time ago, well before your time Sir, we have the very same one upstairs in the museum, that one doesn't work though!" replied Stan, as he felt he had to explain to the Lt., with him being a lot younger than Chuck and himself.

"Thank you for that detailed information, you seem to be a fountain of knowledge Steve!"

"Erm, the name's Stan not Steve Sir!" as he corrected the Lt.

The Lt. just gave him a glance. The ghost who'd accompanied the Lt. quickly turned his head in the direction of Stan, giving him a deathly look, Stan could feel his very soul being dragged kicking and screaming from his body.

"Ok, then! Should we crack on?" Chuck asked as he broke the deafening silence.

"What's his problem?" asked Stan.

All three of the men walked over and stood in front of the machine, they just stared at the flashing lights and the reels of tape spinning around before their eyes. The Lt. pondered, his hand rubbing his chin, as he tried to understand what was going on. The high tech mobile comms device stood beside the antique Radar Module, nothing had been hooked up to it yet. The ghost whispered something into the Lt's. ear, he turned to look at him, raising his eyebrows as he said; "Do you think that will work? We have nothing to lose! What would it take to connect the Radar Module to the comms device?" he asked.

"What do you mean Sir? Connect this to that?" replied Stan.

"Yes!"

Stan looked at Chuck, knowing that as soon as they connected the two devices, it would instantly be connected to Blue-Sky, allowing it to transmit over the whole network. Who knows what might happen then.

"Are you sure that's what you want to do?" asked Stan, as he explained what might happen.

The Lt. looked at the ghost again, his carved facial structure remained unchanged. This told the Lt. that that was the right thing to do. For some reason the ghosts wanted the transmission to be accessed from their command post in Chuck's office. This way they could use their state of the art software and Blue-Sky network connections to monitor the situation.

   The ghost set to work! He walked over to the desk, taking a quick look into the water dispenser as he did so. He took an almighty breath in and blew as hard as he could over the top of the dusty surface of the desk, blowing the few scrap pieces of paper off and onto the floor. He moved the lamp and placed his case onto the distressed wooden surface. His thumb was placed onto the circle of light. The case started to open, transforming like the rest of the cases had done. While this was happening the ghost had walked back over to the Radar Module, unimpressed at his transforming tech, he'd seen it a million times before, but Stan and Chuck were watching its every move. The air was filled with dust particles now, all looking for their next resting place. The ghost did the same to the Radar Module, took a mammoth lung full of dusty air, then with a humongous hurricane of a breath, blew the dusty machine almost clean. The rest of the men were left wafting the air, so they could see and breathe once more, they all coughed with the thickness of the murky atmosphere.

   The ghost was looking for the connection port, the cable that connected this machine to its power source and the one to be able to receive the signal. He looked all over the front of the control panel, there was nothing there. He then turned his attention to the cover underneath, the part where your legs would be as you sat there monitoring the Radar. There were two paint flaked metal panels, the kind that slid behind each other allowing access to one side at a time. He slid one across, revealing a bunch of cables, he then slid the two back across to the other side, this too had loads of cables behind it. The ghost eased the sliding panels into the middle and gave them a pull, they bent in the centre and came away in his hands, he made it look so easy. They had full access now to all the cables which ran the machine, they were all the colours of the rainbow. Stan wouldn't have a clue what he was looking for, the ghost seemed to though, his hand went straight into the mix of colour, moving bunches of wire out of the way, searching for a particular one. His other hand reached into his pocket, pulling out a small cylindrical item, about the size of a pill. He placed it between his teeth and squeezed, gently compressing it, the object burst into light, illuminating the whole of the inside, making his job so much easier.

"Where do you get all these gadgets from, they are amazing, I want some!" Stan said, with the excitement of a little kid.

The ghost slowly worked his way through the jungle of wires, before starting to ease one out, hoping it had enough length on it to reach the front. It did! Keeping this one tightly grasped in one hand, he sent his other one in, not taking as long this time, before pulling it out, holding onto another cable, this one was slightly thicker, it looked like the power cable. Both the cables were free from their entanglement now, they stayed out as the ghost let go and stood up, he then came back to the transformed case, removing two sections, both the same. They looked like tubes, about six inches in length and two inches in diameter. He got back onto his dusty knees under the Radar Module and placed one of the things on the floor. He then opened the other one, it split in half revealing a soft interior, filled with technology. He placed the first wire inside the tube and clicked it shut. He then repeated the same process with the other tube, clicking it around the thicker cable. On the front of each gadget, a circle of light appeared, just like the one he pressed on his case. He held the two tubes and placed his thumb on each one, then released them. A series of illuminated rings lit up in unison, moving down, until they reached the bottom, then they all glowed and flashed, pulsating together as the ghost got back up again, still with no expression on his now dusty face.

His transformed case erupted into life as he rested his thumb on the glowing circle. Two green laser beams cut through the particles hanging in the air, showing them tumbling over and over as they danced through the atmosphere, free from their stagnant resting place. The two beams crossed in the centre of the case, lights started to glow up the sides, across the top and over the front. A glass screen started to rise up from the top of the case, finally stopping, the glass was as thin as a hair. An image appeared on the front, it was the emblem for the 'Space Superiority Systems Wing', making it look like it was hovering just above. It then spun round and disappeared into the top leaving the glass blank for a second, before being replaced by the words;

CONNECTION
COMPLETE...

~~~~~~~

Welcome to the
BLUE-SKY
NETWORK...

~~~~~~~

The ghost's communication device had linked to the mobile comms unit Stan had brought into the room. They now had full and unrestricted access to the whole world network! He began to touch the surface of his case, Stan couldn't see what he was doing exactly, but it looked like he was typing. The screen began to show signs of life again, the ghost was doing things so fast, that items were coming and going from the screen before anybody knew what was happening. His hands came to a stop, he looked at the Lt. and nodded his head towards him. Stan assumed he'd been successful at his task, whatever it may have been.

The Lt. turned to Stan and Chuck and said, "Whatever goes on from here on in, is a matter of a top secret nature, we do not know what we are dealing with and we do not know what is going to happen. We can access all the information from the command post in your office, we have created a link through your mobile comms network. Please take us back there to further assess the situation."

Stan walked towards the ghost's case to take a closer look, as he did so the ghost stepped across his path and looked him straight in the eye, the kind of look that said, "Don't take another step!"
Stan raised up one finger and reached around him, his hand feeling for the old cigar box on the desk, showing it to the ghost before blowing the remaining specks of dust towards the mean looking man, which probably wasn't the best thing to do!

He then followed the Lt. and Chuck out of the dust filled room, closely tailed by the angry man in black, who spoke quietly to the h-Bot as he left the room, "No one is to enter, under any circumstances!" were his instructions, of which nobody heard.

As they returned back to Chuck's office, the ghosts were still busy working away at their stations. The rest of the museum had no idea what was going on, the h-Bots were doing their daily tasks, the tours were all running smoothly. Nobody knew what was about to happen!

Lt. Gen. A. Franklin sat down behind Chuck's stylish desk, in his snug reclining chair, spinning around once more to look out across the forest of erected old space craft, littering the landscape. It was nearly three in the afternoon now, the Lt. had listened to most of the scanned documents as he sat gazing at the metal forest. He had a good idea of what had happened all those years ago now, the details had been documented meticulously by the Chief of the S.I.S. who'd monitored this mission for years after the event, hoping something would come back.

He was shocked, to say the least, these were the documents from a mission which had never been made public, 'The Forgotten Mission!' he thought. "Right let's do this!" exclaimed the Lt. The ghosts all looked round towards him. He gave them a slight tip of his head, this was the authorisation, it was all systems go!

They each faced back round to their stations and stood up in turn, this looked like a drill they'd done many times before, but not for what they were about to do. Stepping to one side they all walked backwards, still facing their transformed cases. Their job was done, just one last thing for the Lt. to do, he stood up and walked over to the main command post, his footsteps heavy, unsure of the task in hand, the world might never be the same again, he thought. He'd been given the authorisation and clearance from the network, as high up as the President and beyond. The public were totally unaware of what was going on.

"Lt. Gen. A. Franklin." were his only words as he waited patiently for a response.

"Voice recognition complete."

~~~~~~~

"Allow signal to transmit."

~~~~~~~

"System connection complete.
Initialising signal…"

~~~~~~~

"CONNECTION COMPLETE WELCOME
TO THE
BLUE-SKY NETWORK"

~~~~~~~

"There's no going back now! It's out of our hands,
all we can do is wait!"
   They didn't have long to wait, the lasers started
beaming into the air above the ghost's work station,
they were creating a three dimensional picture, like
the one of the Lt's head they had done earlier that
day. First, there was a detailed image of our planet,
then the Moon orbiting the Earth, finally there was a
flashing dot just behind the Moon, unable to be seen
from the Earth, a signal, a sign from something.
"WHERE IS THAT COMING FROM?" Exclaimed
the Lt. to one of his ghosts.
There was no response from any of them.
"WELL…FIND OUT!" he shouted, before walking
over to the station to take a closer look.
"Is that the signal the Radar Module has been

picking up?" asked Stan.

"How long did you say this transmission has been happening for?" asked the Lt.

"We're not sure Sir, we only picked up the power leak this morning on preparing the museum for the day!" replied Chuck.

"Whatever that signal is, it's near, very near, hiding on the dark-side of the Moon. Why haven't our posts picked this signal up?"

One of the ghosts finally spoke out, "The transmission is being sent on the old radio wave frequency Sir, that has long gone, Sir."

"Clearly not! They, whoever they are, are still using it…" The Lt. was stopped short by Chuck, "Look!" He pointed to the thin glass screen. A flashing cursor had illuminated in the corner, pulsing, waiting to say something…

..H..E..LL..O…..EA..RT..H….

Stan erupted with excitement, it was all his Christmas mornings coming at once. He'd longed for this day all his life, wondering if we'd ever make contact with one of the infinite number of habitable planets out there.

"Ok, calm down. We need to assess the situation," said the Lt.

Stan tried to calm down! All the ghosts were sitting back down now looking intently at the stations, not really knowing what to do. They had planned for this day, but never really thought it would happen.

The Lt. stayed standing behind Chuck's desk, he spoke to his comms device, "Hello. This is Lt. Gen. A. Franklin, of the Space Superiority Systems Wing! Who am I speaking to?"

…I..KNO..W…W..HO…Y.O.U…A.RE..Lt..
I…A.M…..
S.C.O.T.T…

"Impossible!" he said, his voice shaking as he slowly sat down into the chair.

.W.E…HA.VE….W.AIT.E.D…
HERE….FO.R…YOU..TO ES.T.ABLI.SH…
A…CO.NNEC.T.I.ON…SO…W.E…C.AN…
COMM.U.NI.C.A.TE…B..E.F.ORE…..

.
.
.
.
.
.

The screen when blank, "Before WHAT?" shouted the Lt.

Communication lost.
Re-establishing connection.
~~~~~~~

Then came a message from Blue-Sky…

Communication complete.
~~~~~~~

"BEFORE WHAT?" shouted the Lt. again, as he
waited for the Blue-Sky to send his message,
looking at each person standing, waiting for a
response from whatever was out there.

…THE…RETURN…

. . . .

Coming soon…

The
Forgotten
Mission
~~~~~~~

The Return
Home
~~~~~~~

That was the worst dream I've ever had! thought
Scott as he opened his eyes.

~~~~~~~

Gasping for air Scott awoke from his induced
comatose state, he was coming round after the deep
hyper-cryogenic journey. He could feel the tube,
which had filled his lungs with the cold oxygenated
liquid, slowly being retracted, grating up his raw
dry throat, baulking as it was extracted! His head
was pounding, he felt worse than he'd ever felt in
his whole life! Watching from the corner of his
darkened eye protection, he saw the level of the

jelly-like substance receding, vanishing into the base of his pod. Scott was still unable to move, his arms fixed and moulded tightly into the pod he occupied. He could see the glowing crystal skull still placed above the reclined chrome coloured seat his projected body had occupied at the beginning of his journey. These surreal events played over and over again in his troubled mind. This must all be a dream, it must be!

The craft was motionless, hauntingly quiet and deathly tranquil, as it defied any kind of gravitational pull. It waited with stealth and patience. A long time had passed since they'd left, who knows what may lay ahead when they finally return to the planet.

The skin on the surface of the craft shimmered, then melted away, leaving the deep dark vacuum of space, littered with tiny specks of light, stars, some of which had just been born and some which had met with their inevitable demise. The inside of the craft felt still, but as Scott peered out into space he noticed these tiny dots of the purest light, were moving, they were tumbling very slowly in space as they waited. Then there it was, just coming into view through the translucent skin that cloaked the craft, the most beautiful object Scott had ever seen. This can't be real, it has to be a dream!

~~~~~~~

It was at this moment, he realised it wasn't a dream at all!

~~~~~~~

To be continued…

theforgottenmission.com
themission@theforgottenmission.com
Published by: In House Aliens©
(J Taylor)

16427600R00288

Printed in Great Britain
by Amazon